INTRODUCING
KATIE MAGUIRE

KATIE MAGUIRE was one of seven sisters born to a police Inspector in Cork, but the only sister who decided to follow her father into An Garda Síochána.

With her bright green eyes and short red hair, she looks like an Irish pixie, but she is no soft touch. To the dismay of some of her male subordinates, she rose quickly through the ranks, gaining a reputation for catching Cork's killers, often at great personal cost.

Katie spent seven years in a turbulent marriage in which she bore, and lost, a son – an event that continues to haunt her. Despite facing turmoil at home and prejudice at work, she is one of the most fearless detectives in Ireland.

Also by Graham Masterton

Horror Standalones

Black Angel
Death Mask
Death Trance
Edgewise
Heirloom
Prey
Ritual
Spirit
Tengu
The Chosen Child
The Sphinx
Unspeakable
Walkers
Manitou Blood
Revenge of the Manitou
Famine
Ikon
Sacrifice
The House of a Hundred Whispers
Plague
The Soul Stealer
Blind Panic
The House at Phantom Park

The Scarlet Widow Series

Scarlet Widow
The Coven

The Katie Maguire Series

White Bones
Broken Angels
Red Light
Taken for Dead
Blood Sisters
Buried
Living Death
Dead Girls Dancing
Dead Men Whistling
Begging to Die
The Last Drop of Blood

The Patel & Pardoe Series

Ghost Virus
The Children God Forgot
The Shadow People
What Hides in the Cellar

The Night Warriors

Night Warriors
Death Dream
Night Plague
Night Wars
The Ninth Nightmare

Short Story Collections

Days of Utter Dread

PAY BACK THE DEVIL

GRAHAM MASTERTON

An Aries Book

First published in the UK in 2024 by Head of Zeus,
part of Bloomsbury Publishing Plc

Copyright © Graham Masterton, 2024

The moral right of Graham Masterton to be identified
as the author of this work has been asserted in accordance with
the Copyright, Designs and Patents Act of 1988.

All rights reserved. No part of this publication may be reproduced,
stored in a retrieval system, or transmitted in any form or by any means,
electronic, mechanical, photocopying, recording, or otherwise,
without the prior permission of both the copyright owner
and the above publisher of this book.

This is a work of fiction. All characters, organizations, and events
portrayed in this novel are either products of the author's
imagination or are used fictitiously.

9 7 5 3 1 2 4 6 8

A catalogue record for this book is available from the British Library.

ISBN (HB): 9781837931064
ISBN (XTPB): 9781837931071
ISBN (E): 9781837931040

Printed and bound in Great Britain by
CPI Group (UK) Ltd, Croydon CR0 4YY

Head of Zeus
First Floor East
5–8 Hardwick Street
London EC1R 4RG

WWW.HEADOFZEUS.COM

Nil cara ag cumha ach cuimhne
'No friend for sorrow but memory'

Irish saying

1

'Fidelma!' called Brendan up the stairs to the bathroom, where he could hear her still splashing. 'Would you fancy a mug of scáiltín, and maybe a slice of that brack your mam fetched over?'

Before his wife could answer, the house blew up. Brendan's head was blasted off his neck and hit the front door, which slammed backwards on to the porch, while his left arm was torn away and disappeared into the living room. The staircase shot straight upwards like a fireman's ladder and then broke apart and collapsed on top of him, burying his decapitated body under a clattering cascade of wooden treads and rippling folds of carpet.

The side walls of the house burst out into the garden and bricks went bouncing across the road and on to the grass of Merrion Court. Then, with a hideous groan and a deafening crash, the upstairs floor collapsed at a steep angle to ground level. The bathtub slid down on to the front patio as fast as a toboggan, awash with bloodied water, with Fidelma still sitting in it, or what was left of Fidelma, with her head blown off like her husband's and her intestines dangling over the sides.

The explosion was so loud that the McCarthys' immediate neighbours could hardly hear it. They felt only as if their ears had been compressed, like descending in an airliner. But further away, all across the heights of Montenotte and all over Cork city centre, the boom echoed and re-echoed, and passers-by stopped and looked around in shock.

A boiling grey ball of smoke rolled up into the air and was then swallowed up by the darkness. Immediately afterwards, lurid orange flames flickered up over the treetops.

Less than five minutes later, the wailing of sirens could be heard from the fire station on Anglesea Street, across the River Lee and up Summerhill.

When the McCarthys' house blew up, Katie was chatting to her old school friend Saoirse O'Connor in the Glasshouse bar in the grounds of the Montenotte Hotel.

The Glasshouse was less than five hundred metres away from Merrion Court, although it was further down the hill, and it was shielded from the main force of the explosion by the hotel building itself. All the same, they clearly heard the boom, and all the windows rattled. Everybody in the bar put down their cocktails and every conversation came to a stop.

'Holy Christ,' said Saoirse. 'What in the name of mercy was that?'

A few seconds later, a fine shower of brick and tile fragments rained down out of the evening sky on to the bar's glass roof, followed by a wooden banister post, which bounced off into the gardens.

'It's a bomb,' said Katie. She had heard one less than a year before, when the UCC's School of Pharmacy had been deliberately blown up, and there was no other sound like it.

She reached over to the chair beside her and took her phone out of her bag. Even though she was still on suspension, she had stayed connected to the Garda communications centre at Anglesea Street.

'A *bomb*?' asked Saoirse. 'Who in the name of Jesus would be setting off a bomb in Montenotte, of all places?'

Katie lifted her hand to Saoirse to show that she would answer in a moment. After two or three minutes, she got through to Sergeant Murphy in the communications centre and he sounded harassed.

'Peter? It's Superintendent Maguire. I'm up at Montenotte and we've just heard what sounds like a bomb.'

'The calls are still coming in, ma'am. All we know so far is that it was a house on Merrion Court and that it's been totally flattened. We're not sure yet if it was some kind of explosive device or whether it was a gas leak, you know – same as that blast last week at the Meanys' house on the Lower Glanmire Road. The fire brigade and the ambulance are on their way like, because there's casualties reported, and we've contacted Gas Networks to send their emergency engineers.'

'How about the acting detective superintendent? Does he know about it?'

'DS Ó Broin? I'm told that he's on his way up there already, ma'am, along with DI O'Sullivan.'

'Well, I'm thinking of going up there myself to take a look.'

'Be doggy wide, ma'am. You know – just in case it *was* a bomb, like, and there's a secondary device still waiting to be set off.'

Katie was tempted to tell Sergeant Murphy that she hadn't come down in the last shower, but instead she said, 'Thanks a million, Peter. I'm counting on returning to duty in a week or so, when the Discipline Section have finally made up their minds.'

'You and me both, ma'am,' said Sergeant Murphy quietly, and she could tell by his tone of voice that he meant it.

'Apparently it was a house on Merrion Court that blew up,' she told Saoirse. 'I'm off up there now to take a sconce at it.'

'Shall I come with you?'

'No, love. Just in case. Why don't you stay here and have another cocomintini? I shouldn't be too long and I'll probably need another one myself when I get back.'

She lifted her red duffel coat off the chair beside her, shrugged it on, and gave a wave to the barman before she walked out into the night, mouthing *I'll be back!* in case he thought she was leaving without paying. It was late November, and damp, but it was not too chilly, and at least it had stopped raining, although the pavements were still glistening wet as she walked up the steep slope of Leycester's Lane. An ambulance sped past her as she climbed, with its blue lights flashing, and up ahead of her she could see that smoke was still rising, with floodlights criss-crossing through it like lightsabers. She could smell burning, too, with a curious nutty aroma.

When she reached Merrion Court she saw that the roads that surrounded the grassy area in its centre were jammed with three fire engines, two ambulances, at least four Garda patrol cars and six or seven other unmarked cars. The roads had already been cordoned off with tapes, and they were crowded with firemen and paramedics and gardaí, although she could see that Bill Phinner and his technical team had not yet arrived.

The south side of the court was lined with eight detached houses, except that there was a gap where the seventh house should have been standing, and all that was left of it was a smoking jumble of bricks and tiles and broken doors and window frames. The windows in the two adjacent houses had all been shattered, too, and half the tiles had been blown off their roofs. The chimney of number 5 had crashed down on to the new Volvo estate that was parked in their front garden.

Katie saw Detective Superintendent ó Broin standing beside the police tape, talking to Detective Inspector O'Sullivan. He was thin, Micheál ó Broin, with a hooked nose, and this evening he was wearing a grey woollen beanie and a long black raincoat, which Katie thought made him look even more like a witch than usual. He had a habit of repeatedly jabbing people with his finger when he was talking to them, and she could see that he was doing it now. It was just as well that DI O'Sullivan was plump and wearing a puffer jacket, so he probably couldn't feel it.

'Micheál,' she said, as she walked up to them. And then, to DI O'Sullivan, 'Terry, how's yourself?'

Micheál stared at her as if she were a mirage.

'Kathleen. You shouldn't be here.'

'I don't see why not. I'm nothing more than an innocent bystander, that's all.'

Micheál looked furtively around to see if any other senior Garda officers had arrived.

'You do realize that if it gets reported that I was discussing this situation with you, then it'll look like I was approving what you got suspended for.'

'Oh, don't be so sensitive. In any case, I'm almost sure that my suspension's going to be lifted soon, and then you can go back to Henry Street and forget about all the stresses and strains of solving crime in Cork.'

Micheál ó Broin had been brought in from Limerick to act as detective superintendent while Katie was relieved of duty. He had never concealed his contempt for women being promoted to senior positions in An Garda Síochána. Katie had heard from Detective Bedelia Murrish that he had expressed the hope several times that the officers of the Garda's Discipline Section would find her guilty of serious misconduct and recommend that she be sacked, or even prosecuted.

'What do we think happened here, Terry?' she asked DI O'Sullivan.

'An explosive device of some sort, almost certain,' said Terry. 'The neighbours say that prior to the blast there was no smell of gas at all, like. But now you can smell that almondy smell and I'll bet that's C-4.'

'All right, O'Sullivan,' said Micheál testily. 'This isn't a briefing.'

'Some of the neighbours say they heard a noise like *whoosh!* too, right after the bang,' Terry went on, ignoring him. 'That makes me fairly sure that it was a bomb.'

'Bombs create a vacuum, don't they, when they go off?' Katie nodded, looking at Micheál as if it were likely that he didn't know this. 'And that *whoosh* – that's all the air rushing back in. Like thunder, after lightning.'

'Let's wait until forensics show up, shall we?' snapped Micheál.

'What about casualties?' Katie persisted. By now, she could almost imagine Micheál mounting a broomstick and flying around them in a frustrated rage.

'Two dead,' Terry told her. 'The owner of the property and his wife. A neighbour was struck by a shower of flying glass when he was out in his garden putting out the rubbish, but his injuries aren't too serious.'

'Do we have the names of the two deceased?'

'Hold on,' said Terry. He took out his phone and tapped the screen. 'Yes – here we are. Brendan and Fidelma McCarthy. According to the neighbours, Brendan worked at the Opel dealership in Silver Springs.'

Katie took hold of Terry's hand and angled his phone so that she could see the screen for herself.

'Mother of God,' she said. 'I *know* him. I know him and I know his family. I had a rake of trouble with those McCarthys two years back.'

'So why was that?' asked Micheál in a sharp voice, clearly annoyed at being left out of the conversation.

'They were members of what they called the Dripsey Dozen. We got wind that they were planning to sabotage a coachload of UK tourists on the centenary of the Dripsey Ambush. They denied it, of course, but they found out who had tipped us off and they beat the poor fellow within an inch of his life.'

'Some people can never fecking forgive and forget, can they?' said Terry.

'What are you suggesting, Kathleen?' Micheál demanded. 'This explosion today, it may be connected to the Dripsey Dozen?'

'It's possible.'

'Wouldn't you say that's jumping the gun a little? I'm not being critical, but I've been told by several of your colleagues that your methods have often been – how shall I put it? – less than methodical.'

'I'm suggesting nothing definite at all, Micheál,' said Katie. 'Let's wait until we receive a full report from Bill Phinner.'

'Don't you mean, let's wait until *I* receive a full report from Bill Phinner? Do I really have to remind you that you're on suspension?'

At that moment, a white van marked An Biúró Theicniúil came around the corner and parked right in front of them, followed by a white Garda car.

Three forensic technicians climbed out of the van, all wearing white protective Tyvek suits, like three snowmen who had lost their carrot noses. Then the car door opened and Bill Phinner, the head of the technical bureau, emerged. He saw Katie talking to Micheál and Terry and came across, with a questioning smile on his face and his hand extended.

'Well, well, well! Detective Superintendent Maguire! Welcome back!'

2

When Katie returned to The Glasshouse, took off her duffel coat and sat down, Saoirse said, 'Jesus, girl, the smell of smoke on you! Was it a bomb?'

Katie nodded. 'I'm pretty sure of it. We can't be one hundred per cent certain, not until the technical team have finished sorting through the rubble, but it doesn't seem likely that it was a gas explosion. The house was totally wrecked, like. There's nothing left of it but a heap of bricks. And the husband and wife who lived there, they've both been killed.'

Saoirse crossed herself. 'If it was a bomb, who do you think might have planted it?'

'At the moment, I have no idea at all. But the husband was one of a loose collection of headers who call themselves the Dripsey Dozen.'

'The Dripsey Dozen? I never heard of them.'

'There's about twelve of them, and they all claim to be distantly related to the five IRA men who were captured at Godfrey's Cross back in 1921 and executed. Of course we commemorate the Dripsey Ambush every February with a parade and all, but these fanatics insist that's not enough. They say we should take our revenge on the English for all eternity, because those five boys were taken away from us for all eternity.'

The barman came over and asked Katie what she wanted to drink.

'Another cocomintini, is it?'

'Thanks a million, but no thanks. Right now I could use a double vodka, straight, with a half of a lemon on the side, please.'

She turned back to Saoirse. 'A couple of years ago, some old fellow gave us a tip-off about the Dripsey Dozen. He told us that they'd been responsible for at least two of those terrorist bombings in the UK, back in the 1970s. At the time, the Provos claimed that it was them who'd carried them out, but they had none of the Provos' usual hallmarks, you know, like the coded warnings they used to give before they set them off. We looked into it, but we couldn't find the evidence to take it any further. We must still have a file on it somewhere.'

'So what do you think?'

'I'm not jumping to any conclusions, Saoirse. Maybe they were planning another bombing in the UK but their bomb went off by mistake. It's happened before. Who knows?'

The barman brought Katie's vodka and her lemon half. She took a large swallow of vodka and shivered, and then she squeezed the lemon on to the fingertips of her left hand and patted them under her nose.

'That's better! I needed to get rid of that stink. I'm sure it was a bomb and bombs always leave the smell of death behind them.'

Katie and Saoirse were still talking when Kieran walked into the bar. Katie gave him a wave and he came over to join them. He sat down next to Katie and leaned over to give her a quick peck on the cheek.

'That's a hell of a hullabaloo that's going on outside, isn't it? Fire engines and ambulances and all. We heard the boom even inside the courthouse. I bumped into your Inspector Kelly as I was leaving and he told me that there'd been some kind of explosion somewhere up in Montenotte. I was worried it might have been here, at The Glasshouse.'

'It was in Merrion Court. One of the houses was totally demolished. I went up to take a sconce at it myself and I'm almost certain that it was a bomb.'

'Holy Joseph. Who sets off bombs in a posh area like this?'

Katie told him about the McCarthys both being killed, and her suspicions about the Dripsey Dozen.

Kieran shook his head. 'You really wonder, don't you? Is the past never going to leave us alone?'

'In the rebel county?' said Saoirse. 'You're joking, aren't you? My uncle has a framed photo of Michael Collins on his sideboard, and he still wears white socks.'

'Court finished late today,' said Katie, looking at her watch.

'Tell me about it. We were held up for more than an hour because one of the witnesses in the Darley case had a fainting fit. I was minded to postpone the hearing until tomorrow, but then we would have had to put up seventeen witnesses in a hotel for the night and two of the gardaí had come down all the way from Dundalk, so there would have been all manner of mayhem.'

'So it's all wrapped up now, the Darley case?'

'The jury will be back tomorrow to deliberate, but I don't think there's much doubt that they'll find the Darleys guilty as charged. If they do, I won't be going easy on them, I can tell you. To be honest with you, Katie, it's hard to know what punishment is going to be enough for those two scummers. They ran that orphanage like a brothel for more than five years, and I can't imagine how many young lives they've ruined.'

'How about a stiff drink, Your Honour?' Katie asked him.

The barman came over and Kieran ordered a Jameson's on the rocks. Katie laid her hand on his and gave him a sympathetic smile. She still found it hard to believe how he had come into her life just when she needed him most. After the killing of Justice Quinn, he had been sent down from the Criminal Courts of Justice in Dublin to assist in the courts in Cork. The original arrangement had been for two months only, but the pressure on the courts in Cork had been such that two months had been extended to four, and then six, and because of his relationship with Katie he had found one excuse after another not to return to the capital.

She loved everything about him. He was very tall, at least six foot three or four, with swept-back flax-coloured hair, which was beginning to glisten silver at the sides. He could have been Scandinavian rather than Irish, with a broad forehead and high cheekbones and washed-out blue eyes that looked as if they had faded to that colour because he had been standing for too long on the prow of a longboat, staring out to sea.

Most of all, though, she loved his calmness, and his deep reassuring voice. Whenever she was stressed, it would take only half an hour of talking to Kieran and she would already start to feel stable, and focused, and able to take on the world again.

After half an hour of talking, Kieran finished his drink, put down his glass and said, 'So. Are you ready for the Bon Secours? I called Sister Brogan again and told her we should be there around nine-thirty.'

'It's funny, but I'm nervous,' said Katie.

'Nervous? You?'

'I feel responsible, that's why.'

'Katie, you can't be responsible for the actions that other people take.'

'Yes I am, if they took that action because of me.'

She looked across at Saoirse, but Saoirse simply shrugged and said, 'Go on, girl. You'll be grand.'

They left The Glasshouse and walked to the hotel car park. It had started to drizzle, which had damped down the smell of smoke, but Katie could still see blue lights flashing over the rooftops and hear the rumble of diesel engines running. She said goodbye to Saoirse, giving her a hug and promising to meet again soon for lunch at Isaacs.

She and Kieran climbed into her Audi, and once they had buckled up their seat belts he leaned over and gave her a long, passionate kiss.

'I've been looking forward to that all day,' he smiled, stroking her short bob as if he had never come across hair as red and silky as that before.

'I'm still nervous, Kieran.'

'You really don't need to be. I think you can just be thankful that it didn't turn out to be tragic.'

Katie started the engine and drove them down Summerhill, crossing the River Lee by the Brian Boru Bridge and then heading westward until she turned off at Gaol Walk.

They passed the grim pillared façade that was all that remained of the old Cork County Gaol. Kieran said, 'This is a tad ironic. Do you think that Fate's trying to tell you something?'

He was referring to the five IRA men who had been caught at the Dripsey Ambush. They had all been buried here, in the gaol, after their execution at Victoria Barracks.

Katie glanced up at the prison entrance. 'All I want Fate to tell me right now is that I'm cleared of misconduct and that I can go back to work.'

She pulled into the car park outside the Bon Secours Hospital. She sat behind the wheel for a moment, taking long deep breaths to steady her nerves. Kieran watched her with concern on his face but said nothing. Eventually, she said, 'Right. I'm ready so.' She opened her bag and handed Kieran a face mask, put on her own mask, and they both climbed out of the car.

Inside the reception area, Sister Brogan came out to meet them. Because of the Covid pandemic, visitors were not usually allowed, but Kieran had used his influence as a High Court justice to arrange for the two of them to be admitted.

Sister Brogan was short and tubby and she looked at them over the top of her mask like an inquisitive hedgehog. 'She's on the first floor,' she told them. 'Serious, I think your coming to see her will do her a whole world of good. Dr Crowley, the consultant psychiatrist, paid her a visit this afternoon and told me that she's still feeling pure isolated, do you know what I mean, as if nobody cares about her.'

They went up in the lift together. When they reached the first floor, Kieran said, 'Listen, Katie, I'll wait outside to begin with. You two should have some time alone together. Look – there's a chair down there and I can sit and make a few phone calls. When you're ready, you can give me a wave.'

'Thanks, Kieran,' said Katie. Sister Brogan had already opened the door to the private room and was waiting for her to come in.

'Kyna,' she announced. 'You have a visitor.'

Katie entered the room, and there was Kyna sitting up in bed. She looked ghostly pale, with plum-coloured shadows under her eyes, and her blonde hair was scrunched up into a tight bun on top of her head. Both her wrists were wrapped in thick white bandages, and she was connected to a drip.

'*Katie,*' she croaked, and her eyes were instantly filled with tears.

'Detective Sergeant Ní Nuallán,' said Katie softly. She went up to Kyna's bed, laid her hand on her shoulder, and kissed her. Her lips were dry, but Katie kissed her with as much passion and as much feeling as Kieran had kissed her in the car.

'I never thought that you'd come,' sobbed Kyna. 'I thought that you'd hate me when you found out what I'd done.'

'Kyna, I could never hate you. I loved you before and I love you now and I always will. You have no idea what a fierce shock it was when I heard what had happened to you.'

'It didn't happen to me. I did it to myself. I wanted to leave this world if I couldn't have you and never come back. When I woke up here and realized that I was still alive, I can't tell you how desperate I felt.'

Katie tugged a tissue out of the box beside the bed and gently dabbed Kyna's eyes. 'They tell me it was your landlady who found you.'

'Yes. If I'd remembered to pay my rent I'd be lying in Saint Fin Barr's cemetery right now, and I wouldn't know a thing about nothing.'

Katie pulled over a chair and sat beside the bed, holding Kyna's hand.

'Kyna, sweetheart, if there's one horrendous thing I've learned about life, it's that there's only one of you. Sometimes you have to make a choice and that choice means you have to abandon somebody or something that you dearly love.'

'But all I wanted was *you*, Katie. There was nobody else in my life.'

'I know. But one day you'll meet somebody else you fall in

love with, and you wouldn't have been able to do that if you were lying in a box in Saint Fin Barr's cemetery, would you? You're a beautiful woman, Kyna, and some other woman is bound to be attracted to you. Then I can be nothing more to you than a happy memory.'

At first, Kyna didn't answer, but took hold of the cuff of Katie's blouse and twiddled the button between her fingertips.

After a while, she said in a monotone, 'I swallowed one hundred and twenty tablets of paracetamol and drank a whole bottle of codeine cough medicine. Then I cut both of my wrists with my carving knife. But my landlady tied up my wrists with kitchen towels, and when they brought me here to the hospital they washed out my stomach. Gastric lavage, they call it. It sounds almost romantic, doesn't it, gastric lavage? And I've been on dextrose ever since.'

'How much longer do you think you'll have to stay here?'

'Another three or four days, the doctor told me.'

'And then?'

'I don't know. I don't really have any family to go to.'

'Why don't you come and stay with me for a while at Carrig View?'

Kyna frowned. 'What would your Kieran think about that?'

'Kieran's a judge, Kyna. He's a whole lot more understanding than most men. He's waiting outside, as a matter of fact, if you'd like to see him.'

Kyna twisted Katie's cuff and said, 'Can't we be alone together, just for a little while longer?'

Katie stayed for three or four minutes more, although neither of them spoke. At last, Katie stood up and gave Kyna a quick kiss on her lips, followed by another quick kiss on her forehead.

'I'll come back tomorrow so, to see how you are.'

'Katie—'

'I'm sorry, Kyna, but life isn't a fairy story. You know that yourself, from all your experience in the force. We just have to be thankful for whatever love that others give us, and like I said, I will always love you. But I love Kieran more, and there's nothing I can do about that, so help me God.'

She went to the door and opened it, pausing for a moment to look back at Kyna. The look they exchanged between them could have been accompanied by heart-rending music. Then she closed the door and went to find Kieran.

As they left the hospital, it was raining hard. They hurried across the car park and scrambled quickly into Katie's car.

'Are you coming back to Carrig View?' asked Katie.

'You know I'd love to, but I have to make an early start tomorrow.'

'Maybe the weekend, then?'

'Try and stop me.'

Katie shook the rain out of her hair and then she leaned across and gave Kieran a kiss.

'You're not jealous of Kyna, are you? I told her that I still loved her, but I love you more.'

'And what did she say to that?'

'She's a sad and lonely young woman, Kieran.'

Kieran sat watching the rain trickling down the windscreen and said nothing for a while.

'You *are* jealous, aren't you?' said Katie.

'Maybe a little. I can't say that I wouldn't like you all to myself. But you're fond of her, and she needs your support, so let's support her.'

Katie kissed him again, and then she started the engine.

3

The next morning, Katie overslept until a quarter past nine. When she opened the curtains, she saw that it was a grey day, but bright, and at least it wasn't raining. She made herself a breakfast of smoked salmon slices and scrambled eggs, with a strong black coffee, and sat in the kitchen eating it while her two setters, Barney and Foltchain, sat staring at her as if they still couldn't quite believe that she was going to spend all day with them, instead of leaving them in the care of her neighbour, Jenny Tierney, and going off to work.

There were still no messages from Internal Affairs or from the new chief superintendent, O'Leary, so she decided to take the dogs for a long walk in Marlogue Woods, and maybe down to the beach too.

It was only a fifteen-minute drive to the nature reserve, and as chilly as it was, both her dogs loved to cram their heads out of the passenger-side window and feel the wind blustering in their faces. Katie was sure that as soon as they drove through Ballymore they recognized where they were going, because Barney let out an excited yelp.

There were only two other cars in the car park, and when they began their walk between the oaks and the beech trees, there was absolute silence, not even a chaffinch chirping. Katie felt in a reflective mood and couldn't stop thinking about Kyna. How do you rescue someone you love when you simply can't give them what they desperately need, which is you, yourself?

Foltchain, her red-and-white setter, stopped and looked back at her as if she understood what was troubling her. Katie smiled at Foltchain and called out, 'I'm all right, girl! I'm grand altogether!' and Foltchain scampered off to catch up with Barney.

They emerged from the trees and out on to the stony beach that overlooked the inlet from the Celtic Sea. The water was grey this morning, and the surface was ruffled, but both Barney and Foltchain loved running through the shallows, circling around and around and splashing each other.

Katie was standing on the shingle watching them when her phone warbled. When she took it out of the pocket of her duffel coat, she saw that she was being called by Bill Phinner.

'Superintendent Maguire? I've just been briefing himself about last night's bombing, but I thought I should bring you up to speed as well. Strictly between me and you, like.'

'So it was a bombing?'

'Absolutely. We found residue of RDX so we're talking about an explosive device packed with C-4. We've identified the seat of the explosion and although it was one almighty blast, we're also pretty certain what that explosive device was packed in.'

'Hold up a second,' Katie told him. She could see an elderly couple further along the beach who were walking their spaniel, and Barney and Foltchain were already running off to make its acquaintance. 'I need to call my dogs back.'

She gave a piercing whistle between finger and thumb and her two setters reluctantly turned around and came trotting towards her, tongues hanging out, trying to look innocent.

'Sorry, Bill. I didn't want to find myself breaking up a dogfight. I have enough troubles to contend with.'

'The device was in a cardboard box containing a Hauswirt air fryer,' Bill Phinner told her. 'It was placed on the floor of the kitchen beside the back door. The Hauswirt's one of the largest air fryers, twenty-five-litre capacity, so I'd say it was packed with more than a kilo and a half of C-4. We retrieved multiple fragments from the air fryer's casing and three or four small pieces of cardboard.'

'Does the cardboard have any prints on it? Any DNA?'

'One thumbprint only, but the Good Lord must have been smiling on us. We haven't been able to match it yet, but it's a fine clear print, like, and it was made by neither of the two victims.'

'Well, all we have to do now is find ourselves a suspect and check out his thumb. You don't happen to know if any warning was given, do you?'

'Not so far as I know, ma'am. I asked DS ó Broin but he was kind of tight-lipped about it. All he would tell me was that things were "ongoing".'

'That's annoying. A warning about a bomb can often give you a clue as to who planted it, even if they don't come out afterwards and admit it was them. You know – like the Real IRA used to use the codewords "Martha Pope", just to prove their warning was genuine.'

'This wouldn't have been the IRA, of course. Brendan McCarthy was almost IRA himself, or certainly sympathetic. More likely he'd got on the wrong side of one of the local gangs, like the O'Donnells.'

While she was talking to Bill Phinner, Katie was watching Barney and Foltchain running around in the shallows. She felt so frustrated that she kicked the shingle. If only she had been back in her office in Anglesea Street, she could have immediately launched an investigation into Brendan McCarthy's background. As Bill had suggested, it was quite possible that he had been tangled up in some illegal activity and a rival had wanted him out of the way.

He had been employed by Opel as a salesman, but he could have been dealing in stolen cars and changing their number plates, or assisting a gang of local car thieves by supplying them with duplicate keys and registration documents. She had come across the same kind of organized car-thieving before.

Maybe Micheál ó Broin had started looking into it, but he was a bureaucrat by nature, and a stickler for procedure. All the t's had to be crossed and all the i's dotted before the next step could be taken. That didn't mean that he was a poor detective. He had a very reasonable record of arrests and convictions. It simply meant that he was hypercautious, and not a man to take any chances. Apart from that, he had nothing like Katie's numerous contacts in Cork's criminal and semi-criminal underworld. Neither did he know any of the gangsters' wives and girlfriends who frequently tipped off Katie with some of her most useful and incriminating information.

She whistled again at Barney and Foltchain and called out, 'Come on, you two scallywags! Time to go home for some lunch. And, Bill, thanks a million for the update. If you can let me know if anything new comes up, I'd appreciate it.'

'Before you go, ma'am,' said Bill, 'I thought you ought to know that DS Mullan has gone missing.'

'Conor Mullan? What do you mean, "gone missing"?'

'From what I hear, he was supposed to show up for duty yesterday afternoon, but he never appeared. DS Begley phoned his home, but his wife told him that he'd left at the usual time and he'd given her no sign that anything at all was amiss.'

'And there's no indication of where he might have gone?'

'None at all. His mobile's dead and there's not a trace of his car. He was last seen on CCTV at the junction of the Boreenmanna Road and the South Link Road. After that, nothing. Wherever he went, he probably knew that there were no cameras.'

'That's a real worry, Bill. He's been with us only six months and so far all his work has been first-class. He's been investigating the Dooley gang for smuggling drugs through Ringaskiddy, but I wouldn't have thought the Dooleys would have done him any harm. They're as soft as Gubbeen, the Dooleys. They gave a fellow a serious beating with a hurley last year and almost killed him but afterwards they drove him to the Mercy and carried him into the ED.'

'Well, here's hoping that Mullan's alive and well, like. I've had a couple of my own staff go missing for a few days because of the stress. Fortunately, they both came back.'

Katie whistled again to Barney and Foltchain and then she said, 'I know Mullan's wife, Maeve. He brought her along to that fundraising party we held last October at the Maryborough. Very sweet she was, but shy. I think it might be a good idea if I go over to Douglas and see how she's coping.'

'Okay then, ma'am. I'll let you know if we hear any news of DS Mullan at the station. Ó Broin has been keeping a tight lid on his disappearance, so far as the media's concerned. He says he doesn't want the public thinking that any of his officers might be coming apart at the seams, like, do you know what I mean?'

'Yes, Bill. I'll talk to you later so. *Maith thú*.'

Maeve Mullan looked both surprised and relieved when she opened her front door and found Katie standing outside.

'Oh! Superintendent Maguire! You've heard, then?'

'Yes, Maeve. Bill Phinner just told me. Is it all right to come in and have a chat to you about it? I gather you still haven't heard from Conor.'

'No, nothing at all.'

Maeve was a small, pretty woman with a cherubic face and braided brunette hair. She was heavily pregnant, and Katie guessed by the bump under her oversized green sweater that she probably had less than a month left to go before she gave birth.

A boy of about three years old came out of the kitchen and into the hallway. He clung on to Maeve's sweater and stared up at Katie suspiciously. Katie supposed that everybody who had called on the house in the past twenty-four hours had come with bad news about his father.

'Hey, don't you be rubbing your chocolatey mouth on me, Noah,' Maeve admonished him, lifting her sleeve away from his face. 'Go wipe it off, will you.'

Katie stepped inside and Maeve showed her into the living room. It was quite cramped, with two large armchairs and a leatherette sofa, and wallpapered with pink chrysanthemums. Yesterday's *Examiner* was still lying untidily folded over the arm of what must be Conor's chair. The fire was unlit and still heaped with ashes, although a two-bar electric fire was keeping the chill off.

Hanging over the fireplace was a framed reproduction of a painting of the Old Head of Kinsale, and the mantelpiece was lined with small silver cups and a shield, which Conor Mullan had won for playing golf.

Katie and Maeve sat side by side on the sofa and Katie took hold of Maeve's hand and gave it a comforting squeeze.

'Would you care for a cup of tea, superintendent?' Maeve asked her.

'For goodness' sake, call me Kathleen. And no, thank you, you're grand altogether. I had a coffee before I came out. Has anybody come down from the station to talk to you?'

Maeve nodded. 'Sean and Cairbre came early this morning. There wasn't much that I could tell them. I've had no messages from Conor. Nothing at all. I've phoned his sister and a few of his golfing friends but none of them have heard from him either.'

Katie was silent for a moment, but then she said gently, 'How has your relationship been with Conor lately? Has there been anything that might have led him to take some time away from you? Any disagreements?'

Maeve sniffed and wiped her eyes with the sleeve of her sweater. 'I didn't tell this to Sean and Cairbre, but he's been kind of frustrated. Well, what with me expecting and all, I haven't felt much like you-know-what. I've tried my best to give him some satisfaction, if you know what I mean, but he's still been edgy, like. Banging doors and not talking.'

'Was he like this when you were expecting Noah?'

'A little, but not so much. But there's something else, and I'm pure worried about this. I didn't tell Sean and Cairbre about it because I found out only this morning. I needed some cash so I went to the ATM in Douglas Village but I was declined. I went into the bank and the manager told me that our account had no funds at all. Zero. In fact, he said that Conor had applied two months ago for an overdraft of two thousand euros but that had all gone too. Every last cent of it, and I can't think what he could have spent it on.'

'He'd arranged an overdraft but you didn't know about it?'

'I had no idea at all, Kathleen. Lately, I've never had to use my bank card when I went shopping because Conor always gave me cash. I thought we had a really healthy balance in the bank because he was always so careful. But our current account was empty and so was our savings account.'

'Does he like a bet? Do you think all this money might have gone on the horses?'

'He likes to go to Mallow now and again, but we've always been together and I only saw him place one bet, and that was because a friend of ours had a horse running in the Hilly Way Chase.'

'Maybe he's been betting online.'

'Well, you could ask Sean and Cairbre about that because they took his laptop. Only borrowed it, like, to see if it could give them any clue to where he's gone to.'

'I'm still officially not allowed to get myself involved in any investigations, Maeve. But I'm sure Cairbre will tell you if there's any clue at all.'

Noah came into the living room and sat on the arm of the sofa next to Maeve, looking sad, so Katie changed the subject and started to talk about The Glasshouse and the new toastie menu at Crack Jenny's pub on Lavitt's Quay.

'Strange you should mention Crack Jenny's,' said Maeve. 'That's where I first met Conor. I was out with all the girls from Penneys but he came straight over bold as you like and asked me for a dance. They were playing "Out Of Control" by the Chemical Brothers and he said that was his favourite song.'

'When's Daddy coming home?' asked Noah.

Maeve put her arm around him and gave him a hug. 'Soon, dote. Soon.'

Katie stayed with Maeve for another half-hour. Before she left, she promised her that she would do everything she reasonably could to find out what had happened to Conor.

'And you can call me any time you feel the need to talk to

someone,' she said, taking hold of Maeve's hands outside the front door and giving them a reassuring squeeze. 'I may be suspended from the station right now, but they can't suspend my heart.'

4

'You're quiet, Cillian,' said his grandfather, as they walked hand in hand up Glenheights Park.

'I'm thinking what to buy,' Cillian told him. 'I have only two euros of my pocket money left and I don't know if I want a Tayto cheese-and-onion chocolate bar or a packet of Eskimo Mints. I can't afford both.'

Cillian's grandfather looked down at him and it was all he could do not to smile. Cillian was a skinny little boy of six years old, with curly ginger hair and a snub nose with freckles on it. He was wearing a Spiderman anorak that was two sizes too big for him because it had been passed down from his older brother, Declan. The sleeves were so long it appeared as if he had no hands.

'I'll treat you to the mints, Cill, so long as I can have one.'

Cillian shook his head. 'Ma told me that I mustn't beg you for nothing because you have so little money yourself.'

'Well, it's true that I'm not a millionaire,' said his grandfather. 'You have only to look at this worn-out old tweed coat of mine. My father bought this coat to wear when he married my mother, and that was in the winter of 1954.'

'You should buy yourself some new glasses instead of those ones stuck together with a bandage.'

Cillian's grandfather laughed. 'I can see you perfectly well through these ones, Cill. It doesn't matter how they're held together.'

They passed St Oliver's Church with its tall needle spire and reached Ballincollie Road. Right on the corner was Derry's convenience store, a single-storey pebbledashed building with signs along its walls advertising charcoal briquettes and fresh-made sandwiches.

'It was only butter your ma wanted, wasn't it?' said Cillian's grandfather, as they opened the shop door.

Cillian had no chance to answer before the shop exploded. A devastating blast blew both of them back across Ballincollie Road to hit the stone wall on the opposite side. They were struck by a blizzard of shattered glass and splintered wood and bent tins and bottles and burst-open boxes of cereals. A woman's torso came tumbling out of the shop, too, headless and legless but still wearing a short pink coat.

Derry's store was almost totally demolished, with its outside walls lying in the road in a scattering of broken breeze blocks, mixed with everything that had been stacked on its shelves and kept in its freezer – pizzas and batteries and cartons of cigarettes and frozen peas and bags of sugar and cakes. Somewhere under this rubble lay Derry himself and any customers who might have been shopping in his store.

Cillian was barely marked and he was sitting up against the wall with his blue eyes open, but he was dead. His grandfather lay on his side not far away, but he had lost both his legs and his old tweed coat had been blown open at the front, so that his ribs were sticking through the skin of his narrow white chest.

The bang of the detonation had been heard far beyond Ballyvolane. Even down in the centre of Cork, three kilometres to the south, shoppers had stopped and frowned at each other, and a similar distance to the north, at White's Cross, the customers at Hennessy's Daybreak café had stopped in mid-conversation.

Katie was at home in Carrig View, vacuum-cleaning dog hairs from the carpet in the living room, but at the same time she was half listening to Cork's 96FM. The song 'Secret Love' was interrupted by the breaking news that Derry's convenience store had been destroyed by an unexplained explosion.

Katie switched off her vacuum cleaner. Barney came trotting out of the kitchen and stared at her, whining softly in the back of his throat. Foltchain followed him and stared at her too.

Derry's in Ballyvolane, she was thinking. That shop was owned and run by Derry O'Brien, and she remembered him from the investigation that she had run into the Dripsey Dozen.

Two explosions in two days at properties occupied by members of the Dozen. Could that really be a coincidence? She waited for more news from the radio, but it had gone back to playing 'Secret Love'.

She left Barney and Foltchain with Jenny next door and drove to Ballyvolane. When she reached the corner of Glenheights Road and Glenthorn Drive she found that the road ahead was cordoned off, so she had to pull over and park. Further up the hill she could see fire engines and ambulances and one of the armoured khaki trucks that belonged to the army bomb disposal unit from Collins Barracks.

Two soldiers were standing guard on the cordon. She walked up to them and showed them her ID card, but one of them shook his head and said, 'Sorry, but we've strict orders not to permit nobody at all past this point.'

'What happened up there? Was it an IED?'

'Can't tell you, ma'am. But all the houses up to Glenheights Park have been evacuated, just in case.'

Katie could see the white Technical Bureau van half hidden behind the bomb disposal truck, and she was tempted to call Bill Phinner. She decided against it, though. She had to bear in mind that she was still suspended, and in any case Bill and his technical team must be totally preoccupied sorting through the wreckage, trying to determine what had caused the explosion and how it had been detonated.

It was likely that DI O'Sullivan was up there at the scene too, but she decided not to call him either. If he were to give her any unauthorized information about the blast, he could find himself in all kinds of trouble – especially if Micheál ó Broin became aware of what he had told her.

She went back to her car and drove down to the courthouse on Anglesea Street to see if there was any chance of talking to Kieran. When she arrived, though, she found that he was in the middle of hearing a case against three teenagers charged with a stabbing. She entered the public gallery so that he could see her, but she refrained from waving, and although Kieran nodded in her direction that was all he could do, in case the defence accused him of being distracted. The defence lawyer, Aidan Boyle, knew who she was and it was likely that he also knew about her relationship with Kieran. It was almost impossible to keep any secrets in the legal community in Cork.

Katie drove back to Carrig View feeling empty and useless. It started to rain as she crossed over the Glashaboy River, so hard that she had to switch her windscreen wipers on to what her late husband, Paul, used to call 'fecking full flap'.

After she had returned home, she went next door and collected the dogs, who bounded around her as if she had been away for a week. Then she made herself a coffee and switched on the radio and the television on mute to see if there was any news about the explosion at Derry's.

She was troubled the most by the fact that both Brendan McCarthy and Derry O'Brien had been linked to the Dripsey Dozen. Of course, it was possible that this was a coincidence, or that both of them had political or criminal connections that had gone fatally wrong. Republican terrorists and local drug gangs had both used improvised explosive devices to get their revenge on people who had crossed them, and last year alone the bomb squad in Ireland had been called out to defuse more than fifty IEDs.

Katie wondered if the remaining members of the Dripsey Dozen should be warned that they could all be in mortal danger. Perhaps they had already worked that out for themselves when they had seen the news. Perhaps they even had some idea of who was out to exterminate them.

If she had been in charge of this case herself, she would have tipped all of them off, and cautioned them to keep their eyes open wherever they went, and to search their homes daily, and not to touch any suspicious packages, and to check underneath their cars before they climbed in. But at the moment she had no authority to do so, and no access to the files with their addresses and contact details in them.

She was also worried that Micheál ó Broin would lodge a formal complaint and accuse her of trying to subvert his investigation. A complaint like that might be spurious, but it would do little to encourage the Discipline Section to lift her suspension anytime soon.

She was still thinking about what she should do, if anything, when ó Broin himself appeared on the television screen. He was standing outside the Garda station on Anglesea Street, holding up a large black umbrella. She switched the sound back on in time to hear him saying, '—sadly, three innocent shoppers lost their lives too, and we offer our deepest condolences to their families and their friends. The scene of the explosion is still cordoned off, in case of a second device having been planted there, although we don't believe that's likely. We're working on the assumption that this was personal, since Mr O'Brien had no political connections that we know of.'

Katie felt like phoning Micheál immediately and telling him that Derry O'Brien had been an active member of the Dripsey Dozen, and if that wasn't a political connection then she didn't know what was.

She was fairly sure, however, that Micheál probably wouldn't answer when he saw who was calling him. Even if he did – and even if he were to listen to what she had to say – it was more than likely that he would ignore her. He would tell her again that she was jumping to conclusions with no evidence to back them up, and he had his own systematic way of conducting investigations, thank you, with a seventy-six per cent conviction record to prove it.

She muted the television sound again. She wasn't in the mood to listen to Dáithí and Maura chatting to some psychologist on *Today*. The radio started to play 'I'll Be Missing You', which had been played at Paul's funeral, so she switched that off too. She sat with her coffee growing cold, listening to the rain pattering against the windows. Barney and Foltchain sensed her mood and settled on the floor by her feet, wuffling occasionally but not demanding that she stroke them or playfully tug at their ears.

A few minutes after six o'clock, she heard the sound of Kieran's Volvo drawing up outside. She went to the front door and opened it, and he came hurrying in with a plastic folder held over his head.

'Jesus,' he said, brushing the rain off his sleeves. 'What a hell of a day that was.'

Katie helped him to take off his coat, shook it, and then hung it up next to hers. She stood on tiptoe and kissed him, and he took hold of her head in both hands so that he could give her a long kiss in return.

'I expect I can tempt you to a whiskey,' she smiled.

'Don't bother to pour it out, Katie. Just give me the bottle.'

They went through to the living room, and Barney and Foltchain both stood up with their tails slowly wagging. Whenever Kieran visited they were respectful, because they could tell that Katie was very fond of him, but they were still protective towards her.

'You've heard about that explosion up at Ballyvolane?'

'Heard about it? Two of our ushers were standing outside having a smoke, and they actually heard it. Some convenience store, that's what I heard on the news just now.'

'Derry's. It belonged to a fellow called Derry O'Brien, and would you believe it, he was one of the Dripsey Dozen too.'

Katie poured out a large glass of Jameson's whiskey for Kieran and a vodka and tonic for herself. She sat down on the couch beside him and gave him another kiss.

'You think there could be some kind of vendetta going on?' Kieran asked her.

'There's no way of telling, not for sure. But I was thinking that if I was in charge at the moment, I'd be warning all the rest of the Dozen to be doggy wide, like, and not to touch any packages unless they were sure what was in them.'

'Can you not suggest that to Micheál ó Broin?'

'I doubt if he'd listen. He said on the news that he doesn't believe that it's anything political. Not only that, he seems to think that God created women gardaí for the sole purpose of annoying him.'

'You should try, all the same. People's lives are at stake here, after all. From what I heard on the news, three shoppers were killed, along with the shop owner himself. A woman, a little boy of six years old, and his grandpa.'

'Mother of God. That's tragic. I have an appointment with my solicitor in South Mall tomorrow, so I'll call in at the station afterwards and see if Micheál will give me a hearing.'

Katie paused, and took a thoughtful sip of her drink. Then she said, 'So what made your day so hellish?'

'Two things. You saw those three lads who were up in front of me. They were charged with stabbing another lad, who was dating the ex-girlfriend of one of them. It was a miracle they didn't kill the poor fellow, or they would have been up for murder.'

'I can't believe young boys today. Give them the slightest excuse and they're out with a knife, or a machete. When I was at school, the worst they ever dished out was a lowry – a punch on the nose.'

'I agree with you. But I keep my mouth shut. Remember what happened to Mr Justice Carney during the Wayne O'Donoghue case. He made comments to the media about the proliferation of stabbings, and the case had to go for a retrial.

'But anyhow, what happened today was, one of the accused lads went to the toilet during the lunch break and tried to cut his own throat with a razor blade. How he'd managed to hide it, we have no idea. Thank God the guard who was with him grew suspicious about how long he'd been in the stall, and stopped his bleeding with a handful of paper towels.'

'That's horrifying. That really is.'

'Well, of course, we cancelled the hearing for the rest of the day. We spent the afternoon with the registrar, rearranging our schedule.'

'You said *two* things made your day hellish. What was the other one?'

Kieran put down his drink and took hold of Katie's hands. He looked her straight in the eyes and she knew that he was going to say something serious.

'They want me back in Dublin.'

Katie felt as if cold water had been poured down her back, and she gave an involuntary shiver.

'Serious? Can't you postpone it again? Can't you tell them how badly they need you in Cork?'

Kieran slowly shook his head. 'I tried, Katie, believe me. But Judge Denis Twomey has retired prematurely because of ill health and they need me.'

Tears slid down Katie's cheeks. 'Kieran, what will I do? I'm almost sure they're going to end my suspension very soon, and then I'll be working all the hours that God sends me as usual and I won't be able to come up to Dublin to see you. Maybe I shouldn't go back.'

Kieran put his arms around her and held her tight, breathing in the perfume that he could smell in her hair.

'I know. I'm pure devastated. When they called me this morning and told me, I felt like saying that I quit.'

'You can't, Kieran. You can't quit. Not for me.'

'And you can't quit for me, either.'

They sat in silence for a long time, holding each other close. A log in the fire lurched, and the rain kept sprinkling against the windows.

'What date are you supposed to start?' asked Katie at last.

'January the second.'

'What are we going to do, Kieran? I love you. I can't lose you.'

'Katie, I simply don't know. I love you too. I spend my whole life making decisions, that's my job, but this is one decision that's beyond me.'

When they went to bed that night, well after midnight, they didn't make love, but held on to each other as if they were on board the *Titanic* and it was sinking beneath them.

5

When he came out at nine o'clock the next morning to empty the rubbish bin at the Blackrock Castle car park, Shay Carroll saw that a single car was still parked at the far end of it, as if it had been there all night.

It was a grey Nissan Qashqai with 2019 Cork registration plates. He walked up to it and peered into the window to see if anyone was sleeping in it. This had happened twice before, once when a man had been too drunk to drive any further, and another time when a woman had caught her husband in bed with another woman and hadn't wanted to return home.

There was nobody inside the Nissan, either asleep or awake, but on the passenger seat Shay saw a neatly folded pile of clothes: a pair of dark blue trousers and a dark blue sweater and a light blue jacket. On top of these folded clothes was a pair of brown shoes, each with a sock stuffed into it. On the driver's seat lay a white envelope with something scribbled on it, although he couldn't make out what it was.

He looked around. It was a chilly morning, with low grey clouds, but it wasn't raining. Whoever owned this car, they obviously hadn't come to visit Blackrock Castle, because it didn't open for visitors for another hour. The castle itself stood right on the edge of the River Lee, with a tall crenellated tower, like a castle from a Disney film. It had originally been built to deter pirates from sneaking in and stealing ships from Cork Harbour, but now it was an observatory and a research centre, open to the public.

Since the owner of the car had left his clothes here, Shay wondered if he might have gone for a swim. The river was only a few metres from the car park, and there was no fence. As chilly as it was, he knew that there were enthusiasts who enjoyed going for a swim in the winter, even on Saint Stephen's Day.

He tried the door handle, and to his surprise the car was unlocked. He opened the driver's door and saw that the keys were still in the ignition. He picked up the envelope, took his glasses out of the pocket of his windcheater, and saw that it was addressed to 'Maeve'.

The envelope wasn't stuck down, though, and even though it was addressed to Maeve, he took out the sheet of paper inside and unfolded it. There were only two words written on it, in a spidery scrawl, as if the writer had been shivering.

I'm sorry.

When Katie stepped out of the lift at Anglesea Street, she almost bumped into her personal assistant, Moirin, who was carrying two cups of cappuccino.

'Superintendent Maguire! Jesus, ma'am, I nearly anointed you then!'

'Good to see you, Moirin. How's yourself?'

Moirin lowered her voice. 'I'm grand. But have they lifted your suspension yet? I've sore missed you, if you want to know the God's-honest truth.'

Katie began to walk along the corridor with her, back in the direction of her erstwhile office.

'I've not heard yet, but I'm expecting an outcome soon. I miss this place myself – and I miss you, too.'

'Have you come to see Micheál ó Broin?'

'I'm hoping to. I didn't tell them at the desk downstairs, in case they phoned up and told him that I was there, and he said that he was too busy. I just said I was picking up some papers.'

'I hope you don't mind my asking, but do you and he – well, do you not get along so well?'

Katie couldn't help smiling. 'Let's just say that I'm chalk and he's Ballyhooly Blue.'

They reached Micheál ó Broin's office and because Moirin had both her hands full, Katie knocked. *Knocking at the door of my own office*, she couldn't help thinking. Micheál called out 'Come!' and they both entered, Moirin first, and Katie right behind her.

Micheál was sitting back with his feet on top of the desk, ankles crossed, wearing a black shirt and grey braces. Wedged into a leather armchair on the opposite side of the room was Councillor Ian O'Shea, big-bellied and balding, with a bristling moustache and cheeks like two bruised apples.

Ian O'Shea was a member of Cork County Council's Joint Policing Committee, and Katie had clashed with him several times in the past on questions of strategy, especially when it came to rooting out organized crime. Councillor O'Shea persistently argued that there was very little in the way of organized crime in Cork, and it was one of the safest cities in Ireland. Katie had often wondered if he was being paid by one or more of the drug-dealers and people traffickers to keep the Garda off their backs.

'Kathleen!' said Micheál, swinging his feet off the desk. 'This is an unexpected pleasure. Well, it's unexpected, anyhow.'

Moirin set down the two cups of coffee. Then she gave Katie a quick, nervous smile and hurried out of the office, closing the door behind her.

'I'm kind of involved in a private meeting here, as it happens,' said Micheál.

'I can see that,' Katie told him. She nodded to Ian O'Shea and said, 'Good to see you, councillor. How's the boat repair business? Still afloat?'

Ian O'Shea gave an uncomfortable grunt and said nothing. Whatever he and Micheál had been talking about, it was clear that he was seriously annoyed that Katie had found him here, and that he was expecting Micheál to usher her out of the office with as much haste as possible.

Katie said, 'I was only passing, and I was interested to know if you'd made any progress with either of those two bombings.'

'We've made some progress, yes. But I'm afraid that at this stage it's confidential.'

'Micheál,' Katie retorted, 'I may be temporarily suspended, but I still have security clearance.'

Ian O'Shea levered himself out of his armchair to come across to the desk and pick up his cup of coffee. As he passed, he looked Katie up and down and said, 'Security clearance? You stood by while two women blew the brains out of two prominent local businessmen. And you still have security clearance? Christ on a bicycle.'

'Oh, and what was I supposed to do, councillor? Shoot those two women in cold blood? And that pair of gurriers you describe as "prominent local businessmen" were two of the worst criminals this city has ever known. Thomas O'Flynn and Barry Riordan. Murderers, the both of them.'

'So you say. But they were never convicted in a court of law, were they? And capital punishment for murder was abolished in 1964, as you well know. It wasn't up to you to be the arbiter of life or death.'

Katie said, 'I didn't come here to discuss the rights or wrongs of my suspension. I came here to make sure that Micheál here was aware that Derry O'Brien was also a member of the Dripsey Dozen.'

Micheál had picked up his cappuccino, but now he put it down again.

'No, Kathleen, I did *not* know. But I'm not at all convinced that it's relevant. Earlier this year, in Limerick, two priests were shot dead in the space of a week, one each side of Easter. As it turned out, though, their deaths were entirely unconnected. I didn't automatically conclude that someone was carrying out a vendetta against the Church.'

'Besides,' put in Ian O'Shea, 'who in Cork of all places would wish harm on such dedicated republicans? If you ask me, we should be looking for one of them Romanian gangs. Maybe both McCarthy and O'Brien were mixed up with drugs, or people-smuggling, and got themselves on the wrong side of them.'

'Whatever you think, councillor, I believe it would be sensible to warn all the remaining members of the Dripsey Dozen that their lives may be in danger,' said Katie. 'Some of them may have moved in the past couple of years, but you should be able to find most of their contact details on file, and they all keep in touch with each other, so far as I know.'

'That's all very well, Kathleen. But so far we have no concrete evidence that these two explosions were linked in any way at all, or that they had any connection at all to this "Dripsey Dozen". As Councillor O'Shea rightly pointed out, this is the rebel county and these people are regarded as heroes and heroines.'

'Quite apart from that, I wouldn't want to be causing them any unnecessary alarm. Can you imagine what the media would be saying about us if we went around knocking on their doors, telling them that they were likely to be blown to smithereens – scaring the living shite out of them with no real evidence at all?'

'Oh, really?' Katie snapped back at him. 'And what will the media be saying about us if there's a third explosion, and that explosion kills yet another member of the Dripsey Dozen?'

Micheál looked down to the floor, like a weary headmaster trying to reason with a recalcitrant pupil.

'We can only act on evidence, Kathleen. Not hunches. Not speculation. Solid, provable evidence. We've seen far too many miscarriages of justice in this country in the past few years, and too many times it was down to gardaí putting prejudice first and proof second.'

At that moment there was a light tap at the door and Assistant Commissioner Frank Magorian came in, without waiting for Micheál to invite him. He was tall, Frank Magorian, at least six feet three, with grey wings to his slicked-back hair and a large face that was still as pink as boiled bacon from his last holiday in Gran Canaria.

It was Frank Magorian who had informed Katie, with great reluctance, that she was suspended. Unlike many of his colleagues, he was a strong supporter of diversity in An Garda Síochána, both sexual and racial. His own wife, Syahla, was Indonesian, and a professional violinist, and almost as tall as he was. He had backed Katie's promotion to detective superintendent against fierce opposition, especially from freemasons.

'Well, well, if it isn't Kathleen Maguire,' he said, with a genial smile. 'You're not really supposed to be here, are you?'

'I came in to see if Micheál was making any headway with these two bombings. And to make a suggestion that might prevent any more.'

'Oh, yes?'

Micheál flapped his hand as if he were swatting an annoying fly. 'Kathleen believes that she's worked out the motive already. I mean – set aside the fact that we've yet to receive the full forensic report on the Ballyvolane bombing, and that we don't even know if it was the same kind of device with the same type of explosive.'

'So, Kathleen, what do you think the motive might be?' asked Frank Magorian.

Micheál gave Katie no time to answer. 'It's tenuous, to say the least. It seems as if Derry O'Brien was a distant descendant of one of the men who was executed for his involvement in the Dripsey Ambush, and so was Brendan McCarthy, and that's enough for Kathleen to assume that there's some sort of vendetta going on. Jesus, it's at least four generations since that ambush, and those men must have hundreds of descendants by now. Thousands, even.'

'But there's only twelve of them in the Dripsey Dozen,' said Katie. 'Well – only ten of them now. I came here to suggest to Micheál that we might advise those remaining ten to keep sketch for any suspicious packages or anything that might look like an IED.'

'Crying wolf, if you ask me,' put in Ian O'Shea.

'Wolves may be dangerous, councillor,' said Katie, without looking at him. 'As a rule, though, wolves don't bear grudges. And they're not too handy when it comes to making bombs.'

'Well, I'll leave you two to sort this out between you,' said Frank Magorian. 'Meanwhile, I've come to tell you that DS Mullan's car has been found.'

'Serious?' asked Micheál. 'Where?'

'It was left in the car park at Blackrock Castle, apparently overnight, and his clothes and shoes were discovered inside it, along with a note addressed to his wife.'

'Holy Mother,' said Katie. 'Do you know what the note said?'

'Not yet. I ran into Brian Keane downstairs and he said that the call had only just come in. The fellow who found his car spent about half an hour looking for him, because he thought he might have gone for a swim.'

'In the Lee, in November? And after leaving a note for his wife? Was this fellow thick or not?'

'Pff! I wouldn't have left a note for my wife,' said Ian O'Shea. 'I might have left one for my bookie, though, telling him to go to hell.'

Frank Magorian ignored him. 'Apart from our own search team, we've alerted the coastguard, and of course the Cork City Missing Persons Search and Recovery. They'll be taking their inflatable boat out, with the sonar.'

'I saw Maeve Mullan yesterday afternoon,' said Katie. 'She was in flitters. Is anybody going to tell her that Conor's car has been found?'

'Brian said that two officers had already been sent to bring her up to date. And console her, of course.'

'I'll dispatch O'Sullivan and Coughlan down to Blackrock, too,' said Micheál. 'I mean, Jesus, as if we haven't lost enough detectives with the Covid, and Mullan's one of the best. Well, he *was* one of the best.'

'He's not been found yet,' Katie said quietly. 'Let's not jump the gun.'

Micheál gave her a sour look, but Katie simply smiled back at him.

'Can we have a quick word, Kathleen?' said Frank Magorian. 'Outside?'

Katie lifted her hand to say *slán go fóill* to Micheál and to Ian O'Shea, and then she went out into the corridor with Frank Magorian. They walked as far as the lift, to make sure they were completely out of earshot, and then Frank Magorian said, 'I was intending to text you later, but since you're here you've saved me the trouble. And it's grand to see you. You may have been itching to get back to work but it looks as if the time off has done you no harm at all.'

'You've heard from Internal Affairs?'

'Not officially. But Pat Devain called me this morning and said that Muireann Nic Riada and Megan Riordan will be coming up for sentencing next Tuesday. Of course, they both pleaded guilty to killing Thomas O'Flynn and Barry Riordan. With all the witnesses, including you, they didn't have much alternative. But once the officers appointed to look into your case have heard what sentence Judge Finnegan has decided to hand down, they'll be making a final decision on your suspension.

'Pat said nothing definite, and he told me not to get your hopes up. But the feeling seems to be that both women had a rake of justification for killing those two reprobates, considering the way that they'd been treated. Your refusal to shoot them may have been a difficult moral decision, but it was the right one. You were not going to kill two good women to save the lives of two bad men.'

'So when do you think I might hear something definite?' asked Katie.

'By the end of next week, with any luck,' said Frank Magorian. He turned around and looked towards the door of Micheál's office. 'I didn't want to say anything in front of himself, because I'm aware that he quite fancies the idea of staying on here in Cork as detective superintendent, instead of going back to Limerick. He's not a bad fellow at all if you can get past his ego, and he's been a first-rate detective, too, although he works in a totally different way from you. Much more by the book.'

'I'll wait to hear, then,' said Katie. 'Whatever the Discipline Section decide, though, I'd like to thank you, sir, for all your support.'

'Kathleen, you're that rare creature, a highly efficient detective with heart. If I didn't support you, I'd be cutting off my nose to spite my face.'

6

Katie drove to Blackrock Castle. When she arrived, she found that the car park had been cordoned off and that it was jammed with Garda cars and vans as well as an ambulance, and teeming with gardaí in fluorescent jackets and volunteers from the search and recovery team in their distinctive red lifebelts.

Gathered behind the police tape she recognized reporters from the *Examiner*, the *Echo*, Cork Beo and RTÉ. After she had parked and climbed out of her car, Dinny O'Rourke from the *Echo* shouted out, 'Detective Superintendent Mag-*why*-aah! Have ye heard any news about your suspension?'

Katie gave him a wave and shook her head. Then she ducked under the tape and crossed over to the far end of the car park, where she had spotted Inspector Barry Walsh. He was standing close to the river's edge, talking to a grey-haired member of the CCMPSR.

She liked Barry Walsh. He had a good sense of humour, even in the most tragic of situations. In fact, he reminded her in appearance of the comedian Tommy Tiernan, without the beard.

'Well, well,' he said, as she walked up to him. 'And how's yourself?'

'I'm grand, thank you, Barry. Enjoying a well-deserved rest from you and all the other Anglesea Street reprobates.'

'Oh, yes? I'll believe that when the swans start to sing "Amhrán na bhFiann".'

Katie looked out over the river. Close to the opposite bank she could see the *Nora Flynn*, the blue dinghy that CCMPSR used to search for missing persons who were thought to have drowned.

'Any sign of Conor?' she asked. 'I know that his car was found here, with his clothes, and a note to his wife, although I don't know what he'd written to her.'

'Well, it's not too hopeful, I'm afraid. All he said in the note was "I'm sorry". We don't know what he was saying he was sorry for, and his wife herself couldn't tell us. She's right over there, with Caitlin Creevy taking care of her.'

'We found fresh footprints in the mud, and they was leading towards the river,' put in the grey-haired volunteer from search and recovery. 'There wasn't no footprints coming back, like, but it's too early to make assumptions. We never do, when it comes to missing persons. For all we know, your man swam across the river and climbed out the other side, just to leave his old life behind. You'd be surprised how many of *them* we get.'

'That would be one hell of a swim, though, in this weather, with no clothes on,' said Katie.

'The tide's coming in, so if he didn't make it, we'll probably discover him floating around and around in the Tivoli docks. You can see that our boat's headed in that direction now.'

Katie was struck by the tone of fatality in the volunteer's voice, but it also had a note of sorrow in it. She could imagine how rewarded he must feel when the CCMPSR managed to find a missing person alive, or even when they found them dead. Even if they were dead, it would at least give their relatives closure.

She left Barry Walsh and walked further up the car park

until she found Maeve Mullan, sitting in the passenger seat of a Garda car with the door open, holding a plastic cup of tea in both hands. Garda Creevy was standing beside her, and she gave Katie a nod of acknowledgement as she approached.

'Can you give us a moment?' asked Katie, and Garda Creevy said, 'I will, sure,' and went over to talk to two more gardaí who were standing beside the ambulance.

Maeve was wearing a thick brown shawl-collared sweater and she was puffy-eyed, as if she hadn't slept, and as if she had been crying too.

'They said I could go home and they'd call me as soon as they had any news about Con,' she told Katie. 'But I have to be here when they find him. I've left young Noah with my sister.'

'They'll find Conor all right. I've worked with these search and recovery people plenty of times before, and they're amazing.'

'I can't imagine Con drowning himself. He would know how much it would hurt me, and the day we were married he swore that he'd never ever hurt me. Of course we've had our carry-ons, like all married couples, but he's never lifted his hand to me, not once.'

'Have you told Inspector Walsh about how much he was in debt?'

'No – no, I haven't. And please don't yourself. I can't see how that would help to find him, and what if he's still alive, please God? He would never forgive me for telling how much money he owed. He didn't even tell *me* about it, did he, so he must be fierce ashamed about it.'

'Have you found out any more about why he borrowed so much?'

'No. I asked Cairbre if there was any clue on his laptop as to why he'd disappeared, but she said nothing at all, so far. He'd been googling hurling results and holidays in the Canaries and where to find spare parts for his motorcycle, things like that, but nothing more.'

Katie almost told Maeve *I'm sorry*, but then she thought of what Conor had written in his note, and so she said nothing. She strongly suspected that Detective Mullan's disappearance was connected with the enormous debts that he had run up, and if she were in charge of finding him she would be searching for any clue as to where all that money had gone. But for the moment she respected Maeve's plea not to tell Barry Walsh about it.

She also strongly suspected that Conor would be found drowned in the river. He would be beyond shame then, and beyond embarrassment, no matter what he had spent his money on.

Katie waited with Maeve until it began to grow dark. It began to drizzle too, although the search and recovery team continued to scan the river in their dinghy, inch by inch. Once they had disappeared in the direction of Tivoli docks, though, Katie said, 'Come on, girl, I'll take you home. Your Noah will be wondering where his mummy is, and you can comfort each other.'

Maeve gave a reluctant nod, and she and Katie ducked back under the Garda tapes and climbed into Katie's car. Just as Katie put the key into the ignition, though, her phone played 'The Parting Glass'. It was Kieran calling her.

'I'm at your place, sweetheart,' he said. 'The court finished early and so I came down to see you. I should have had the sense to call you before, shouldn't I? I didn't realize that you wouldn't be in.'

'I'll be back in about half an hour,' Katie told him. 'I'm at Blackrock Castle and I'm just running Maeve Mullan home to Douglas.'

'Don't worry. I'll keep the engine running to stay warm and listen to the news.'

Katie drove Maeve home. After Maeve had unlocked her front door, she gave her a hug and said, 'Call me anytime if it all gets too much for you.'

'Do you really think they'll find him?'

'I'm sure of it, Maeve. But I'll be saying a prayer for you tonight.'

Katie drove back to Carrig View feeling deeply sad. She couldn't help remembering the morning she found her little Seamus cold and lifeless in his cot, and her overwhelming sense of loss, as well as her disbelief that she would never see him again, no matter where in the whole world she travelled.

When she turned into her driveway, she saw Kieran sitting in his Volvo with the interior light on. He had his eyes closed and his head tilted to one side, so she went over and tapped on his window. He jerked, opened his eyes, and then blinked at her and smiled.

'They've not yet found Detective Mullan, then?' he asked her, as they went into the house.

Katie switched on the living-room lamps. 'Not yet. But I'm almost certain that he's drowned himself. I've had so many cases like this before. Whatever led him to take his own life, he must have felt that he couldn't confide in anyone about it, not even his own wife. He was up to his ears in debt, although she has no idea at all where all the money might have gone to.'

'It's hard to imagine being so desperate about anything that you'd want to kill yourself.'

Katie went into the kitchen and filled the kettle. 'I feel like a large vodka, to tell you the truth, but I'm going to be saintly and have a cup of tea. Listen – why don't I give you a spare key, so that if you turn up here when I'm out for any reason, you can let yourself in. Better than dropping off to sleep in your car.'

She went through into the spare bedroom, which she used as an office, took a key out of her desk and handed it to him. It had a fluffy pink heart on it as a keyring, and she said, 'You can take this off. That's unless you want any of your fellow judges thinking that you're more interested in them than you are in me.'

'I will, yes. I think there's one of them who fancies me already. I won't tell you which one it is. I don't want to be up for slander.'

'How hungry are you?' she asked him. 'I have some leftover beef and Beamish pie if you fancy it, or else I could call Apache's and have them deliver a pizza.'

'I'm not that hungry, to be honest with you. I had lunch with Judge Boyle at The Metropole but even then I didn't have too much of an appetite.'

They were standing in the living room now, like two strangers who had just been introduced, and didn't quite know what to say to each other.

'I'll make us a sandwich, in that case,' said Katie. 'We can't go to bed with our stomachs empty. We'll have nightmares.'

'Katie, sweetheart, it's enough of a nightmare knowing that I have to go back to Dublin.'

All the same, Katie went into the kitchen, switched on the kettle, and opened the bread bin. She made them both a Reuben sandwich with corned beef brisket and Swiss cheese and sauerkraut on Martin's potato bread. She grilled them on each side until the cheese melted and then carried them into the living room.

They sat side by side on the couch, with the TV on, but muted, trying to eat their sandwiches but both of them too choked up to swallow. Katie's eyes were filled with tears and after a while Kieran shook his head and said, 'Sorry, sweetheart,' and down put his plate with his sandwich less than half finished.

'Maybe you could get yourself transferred to Dublin,' he suggested, as he watched her tip their plates into the kitchen wastebin.

'I don't think that's very likely. Chief Superintendent Mulligan at DMR thinks that female officers were purposely recruited by Satan to get on his nerves, and Detective Superintendent Dempsey has only been in the job for little more than eighteen months, so he's not going to be willing to step aside.'

They went through to the bedroom. Kieran took Katie into his arms and kissed her, gently at first, but again and again, and ran his fingers into her hair. In return, Katie started to kiss him more fiercely, pushing her tongue into his mouth. Then they stood, holding each other close, each of them staring into the other's eyes, Katie's green and Kieran's blue.

'We'll find a way,' said Kieran at last. 'Other people do, don't they?'

'Other people aren't judges and detective superintendents.'

Kieran started to lift Katie's sweater and she raised her arms so that he could take it off over her head. He dropped it on the bed and then he unfastened her skirt, so that she could step out of it. He kissed her again, before reaching around her back and opening the catch of her bra.

'You're my angel,' he told her. 'Do you know that?'

'My breasts are too big to be an angel,' she smiled, kissing him on the tip of the nose. 'I'd never be able to get off the ground, let alone sit on a cloud.'

She unbuttoned his waistcoat, peeling it back off his shoulders, and then she unbuttoned his formal white shirt. She kissed his bare chest, nipping his nipples between her teeth. When she unbuckled his leather belt and reached inside the front of his trousers, she found that he was already hard.

They finished undressing quickly. Katie sat on the bed and pulled off her tights, while Kieran kicked off his patent leather shoes and let his trousers fall to the floor.

Katie lay back on the blue patchwork quilt and said, 'Your socks. There's nothing less sexy than a naked man with his socks on.' She had left on her red satin thong, though, because she knew that Kieran liked to take it off.

They made love slowly, as if elegiac music were playing, and Kieran was sliding in and out of her in time to it. 'An Evening of Regretful Love', played adagio. Katie climaxed first, unusually. As she started to quake she gripped Kieran's shoulders, digging her fingernails into him, and she couldn't stop herself from crying out. Then Kieran came, grunting and shaking his head from side to side.

Afterwards they both lay back, side by side, with their arms around each other, looking up at the ceiling. Katie had stuck silver stars there, many years ago, to celebrate a Christmas. She had often thought of peeling them off, because they reminded her of Paul, and of Seamus, but then she decided to leave them. She knew she couldn't go back and change the past, and it would be as pointless as trying to take the stars down out of the sky.

All the time she was thinking that, Kieran was stroking her

slippery clitoris so lightly that she could barely feel it, and dipping his fingertip between the waxed lips of her vulva. It aroused her again, but it relaxed her too, almost as if she could imagine that this dreamlike sensation would last for ever.

Eventually, she said, 'Let's take a shower,' and they both climbed off the bed and went through to the bathroom. In the shower, they soaped each other with shower gel, and kissed, and washed each other all over.

'I think I've stopped being a saint,' said Katie, as they towelled each other dry.

'What do you mean?'

'I'm going to treat myself to a vodka. I deserve to drown my sorrows, don't you think so?'

'I'll tell you what I *do* think, sweetheart,' Kieran told her, glancing into the kitchen as they went through into the living room. 'I think I'm hungry.'

7

When Aiden and Shauna O'Farrell returned from their walk, they found that their gate was wide open. Not only that, but the fibreglass leprechaun who usually stood in the flowerbed in front of their terraced house was lying on his back, smiling inanely at the sky.

'Oh, poor Potluck,' said Shauna. The leprechaun had been given to them by her brother on their wedding day and he had brought them good luck ever since. They had won the lottery twice – only a few hundred euros, but enough to take weekends away at a grand hotel in Kerry.

'Well, the wind's not strong enough to have blown the little fellow over,' said Aiden, as he put the key into the front door. 'I'll bet it was that young gurry from next door with his catapult. At least he didn't crack the fecking car window like he did the last time.'

He whistled to their brown-and-white springer spaniel, who was snuffling around the front gate, and called out, 'Come on, Harvey! How d'ye fancy some turkey sausage?'

Harvey came trotting up to the porch with his tongue lolling out. He was about to step over the threshold into the hallway when he stopped, and lifted his head, and sniffed.

'Move your arse, Harvey, we don't have all day,' Aiden chided him. But Harvey stayed where he was, sniffing again and again. At last he looked up at Aiden and made a thin creaking noise in the back of his throat.

'What's the matter, boy? Don't tell me you smell *money*? We didn't win the lotto this week, I'm sorry to tell you. Now will you get your tail inside so that I can fix you your dinner?'

Harvey still refused to move, and after taking a few more sniffs he started to back away, although he kept his eyes fixed on the open front door. Shauna had finished packing soil around Potluck's feet so that he was standing upright again. When she saw Harvey slowly retreating down the driveway, she looked across at Aiden and said, 'What's got into him? He looks like he's seen the devil himself.'

'I don't know. Maybe he can still smell those kippers we had for breakfast.'

Shauna went over to Harvey and said, 'What's the matter, boy? Come on, get yourself inside and you can have something to eat and a cuddle.'

Harvey not only refused to respond, but he edged his way even further back down the yard, his claws scratching on the paving stones, still staring at the front door as if he expected a banshee to come jumping out of it.

Aiden came down the yard, took hold of Harvey's collar and tried to pull him up the slope towards the front door. Harvey struggled and barked and stiffened his legs so that it was almost impossible for Aiden to move him.

'All right, you canine header!' Aiden snapped at him. 'If you won't conduct yourself, you can stay out here and starve! See if we care!'

Shauna couldn't help laughing. Aiden went to the front gate and made sure the latch was fastened, but when he returned to the front door he left it a few inches ajar, so that when Harvey stopped behaving so stubbornly he could push his way back into the house.

Aiden was almost sure it was the lingering smell of kippers that had put Harvey off. Harvey had a sense of smell that was beyond hypersensitive, even more sensitive than most dogs. The O'Farrells had adopted him when he was retired as a sniffer dog for the revenue officers at Cork airport. He had been one of their best – so well trained that he could smell not only cannabis and heroin but 100-euro notes.

Shauna went straight through to the kitchen because she had bought two pork rib bodices at Malone's supermarket, and she was going to boil them this evening for their supper. Aiden hung up his windcheater and then he opened the box on the back of the front door to see if the postman had been.

'Here,' he said, coming into the kitchen. 'We've a letter from the IVF clinic.'

'Really? *Really?* Go on, open it, then! My hands are all porky!'

Aiden tore it open. It was a letter from the Sims clinic in Mahon, telling them that a suitable surrogate mother had been found for them. Her name was Roisin, she was thirty-two, and she had three children of her own already.

'At last!' said Shauna, and she burst into tears. She came round the kitchen table and wrapped her arms around Aiden, although she held her hands well away from his sweater. 'Oh, darling, it's a dream come true! Imagine our own little wain!'

'I'll bet Harvey will be mortified,' said Aiden, kissing her forehead. 'He won't be our bar of gold any longer.'

'Of course he won't be upset! He'll love having a playmate!'

'You think so? If the smell of kippers gives him as much bother as this, Jesus only knows how he's going to react to the smell of nappies!'

'Aid, honestly! We're going to have a girl and we'll christen her Orla, after my granny!'

'I don't care if it's a him or a her, so long as I can bring it along fishing.'

Shauna laughed, and she was about to protest when the house blew up. The explosion was centred in the kitchen, so that both Aiden and Shauna were blasted instantly into bloody shreds. A U-shaped hole was blown out of the centre of the terrace, sending bricks and floorboards and lumps of concrete tumbling down their front yard and into the road. The party walls on both sides of the O'Farrells' house collapsed, so that their neighbours' bedrooms and bathrooms could be seen from the street.

The bang was deafening, and it was heard as far away as Dripsey Cross, four kilometres to the east. Debris showered high into the air, followed by a rolling column of brown smoke that looked like a giant genie rising out of the ruins.

There was a few seconds' silence, interrupted only by the intermittent clatter of broken bricks dropping out of the sky. Almost immediately, though, all the front doors along the terrace opened up, and the other residents emerged from their houses, looking stunned. Several cars stopped along the road, and their drivers climbed out to stare at the billowing smoke.

Where the O'Farrells' house had been there was nothing left but a cavity heaped with rubble, and as the neighbours approached they could see right through to their back garden, where their tattered clothes were still hanging on their rotary washing line.

All that was left of Aiden and Shauna was their torsos. They were lying in the flowerbed next to Potluck the leprechaun with their ribcages interlocked, and ribbons of bloody flesh dangling off them. Not far away lay the two pork bodices that Shauna had bought for supper.

Harvey was standing beside the flowerbed, shivering with shock. When the first of their neighbours came up the yard, a stout middle-aged man who worked for Cooney's Garage just along the road, Harvey looked up at him and let out a long howl of grief that sounded almost human.

Katie had just come back into the kitchen from emptying her rubbish bin outside in the garden when her phone warbled. It was DI O'Sullivan, and he sounded breathy, as if he was in a hurry and didn't want anyone else to overhear him.

'Terry? What's the form?'

'I thought you ought to know, ma'am. There's been another bombing. Out at Coachford this time. Two fatalities, from what we know so far.'

'Mother of God. You don't have any names yet?'

'No, but I can tell you where it went off. About half a kilometre before you get into Main Street on the R618. An entire house flattened from what we've been told. I'm off there now.'

'I'll probably see you there, then. Take care.'

Barney and Foltchain came trotting into the kitchen. They looked up at her in that inquiring way they always did when they sensed that she was upset.

'I'm sorry, children. I know I promised to take you to Ballyannan Woods this morning, but something's come up. Or should I say something's blown up. But you don't mind going to Jenny's, do you?'

Immediately, the two dogs turned around and scampered

to the front door, where they stood with their tongues out, panting expectantly.

'Christ in the marketplace, I know you love Jenny, but will you at least give me the chance to brush my hair and fix my make-up and put on my coat?'

Once she had taken Barney and Foltchain next door, Katie headed out west. She drove through the Jack Lynch Tunnel, 'Jack's Hole', and then through Wilton and Farran, crossing the narrow River Lee bridge that took her directly up to Coachford. She chose that route because she suspected that the main R618 from Dripsey would be cordoned off.

She was right. She was able to drive only as far as the Coachford Hair & Beauty Salon before she reached a Garda barrier across the road. On the other side, she could see a khaki bomb disposal truck, a fire engine, an ambulance, a van from the technical bureau, and at least eight Garda cars and vans.

She walked up to the barrier and showed her identity card to the two gardaí who were standing there shuffling their feet and looking bored. They moved the barrier aside and let her through without any argument. As she made her way towards the terrace where the explosion had occurred, she was shocked by the gaping hole where the house had been, and by the amount of bricks and floorboards and other debris that was scattered all down their front yard and across the road. A pine wardrobe was lying on its side on the pavement with one door open, still crammed with dresses and jackets and women's shoes.

Standing among all this wreckage were Micheál ó Broin and Terry O'Sullivan, as well as Superintendent Pearse and Inspector Hackett. On the far side of the cordoned-off area, Katie could see Dan Keane from the *Examiner* and Rionach

Barr from the *Echo* and also Fionnuala Sweeney from RTÉ Six One News. There were some other faces that she didn't recognize, and she guessed they were Instagrammers and TikTokers, trying to sneak pictures for their podcasts.

'Couldn't keep away, then, Kathleen?' asked Micheál, without even looking at her.

'Two people met their Maker,' Terry intoned, as if he were saying a prayer, even though he had already told Katie about the fatalities.

'Do we know who they were yet?'

'They were the young married couple who owned the property, so far as we can tell. We'll have to wait, though, for the coroner to give us a formal identification. He'll need the DNA to be sure, like, and the dental records. Both of them were pretty much blown to smithereens.'

'We could have *warned* them, Micheál,' said Katie. She made no attempt to hide the bitterness in her voice. 'What did I say to you? They need to be warned, the Dripsey Dozen, all of them. We have their names and their contact details. How many more are you going to allow to be killed? Or is it that you simply don't care?'

Micheál still refused to look at her. He was watching a female garda who was crouching down next to an elderly springer spaniel, stroking his back and trying to calm him down. The dog was still trembling uncontrollably, as if he were freezing cold.

Micheál said, 'If it *was* the husband and wife who lived here – and we have no reason to believe otherwise – then we're not talking about any of your "Dripsey Dozen". Their names were Aiden and Shauna O'Farrell, and none of the Dripsey Dozen are called O'Farrell.'

'Then do we have any idea why their house was blown up?'

'Kathleen – we still don't know for sure why bombs were planted in *those* two properties, do we? And until the technical team have completed their examination of the scene here today, we can't know if the same type of explosive was used to bring down this house – or even if it *was* explosive, and not a gas leak. The bomb disposal team say that it has all the appearance of an IED, but it's still far too soon to jump to conclusions.'

'So you're still not going to tell the remaining members of the Dozen that they could be in mortal danger?'

'Perhaps I should walk up and down Pana all day, warning every shopper to keep sketch when they're crossing the road, in case they get run over by a bus?'

'Is that supposed to be funny?'

Micheál turned at last and looked at her. 'I'm leading this investigation, Kathleen, and I'll proceed in the way that I always proceed. The three Fs. Follow the fecking facts.'

'Oh, really? I thought you believed in the two Ls. Logic before lives.'

Katie and Micheál stared at each other for a few seconds with undisguised hostility. Then Bill Phinner called out to Micheál from the heap of bricks that used to be the O'Farrells' kitchen, where he was standing with Commandant Brophy of the bomb disposal team. Micheál left her without another word and climbed up through the wreckage to see what they wanted to show him.

Katie gave Terry a noncommittal shrug. Then she went over to the garda who was looking after the springer spaniel and bent down to stroke the dog gently under his chin. The garda lifted up the metal disc on his collar and said, 'His name's Harvey. Look, on the other side it says Revenue, *Cáin agus Custaim na hÉireann*, so I'm guessing he used to be a sniffer dog. Poor creature, I can't stop him from shaking.'

It was impossible for Katie to tell if Harvey could smell Barney and Foltchain on her, but he raised his eyes towards her with the most mournful expression.

'Maybe I could take care of him,' said Katie. 'I have two dogs of my own who would treat him like family, now that he's lost his. Give me a few minutes. I'm just going over to have a chat with the media.'

She crossed over to the far side of the cordoned-off area to talk to Dan Keane and Fionnuala Sweeney and the rest of the reporters. Some of the local residents were there too, looking distressed. One woman was sobbing and tearing a tissue into shreds.

'Well, now, DS-as-was Maguire,' Dan Keane greeted her. 'What way are you?'

'DS-as-was, Dan, and DS-as-will-be-again,' Katie retorted. 'I've been following these bombings closely, and it's my working supposition that they're linked.'

'Linked how, exactly?' asked Fionnuala Sweeney.

'I'm telling you this in confidence, because we're lacking firm evidence so far. But both the McCarthys at Merrion Court and Derry O'Brien at Ballyvolane were direct descendants of the men who were executed for the Dripsey Ambush.'

'The Dripsey Dozen,' said Dan Keane. 'Yes, I've heard of them, of course. But what about the couple who were killed here today, the O'Farrells?'

'I don't know yet what their connection might be. But I intend to find out.'

Fionnuala Sweeney turned to the woman who was still dabbing at her eyes with her ragged tissue. 'I've been talking to this lady here. She was their next-door neighbour. Mrs Blaney – this is Detective Superintendent Maguire. Maybe you can tell her something about the O'Farrells.'

Mrs Blaney crumpled her tissue into her hand and pulled her grey shawl tighter around her shoulders.

'Has no other officer spoken to you yet?' Katie asked her.

'No, not yet,' said Fionnuala Sweeney. 'They just wanted everybody to clear the area, in case there was a second device.'

Mrs Blaney sniffed and shook her head. 'Shauna and Aiden, they were such good skin, the both of them. I can't believe they're gone. This has scalded the head off me, I can tell you. Our own house has had the upstairs wall blown right open. I don't know where we're going to stay tonight. You can stand in our bathroom now and see all the way to Old Town.'

'Did you know anything about their family connections?'

'I met Shauna's ma once. I was invited round for tea. Shauna was desperate for a baby and she was asking her ma for advice. But I didn't meet any other members of her family, or Aiden's. They'd been living there only since Easter.'

'Really?' said Katie. 'Who was living there before?'

'It was empty, that house, for about a year before Shauna and Aiden bought it. The couple who lived there before were called Tim and Nola.'

'What was their surname, do you know?'

'I can't remember, to be honest with you. I just knew them as Tim and Nola. Hold on, I'll ask Pat.'

She turned around and called to a man who was standing under a tree smoking a cigarette, 'Pat! What was Tim and Nola's name?'

'Tim and Nola. Why?'

'No, you gom. Their surname!'

'Oh. Lyons. Tim and Nola Lyons.'

Katie looked at Fionnuala Sweeney and Dan Keane. 'John Lyons was one of the men executed for their part in the Dripsey Ambush. Maybe it's a coincidence. But maybe the Lyonses are members of the Dripsey Dozen and whoever planted that bomb in the O'Farrells' house was under the impression that they still lived there.'

'Bit of a stretch, that, even so,' said Dan Keane.

'Perhaps it is,' said Katie. 'But it's worth following up as a line of inquiry. And if the bomb *was* meant for the Lyonses, they need to be found as soon as possible and warned. Once the bombers know that they've killed the wrong people, they're sure to be out looking for them.'

'What does himself think about that?' asked Dan Keane, nodding towards Micheál, who was climbing down now from the rubble, along with Bill Phinner and the bomb disposal officer.

'You'll have to ask him,' said Katie. 'He and me, we have a different approach, that's all I can say. He's more chess and I'm more ouija.'

She went back up the yard. Bill Phinner gave her a salute and said, 'This one has a pure close resemblance to the other two, no question about it. It was C-4 all right, you only have to smell it and see the blast pattern. Unlike the others, it was packed in a Sharp microwave oven, although the use of a kitchen appliance is similar.'

Micheál gave him an irritated look, as if he shouldn't be telling Katie any of this.

Katie said, 'Maybe that's not the only similarity. Before the O'Farrells bought this house, it was owned by a couple called Tim and Nola Lyons. And Lyons is one of the family names with a Dripsey connection.'

'There you are, hopping to conclusions again,' said Micheál. 'Lyons is one of the commonest names in the country. How many people do you think there are in Ireland called Lyons?'

Bill Phinner took out his phone, prodded it for a moment

with both thumbs, and then said, 'Nine thousand five hundred and forty-four.'

Micheál smiled at Katie triumphantly. 'There, you see. Fair play to you, there's a remote possibility you *could* be right. One chance in nine thousand five hundred and forty-four. But first of all we need to establish for certain who's behind these bombings and whether the O'Farrells might have provoked them in some way.'

Katie exchanged a long look with Bill Phinner but didn't respond to what Micheál had said. All she said was, 'I'll be off now. Unless you have any objection, I'll be taking that poor dog with me. He's been fierce traumatized, by the look of him, and I can calm him down. If any other family member wants to claim him, give me a call.'

She went over and stroked Harvey again, tugging at his ears. 'Come on, you sad little dote. Let's take you home and give you a nice warm bath and a cuddle.'

8

'What in the name of Jesus do you call this, Flora?' asked Declan, picking up the drawing from the desk and waving it in front of her face.

Flora was busy with her crayons, vigorously scribbling a picture of a huge rabbit with goofy teeth and rainbow-striped ears, and she didn't look up.

'It's a shite fairy,' she said.

'Well, that's for sure,' said Declan. The drawing showed an angry-looking fairy rising out of a lavatory, her face and dress streaked with brown and blobs of what could only be excrement dropping from her wings. 'But, come on, who told you there was such a thing as a shite fairy, for the love of God?'

'Ma did. She said that if I forgot to pull the chain, the shite fairy would come out looking for me and drop all my dolls down the toilet.'

'Oh, your ma's pure class, isn't she?'

Declan glanced up at the clock on the office wall. His estranged wife, Neala, was in the Mater Private Hospital today undergoing a hysterectomy, and so he had agreed to take their daughter, Flora, to work with him. He had not found it easy, though, having a singing, chattering six-year-old sitting in his office with him all morning. He was a savings and investment advisor at Inspirational Finance, and his job required unbroken concentration, his eyes on the ups and downs of Euronext Dublin, the Irish stock exchange, and his ears on what his dozens of impatient clients were demanding.

At twenty past twelve, he decided he needed a break. It was cloudy outside, but bright, and so he opened his desk and took out the Tupperware box of cheese sandwiches that he had made that morning, along with two packets of Taytos.

'Come on, sweetheart. How about we go for a picnic?'

'Can we feed the ducks?'

'So long as they say grace.'

He shrugged on his anorak, and zipped Flora into her pink puffer jacket. Hand in hand they left the IF office building and crossed over the road to the wild grassy verge that led to the river. A soft breeze was blowing, and the surface of the water sparkled in the sunlight. From here, on Little Island, they could see Blackrock Castle on the opposite bank of the river.

They walked along the flat muddy stretch by the river's edge. In her high, piping voice, Flora was singing the song from the Disney film *Moana*, about always coming back to the water, although she didn't know all the words. Declan was suddenly overwhelmed by a feeling of emptiness. Is this what his life had become? A morning of market fluctuations followed by a scove by the Lee with a six-year-old girl and a box of misshapen sangers?

Further along the riverbank stood a wooden bench where they could sit and eat their picnic. As soon as she had settled down next to him, though, Flora tugged at Declan's sleeve and said, 'Look, Dada! Ducks! Can I go give them some bread?'

A family of six or seven tufted ducks were gathered by the water's edge about fifty metres away, half hidden behind a tangle of dry weeds. Declan prised open his sandwich box, took out the thickest sandwich, and after he had peeled out the slice of cheese, he gave the bread to Flora to feed them.

'Just be careful you don't fall in the water. I don't fancy going for a swim to fish you out.'

Flora skipped off towards the ducks, while Declan sat back, took out a cigarette and lit it. He had given up smoking seven years ago when Neala fell pregnant, but after their separation he had lit up just one to calm himself down, and within a day one had become ten, and then twenty.

'I can't think what possessed me to marry you,' Neala had snapped at him. 'You're all looks and no fun at all.'

He saw Flora tearing off bits of bread and tossing them to the ducks, but then suddenly she stopped. She hesitated for a moment, and then she came running back to him, still holding half of the sandwich. She looked distressed.

'What's wrong, sweetheart? Did the ducks want to know where the cheese was?'

'There's a man!' Flora panted. 'He's lying down on the ground and he doesn't have any clothes on! I thought he was waving at me! I don't know if he's real or if he's made of rubber!'

Declan stood up. 'A man? Why did you think he was waving at you?'

'He had his arm up, like this. But I don't know if he's real or if he's made of rubber!'

'Sit down here and wait for me,' Declan told her. Then he walked along the river's edge towards the ducks. They reluctantly hopped and fluttered out of his way, and two of them flapped their wings and flew up into the air.

The man was lying on his side among the weeds, with his back turned and his left arm raised because it had been snared by a leafless bush. He was white and bloated, and Declan could see why Flora thought that he might have been made out of rubber.

As he came closer, however, he could see that this was a real man. His face was puffed up and his eyes were milky. His hair was dark but cropped very short, and he had a crucifix of dark hair on his chest. On his upraised forearm, Declan could see a tattoo of a badge of some kind, and the name *Maeve*, surrounded by a heart.

He turned round and Flora was standing close behind him.

'I thought I told you to sit down and wait for me.'

'He's a real man, isn't he? He must have drowned. Look, his bottom's all wrinkly.'

'Yes, he's a real man and yes, he must have drowned. Now go back to the bench, will you, while I call the guards.'

Declan took out his phone. His hands were shaking as he prodded 112. The emergency service operator answered immediately and asked him which service he needed.

'The Garda, I'd say. I'm on the shore of Little Island, opposite the entrance to the Hoffmann Park industrial estate. There's a fellow lying dead here like he was probably washed up by the tide.'

'Can you tell me your name?'

'Declan. Declan Croke.'

'Don't worry, Declan. Stay where you are and there'll be help coming before you know it. Stay on the line, please.'

Declan walked back to the bench where Flora was sitting. Her hands were clasped together in her lap and she was singing that *Moana* song again, very softly. Declan stood watching her and he found her singing quite eerie. Maybe this was what marrying the wrong person did to people, he thought. It detached them from reality, and out of the normal world, not only them but their children, too, and none of them would ever be the same again.

Katie was out in her back garden with Barney and Foltchain and Harvey when her phone played 'The Parting Glass'.

Barney and Foltchain had accepted Harvey without any hesitation at all when Katie brought him round to Jenny's house to collect them. They had sniffed all around him while he stood in Jenny's hallway, still shivering and bewildered, but it was obvious they thought that if Katie had taken him in, then she must like him, and so they would grow to be fond of him too. The way that Foltchain nuzzled him was almost motherly.

It was Sergeant Murphy calling her, from the communications centre at Anglesea Street.

'I thought you ought to know, ma'am, a body's been found by the river at Little Island. It's Conor Mullan, for sure.'

'Oh, sweet mother of God. Has his wife been informed?'

'Yes, she has, and she'll be on her way over to CUH in an hour or two to identify him formally.'

'I'll call her myself. She's going to need some fierce support right now. Do you know who found Conor?'

'It was a fellow from one of the offices at Hoffmann Park. It seems like he was taking his young daughter to feed the ducks, and she was the one who discovered him.'

'Poor girl. I hope she doesn't have nightmares about it.'

Sergeant Murphy paused, and then he said, 'You won't be letting on that I called you?'

'No, Peter. Why would I?'

'It's just that DS ó Broin has given out this memo that nobody should pass you information on any pending investigations – not until he's authorized it himself.'

'You're joking.'

'I am of course. And did I ever tell you how we know that Christ was Irish?'

Katie put down her phone and watched Barney and Foltchain and Harvey snuffling around her garden. Harvey looked much more settled already, and when Foltchain came up to him they exchanged friendly licks. Katie was reluctant to leave them, but she wanted to make sure that Maeve Mullan had all the care she would be needing now that Conor's body had been found. Unless he had been the victim of a very elaborate homicide, there was little question that he had drowned himself. Every year, an average of twenty-nine people committed suicide by drowning themselves in the River Lee, so it would not have been unusual.

She called Maeve, but there was no answer. Despite that, she took the three dogs around to Jenny's again. Jenny was out shopping but her son Reilly was home from college with a cold, and he was more than happy to look after them.

'I'll take them all for a walk down Pebble Beach. Beats studying economics, like.'

Katie drove to Cork University Hospital in Wilton. When she walked in, she found that DI O'Sullivan was there already, sitting in the waiting area with Detective Coughlan and Garda Creevy and two other uniformed gardaí.

'Have you seen him?' asked Katie, nodding towards the double doors that led to the mortuary.

Terry nodded. 'It's him all right. But his poor wife should be here any minute, to make it formal. Myself, I can't think why he would have wanted to end it all. He'd collected almost as much evidence as he needed to bring in those two fecking Cafferty brothers, and if he'd got a conviction, Jesus, what a feather in his cap *that* would have been.'

Katie pushed her way into the morgue. It was chilly and echoing, with its high church-like windows letting in the washed-out daylight, and with every breath she could smell formaldehyde, like strong sweet pickle. On the left side, three bodies were lying on trolleys under neatly pressed green sheets. On the right, Conor Mullan was laid out naked on the stainless-steel examination table. Dr Mary Kelley was leaning over him, carefully applying make-up to his face, and one of her young assistants was sponging his abdomen.

Conor's skin had already turned a pale greenish colour, with purple bruises around his thighs, and Katie could see that the fish had been nibbling at his ears. She knew from experience that Dr Kelley would cover up his ears before he was rolled through to the relatives' room for Maeve to identify him. She was adept at making crushed and mangled corpses look the way that their loved ones would want to remember them.

'Kathleen,' said Dr Kelley, looking up. 'All belonging to you?'

'I'm grand, thanks, Mary. How's yourself?'

'Overworked and underpaid, as usual. And would you believe this is the third drowning we've had this month already – two children among them, too, seven and three years old. Tragic.'

She finished patting powder on Conor's puffed-up cheeks, and then she said, 'They've reinstated you then?'

'Not yet, no, but my star signs look promising.'

'Between you and me, I'll be delighted when that Micheál ó Broin goes back where he belongs. He has about as much charm as a coal-cellar door.'

'Conor was drowned, then? No sign of any other cause of death?'

'I've still to carry out the full autopsy, of course. But there's nothing obvious. No stab or bullet wounds or contusions or broken bones. The bruises probably came from knocking against the dockside when he was floating around. I've seen similar bruises plenty of times before.'

Terry appeared at the doors and beckoned to Katie.

'Mrs Mullan's arrived.'

Mary reached down to the sheet that was folded over Conor's knees and drew it up to his neck. 'Give me ten more minutes, Kathleen, and I'll have him ready for viewing. I'll call you.'

Katie went back out to the waiting area. Maeve Mullan was standing talking to Caitlin Creevy. She looked pale and tired, and she had fastened all the wrong buttons of her bobbly wool coat. When she saw Katie, she shook her head and burst into tears.

'I'm so sorry,' Katie told her, hugging her close. 'I'm so, so sorry. Of all the ways in the world that this could have turned out, this is the worst.'

Maeve took several quivering breaths, and then stepped back and took out a handkerchief to wipe her eyes.

'I don't know if I want to set eyes on him or not. I know that he's gone, but there's a tiny spark of hope in me that it isn't him at all, and that it's all been some terrible mistake.'

'I'm afraid that it is him, Maeve. Dr Kelley will be calling us in just a while and you'll be able to see for yourself.'

Maeve twisted her handkerchief as if she were wringing a chicken's neck. 'I only wish that Con could have confided in me. He was pure ashamed, I know that for sure now, but I would rather have had the father and mother of all ructions than for him to go out and take his own life.'

'You know *why* he was so ashamed? Was it something to do with all that debt that he'd got himself into?'

Maeve nodded, and looked over towards Terry O'Sullivan and the rest of the officers, who were all standing within earshot. She took hold of Katie's elbow and said, 'Can we talk in private, like?'

They went out of the front doors of the hospital and stood together on the steps. Two pigeons strutted up to them, as if they expected to be tossed a handful of crumbs.

Maeve sniffed, and then she said, 'By rights, I suppose I should tell Terry O'Sullivan about this. But it would ruin Con's reputation for ever, and I couldn't bear that. What if Noah found out about it when he was older, him and this poor fatherless daughter that I'm carrying inside me now? What would I say to them, when they asked me why their friends all had a da and they didn't?'

Katie said nothing, but waited patiently for Maeve to continue. She had learned from long experience never to press anybody who was making a painful confession. Meanwhile, the pigeons had realized that they would be given nothing, and had strutted off in disgust.

'Yesterday afternoon, when I was clearing up, I dropped my brush by accident into the dustbin. I tipped the bin over on to its side, like, so that I could get my brush back, but then I found a phone, all wrapped up in one of Con's old T-shirts. I'd never seen it before, this phone. Its glass was broken, like it had been hit with a hammer, and it had no charge in it, but when I plugged it in it still worked.'

Maeve paused again, and glanced back at the hospital doors, almost as if she was worried that Conor would come storming out and light into her for blabbing his secrets.

'I tried three or four passwords, but none of them worked. Then I remembered that Con always wrote his passwords down in his diary, because he thought that somebody would hack them if he stored them online. His diary was still in his desk, and there it was, the password. Eveam34. My name backwards and my age at my last birthday.

'I think he must have been panicking when he threw that phone away, do you know what I mean? Otherwise, I'm sure that he would have taken much more care to destroy every single trace of what he'd been doing. He's a detective, for the love of God.'

She paused again, and then said, '*Was* a detective.'

'So, you looked through this phone, and what did you find?' Katie asked her, as gently as she could.

'Videos. Videos of Con that turned my heart sideways. You'll have to see them for yourself to believe them.'

'Sexual?'

'Yes. With young women. Very young women, and more than one at a time. And doing things that actually made me gawk.'

'You think that someone might have been blackmailing him?'

Maeve nodded furiously. 'That was my very first thought. I don't know when or where he might have been meeting these young women and doing these things, but of course he was often out late and he didn't need an excuse because I always imagined he was caught up in some case or other.'

'You do realize that the coroner will be holding an inquest into why Conor died, and that this all may have to come out?'

'Isn't there any way we can keep it secret?'

'Well, let's take one thing at a time. Are there any messages on his phone to suggest that he was being blackmailed? Any demands for money?'

'I couldn't bring myself to look any further than those videos. I'm still craw sick thinking about them.'

'Do you have the phone with you?'

Maeve shook her head. 'I couldn't bear the thought of having it on me when I came here to see if it really is Con. It would have been like betraying him, do you know what I mean? Whatever he's done, Kathleen, he's still my husband and the father of my children and I still love him.'

'I'll come over to Douglas later, then, if that's all right, and pick it up.'

'Sure, like. I wish you would. If some evil gowl *has* been blackmailing him, and you can find out who it is, and punish them for it without anybody else knowing what he did, then I'll be in your debt for ever after, and so will he.'

'Maeve – I'm sorry. I can't make you any promises.'

At that moment the hospital doors opened and Caitlin Creevy called out, 'Dr Kelley's ready for you now, Maeve.'

Maeve crossed herself and said, 'Dearest Lord, please may it not be him.'

9

Maeve came out of the viewing room as white as a ghost, unable to speak. Katie took her arm and led her out to her car, opening the passenger door for her and fastening her seat belt. She drove her back home to Douglas, and on the way there Maeve stared silently out of the window with tears sliding down her cheeks.

After they had arrived at her house in Belgard Downs, Katie spent an hour with her, saying very little but holding her hand, until her sister arrived with Noah. Before Katie left, Maeve handed her Conor's phone with its cracked glass screen.

'I never want to set eyes on that cursed thing again, God help me. Once you've finished with it, you can send it to hell where it belongs.'

Katie returned home to Carrig View and collected Barney, Foltchain and Harvey from Jenny next door. Once she had fed them, she sat down in the living room and started to scroll through the phone to see why Conor might have considered suicide. Maeve had been right when she said that he must have been panicking when he smashed the phone and dropped it in the dustbin. As a highly trained detective, he should have deleted every trace of everything on it, and then destroyed it beyond repair.

She found seven different videos, each lasting more than

five minutes, in which she could clearly see Conor having sex with no fewer than three young girls at once, and in two of the videos with three girls and two young men, one white and one black. All the videos had been extreme, with oral and anal sex, bukkake, bondage, whipping and urination. Katie was hardly surprised that they had turned Maeve's stomach. They made her feel queasy herself.

Apart from the videos she found no emails or text messages, but a list of at least twenty phone calls, most of them from the same number. Tomorrow she would contact Sergeant Murphy and see if he could trace the subscriber for her. She could do it herself, but she was wary of alerting the caller and having them disappear before they could be identified.

Kieran arrived a few minutes after seven o'clock. Katie had been planning to cook him stuffed pancake rolls this evening, but after seeing Detective Mullan's bloated body in the morgue she had been unable to face it. Instead, she had ordered a cheese pizza to be delivered later from the Grand Italia Pizzeria in Cobh.

'Don't worry,' said Kieran. 'I've not too much appetite myself. I've been hearing a nasty case of domestic abuse today. You can't believe the wretched way some husbands treat their wives. You wouldn't treat a dog so badly. Well, I know *you* wouldn't. You treat them like they're kings and queens.'

'I'm sorry, but I'm about to make your day even worse,' Katie told him. She explained how Maeve had found Conor's phone in the dustbin, and then she showed him some of the videos. After he had watched three of them, he could only shake his head and hand the phone back to her.

Katie said, 'I'm in a real jam here, Kieran. I should be passing this phone over to Micheál ó Broin, but Maeve gave it to me on trust, and she's in bits as it is.'

'Yes, sweetheart. But there's no doubt they're going to lift your suspension, is there? It may be this week, even, from what you've told me. You won't have to bother then about showing it to Micheál, will you? *You*'ll be in charge.'

Katie sat down on the couch next to him and leaned over to rest her head on his shoulder. 'I can't help wondering how poor Conor got himself into such a fierce mess. He would have known the risks.'

'Come on, Katie. Both you and I know that when lust walks in the door, common sense jumps out the window.'

'Yes. And it seems fierce likely that Conor was being blackmailed. Maeve showed me their bank balance and it's two thousand euros in debt, with nothing to show for it. Plus all their savings had gone, and that was another seven and a half thousand.'

'So what are you planning to do?'

'If this is the kind of extortion racket that I think it is, I need to find out who's running it and then I need to set up some sort of entrapment. Conor took part in those sex sessions voluntarily. Well, he must have done, to take part in so many, and you've seen for yourself how much he's enjoying them. They're not illegal in themselves. If five people want to get together and have an orgy, good luck to them. But if payment is either offered or demanded, as you very well know – that's an offence.'

The doorbell rang and the three dogs immediately jumped up and scrambled to the front door, their tails thumping against the walls.

'It's our pizza, you silly mutts,' Katie chided them. 'You've already had your meaty treats and you don't like cheese.'

She was slicing the pizza in the kitchen when her phone rang. She picked it up with her knife still in one hand and it was Assistant Commissioner Frank Magorian. He sounded unusually solemn.

'Kathleen? I presume you've seen the seven o'clock news.'

'No, I haven't had the chance. What's the latest?'

'You were mentioned by name.'

'You're joking. What have I done now?'

'The lead story was all about that house that was blown up in Coachford. Fionnuala Sweeney said that she had spoken to you, and you suspected it had been bombed because the perpetrator was under the mistaken impression that the owners were members of the Dripsey Dozen.'

'Jesus Christ. I told her that in confidence.'

'That was bad enough, but she had an interview afterwards with Micheál ó Broin. He said that we had no concrete evidence so far that the Coachford bombing or the other two bombings in Montenotte and Ballyvolane were connected. He agreed that there were similarities, but nothing so far to prove beyond doubt that there was any kind of vendetta being carried out against the descendants of the Dripsey Ambush.

'He said that you were on suspension and therefore you didn't have access to all the facts and forensic evidence. So far as he was concerned, your remarks were highly irresponsible and could seriously hinder his efforts to find the real perpetrator.'

'Jesus.'

'You realize the gravity of this, Kathleen? You did actually say that to Fionnuala Sweeney?'

'Yes, I'm not denying it. But like I said, I told her in confidence. And as it turned out, I found out from telling her that the previous owners of the Coachford house might well have been members of the Dripsey Dozen. The Lyonses, they were called. I passed that information on to Micheál, too – not that he seemed to be interested.'

'What concerns me is that the members of the NBCI will have seen this and might well consider prolonging your suspension while they look into it, or even decide to relieve you of duty altogether. I'm going to call Judge McCabe tomorrow to see what their reaction has been.'

'Do you know something? This morning I saw Conor Mullan lying dead in the morgue. This is all I need to top off my day.'

'I'm really sorry, Kathleen. I'll do my best to put in a good word for you.'

That night, as they lay in bed together, Kieran said, 'I've a confession to make.'

Katie didn't answer until the clock in the hallway had finished chiming midnight. Then she said, 'Don't tell me you've found another woman. It's not that court usher, is it? That Briana?'

Kieran grunted in amusement, and shifted himself sideways to kiss her on the forehead. 'No. There's not a woman in the world who could ever replace you, sweetheart. But I'm afraid I've been secretly wishing that you don't get reinstated.'

Katie said nothing, but took hold of the Saint Ivo medal that he wore on a chain around his neck and started to twiddle it. It was her way of showing him that she really didn't want to hear any more.

Despite that, he carried on. 'I know full well what your job means to you. I know that it's been your whole life. But since we've been together, you've become *my* whole life, and the thought of us parting is more than I can bear.

'I want you to marry me, Katie, or for us to live together, at least. If you really can't give up the Garda, maybe you could arrange for a posting in Dublin. I've talked to Justice Ryan to see if I could stay here in Cork, but she was adamant. They need me up at Parkgate Street and that's all there is to it.'

Katie gave his medal one last twist and then let go of it, and kissed him. 'You don't have to feel so guilty about it, darling. I've been wondering myself if you could retire as a judge. But I suppose this is what happens when you devote yourself to serving your community first and your own passions second. Or third. Or maybe even further down the list.'

'We could both give up our careers and go and live in a *teachín* in the country,' said Kieran. 'But what would we do for money? I'm not at all skilled when it comes to raising animals. Even my pet rabbit died because I fed the poor creature on daffodils.'

'Let's talk it over in the morning, shall we?' said Katie. 'I'm banjaxed.'

She gave Kieran a hug and another kiss and then she turned over. As she made herself comfortable, though, there was a loud crash from the room that she still called the nursery.

Both she and Kieran scrambled to sit upright, pushing back the duvet. Katie switched on her bedside lamp.

'What in the name of Christ was that?'

They both climbed out of bed. Katie could hear the pattering of paws in the hallway, and her dogs growling and wuffling. She was wearing only her pink starry nightshirt, so before he opened the door, Kieran took down her flannel dressing gown and handed it to her.

'Hallo?' he called out, into the darkened hallway. 'If there's anyone there, you'd better make a run for it, I warn you.'

There was no reply. All Katie could see in the darkness were Foltchain's brown eyes, reflecting the light. But the nursery door was half open, and from inside she could hear more growling.

Kieran went into the hallway, switching on the light, and then he pushed open the nursery door wider. Inside, Katie saw that the top drawer of the dresser had been pulled out and dropped down on to the floor, which must have made that crashing noise. All its contents had been scattered across the carpet – notebooks and ballpoint pens and scissors and rolls of Sellotape – as well as Katie's Smith & Wesson Airweight .38 Special and a box of PPU cartridges. Although she was on suspension, she had been allowed to keep her handgun for personal protection, since none of the Cork criminals who bore a grudge against her would care if she was suspended or not.

Sniffing and growling at this small stainless-steel pistol and its ammunition was Harvey, with his tail flapping from side to side in what Katie could only interpret as a sign of self-satisfaction.

'Holy Saint Joseph,' said Kieran. 'He's found your gun and your bullets. He must have pulled the drawer out somehow. But how did he know it was in there?'

Katie crouched down next to Harvey, picked up her revolver and the box of cartridges and tickled him under his chin. 'Good boy, Harvey. He must have smelled they were there. At one time he used to be a Revenue dog, so maybe he was trained to sniff out explosives.'

'That's unbelievable.'

'Oh, you should never underestimate a sniffer dog. They gave me a demonstration once at the airport, and one of their dogs sniffed out that I had a single 100-euro note folded in my pocket.'

Kieran lifted up the drawer and slid it back into the dresser. 'You'll have to put that somewhere out of reach, where he can't smell it. Otherwise we'll never have any peace, God help us.'

Katie shooed Harvey through the kitchen and into the utility room where the dogs all slept. Once Harvey had settled down in his bed, she closed the door to make sure that he was unable to see her. Then she prised open an empty Kimberley biscuit tin, placed the revolver and the box of cartridges in it, and shut it in the top cabinet over the kitchen sink.

'If he can smell it and reach it up there, he's supernatural,' she said. 'Now, let's get some sleep, shall we?'

The next morning, rain was lashing against the windows and they could hear the grumbling of distant thunder. Katie made them a breakfast of puff pastry squares with tomatoes and maple syrup, with what she called 'horseshoe' coffee – coffee so strong that a horseshoe would float in it.

Kieran said very little, and she could tell he was thinking that their days and nights together were flickering past much faster than he would have liked.

'I've more witnesses to hear in that domestic abuse prosecution today,' he told her, as he buttoned up his raincoat and opened the front door. 'At least it takes my mind off losing you.'

'Kieran, you won't lose me. One way or another, we'll manage to stay together.'

She watched him drive away, and then she went back into the living room and picked up her phone. She needed to talk to Fionnuala Sweeney. She had tried to call her yesterday evening after Frank Magorian had told her about her news bulletin, but it had been too late and Fionnuala had already left the RTÉ studios on Father Mathew Quay.

This time, she was put through. The first words Fionnuala

said to her were, 'I was wondering when you'd be after me, Superintendent Maguire.'

'Are you surprised? You know full well I'm on suspension and that I'm not supposed to be getting myself involved in any ongoing investigations. There's a real risk that this could jeopardize my chance of being reinstated.'

'I'm truly sorry, believe me. I'm well aware that you should be keeping yourself out of current cases, but I was faced with a moral dilemma, if you know what I mean. You went a long way to convincing me that you're right, and that for some reason someone is out to kill off the Dripsey Dozen. If that's really true, then they need to be alerted to the fact that they're in mortal danger, and the best way that I could warn them was on the news. Well, it was the *only* way that I could tell them.'

'But why did you have to mention my name?' Katie demanded.

'Because you're so well known and respected in Cork for the way you've cleaned up so much crime, and your name gave that warning real authority. If I was one of the Dripsey Dozen who haven't been blown up yet, and I'd seen that report – I'd be taking precautions already. I might even be thinking of leaving Cork for a while, until I heard that the bomber had been caught.'

'I saw your interview with DS ó Broin, saying that he doesn't necessarily agree with me.'

'I'm not saying that I don't respect his point of view,' said Fionnuala. 'He's the acting detective superintendent, after all, and he has a solid reputation, for sure, especially for cleaning up the drug gangs in Limerick. But then I thought to myself, even if you're wrong and he's right, and there's nobody out to kill off the Dripsey Dozen, there's no real harm done by giving them a warning. Maybe the Garda would suffer some public embarrassment, but so what? If you're right, which I believe you are, then you could be saving some lives.'

'I can't really argue with that,' Katie told her. 'All the same, it may have caused me some delay in getting my job back, and that's if I get it back at all.'

'Oh, I'll bet money that you will,' said Fionnuala. 'As a matter of fact, I was going to call you this morning myself. Those neighbours told us yesterday, didn't they, that a couple called Tim and Nola Lyons owned their house before the O'Farrells.'

'That's right.'

'I managed to find the estate agent who sold the O'Farrells their house, Sherry O'Leary, and she was able to give me a contact number for the Lyonses. They're living in Ballincollig now. I phoned them, and they'd already seen what had happened to their house in Coachford on the Six One News. It gave them an awful land, I'm telling you. I asked Tim Lyons outright if he belonged to the Dripsey Dozen, but he wouldn't tell me. He didn't say yes and he didn't say no.'

'What did he say?'

'He said, "You never know what's around the fecking corner, do you?" and then he put the phone down. I tried to call him back, but it was engaged.'

'You have the Lyonses' address, though?'

'Barley Grove, The Maltings, Ballincollig. I was thinking of going there, but I have to cover the mayor's daughter's wedding this afternoon, and all kinds of famous people are going to show up. Anna Mieke, for one.'

'I may go and talk to the Lyonses myself so,' said Katie.

'Do you want their number?'

'Yes, please. But I won't call them first. I want to make sure that I meet them face-to-face. Thanks for the information,

Fionnuala. I can almost forgive you for taking my name in vain. If and when they lift my suspension, you wouldn't want to join my team of detectives, would you?'

'Oh, I would, yeah,' said Fionnuala, which was always the Cork way of saying an emphatic 'no, I wouldn't, under any circumstances whatsoever, so help me Jesus'.

10

Katie took the three dogs out for a walk. The rain had eased off now, although the pavements were still glistening wet and the hedges were dripping, and she could hear the deep grumbling of distant thunder over Cloyne, like God's indigestion.

Foltchain kept stopping and looking back at her as if she could sense that she had an anxious head on her, and Harvey kept stopping too, to sniff at every fence and lamp-post as if he were checking for drugs or explosives. After a while, Katie had to clip his lead back on and tug him away from every smell that caught his attention, or else their short walk up to the Passage West ferry terminal and back would have taken more than an hour.

Foltchain was right: she was anxious. She knew she should be passing on to Micheál ó Broin the information that Fionnuala Sweeney had given her about the Lyonses. She should also have informed him about Conor Mullan's overwhelming debts and handed him his phone, with all its videos. But some instinct was telling her that she should keep all this information to herself until she had irrefutable proof.

Micheál's methodical style of detection might have corralled most of the serious drug-dealers in Limerick, but in her experience terrorists of any kind were far more wily than drug-dealers, and far more elusive. It took ingenuity and surprise to catch them, rather than doggedness. And if Conor Mullan really had been blackmailed, it was likely that his blackmailers would melt away as soon as they had the slightest suspicion that they were close to being identified.

Once Katie had fed and watered the dogs, she took them next door. Jenny's son Reilly was still at home with his cold, and he was delighted to see them. Katie gave the three of them a goodbye hug, and then she went back to retrieve her revolver from the biscuit tin in the kitchen. She loaded it and tucked it into her inside coat pocket. She had not wanted to do it with Harvey around, in case he became overexcited with himself by the smell of ammunition.

When she had left Jenny's house, she had noticed a silver Honda Accord parked about fifty metres further down Carrig View, with two of its wheels on the pavement, because the road was very narrow here. As she backed her Audi out of her driveway and turned north, she glanced in her rear-view mirror and saw the Honda start up and appear to follow her. It kept its distance, so she doubted at first if it was actually tailing her, and when she turned off the East Cork Parkway to drive through Jack's Hole and join the South Cork Ring Road, she lost sight of it altogether behind a huge blue Crowley Transport truck.

As she passed Douglas Village, though, she looked in her mirror again and saw the Honda overtaking the truck and settling down behind her once more. It still kept its distance, but when she speeded up to eighty for the next three kilometres, it speeded up too; and when she reached the Magic Roundabout, where the Kinsale Road crossed over the ring road, and she was forced by the heavy traffic to slow down to a crawl, it still kept well back. She was already convinced that it was following her by the time she turned off at Greenfields

Allotments to drive into Ballincollig, and sure enough she saw it turning off behind her.

Instead of driving straight to Barley Grove, though, Katie went to the centre of Ballincollig and parked in the huge car park next to the Farmers' Market. She sat and waited for the Honda to park there too, so that she could confront the driver and demand to know why he had been shadowing her.

She waited for over ten minutes, but the Honda failed to appear. Katie climbed out of her car so that she would have a wider view of the car park, but there was no sign of it anywhere. She began to wonder if it had simply been a coincidence that it had tailed her all the way from Carrig View to Ballincollig.

She waited another five minutes, and it started to rain, very softly, so she got back into her car. She could give up her attempt to talk to Tim and Nola Lyons, and drive back home, but the Honda seemed to have given up following her, and there was no reason to think that it had any connection to the Dripsey Dozen. It was quite possible that the Lyonses had no connection to them either, and that the bombing of their house in Coachford had been a catastrophic mistake. Or maybe Micheál had been right after all, and the O'Farrells had upset some vengeful gowl who had been determined to punish them for it.

She drove to Barley Grove and parked across the road from the Lyonses' house. She waited another few minutes before she went to knock at their door, in case the Honda reappeared, but the only vehicle that came around the corner was a green An Post van.

Barley Grove was a private estate, and the houses were all new, neat and semi-detached. The Lyonses' house was painted white, with a scarlet front door. Katie knocked, and almost at once Nola Lyons appeared in the living-room window, staring at her like a goldfish staring out of its tank.

Tim Lyons opened the door. He was a big man, late fiftyish, with tousled grey hair and bags under his pale-blue eyes. He was wearing a sagging green cardigan and drooping grey flannel trousers.

Before Katie could introduce herself, he said, 'Sorry, love, sorry. We don't buy nothing on the doorstep, and we've donated already to the donkey sanctuary.'

Katie held up her identity card. 'I've not come to sell you anything, Mr Lyons. My name's Detective Superintendent Kathleen Maguire, from the Cork city Garda station. If you've no objection, I'd like to ask you one or two questions.'

'What about? Not our old house in Coachford getting blown up, is it? We don't know nothing about that at all. Nothing whatsoever.'

'But, come on. You knew Brendan and Fidelma McCarthy, didn't you? And you knew Derry O'Brien?'

Katie was doing something that Micheál ó Brion would never have done. She had no evidence at all that Tim Lyons was one of the Dripsey Dozen, apart from his name, but she was making him think she was quite certain that he was. If it turned out that he wasn't, he would be totally baffled by what she had just asked him, but there would be no harm done.

For almost ten seconds he simply stared at her, saying nothing. Then he said, 'You'd best come inside.'

Katie stepped in through the front door. Tim Lyons's wife had been hovering behind him in the hallway, and he introduced her. 'This is the mot, Nola. Nola, love, this is Detective Superintending Maguire.'

Nola Lyons was dumpy and curly-haired and could have been the twin of Brenda Fricker, the actress who had played

Christy Brown's mother in *My Left Foot*. She ushered Katie into the living room and the three of them sat down, with Nola perched uncomfortably on a leather pouffe.

'Is this about the house in Coachford?' she asked, biting her lip.

'Well, it could be. You belong to the Dripsey Dozen, don't you?'

'We used to call ourselves that, sure,' said Tim. 'We still meet now and again, and of course we still join the memorial parade every year at Dripsey Cross. But we don't do nothing *active*, like, if you know what I mean. Not like some of our parents and our grandparents did. We get together now and again and we have a few gats and we talk about the Uprising in the twenties and the Troubles in the sixties and we look over some of the old family photos that we might have come across, but that's about it.'

'When you say "nothing active", what do you mean, exactly?' Katie asked him.

Tim looked over at Nola and Nola gave him the slightest shake of her head.

'You know – political protests, like,' said Tim. 'Shouting out "Feck Margaret Thatcher!" in the Dáil and painting slogans like "Never Forget Dripsey" on the walls of Collins Barracks. We don't do nothing like that no more.'

'Okay, I have you,' said Katie, as if that satisfied her. She made no mention of the investigations that the Garda had carried out two years ago into the allegations that the Dripsey Dozen might have been responsible for bombings in the United Kingdom in the early 1970s. To be fair, that investigation had never come up with any conclusive proof, and the last thing she wanted to do was to put the Lyonses' backs up.

'When you heard about the McCarthys, though,' she went

on, 'and then about Derry O'Brien, and then you heard that your own house in Coachford had been bombed, what did you think?'

'We weren't sure, to be honest with you. The last time I saw him, Derry told me that he'd been having some trouble with the O'Dwyers, so I had to wonder if they had something to do with it.'

'Really?' Katie asked him. 'I can see the O'Dwyers beating him half to death with a hurley or shooting him, even, but I'm not so sure I can see them blowing up his shop.'

She was more than familiar with the O'Dwyer gang. Over the past decade they had been the leading dealers in heroin and cocaine in Cork city, and they may have been responsible for the murders of at least five rivals. She had arrested three of them herself on various charges and succeeded in having them jailed, one of them for fifteen years.

Tim said, 'I couldn't be sure about Brendan, either. I heard that he was into some funny business with bitcoins, although I couldn't tell you what.'

'So you don't think that someone may be trying to take out the Dripsey Dozen, one at a time?'

'You'd have to ask yourself who would want to, wouldn't you? And why? And why would they do it by blowing up their houses? There must be a fierce risk in planting a bomb. Why not do what the O'Dwyers do – knock on their door and shoot them when they open it?'

'So far, we don't have any substantive proof,' said Katie. 'But I think it would be a good idea if you were to warn all the other members of the Dripsey Dozen that they could be next. Better to be cautious than blown up.'

'Tim's already talked to three or four of them about it,' put in Nola. 'And I've talked myself to Margaret O'Mahony. She's the wife of Liam O'Mahony, who runs O'Mahony Motors down at Ballycureen. We're all of us worried about it, but like Tim says, it's not so easy to believe, is it? Who would want to be doing such a thing?'

'Have any of the others been given a warning of any kind?'

'Not that they've told me about,' said Tim. 'But I'll do what you suggest, like. I'll call the rest of the Dozen who are still in the country and tell them to keep sketch for anything that looks suspicious, if they're not doing it already. I know that the Boyles are in Tenerife at the moment, so I don't think they're likely to be blown up there.'

'In particular, tell them to watch out for air fryers or microwave ovens,' Katie told him. 'Kitchen appliances packed with explosives were used in all three bombings. If your friends have one delivered that they haven't ordered, or if they mysteriously find one somewhere in their house and they don't know where it came from, warn them to go nowhere near it. They should leave the house immediately, take themselves as far away as possible, and call 112.'

'Would you care for a cup of tea in your hand?' Nola asked her.

'Thank you, Nola, but no. I have to be going. I only came to make sure that Tim and you and the rest of the Dozen were fully aware of the possible danger. We don't want any more houses blown up and we don't want to lose any more lives.'

She stood up. 'There's one thing you can do for me before I go, though. Do you have the addresses and the contact numbers of all the other members? We have some of their details on file at Anglesea Street, but it's possible that some of them may have moved house in the past two years, like you did.'

'There's been two or three changes, yes,' said Tim. 'The

O'Mahonys have upped sticks to Clon, I know that. But I'll go through my address book just to make sure. If you let me have your email address, I'll send them to you.'

Once Katie had pencilled down her address for him in the margin of *The Irish Sun*, Tim saw her to the door. He looked regretful and confused.

'If somebody *is* after killing us all off, then it's a pure tragedy. Nobody in this country can never forget nothing, can they, even after a hundred years? I reckon it must be genetic. I know for sure that I can't wipe the past out of my mind. I still think of John Lyons on that last day of February in 1921 being blessed by Canon O'Sullivan and Father Willie O'Brien and then walking out into the barracks yard to face the firing squad. To me, it's as painful and personal as if it happened only yesterday. John Lyons was my flesh and blood.'

Katie laid a hand on his sleeve. 'Keep your eyes open, Tim, that's all I can say to you. God be with you.'

She crossed the road and unlocked her car. As she did so, she caught sight of a silver Honda Accord parked around the corner, half hidden behind a tree. There was no way she could tell for sure that it was the same Honda that had followed her from Carrig View, but how likely was it that somebody visiting Barley Grove this morning had exactly the same model and colour of car?

She climbed behind the wheel, switched on the engine and checked her sat-nav screen. She could see that if she drove off in the opposite direction, she could circle all the way around the estate until she came up behind the Honda. Keeping a watch in her rear-view mirror to make sure the Honda did not start to follow her again, she steered away from the kerb, drove two hundred metres along the road, and then turned right, and right again.

When she turned the last corner, she saw that the Honda was still parked next to the tree, and a man had opened the driver's door and already swung one leg out. As Katie drew up behind him, though, he must have seen her, because he pulled his leg back in, slammed his door shut and started his engine. With a squittering sound of tyres, he pulled away from the side of the road, swerved around the corner in front of the Lyonses' house, and then accelerated along Barley Grove at nearly sixty kph.

Katie jammed her foot down and sped after him. The last time she had driven like this was during her driver training at the Garda college in Templemore – fast and risky but highly controlled. The Honda slewed out of Barley Grove into Station Road, colliding with the kerb on the opposite side before it started to speed south. Katie took the same turn much tighter, so that she began to gain on it. By the time the Honda reached Station Cross, her Audi was less than a metre away from its rear bumper.

As it came to the T-junction with Carriganara Road, the Honda was going too fast to stop. Katie stamped on her brakes, but the Honda hurtled through a red light, colliding with the back of a truck laden with logs, spinning around, and then crashing into the wrought-iron gates next to Posh Paws dog grooming cottage.

Katie mounted the pavement by the side of Station Road, stopped, and climbed out. The log truck and five or six cars had all come to a halt, and so she was able to cross the junction towards the wrecked Honda. Before she could reach it, though, the driver's door was kicked open and a man struggled out. He was tall and bald and dressed entirely in black – a black leather jacket and black jeans.

'Stop right there!' Katie shouted at him. 'I'm an armed guard! Stop!'

The man ignored her, and started to run away, although he was limping. Katie ran after him, shouting '*Stop!*' yet again.

After running about a hundred metres, the man did stop. He turned around to face Katie, and at the same time she could see him pull something out of his jacket. In case it was a gun, she stopped herself, and tugged her own revolver out of her inside pocket.

'Drop that, and put up your hands!' she ordered him, almost screaming.

She took a step forward, but as she did so there was a devastating bang right behind her – so powerful that she felt the blast against her back, as if some hefty man had come running up and given her a violent push. She turned around to see that the Honda had been torn apart, and it was burning fiercely. The blackened wreckage of its roof was sticking upwards out of the flames like the figure of Death with his scythe.

A green Toyota that had stopped on the opposite side of the road had its windows smashed and its doors dented inwards. The ropes on the back of the truck had been ripped into shreds, so that six or seven immense ash logs had rolled off on to the ground. The truck driver must have climbed out of his cab when he saw the Honda crash, because he was lying on his side next to his truck and his face and his hands were smothered in blood. He was lucky that none of the logs had toppled off on top of him.

Katie turned around again to see that the man in black was running off down the road, swinging his left leg in an exaggerated limp. She let him go. She had his description and he wouldn't be able to get far. Tucking away her revolver and taking out her phone, she called Sergeant Murphy.

'Peter, this is Superintendent Maguire. There's been a

car bomb by the look of it, junction of Station Road and Carriganara Road, south of Ballincollig. We'll need the fire brigade and an ambulance, urgent-like, because there's been some injuries. And the bomb squad. And a suspect is trying to get away on foot heading west. Fiftyish, six foot something tall, bald, dressed all in black.'

'I'll stay on the line,' she told him.

Still holding her phone to her ear, she crossed back over the road to the damaged Toyota. In the two front seats an elderly man and woman were sitting, both of them deeply shocked. Their faces were criss-crossed with bloody scratches, their white hair was standing up as if they had been frightened by a ghost, and their laps were heaped with shattered glass.

'Sit tight,' Katie told them. 'Help will be here before you know it.'

The man stared at her. 'What's happened? I can't hear you.'

Katie could only give him a thumbs up and lift both hands reassuringly. Then she went over to the truck driver. He was sitting up now, and two women had come out of the Posh Paws cottage to help him. One of them was dabbing the blood from his face with a kitchen towel and the other was holding a cup of water for him.

'What in the name of God?' asked one of the women.

Katie looked at the wreckage of the Honda, still fiercely ablaze, with black smoke piling up into the sky. *Don't jump to conclusions*, Micheál had admonished her. But she was already convinced that the Honda driver had somehow known she was going to talk to the Lyonses, and he had followed her so that he could discover where they were living.

He had been carrying an explosive device with him, which was capable of being set off remotely. Katie had little doubt where he had intended to plant it, before she had scared him off.

Over ten minutes passed before she heard the sound of a fire siren. Ballincollig fire station was manned only by a part-time crew, and they would have had to respond to a call from their personal pagers, drop whatever they were doing and rush to Leo Murphy Road to climb aboard their engine.

Almost at the same time as the fire engine came speeding down Station Road, two ambulances appeared, their blue lights flashing, followed by three Garda patrol cars. A sergeant came over to Katie, staring first at the burning Honda, although its flames were beginning to die down now, and then at her. She had met this sergeant before, although she had temporarily forgotten his name. She remembered his little clipped moustache, and that she had thought that if Hitler had been ginger, he would have looked exactly like this.

It was plain from the look on his face that he was not sure what to say to her. But it was also plain that he was thinking, *You're suspended, aren't you? What the feck are you doing here?*

11

When Detective Inspector O'Sullivan arrived with Detectives Coughlan and Malloy, he must have been asking himself the same question. The difference was that he said it out loud.

'Well now, Kathleen. I'm surprised to see you here.'

He turned to look at the Ballincollig firefighters spraying the shattered wreckage of the Honda with foam. Then he turned back to Katie and said, 'Would this have any connection with them other bombings, by any chance?'

'To be honest with you, Terry, I believe it does.'

'But they're blowing up cars now, as well as houses?'

Katie hesitated for a moment, but she realized this was not an investigation she could carry out entirely on her own, and that she would need all the assistance that her one-time team could give her.

As succinctly as she could, she told him how she had found out where Tim and Nola Lyons were living now, and that Tim had confirmed that he was one of the Dripsey Dozen. She explained how the Honda had followed her all the way here from Carrig View, and how she had surprised its driver.

'It's my guess that he was carrying an IED, intended for the Lyonses. But when Bill Phinner shows up, he'll be able to tell us for sure. If there are any bits and pieces of microwave oven or air fryer in there, that'll be a dead giveaway.'

'With respect, ma'am, you know that DS ó Broin is not going to be too happy about this.'

'I didn't come looking for the Lyonses to make Micheál ó Broin happy. I came to make sure they knew that they could be in mortal danger. Them and all the rest of the Dripsey Dozen, or what's left of them. There's no question in my mind at all that someone's out to kill them all off.'

Terry looked around again, and then he said, 'We have three units out looking for the suspect you described. Tall, bald, and dressed in black, was that it? We'll check the Honda's number plate, too, but it wouldn't surprise me if it's fake, or the car's stolen.'

Bill Phinner's car and two vans arrived, one van close behind the other. One was from An Biúró Theicniúil and the other from RTÉ news.

Katie said, 'Look, I think I'm going to make myself scarce. I don't want that Fionnuala Sweeney seeing me here and dropping me into any more shite. If you need any further information, Terry, give me a call. Or I can come up to Anglesea Street, any time at all.'

As she crossed back over to her car, she could see a low-loader slowly approaching along the Carriganara Road. It was carrying a digger fitted with a forestry grab, for lifting up the logs that had rolled off the truck. Both ambulances had left, taking the truck driver and the elderly couple to hospital, and what was left of the Honda had now been buried under a billowing heap of white foam. She was satisfied that everything was under control, and that there was nothing more she could usefully do here, so she climbed into her car, reversed up Station Road, and started to head for home.

It was only when she joined the south ring road that she realized her hands were shaking.

★

About an hour after Katie had returned to Carrig View, Sergeant Murphy called her. She had been watching RTÉ news but so far there had been no report about the bomb blast at Ballincollig.

'I've tried to trace that phone number you gave me, ma'am, but no luck at all, I'm sorry to tell you. More than likely it was a burner.'

'I see. Well, thanks a million for trying, anyhow.'

'I've had a few messages in from Ballincollig, if you want an update. The units out looking for that suspect you described, your bald feen dressed in black, they haven't seen hide nor hair of him. They're saying that he could have hidden himself somewhere, like, maybe in someone's garden shed. Or maybe he called an accomplice to pick him up and whisk him away.'

'I haven't seen anything about it on the news yet.'

'Well, Station Cross is still cordoned off, and it's likely to stay that way for a few more hours yet, because the technical team have still to complete their work there. Oh – and just between you and me, ma'am, DS ó Broin is in the fouler to end all foulers.'

'I didn't think he'd be delighted. I imagine he's found out that I was there.'

'He has, yes. It wouldn't surprise me if you had a call from him soon. He's set up a press conference for later, and he won't want to be caught out with any awkward questions, like what was a suspended detective superintendent doing at the scene of a car bomb blast in Ballincollig?'

'Oh, God,' said Katie, and Harvey looked up at her and cocked his head on one side.

Once she had finished talking to Sergeant Murphy, she

went into the kitchen to make herself a sandwich, but after she had taken the cheese out of the fridge, she decided she wasn't really hungry, and so she put it back in again. The dogs were all following her from room to room now, because they obviously sensed that she was worried.

There was little more she could do about her investigation into the Dripsey Dozen – not until Tim Lyons emailed an up-to-date list of all their contact details. She took Conor Mullan's phone out of her drawer, and although some of the scenes of sexual activity made her shudder, she sat down and ran through all seven videos over again.

In the third video, Conor was standing in what looked like a hotel bathroom, with nothing on but a tartan shirt, unbuttoned. Three naked girls were crowded into the bath. One of them was wearing a black leather mask with a zip across the mouth. The other two were handcuffed together.

One of the girls said, 'We're dying for a shower, Conor, baby! We're so dirty! Give us a shower!' She had a distinct Sligo accent, pronouncing 'us' as 'ush'.

Conor started to urinate on them, splashing each girl in turn. The girl who had begged him for a shower lifted up her face and opened her mouth wide so that he could spray between her teeth and on to her tongue. For a split second, as the video turned to focus on her, Katie glimpsed that a towel was folded over a rack next to the bath, and that the towel had a name embroidered on it.

She stopped the video, reeled it back, and froze it when she came to that scene again. Even though the glass on the front of the phone was cracked, she could make out the name clearly, green lettering on a white towel. Abhaile ó Bhaile Hotel. Katie knew it all too well. It was right in the centre of the Victorian Quarter in Cork city, on Leopold Street. A cheap, shabby hotel, even though its name meant 'home from home'. It was frequently used by prostitutes and drug addicts, although its owner ruled the hotel so strictly that the Garda rarely interfered with what was going on there, because it was better that they had somewhere safe to go, and it kept them off the streets. Almost unbelievably, its owner had once been a priest.

Katie checked the date on the video. It had been taken four months and two days ago. The other six videos had been taken over an eighteen-month period, with the last dated only three weeks before Conor Mullan had drowned himself in the Lee.

Now she had the possibility of a lead. If she could find out who had booked the room that day at Abhaile ó Bhaile, she might be able to discover if Conor was being blackmailed, and if he was, who had been extorting money from him.

She went into the hallway and was taking down her coat when her phone played 'The Parting Glass' again. She could see at once that Micheál ó Broin was calling her. She was tempted not to answer, but then she thought that would be cowardly and would not help her make any progress with her investigation at all. It was unlikely, but he might even be calling her to be conciliatory.

'Kathleen? Micheál. Have I caught you at a bad moment?'

'No, Micheál. No more than usual.'

'I want to make this as friendly a request as I can. You were present, were you not, when that car bomb detonated at Ballincollig this morning? Terry O'Sullivan has told me how you came to be there.'

'I was simply checking if the Lyonses who live there belong to the Dripsey Dozen. It turns out they do, and so that may have been the reason the O'Farrells' house was blown up. I was intending to pass that information on to you in any case.'

'Why did you not simply tell me that you had found out where the Lyonses had moved to, and leave it to me to get in touch with them?'

'Because you seem to be so reluctant to believe that somebody is out to kill off the Dripsey Dozen, that's why.'

'You're making an unfounded assumption, Kathleen. It makes us look as if we're scaremongering. It could well be a complete coincidence that both the McCarthys and Derry O'Brien were related to the Dripsey Dozen. The casing used for the IED that blew up the O'Farrells' property was totally different from the other two. Not only that, we still haven't yet completed our checks into Aiden O'Farrell's background, to see if there might have been any reason why somebody should have wanted him out of the way. Him, himself, and not Tim Lyons.'

'I saw no harm at all in warning the members of the Dozen that they could be in danger.'

'I know that's your opinion for sure. Fionnuala Sweeney came out with it loud and clear on the news.'

'So what's this "friendly request" that you're making?' asked Katie, trying her best not to sound sarcastic.

'It's not really a request,' Micheál told her. 'It's more of a caution for you not to interfere any further in this inquiry, or any other. I don't have to remind you that you're suspended from duty, and while you're suspended you have no authority to act on behalf of the Garda Síochána in any capacity whatsoever. In fact, you're obstructing our investigation, and I'm sure you know the Criminal Justice Act 2006, subsection 16, equally as well as I do.'

Katie closed her eyes for a moment, trying to think how to reply. Regardless of her being suspended, Micheál could have done himself a favour and taken advantage of her experience and expertise. But he was making no secret of his hostility, and his attempt to isolate her. Maybe he was simply misogynistic, like many other Garda officers who had openly resented her promotion. Maybe it went further than that, and he was determined that she should never be reinstated, and that he should remain as detective superintendent at Anglesea Street, instead of being obliged to return to Limerick. Frank Magorian had suggested as much, after all, and Frank Magorian was a shrewd judge of character.

'Very well, Micheál,' she told him. 'I hear what you're saying. *Slán.*'

She switched off her phone and stood in the hallway for a while, and although she knew Kieran loved her, and that she had three affectionate dogs, she suddenly felt unbearably lonely. If she lost her career, it would be as painful as a bereavement.

That afternoon she drove into Cork city to talk to the owner of the Abhaile ó Bhaile Hotel. Before she went to Leopold Street, though, she went to Tesco in Paul Street to buy coffee and Gubbeen cheese and meaty treats for the dogs. Then she called in to the Bon Secours Hospital to see Kyna.

As Katie knocked and came into her room, Kyna said, 'Katie! Jesus! I was going to call you but I wasn't sure if I ought to.'

She was sitting by the window now, although she was still connected to a drip. She was still pale but at least her eyes no longer looked as if some angry lover had punched her in the face, and her blonde hair was neatly wrapped up in a bun. The thick white dressings had been cut off her wrists and replaced with pink foam-backed plasters.

Katie came over to give her a hug and a kiss.

'You're pure mental, you are, bird!' Katie told her. 'You can call me at any time, day or night! You should know that!'

'I don't want to cause grief between you and Kieran, that's all.'

'You won't, sweetheart. Like I told you before, Kieran's the most understanding man in Ireland. In fact, I think he finds the idea that you and I were so close together a bit of a secret turn-on. Here – I fetched you some of your favourite chocolates. You could do with putting some weight on. You don't have a pick on you.'

Katie gave her the box of Lily O'Brien's salted caramel truffles that she had bought at Tesco. Kyna smiled and gave Katie another kiss. This time the kiss lingered a little longer, and when it was over, Kyna stared into Katie's emerald eyes as if she were trying to see if she still loved her, and if she did, how much.

'When are they going to discharge you?' asked Katie. 'Do you know yet?'

'The day after tomorrow, if they're happy with my blood tests.'

'And where will you go?'

'My friend Moira said she'd put me up for a week or two.'

'Oh, Moira. She's that schoolteacher from Scoil Aislinn, isn't she?'

'She can't let me stay longer because her sister's coming to visit and fetching her brood with her.'

'I told you before. You can always come to stay with me.'

Kyna looked out of the window. Seven or eight hooded crows had perched in a row on the roof of the hospital wing opposite, and were pecking at each other and fluttering their tattered black feathers. Katie saw them too, but said nothing.

Her grandmother had always told her that hooded crows were a symbol of change or transformation, but they could also be an omen of bad luck or death, especially when they gathered together in a murder.

'Think about it, Kyna, anyhow. You're always welcome. And it'll give you time to recover and decide what you want to do next.'

Kyna shrugged, and gave her a bitter smile. 'I should have been in Heaven by now, sitting on a cloud and playing a harp. And you're asking me what I want to do next?'

'It's possible that the Garda will take you back, if you're interested. You'd probably have to have a psychiatric test first, just to make sure that you're stable.'

'I'm not so sure I could handle it, Katie. I couldn't stop myself from trying to murder myself, could I? How could I be expected to stop anyone else from doing away with someone they hated?'

'You're a smart detective, Kyna. You have everything it takes. Intelligence, inspiration, and such a quirky way of looking at a crime scene. It would be so sad to lose you.'

'I don't know. Even if I did go back, I don't think I could bear to be posted at Anglesea Street, not with you. To see you every day, and to work with you, but not to be able to go home with you at night and show you how much I love you – Holy Mother of God, that would be some kind of torture.'

Katie and Kyna talked for another half-hour. Kyna had seen the news about the car bomb at Ballincollig, and Katie told her all about her meeting with the Lyonses and about the hostile call she had received this morning from Micheál Ó Broin. However, she said nothing about her investigation into the apparent suicide of Conor Mullan, or why she had come to the city this afternoon. She had promised Maeve that she would protect Conor's reputation for as long as she possibly could, and a promise was a promise, even to someone she loved and trusted as much as Kyna.

Eventually, she leaned over and gave her another kiss, and said, 'Let me know when they're ready to release you, and I'll come and fetch you. Don't be afraid.'

Kyna nodded, her eyes glistening with tears. She didn't have to speak.

Katie drove over Patrick's Bridge and turned left into Leopold Street. It was a short, scruffy thoroughfare lined with bookmakers and oriental spice shops and the City Laughs comedy club. The Abhaile ó Bhaile Hotel was right at the end, on the corner of Connacht Street – a wide, three-storey building painted pale green with the letters HOT L over the front door.

Once she had parked outside Jerh O'Donnell's funeral directors opposite, Katie crossed the road and went into the hotel lobby. It was gloomy inside, with a worn-out carpet, a mahogany reception desk, and a framed reproduction on the wall of *Men of the South*, the famous painting of the men of the IRA flying column of the 1920s.

There was a musty smell in the lobby, of dust and cigarette smoke and a cheap women's perfume, which Katie recognized as Story of Roses.

There was nobody on the reception desk, although the door behind it was open and she could hear Cork's Red FM playing on the radio. She pinged the bell on the counter, and after a few moments the owner appeared, holding up a ham roll as if it had fallen from the ceiling and he had just caught it.

'Ah,' he said, because he obviously remembered Katie from

her previous visits. 'And what fearful crime do you suspect that I've committed this time?'

'How's yourself, John?' said Katie. 'Don't worry, this is a courtesy visit, nothing more. I'm sorry if I've interrupted your lunch.'

The owner stared at his ham roll and then back at Katie. His name was John Quinn, and although he had once been a priest, he could easily have been mistaken for a retired heavyweight boxer because he was so much bigger than other men. He was bald, with small rimless glasses, and he was wearing a tight black turtleneck sweater.

'Detective Superintendent Maguire, unless my memory's failed me. You never paid me a courtesy visit before – it was always business. What brings you here now?'

'Well, it's part courtesy and part looking for a squinchy bit of information. I'm investigating quite a serious case and it would help me to know who might have booked a room here on July the twelfth.'

John Quinn set down his ham roll on the leather-bound visitors' book in front of him. 'Have you a court order for that?'

'No, John. I'm only looking for a little voluntary help. I'm afraid I can't tell you why I need to find out who might have booked a room on that day in particular. But I can tell you that the case I'm looking into involves a tragic loss of life.'

'Why can't you tell me why you need to find out?'

'Because I'm protecting someone's reputation, that's why.'

'Well, I'm sorry, but it's my duty to protect the privacy of everyone who stays here. You know as well as I do that I offer a sanctuary to all and sundry, no matter what the world outside might think of them. Jesus loves every man and every woman, even when they've sunk down deep into the bog of iniquity. I'm no longer a priest, but I still represent Jesus and always will.'

'John, I know all that, and I respect what you do. But in this case, I'm not only seeking justice for someone who tragically ended their own life, I'm probably making sure that it never happens again to anyone else.'

'I understand where you're coming from, Detective Superintendent Maguire. But even if nobody else finds out that I've betrayed a trust, God will know.'

'So you're not going to tell me who booked rooms on that date?' said Katie. She paused, and then she said, 'You're not even going to take your lunch and leave me alone with that visitors' book here so that I might be able to leaf through it myself?'

John picked up both his ham roll and the visitors' book and wedged the book tightly under his left arm. 'I can't. That would compromise the whole meaning of Abhaile ó Bhaile.'

'Well, fair play to you, John, but I pray that nobody else decides to end it all because of something that happened here.'

They stood staring at each other for almost a quarter of a minute, with neither of them saying another word. Then Katie lifted her hand in a silent and dismissive goodbye, pushed open the front door and stepped out into the street. The air outside seemed pleasantly fresh after the hotel lobby.

She was about to cross back over to her car when a man's voice called out, 'Sabrina?'

She ignored it, but then a middle-aged man in a khaki anorak came hurrying up to her.

'Sabrina?' he repeated. He was obviously flustered.

'I'm sorry,' smiled Katie. 'I think you think that I'm somebody that I'm not.'

'Oh,' said the man. He reminded Katie of her former bank manager. 'You look so much like Sabrina. You really do.'

'Sabrina?'

'Sabrina from the website. She told me to meet her here, outside the hotel. Maybe I'm a bit too early.'

'Sorry, what website?'

The man looked around the street, and then back at Katie. 'You know, Extreme Dreams.'

'Well, I may look like this Sabrina from Extreme Dreams, but I can swear on the Bible that I'm not her.'

'Okay, then, okay,' said the man distractedly. He left her without saying anything else and went back to the hotel entrance.

Katie climbed into her car but sat and waited with her keys in her lap before she started up the engine. She watched the man pacing up and down, checking his wristwatch again and again. She was interested to see if this Sabrina was going to show up, and if she did, if she really looked so much like her.

After a few minutes, two more men arrived, and Katie could see that they were introducing themselves. Then three girls joined them, one blonde and two brunettes, all in very short skirts. Then a black girl, with dreadlocks and bangles. They were all talking to each other when a red-headed woman came strutting along the street, wearing a tightly belted black leather coat and black high-heeled boots.

Katie had to admit that, yes, the woman did look like her – not that she would ever have dressed like that. Her hair was cut in a similar bob and she was quite bosomy, and about the same height.

As she arrived, the men and the girls greeted her with smiles, and then all eight of them filed in through the hotel entrance and closed the door behind them.

Katie took out her phone and googled Extreme Dreams.

12

When Nessa O'Callaghan entered the dining room of the Blue Marlin Hotel carrying a huge snow-white cake with forty candles on it, everybody stood up and raised their glasses and started to sing 'Happy Birthday to You'.

Shantene burst into tears and let out a wail like a strangled cat. Her husband, Liam, put his arm around her and gave her a kiss and said, 'What are you howling for, darling? Look how much everybody loves you!'

'But I don't want to be forty! Forty's so *old*!'

'Not if you're eighty-six it's not!' called out her grandmother from the other end of the table.

Shantene's sister Blanid took a tissue out of her bag and dabbed her eyes for her. 'There, sis. Give us a smile, will you, and blow out your candles!'

Nessa O'Callaghan set the cake down in front of her and clapped her hands together. 'All in one breath, remember! That's if your wish has any chance at all of coming true!'

'Jesus, Nessa, with that many candles? I'll be dead for lack of oxygen before I can even think of a wish!'

Her birthday guests had gathered around her now, all thirty-three of them – her grandmother, her father and mother, her five brothers and sisters, her uncles and aunts and seven of her cousins, her next-door neighbours from both sides, her old schoolteacher Mrs Byrne, as well as Father Rafferty from the Church of the Sacred Heart. They were all smiling and their eyes were sparkling in the reflected light from the candles.

Shantene took a deep breath, exhaled to let it all out, and then took a second breath, even deeper, so that her cheeks were bulging and her eyes were popping.

Before she could release it, though, there was an ear-splitting bang and the whole back wall of the dining room was blasted into the assembled guests. An oil painting in a heavy gilded frame came flying through the air and struck Shantene directly in the face, taking out her right eye before she pitched backwards on to the floor. A brick hit Liam in the back of the head and his skull burst apart like a melon hit by a shotgun.

The force of the explosion knocked down the front wall of the hotel, too, so that its bricks were scattered across the street. Shantene's birthday guests were ripped into a hellish chaos of bloody flesh and shattered bones and bowels that were looped from one broken chair to another.

After the bang had echoed and re-echoed down Pearse Street, there was a moment's silence. Then, with a loud creak, followed by a deep thunderous rumble, the three upper floors of the Blue Marlin Hotel collapsed one on top of the other, down to the ground. Apart from an avalanche of bricks and floorboards, they brought with them wardrobes and beds and bathtubs and whole flights of stairs. A cloud of dust and smoke rolled up into the afternoon sky and hung there for a while, shuddering in the breeze from the harbour, like a phantom.

Three dead guests were later dug out of the rubble, one sixtyish man who had come to Kinsale to hire a yacht and take it out fishing, and a married couple who were celebrating their woollen wedding anniversary and were both wearing brand-new Aran sweaters, thick with grit.

By some freak of physics, the first shock wave had blown Shantene's birthday cake into the street. Now it lay on the pavement – badly lopsided, and with all forty candles clustered together, but all blown out.

Katie had continued her investigation into Extreme Dreams until late last night, and this afternoon she felt she was ready to set up a sting.

Extreme Dreams' website featured provocative pictures of sexy girls in tightly laced black leather corsets, stockings and suspenders and stiletto heels, as well as muscular young men in bulging briefs, two of them wearing bondage masks. The text read: 'Ever had an extreme dream, but never thought that it could ever come true? Ever envied those men and those girls in erotic movies, and wished that it could be you? Now it can! Extreme Dreams organizes parties in which you can indulge your wildest and kinkiest desires – no holds barred!'

Further down, there was a picture of Sabrina, who called herself 'The Dominatrix of Extreme Dreams'. Apart from her false eyelashes and her pouting scarlet lips, and the fact that her eyes were grey instead of green, she resembled Katie so much that Katie couldn't help giving a little shiver.

Sabrina promised to bring together men and girls who had similar sexual fantasies, everything from bondage and sado-masochism to anal intercourse, wet sex and foot fetishism. All these parties would be carried out in 'luxurious and discreet surroundings', and every participant would have had to guarantee that they were free from STDs.

The cost was €250 per person, payable in advance, plus extras for any non-reusable bondage gear or soiled underwear or sexual devices, such as dildos.

Katie made herself a cup of coffee and a grilled cheese sandwich, and then she sat down to invent a man who would be eager to attend one of Sabrina's get-togethers.

She realized that what Sabrina was offering could be seen as a violation of the Criminal Law (Sexual Offences) Act 2017, which ruled that 'any person who pays another person money or gives them any other consideration for the purpose of engaging in sexual activity with a prostitute shall be guilty of an offence'.

Pimping and keeping a brothel were also against the law. Yet on the face of it, all the men and women who came to her Extreme Dreams parties seemed to be nothing more than ordinary people with an itch to try something kinky, and not professional sex workers. In that case, it might be argued that Sabrina was doing nothing illegal. She was only charging a few people to take part in social events – even if those social events did turn out to be sado-masochistic orgies. Her fees she could put down to expenses – hiring hotel rooms and providing refreshments – and not the profits of prostitution.

Where she would be committing a serious felony was if she were using videos of these orgies to blackmail the people who had taken part in them, like Conor Mullan. There were two laws that covered that in Ireland, the Theft and Fraud Offences Act and the Non-Fatal Offences Against the Person Act.

Katie logged in to Extreme Dreams and started to fill in the details of her imaginary applicant. His name was Sean Delaney, and he was thirty-three years old, and single. He lived in Carrigaline and worked as a vet for the Riverview Animal Hospital. He was interested in BDSM, especially in being whipped by women. 'I think I deserve it, for all the dirty and disrespectful thoughts that I have about them.'

The application form requested a photograph, so Katie

attached the picture of a young car thief that she had on file. He was quite good-looking, with a smile and hair that stuck straight up, but he had died in a car crash in Kerry three years ago.

Katie went into the kitchen to feed the dogs. When she came back, she found that Sabrina had already acknowledged Sean Delaney's application. She said that she would contact him within forty-eight hours to tell him when a date for his Extreme Dreams party could be arranged, since she would have to find more women who were happy to give him the punishment that he craved. She had only one on her books so far.

She added that there were a number of conditions to which he had to agree before his application could be finally accepted. He was to tell nobody about his attendance at the party – not even his family or his closest friends – and neither should he mention it on any social media like Twitter or Facebook or TikTok. Most importantly, he would have to agree that a video record could be taken of the party, to prove that all the participants had been willing and that nobody had been coerced to perform a sexual act of any kind.

Sean Delaney immediately accepted all these conditions, adding that he couldn't wait to feel the lash of a whip.

As usual, Katie had been keeping her television switched on, tuned to the RTÉ news channel, but mute. It enabled her to keep half an eye on the latest events, and it also entertained the dogs. Harvey in particular sat transfixed for hours in front of the screen, occasionally jumping up and wuffling if he saw another dog, or somebody running.

Only a few minutes after Katie had sent her acceptance back

to Sabrina, she saw a reporter standing in what she recognized as Market Street in Kinsale. Behind him, bricks and rubble and a broken door frame were scattered across the junction with Pearse Street. Two fire engines were visible, with flashing blue lights.

Immediately, she picked up the remote and turned on the sound. She was just in time to hear the reporter saying, '— bomb disposal unit have cordoned off all the streets around here in case of a second device. The total number of dead and injured isn't known yet, but apparently a birthday party was being held in the hotel at the time and so it's almost certain that there's been some fatalities.'

Mother of God, she thought. *That's the Blue Marlin Hotel.* She knew it well, not only because she had once had lunch there when she and her late husband, Paul, had visited Kinsale. She remembered from their investigation into the Dripsey Dozen that the owner of the Blue Marlin, Bryan O'Callaghan, was one of them.

And now, God help us, someone's blown it up. If this didn't convince Micheál ó Broin that somebody was out to kill off the Dripsey Dozen, one by one, then nothing would.

Still watching the television, Katie called Sergeant Murphy. His phone rang and rang, and eventually it was answered by Garda Christina O'Donnell.

'Sergeant Murphy's not here this afternoon, ma'am. He's attending his father's funeral.'

'I see. But can you tell me what's happened in Kinsale? I've just seen it on the news and it looks like another bomb.'

'I'm not sure I should be giving you any information, ma'am. I'm sorry.'

'They said it was a hotel that got blown up, and it looked like the Blue Marlin. Can you at least confirm that?'

'Yes, ma'am, it was the Blue Marlin.'

'Have you been given any indication of how many casualties we're looking at?'

'Not yet. But Superintendent Gaffney from Bandon is on the scene there already. Detective Inspector O'Sullivan is on his way there too, with Detective Sergeant Begley and three detective gardaí – Malloy and Coughlan and Hickey, I think they are. I should be hearing from them any time now. And I really shouldn't have told you any of that, so please don't let on that I did.'

'I won't, Christina, I promise you. But I won't forget this when I'm back in the saddle.'

'Do you mind me asking you when you're coming back?'

'It's still wait and see, I'm afraid. But it shouldn't be too long.'

'The sooner the better, ma'am. That's all I can say.'

Katie was tempted for a second to ask Garda O'Donnell if Micheál ó Broin had upset her in any way, but she knew that would put the poor girl in an impossible position. In any case, the blowing up of the Blue Marlin Hotel was a much more urgent priority. Micheál may have warned her to keep her nose out of any investigation, but she needed to drive over to Kinsale as soon as possible and see the damage for herself. If there were any survivors, she wanted to talk to them about what they might have seen or heard before the bomb went off, and she also wanted to talk to any witnesses who might have seen the explosion from the street.

Jenny next door was out, so she had to take the dogs with her. They jumped excitedly into the back of her car, obviously believing that she was going to take them out to the woods or the seashore for a walk.

It took her three-quarters of an hour to drive to Kinsale. She kept the radio news on, and as she drove she heard frequent updates on the Blue Marlin bombing. So far, twenty-eight people had been found in the rubble, fatally injured. Three more were seriously hurt and had been taken to hospital in a life-threatening condition. Among the dead were the hotel's owners, Bryan and Nessa O'Callaghan.

It was the worst bombing on the island of Ireland since the Omagh bombing in 1998, which had killed twenty-nine and injured two hundred and twenty. Assistant Commissioner Frank Magorian gave a preliminary statement to the media to say that it was a 'heart-rending tragedy' and that no warning had been given to the Garda, either coded or open. Katie could tell by his voice that he was badly shaken.

When she arrived in Kinsale she had to park around the corner from the scene of the bombing, in Market Quay, outside the library. The whole of Pearse Street and Market Street had been cordoned off now, and the junction was crowded with fire engines and ambulances and Garda patrol cars and the van from the bomb disposal unit.

She left the dogs in the car with the window a few centimetres open to give them air, and then she walked up to the cordon that was stretched across the street. She could see Terry O'Sullivan talking to one of the bomb disposal officers, so she called out to him and gave him a wave. He waved back, and then he came over to the tape. He looked as shaken as Frank Magorian had sounded.

'Ma'am – I realize that you can't help having a fierce interest in a major incident like this, but there was no real need for you to attend in person.'

'But, Terry, it's one more murder of Dripsey relatives, the O'Callaghans. God help us, if only they'd been warned.

Maybe none of these other poor souls would have lost their lives either.'

'The O'Callaghans? *They* were members of the Dripsey Dozen?'

'We never got around to interviewing them personally, but yes, they were on the list. I remembered because they ran the Blue Marlin.'

'Jesus Christ.'

'Micheál needs to download that file urgent-like, find their addresses, and contact all the rest of them. He needs to advise them that they're in mortal danger, and their houses could be blown up at any time. They should move, all of them, at least for the time being, and if they can't be persuaded to move, we should think about posting a twenty-four-hour guard on each of their homes.'

Terry bit his lip and looked distinctly uncomfortable. 'The problem is, ma'am, that I've been given strict instructions not to discuss this investigation with you. This investigation or any other investigation, for that matter. DS ó Broin is on his way here and if he finds out that I've been talking to you about it – well, to say that he'll be bulling is an understatement.'

'I was hoping to talk to any witnesses,' said Katie, looking around.

'I'm pure sorry, ma'am,' said Terry. 'If it was up to me, you'd be more than welcome. But I can't let you do that.'

Katie gave him a wry smile. 'Fair play to you, Terry. I don't want to get you into trouble. I'll just have to follow the news, won't I?'

They heard a shout from the ruins of the Blue Marlin Hotel. It was a rescue worker from the fire brigade, who had found another body.

'I'll have to go,' said Terry. Katie nodded, and watched as he hurried off. Again, she felt a surge of helplessness and frustration.

She returned to her car. The three dogs were all panting and scrambling from side to side on the back seat, and so she opened the door and let them all out.

'A short scove before we go home again,' she told them. 'And make sure you do whatever you need to do.'

She took them along Pier Road, in the opposite direction from the scene of the bombing, and along to the bank of the River Bandon. On the way there, Harvey stopped for a moment, turned his head, and sniffed two or three times. Katie wondered if he could still smell explosives in the air.

The water in the river was the same dull grey as the clouds. Katie stood and watched a small motorboat puttering out towards the Old Head of Kinsale and the open sea, while the dogs anointed the nearby lamp-posts.

She whistled at them, and was about to start walking back to Market Quay when she caught sight of a man coming out of the public toilets and crossing the road to the car park. She was shocked to see that it was the tall bald man in black who had blown up his Honda in Ballincollig, and then got away. There was no mistaking him.

For a split second, Katie felt the urge to run after him. She was not carrying her gun, but she reckoned she could knock him off his feet with a taekwondo kick and pin him to the ground. But he could be armed, and she had to think about how she was going to keep him pinned down and call for backup at the same time, and how long it might be before that backup arrived.

The bald man went over to a dark maroon Toyota and opened the driver's door. Before he climbed in, though, he turned and looked around. Katie couldn't be sure if he had recognized her or not, but he slammed the door, started the engine and backed out of his parking space with his tyres squealing, as if he was in a hurry.

Katie pulled out her phone and before he could drive off, she took a picture of his number plate. Then she immediately called Christina O'Donnell at Anglesea Street to send out an all-points bulletin to cover the surrounding area in both Bandon and Cork. After that, she rang Terry O'Sullivan.

'Terry – would you believe I've seen the same suspect I saw at Ballincollig? That's right, that lofty bald feen in black. He's gone speeding off in a reddish Toyota and I'm attaching a picture of it for you.'

'Which way did he go?'

'Well, since the middle of the town's all cordoned off, like, my guess is that he'll be heading away on the R600. I've called the station for an APB but you might want to send a couple of units after him from here.'

'Hold on. DS ó Broin's just arrived, and it looks like he's in a fouler already. This is going to take some diplomacy for sure. If I'm sending cars out looking for your man, he'll want to know where I get my information from.'

'Terry, twenty-nine people have been killed. Diplomacy doesn't come into it. This fellow has to be caught.'

'I know, ma'am, I have you,' said Terry miserably. 'But did you ever hear about rocks and hard places?'

13

Katie drove back to Carrig View. The bombing of the Blue Marlin Hotel dominated the radio news all the way back, and when she arrived home and switched on the television, the coverage of the death toll in Kinsale was continuous.

The number of fatalities equalled that of the Omagh bombing, although far fewer bystanders had been injured because the explosion had taken place inside a building rather than the open street.

To Katie, this bombing reinforced beyond any reasonable doubt her belief that someone was carrying out a systematic campaign of murder against the Dripsey Dozen. She was sorely tempted to call Fionnuala Sweeney at RTÉ and tell her, but she knew that Micheál ó Broin would see Fionnuala's report on the news, and she was reluctant to put his back up any more than she had already. Yes, she still thought that his methods were frustratingly lacking in inspiration, but at least he was carrying out a meticulous step-by-step analysis of every bombing, and if he eventually managed to identify and arrest the perpetrators, he should have a case that stood up well in court.

She was well aware that he had cautioned every member of staff at Anglesea Street not to share any information with her, but she had asked Christina O'Donnell in the communications centre to call her if she received any news about the bald-headed man in black.

However hostile Micheál might be to her, Katie knew that she needed to go to Anglesea Street and talk to him. After all, she was the only witness who had seen the bald-headed man at both Ballincollig and Kinsale, and she would be able to give a description to Detective Kevon Doyle, their EvoFIT artist. Since An Garda Síochána had introduced the new software, the likenesses that Detective Doyle had created from witness descriptions had led to the arrest of sixty per cent of the suspects that they were looking for.

All the same, she was reasonably hopeful that all the surviving members of the Dripsey Dozen would have seen the news, and realized by now that their lives might be in mortal danger. The Blue Marlin bombing had been so devastating that reports of it must have gone around the world, and they could hardly have missed it.

A few minutes after four o'clock, Christina O'Donnell called her.

'This won't be on the telly, ma'am, so I thought I'd tell you myself. That car you described, that Toyota, it was found abandoned about twenty minutes ago round the back of Walton Court hotel near Ballinaclashett. The technical team will be towing it in for fingerprints and DNA testing.'

'Thanks a million, Christina. I appreciate it. No sign of the driver, though, I imagine?'

'No, ma'am. And Walton Court's been closed for a while now, so there was nobody there who might have seen where he went.'

Katie thought of calling Micheál right away, but she knew he would be up the walls at the moment, trying to deal with all the incoming evidence about the bombing, and with the media, too, who would be clamouring for updates. She had been through that experience enough times herself. His response to her calling him would be sure to be impatient and ratty, even if he answered, so she decided to leave it until the morning.

She was brewing herself a cup of lemon tea in the kitchen when her phone pinged, and it was a text from Sabrina at Extreme Dreams. Sabrina was delighted to tell Sean Delaney that she had already found another willing girl to take part in his punishment party, as well as two fit young men. They would meet at the Abhaile ó Bhaile Hotel on Leopold Street in Cork's Victorian Quarter three days from today, at three in the afternoon.

Believe me, Sean, you'll have a whip-round you'll never forget!

All he had to do now was send €250 to Sabrina's PayPal account.

Kieran arrived well after ten. He had already had dinner at the Elbow Lane Brew and Smoke House with Rory Mullican, a special counsel who had recently been appointed as an ordinary judge.

He was tired. It had been a long and difficult day in court, with one of the most appalling cases of domestic abuse that he had ever had to hear. Of course, he had heard about the Blue Marlin bombing, and Katie had texted him to tell him that she would be going to Kinsale. She had also told him that she had seen the bald man in black.

'I'm not so sure you shouldn't be keeping yourself out

of this,' he said, as he watched her pouring him a glass of Jameson's Black Barrel.

'How can I, Kieran? It's in my blood. And it's quite possible that the investigation could still be going on when I'm reinstated, so I need to keep up to date with it.'

'Whoever's planting these bombs, though, and for whatever reason, they're fierce dangerous people. I don't want you putting yourself at risk when you really don't have to. If they're anything like the Real IRA up in Belfast, they consider the police to be fair game, and they won't care two hoots if you're on suspension or not, even if they're aware of it, which they're probably not. And this baldy fellow, he knows what you look like and it's almost certain that he knows who you are.'

'Kieran, that's an everyday risk of being a guard. If I had a hundred euros for every threat that's been made against me by the Kinahans, for instance, I'd be a wealthy woman by now.'

'Or a dead one.'

'You've no need to worry, sweetheart. I can take care of myself.'

'I only wish that you'd let me take care of you.'

They sat on the couch and watched the late-night television news together, Kieran sipping his whiskey and Katie's head resting on his shoulder. It was dark now, but Kinsale was lit up with halogen lamps and flashing blue lights, and behind the news reporter they could see a mechanical digger shovelling up the heaps of broken bricks, plaster walls and splintered joists.

It was nearly midnight when Katie and Kieran each took a shower. When they went to bed, they held each other close, but they were too tired and their minds were too churned up by the day's events to make love. Not only that, neither of them had been able to rid themselves of the dull underlying dread that it would not be long before they would have to separate.

When the clock in the hallway chimed one, they were both still awake. Kieran reached over and stroked Katie's hair away from her face. She could just see his eyes reflecting the light from the bedside alarm.

'Marry me, Katie,' he said, with a catch in his throat. Then he coughed, and said again, 'Marry me.'

Katie could hardly think what to say. Of course she would love to be married to him. But if they were married, and wanted to live together, one of them would have to give up his or her career, or at least change it dramatically. Was Kieran really asking because he loved her so much that he couldn't be without her, or was he trying to find a way of persuading her to leave the Gardaí? If he was, maybe he was doing it because he feared for her safety, but maybe he simply wanted to have her in his life without having to resign from the bench.

Then again, maybe she was thinking like a detective instead of a lover, and she was questioning his proposal as if he were a suspect in a fraud case. If that were true, she thought, she should be ashamed of herself. A handsome judge had asked her to marry him, and she was immediately suspicious that he might have some devious ulterior motive.

A whole minute went past.

'You did hear what I said?' Kieran asked her.

'I did of course.'

'It's just that you're taking your time in saying yes or no.'

'It came as a shock, that's all, darling. I mean, a surprise anyway. And I was almost asleep, so I wasn't sure if I was dreaming.'

'It's not a dream. Well – it surely *would* be a dream if you agreed to be my wife. Mrs Kathleen Connolly. Rolls off the tongue, don't you think?'

'Yes. Yes, it does.'

'So is that a yes?'

'Yes.'

Kieran kissed her, and then kissed her again. 'Katie, sweetheart – you have just made me the most ecstatic judge who ever drew breath.'

Twenty minutes later, he was asleep, breathing very deeply, as if he were wearing an aqualung and was several fathoms underwater. Katie herself found it impossible to sleep. The idea of being Mrs Connolly rolled around and around in her mind, along with every change in her life that being married to Kieran would bring to her. She wondered if they might consider having a child together, or even more than one. And then she thought of little Seamus lying lifeless and cold in his cot that morning.

Strangely, after that, she found herself thinking about Sabrina and Extreme Dreams. She was not going to send her the €250 fee that she had asked for, because she wanted to see what Sabrina's reaction would be.

She heard the clock strike four before she eventually fell asleep, and she was woken up less than two hours later by the sound of rain against the bedroom window.

It was still raining when she took the dogs for a walk up to Flowerhill and back. She couldn't get Kieran's proposal off her mind, and she wondered if she had been too hasty in accepting it, simply because she hadn't wanted to hurt his feelings. She loved him, but she remembered only too painfully what it had been like being married to Paul.

While she couldn't deny that Kieran was a calm and considerate man, and he did everything he could to make her feel loved and looked after, he was still a dominant personality, and she wondered if she might come to regret being tied to him legally. She knew from experience of marriage that even a disagreement about what CD to play in the car could turn into a shouting match.

She took the dogs back to Jenny's, and they stood in her porch and violently shook the rain off themselves.

'How's yourself, Katie?' frowned Jenny. 'If you don't mind my saying so, you look like a tree over a blessed well.'

Katie gave her a weak smile. 'I've not too much to be cheerful about right now, to be honest with you. I was over in Kinsale yesterday after that bombing.'

'Oh Jesus. What a tragedy. Do they still not know who did it?'

'Not as far as I know. But I'm going in to the station this morning to see what the latest news is.'

'I saw your man this morning, as he was leaving. He gave me a wave. He's a fine-looking fellow, isn't he? I'd hang on to him if I was you.'

Katie smiled again. 'I intend to, Jen, believe me.'

She went next door to her own house and changed into her grey tweed suit, with thick black tights. If she was going to meet Micheál, she wanted to look formal. Once she had buttoned up her overcoat she went to the front door, but then she hesitated for a moment and went back into the kitchen. She took her Smith & Wesson revolver down from the cabinet and tucked it into her inside pocket. The chances of her seeing the bald man in black again were probably one in a trillion, but then what had been the chances of her running across him in Kinsale yesterday?

She drove into Cork city and as she passed by Tivoli docks the ragged grey clouds began to clear away to reveal an anaemic winter sun. She tried to persuade herself that this was a good omen. Once she had parked behind the station in Anglesea Street and pushed her way through the doors into the reception area, she was relieved to find that DI O'Sullivan was down there, talking to the duty officer on the front desk.

She waited until he had finished what he was saying, and then she went up to him and said, 'You don't have to tell me anything, Terry. I don't want to get you into the shite with himself.'

'You've seen the TV news this morning?'

'Of course. Claire Byrne said that it was a bomb all right, but nobody had claimed responsibility for it and you still have no idea who might have planted it.'

'Well, yes, that's about the sum of it. There isn't much more I can tell you, even if I was allowed to. It was C-4 packed into an air fryer and set off remotely, like the device that killed the McCarthys and Derry O'Brien, and probably the O'Farrells too, and that Honda that was blown up at Ballincollig.'

Katie glanced quickly around the reception area to make sure that no other officer was watching them or trying to overhear what they were saying.

'How about the baldy fellow? Any luck with tracing him?'

Terry shook his head. 'We've called off the APB. Bill Phinner's team are still examining his car, but even if they find a rake of fingerprints and DNA, they'll be of no use at all if we have nothing on file to match them with.'

'I'll be giving a description of your man to Kevon Doyle,' said Katie. 'There's a chance that somebody might recognize an e-fit. But I have to talk to DS ó Broin first. I think he and I desperately need to come to some kind of mutual understanding about these bombings. Is he here?'

'He is, yes, but he told me he was shooting out to meet the mayor. They're going to be discussing this new extortion racket that the Real IRA gang have been running against criminals. You know – pay us a share of your ill-gotten gains or you'll finish up shot dead like Aidan "The Beast" O'Driscoll.'

Katie couldn't help grimacing. 'I was really making some progress with that bunch of gowls. I only hope that Micheál ó Broin hasn't made a bags of it. His idea of progress is one step forward and then turn around and take two steps back, just to make sure that when he took the one step forward he was heading in the right direction.

'Still and all—' She was about to admit that Micheál had an impressive service record and that it was unprofessional of her to complain about him when the lift doors opened and Micheál himself appeared. He was obviously in a hurry, buttoning up his long witch-like raincoat as he stepped out into the reception area.

'Micheál!' Katie called out. 'Micheál, can you spare me a minute or two?'

'I can't, no,' Micheál snapped back. 'I'm late for my meeting as it is. What way are you, anyhow?'

Katie followed him to the front doors. 'I need to talk to you. And I mean urgently. It's about the bombing in Kinsale, and all the other bombings besides.'

'My investigation is well in hand, Kathleen, thank you.'

'I'm sure it is. And I know you don't believe in speculation. But I really believe that this is the time for you to be making an inspired guess or two.'

They went down the steps in the front of the station together.

A taxi was waiting for Micheál, and as they came through the open gates the driver climbed out.

'Kathleen, guesses don't stand up in court. And that's all I have to say to you.'

He turned towards the taxi, but as he did so a large black Mercedes came speeding down Anglesea Street. It slithered to a stop right next to them, and the passenger window was rolled down.

Katie saw a man holding what looked like a gun, and he was pointing it at them. She shoved Micheál in the back as hard as she could with both hands and screamed, '*Down!*'

Micheál stumbled and dropped flat on his stomach on to the pavement. As he did so, Katie heard a sharp, suppressed shot, like a pistol with a silencer; and then another; and another.

14

Katie ducked down behind the side of the taxi and dragged her revolver out of her inside pocket. At the same time, still lying on the ground, Micheál rolled himself back through the open gate, his raincoat flapping, trying to reach the station steps.

A man wearing a black balaclava and a dark-brown sheepskin jacket climbed out of the Mercedes and stalked towards Micheál, pointing an automatic at him. Katie, crouching against the side of the taxi, fired at him, twice. She hit him in the shoulder, so that his jacket flew up like an epaulette, and then she hit him in the hip.

The man staggered, too stunned to turn around and see where the shots had come from. Katie heard him say '*Feck!*' and then he hobbled back to the Mercedes, heaved the door open again, and pitched back into the passenger seat. The Mercedes screeched away before he had even closed the door, and his left shoe was still trailing along the road. The car took a sharp right when it reached Copley Street and disappeared around the corner.

Katie climbed to her feet and went across to help Micheál up off the pavement. The taxi driver was cautiously peering out from behind one of the Garda cars parked behind his Volvo.

'He didn't hit you?' Katie asked Micheál.

'No, no, I'm grand,' he said, waving her hand away. 'But for the love of God, you opened fire on him.'

'What was I supposed to do, tell him to conduct himself?'

Micheál stood up and started fussily brushing down his raincoat. 'You know the procedure.'

'Sorry? The *procedure*?'

'Yes. You should have ordered him to put down his weapon and fired a warning shot if he wouldn't. Only if he still refused to put it down should you have opened fire to neutralize him.'

'Micheál, he was about to shoot you dead. There was no time for all that fancy rigmarole.'

'Well, we shall never know, shall we, because you didn't give him the chance. It seems to me that your whole modus operandi is to shoot first and don't even bother to ask questions afterwards. Why do you think you're on suspension?'

Katie could hardly believe what he was saying to her. She wanted to tell him *I've just this minute saved your fecking life, you ungrateful gobshite*, but she was too shaken by having been shot at and shooting back. She could only stare at him and wonder how anybody could be so pedantic, especially after having such a narrow escape.

The taxi driver came jogging up to them, carroty-haired, podgy and panting. 'Holy Christ, that was like some cowboy fillum! Did you kill that feller?'

'Well, there's no way of knowing,' said Micheál. 'And I must insist that you keep what you saw to yourself. You may have to give evidence about it later in a court of law, or a tribunal.'

'Whatever you say, sir. I was keeping my head down so I didn't see too much, any road. I heard only that *bangity-bang*!'

He paused for breath, and then he sniffed and said, 'Would you still be wanting to go to County Hall?'

'No. No, of course not. I'll have to postpone my meeting and go back inside to report this. My assistant will call you later if I need you.'

Now DI O'Sullivan and Detective Coughlan and four uniformed gardaí came bursting out of the station doors and down the steps.

'Was that gunfire we heard then?' asked Terry, looking up and down the street. 'Sergeant Beary here said it sounded more like fireworks.'

'It was gunfire all right,' said Micheál. Despite the way he had spoken to her before, Katie could tell that he was finding it difficult to keep his voice steady. 'A fellow drew up in a black Mercedes and took a couple of potshots at me.'

'Serious? Jesus!'

'He had a suppressor, so you wouldn't have heard them, and he missed me, thank God. But when he got out to try and finish the job, Kathleen shot him. That was the gunfire you heard – Kathleen's. No warning. No "drop it and put up your hands"! She just – shot him.'

Terry glanced at Katie as if he couldn't understand why Micheál had said that, because he would probably have done the same.

'Your man was only wounded,' said Katie. 'He got back into the car and they headed off down Copley Street. We need to put out a call asap. Black Mercedes, 350SL I think it was. They'll have it upstairs on CCTV.'

'Here, I'll go and give Peter Murphy the heads-up,' said Detective Coughlan, and he hurried back up the steps.

Micheál peered around the pavement, his eyes narrowed. 'We need to tape this area off for forensics,' he told Sergeant Beary. 'I can't see any stray bullets lying around, but see, look, that gatepost's freshly chipped.'

Sergeant Beary nodded to two of the uniformed gardaí. They lifted the boot of their patrol car, took out rolls of tape and started to cordon off the front of the station.

Micheál watched them for a while. Katie thought that he looked dazed, as if he could hardly believe that he had been shot at, and it had all been a dream. But suddenly he snapped out of it, turned around and said, 'Right! I need Moirin to call the mayor's office and let him know that I've been unavoidably delayed.'

He marched back up the steps into the station and Terry followed close behind him. Katie, uninvited, went with them, and joined them in the lift. As they went up to Micheál's office, he continued to stare at her as cold as a codfish, but he could hardly object. He would need a statement from her about the shooting and she would have to hand over her revolver for forensic examination.

She was quite aware that there would have to be a formal inquiry into the shooting, especially if the man she had shot had suffered life-changing injuries, or died. She had been allowed to keep her revolver during her suspension for self-defence. Yet she wondered if shooting that man had legally counted as self-defence. He had not been shooting at her, and she had opened fire without warning him.

When they reached his office, Micheál sat down behind his desk, opened the bottom drawer and took out a bottle of Paddy's whiskey. He poured himself a glass and knocked it back all in one, and then he poured himself another, and sat staring at it. He didn't offer one to Katie or Terry.

'I never thought they'd fecking try it after I'd moved down here,' he said, to nobody in particular.

'Who's "they"?' asked Katie. She was standing by the window, looking out at the view that used to be hers. Three or four hooded crows were perched on the rooftop opposite and she wondered if they had followed her from the Bon Secours.

'I'm sure it's them, anyway. The Rathkeale Mob.'

Katie knew all about the gangs who operated out of the town of Rathkeale, south-west of Limerick city. They were heavily involved in drug trading and money laundering and fraud, and they ruled the town with impunity. Last Christmas they had smashed up dozens of SUVs in the streets and mutilated rival gangsters with machetes. Once they had persuaded a rival to hand over his assets by nailing his foot to his kitchen floor. It had even been suggested that the army should be called in to Rathkeale to restore order.

Katie could only assume that while he was serving as a detective inspector in Limerick, Micheál had done something that had seriously earned their displeasure, such as having the gall to arrest some of them, or seize their drugs.

After a while, she said, 'There's one question we have to ask ourselves, Micheál.'

'Oh, yes? And what's that?'

'How did those gowls know exactly when you'd be coming out of the station – I mean, to the very second? You need to have a serious word with that taxi company, and that driver. Like, who else knew you were off to see the mayor, and at what time?'

'You *shot* him,' said Micheál, still staring at his glass of whiskey as if it were a crystal ball and he would be able to see his future in it.

'I don't know what else you expected me to do. But I'll give Terry here a statement and then I'll take my gun down to Bill Phinner.'

'They'll be coming back. The Rathkeale Mob, I mean. You shot him, so believe you me, they'll be coming back. And you can mark my words, this time they'll be wanting their revenge ten times over.'

Katie came over to his desk and looked down at him. *You're frightened*, she thought. *For all your arrogance, you're scared sideways. Is this the real reason you don't want me to be reinstated here at Anglesea Street, because you're terrified of what might happen to you if you're posted back to Limerick?*

She went down to the photographic studio to see Detective Kevon Doyle. He was in a good mood as usual and eating a ham roll while he was scrolling through pictures taken at the scene of a fatal car accident at Ballyhooly.

'Well now, super!' he said cheerily. 'How's yourself?'

'Itching to get back here, if you must know, Kevon.'

'No news yet from Internal Affairs? They're taking their own sweet time deciding that you did nothing wrong at all, aren't they?'

'I should hear quite soon, don't worry.'

'That's grand. It's probably not my place to say so but your acting DS is not exactly the easiest fellow to be getting along with, like. If you ask me, he'd cross the street to be offended.'

Katie rolled an office chair over to Kevon's desk and sat down next to him in front of his computer screen. 'I need an Evo-FIT of a suspect who could be connected with that bombing in Kinsale. Maybe those other bombings, too. I've seen him twice myself, clear enough to give you a good description.'

Kevon loaded the Evo-FIT software, keeping his ham roll clenched between his teeth. When he was ready, he took out the roll and said, 'Male, yes, roughly what age are we talking about? Fiftyish, you said? Fat? Thin? What sort of bazzer?'

A series of sixty faces appeared on the screen and Katie picked the one that most closely resembled the bald man in black. Kevon then downloaded a second generation of faces so that she could direct him to make minor refinements in shape and texture, lowering his eyebrows and flattening his ears against the sides of his head.

Finally, the software enabled him to adjust the man's demeanour. He altered it from bland and expressionless to frowning and vengeful. He now had the same expression that he had given Katie when he detonated that car bomb at Ballincollig.

By the time he had finished the Evo-FIT, Katie felt that she was looking at an actual photograph. She found it genuinely unsettling, the way the bald man was glaring at her from out of the computer screen. She could almost believe that wherever he was, he could sense somehow that she had created a likeness of him, and that she would be doing everything she could to hunt him down.

'You're a pure genius, Kevon,' she told him. 'Now, if you can send that down as quick as you like to Mathew McElvey in the press office, we can get that out to the media, RTÉ news and Cork Live and the papers.'

Before she left for home, Katie went to see Sergeant Patrick Bowlan in the armoury. Her Smith & Wesson revolver would be held for examination by the technical bureau for at least a week, so in the meantime she would need a replacement firearm to protect herself. Sergeant Bowlan issued her with a Sig-Sauer subcompact automatic.

He also gave her two boxes of spare 9mm ammunition. 'Just in case every gurrier you ever riled comes after you.'

'You're every woman's dream, Patrick, believe me.'

After that, she went above to the communications centre. She wanted to thank Sergeant Murphy and Garda O'Donnell for continuing to update her on the progress of the bombings, even though Micheál ó Broin had cautioned them not to.

'Sure it does no harm at all to give you the heads-up and it makes good sense,' said Sergeant Murphy, although he kept his eyes fixed on one of the forty CCTV screens in the room, where a van driver was making a holy bags of parking outside Hickeys on Oliver Plunkett Street, and had already collided with another vehicle twice. 'You'll be back in harness before we know it, ma'am, and you'll need to be up to speed.'

Katie smiled, and patted his shoulder, although she suddenly thought of Kieran lying in bed next to her and saying *marry me*.

She was still thinking about Kieran as she drove back to Carrig View. Never in her life before had she wanted two contradictory futures so much. Looking out of the window of Micheál's office, she had felt as if she had come back home, and she couldn't wait to involve herself in the bombings and all the other serious investigations that were pending. At the same time, though, she could imagine herself and Kieran living happily in a house in Dublin, going out to restaurants and concerts and entertaining all kinds of interesting guests at home. She could picture them going on exotic holidays together, and even having a child, or children.

My little Seamus, who art in Heaven, she thought. *You could have a brother or a sister.* If only I could separate myself into *two* Katie Maguires, like twins – Katie the detective superintendent and Katie the wife.

Her three dogs, as usual, were overjoyed to see her, as if she had been away for a month, rather than a few hours. Even

Harvey was jumping up and down and wuffling excitedly. Once she had given them some meaty snacks, though, she caught Harvey standing quite still, not eating, staring out of the living-room window as if he were expecting Aiden and Shauna O'Farrell to appear outside.

She stroked him under his chin. How do you tell a dog that the people who loved him enough to adopt him are dead, and are never coming back?

Her phone pinged. It was a message for Sean Delaney, from Sabrina at Extreme Dreams. Sean had not yet paid his €250, without which Sabrina would not be able to book his whipping party at the Abhaile ó Bhaile Hotel. Had he simply forgotten to make his payment, or was he having trouble raising the money? She would give him twenty-four hours to pay, after which 'regretfully' she would be forced to consider 'alternative measures'. What these 'alternative measures' might be, she didn't say. All the same, Katie suspected they would be more than simply cancelling his party and calling it a day.

Sabrina would have seen that 'Sean' had read her text, but 'Sean' sent her no reply. Katie wanted to see what she would say and do next, and what her 'alternative measures' might be.

She sat down with a mug of tea to watch the Six One News. As she expected, the headline story was all about the shooting outside the Anglesea Street Garda station.

'Thankfully, the attempt on the life of Detective Superintendent Micheál ó Broin was a failure,' said the reporter. 'The gunman fired three times, but missed.' What surprised Katie was that he made no mention of her shooting Micheál's assailant, and neither did he say that Micheál was sure he had been attacked by gangsters from Rathkeale, looking for revenge.

She guessed that Micheál had given Mathew McElvey

instructions not to mention that she had saved his life, and not to name the Rathkeale Mob in case it riled them even more.

The last item on the news was the Evo-FIT picture of the bald man in black. 'Have you seen this man?' asked Caitríona Perry, the presenter. 'The Garda want to talk to him in connection with the bombing of the Blue Marlin Hotel in Kinsale. If you've seen him, or you know where he is now, call this number, or 112. You are advised, though, not to approach him.'

Harvey was sitting on the couch next to Katie, and when the Evo-FIT picture appeared on the screen he lifted his head and let out a little snuffling sound.

'Do *you* recognize him, Harvey?' said Katie. 'Here – do you want a lend of my phone so you can tell Micheál about it?'

Half an hour later, Kieran called to say that he was going to stay in the city that night. It had been a long exhausting day in court, and he had an early breakfast meeting tomorrow.

'You've not changed your mind, though?' he asked her.

'About what?'

'About "Mrs Kathleen Connolly".'

'No, Kieran. I haven't,' Katie reassured him, although she felt a disturbing sense of unease, as if she hadn't been completely honest with him. *I want so much to be your wife, but—*

She took the dogs for a last walk up to Flowerhill in the chilly evening fog, and then she took a long hot balsam bath and went to bed. She read for a while, a new history of the Troubles, *Revenge Is Green*, to see if it could give her any more insight into the Dripsey Dozen.

At the beginning of the book there was a quotation from Éamon de Valera, the former president of Ireland, from the time of the Uprising. 'England pretends it is not by the naked sword, but by the good will of the people of the country that she is here. We will draw the naked sword to make her bare her own naked sword.'

A sword against a sword, she thought, before she closed the book and switched off her bedside lamp. *An eye for an eye, a tooth for a tooth, a bombing for a bombing.*

15

It had started to drizzle again as Tommy O'Mahony turned into the driveway of his bungalow in Berrings. He switched off the engine of his Toyota Hilux but sat behind the wheel for a few moments, quietly burping. His friend Tadgh had bought him one more glass of stout than he usually allowed himself and he hadn't eaten since breakfast.

At last, he climbed out of the cab and made his way to the porch. He had his key poised to unlock the front door when his wife, Bridget, opened it, holding a sweeping brush. Her grey hair was knotted into a businesslike bun, and she was wrapped up in her usual flowery apron.

'Don't tell me,' she said. 'You stopped at O'regan's just to make sure they hadn't run out of Murphy's.'

'I had to see Tadgh about mending the fence behind the haggart.'

'And of course you couldn't discuss it without having a few gats.'

'I owed him one, Bridget, and I couldn't let him drink it on his own.'

'You bought the potatoes, though, and that brown flour, and that Clonakilty pudding I wanted?'

'I did of course. Oh – I've left them in the truck. Hold on, I'll fetch them.'

'Jesus, I swear you'll forget your head one day. But never mind. You're forgiven for once. That air fryer, that's such a surprise. When did you order that?'

Tommy had opened the door of his pickup to retrieve the groceries that he had left on the passenger seat, but now he turned back and blinked at Bridget through the drizzle and said, 'What are you talking about? What air fryer?'

'The fellow delivered it not half an hour ago.'

'I ordered no air fryer. Why would I order an air fryer?'

'Oh. I thought it was a gift, like. I thought you'd bought it for me because Mona Boylan has one and I was telling you what a blessing they are when you're cooking only for two.'

'I did no such thing. I've had all that fencing to pay for this month anyway. I'm broke as a joke.'

'So broke that you could buy Tadgh and yourself a gat or two? Or three, by the sound of you.'

Tommy frowned and lifted one finger as if he were recalling something important. 'Hold your horses. Tim Lyons was on about air fryers, when he called me yesterday morning.'

'You never told me that.'

'Well, you were out with that Denise, weren't you, and I forgot.'

'Why would he call you about air fryers? That's not exactly a manly conversation, is it?'

'We were talking about those bombings. You know, Brendan McCarthy and Derry O'Brien and now Bryan and Nessa down at Kinsale. Tim said that a Garda detective had called to the door and warned him that somebody could be after killing off the Dripsey Dozen. Well, it's been on the news too, hasn't it?'

'So what do air fryers have to do with that?'

'This detective told Tim and Nola to keep sketch for anyone

delivering an air fryer or a microwave oven, or if someone's managed to leave one in their house somehow. That's what them bombs were made of – air fryers and microwave ovens with the plastic explosive stuffed inside them.'

Bridget looked back into the house. 'Holy Mary, Tommy. You don't think—'

'I didn't order it, *a ghrá*. I think you need to come outside here, and for both of us to stay well away from the house while I call for the guards.'

'But surely—'

'But surely nothing at all. Why in God's name would anyone give us an air fryer, anonymous-like, without telling us who they are and when it was going to be delivered?'

'Look, it's raining rotten now,' said Bridget. 'Let me nip in for my coat.'

'No! Just close the door and come out here now. We can drive a safe distance down the boreen and sit and wait for the guards in the pickup.'

'But Tiernan! What about Tiernan?'

'Bridget, I'm not having you risk your life for the sake of a cat!'

'We can't leave him inside if there's a bomb!'

'He's a cat, for feck's sake!'

'Yes! And he's one of God's creatures! And I love him!'

Bridget turned around and went back in through the front door. Tommy said, '*Shite!*' and immediately went hobbling after her. He could hear her calling for Tiernan, who was usually sleeping in the press, because it was warm.

'Bridget!' he shouted, standing in the front doorway. 'Bridget, come back out here this instant!'

He hesitated for a moment, cursed again, and then he stepped inside. The second he entered the hall, the bungalow blew up. The entire triangular roof jumped up three metres into the air before it shattered apart in a blizzard of brown tiles. The front walls were flattened, and huge chunks of brick went bouncing into the driveway, knocking down the front fence and rolling across the road.

The explosion was so powerful that Tommy's Hilux was blasted vertically upwards and then sent crashing back down on to its roof with its wheels in the air.

The inside of the bungalow was devastated. Every room was filled with rubble and broken furniture. Strangely, a single lampstand stood intact by the fireplace, with the fringes of its shade smoking, but the chimney had gone. The kitchen had suffered the worst damage, and the double oven was lying outside in the back garden, next to the fence that Tommy had been intending to repair.

Tommy and Bridget were both buried underneath the wreckage of their day-to-day lives. Bridget was wrapped up almost intact in a shroud made of flower-patterned living-room curtains. Tommy's head and torso were perched on top of the gas meter in the hall, with his intestines drooping down around him in a hideous parody of some science-fiction villain, half-man, half-robot. His pelvis and legs were leaning upright, tangled among his golf clubs.

Only a few seconds later, the fractured gas pipes were ignited by a smouldering newspaper. Despite the rain, the bungalow began to burn, with thick grey smoke piling up to meet the low grey clouds. China and glass crackled and wood began to whistle and sing.

Within a few minutes, the residents of Berrings had gathered in the boreen outside, standing in shock. Some of them had come out of O'regans still holding their drinks. They were helpless to do anything but wait for the emergency services to arrive from Ballincollig, at least fifteen minutes away, and from Cork city, which would take almost thirty minutes at best.

They were still standing in the rain when a ginger cat came limping around the side of the garden, wet and bedraggled. It approached them, mewing pitifully, and one young girl crouched down, holding out her arms to it.

'Tiernan! Tiernan, you little dote! You're soaking! Come here, you poor creature! God love you, where have you been?'

Katie was coming into her kitchen with a bunch of chervil that she had snipped out of her garden when her phone played 'The Parting Glass'.

It was DI O'Sullivan from Anglesea Street, and he sounded almost furtive, as if he were making sure that nobody could overhear what he was saying.

'Have you seen the news?' he asked her.

'Not yet, no. What's happened?'

'Another bomb, out at Berrings. Two fatalities, Thomas and Bridget O'Mahony. I don't have much in the way of any details yet, but Thomas O'Mahony was related to Patrick O'Mahony, one of the Dripsey martyrs. Whether he was one of the Dripsey Dozen I don't know yet for sure.'

'Jesus. What time did this happen?'

'Only about an hour and a half since.'

'Do you know of any witnesses?'

'Not yet, no. DS ó Broin's gone out there himself, along with Coughlan and Murrish.'

'I'll take a look at the news.'

'I'll keep you up to speed when I can, ma'am. But there's something else. We've had a response to that Evo-FIT.'

'Really? That was quick.'

'A check-in agent for Ryanair has just called us to say that she was sure the same fellow boarded their flight to Birmingham yesterday afternoon. The fellow's name is Martin Bracken. She didn't see his picture until this lunchtime when she came home from the airport and saw it on the one o'clock news.'

'Does DS ó Broin know about this?'

'He does of course. But I can tell you that he was not at all happy that Mathew McElvey sent the Evo-FIT to all the media without informing him about it first. Well, that's the understatement of the century. He was up to high doh about it. His exact words were that nobody else has claimed to have seen this alleged suspect but you, and that you have a vested interest in meddling with his investigation.'

'Meddling? Was that what he said?'

'Well, not exactly. It was a stronger word than that, like. Two words, and the second one was "up".'

'So what action is he taking about this fellow being recognized?'

'None, for the time being. He said that if the fellow's gone off to the UK, then he's out of our jurisdiction.'

'That's mental. We've always had a grand relationship with the West Midlands police. Why doesn't he contact them and send them his name and the Evo-FIT?'

'Because he says the only witness is you and he doesn't want to make a holy show of us if it turns out this fellow is only an innocent businessman or a priest, even.'

'A *priest*?' Katie couldn't even begin to think of an answer to that. Micheál's attempts to undermine her were now becoming so desperate that they were absurd. Worse than absurd, they could well be fatal, especially to those Dripsey relatives who were still threatened by serial bombings.

'This Ryanair check-in agent, would she have a record of the fellow's passport number?'

'She would if that's what he used for ID. He wouldn't have needed a passport to fly to the UK, of course, but Ryanair expect you to show some identification when you check in, either your passport, like, or your national identity card.'

'If she has his passport number, ask her to send it to you. If it's Irish, you can contact the passport office in Dublin, or if it was issued in the UK you can get in touch with the passport office in London. Find out what address he gave when he took out his passport, and we'll see where we can take it from there.'

'DS ó Broin won't like this at all.'

'He doesn't have to like it,' said Katie. 'He doesn't have to know about it.'

She hesitated for a moment, and then she added, 'I totally understand that this is putting you in a fierce difficult position, Terry. But we rely every day on information or witness statements or suggestions from the public, don't we? Forget for now that I'm a detective superintendent on suspension. Just pretend that I'm a helpful bystander. A widow from Cobh who just happened to be in the wrong place at the right time.'

Terry was about to answer when he said, 'Hold on. He's just come in the door. I'll have to go.'

'Let me know if you make any progress with the passport, Terry. If you can find out where this fellow lives, I'll go after him.'

'In the UK?'

'Wherever in the world, Terry. I don't care if he comes from Outer Mongolia.'

Katie switched on the news, which was still running a live

report on the bombing at Berrings. She saw the O'Mahonys' devastated house and the upturned Hilux, but the RTÉ reporter knew no more than Terry O'Sullivan about who might have planted the bomb, or why they might have planted it.

There was nothing that Katie could do except wait for Terry to call her with more information. It seemed almost certain that this was another attack on the Dripsey Dozen, and she found it incredibly frustrating that she could not be there at the crime scene herself.

Back in the kitchen, she received two more calls within the space of the next ten minutes. The first was from Kieran. He had heard about the bombing at Berrings too, but the reason he was calling was that the jury in the case over which he was presiding today was already out, considering their verdict. He expected to finish early, and so he would like to take her to dinner this evening at the Titanic Bar and Grill in Cobh.

'Well, that's a very attractive offer, but I was planning on cooking us salmon this evening, with that sauce vierge you like. I've just been out in the garden picking the chervil for it.'

'It'll keep until tomorrow, won't it? I feel like celebrating our engagement, that's all.'

'Engagement? That makes us sound like a couple of twenty-year-olds.'

'I've asked you to marry me and you've said yes. What else would you call it?'

'All right,' said Katie. 'Do you want me to book us a table?'

'Don't worry. I've done that already. And I have a surprise for you.'

After Kieran had ended his call, Katie stood for a moment looking at the bunch of chervil on the chopping board and thinking, this is what I planned to do this evening and now he's making me do something else altogether. Not that I mind being taken out for dinner, especially at the Titanic. It will be a treat. It's only that I've being living on my own for so long and I'm so used to doing what I want, whenever I want, and now I have to face the fact that it's going to be different.'

She could guess what the surprise was going to be. She would bet money that Kieran had been to Kenny's, the jewellers on Oliver Plunkett Street, and bought her a ring.

Her phone rang again. This time it was Kyna, and she sounded a little breathless.

'Guess what? They're letting me out tomorrow morning.'

'So where are you going to go?' Katie asked her.

'You did say that I could come and stay with you for a while. Is that offer still open? I don't want to be a burden to you.'

'Holy Mother of God, Kyna, you'll never be a burden. In fact, you'll be more help than you know. Jenny next door will be away next week to visit her sister in Kenmare and so I'll be needing someone to babysit my three hairy children.'

'I'd be delighted. That Foltchain, she's such a darling. She's like a mother to me.'

Katie drove up to the Texaco garage to fill up her Audi and to buy some more Kimberley biscuits and teabags at the Londis store. Afterwards, she let the dogs have a short run around the nearby rugby field, standing on the touchline and whistling at them like a referee. But while she was watching them scamper around, her phone pinged and she received a text from DI O'Sullivan. It said nothing more than *5 Wood Close, Erdington B24 9AE*. He had obviously been given the bald man's address by the passport office in London, but he had not wanted to take the risk of saying what it was.

As she drove back home, she thought, *Erdington*. When that old man had tipped off the Garda two years ago that the Dripsey Dozen might have been responsible for two pub bombings close to Birmingham city centre, one of the pubs he had named was The Huntsman on Kingsbury Road, Erdington. The bomb had been detonated while the customers were watching a Saturday afternoon football match in November 1972. Seventeen had been killed, with thirty-eight seriously injured.

So what was she going to do? She could tell Micheál that the bald man lived in Erdington, and therefore might have a historical motive for revenge against the Dripsey Dozen. But Micheál would almost certainly dismiss it as one of her wild suppositions, and not worth the time and expense and possible embarrassment of investigating it.

When she was back at home, she looked up Wood Close, Erdington, on Google Maps. It was a narrow terrace off Wood End Road, and number 5 was in the middle of a terrace of red-brick houses. The only unusual aspect about it compared to the houses on either side was that all its curtains were closed.

Katie called Kyna.

'What time are they going to let you out tomorrow?'

'Early, so far as I know.'

'I'll come and pick you up. But it's likely you'll be on your own the first night at least, because I'm thinking of going to England to follow up on these bombings. So long as you don't mind that.'

'Not at all. That'll be grand altogether. I'll have the woof-woofs to keep me company, won't I? You have your job to do. I miss working along with you, the way we did before.'

After that call, Katie opened her laptop and booked a seat on tomorrow's Ryanair flight from Cork to Birmingham, as well as a rental car at Birmingham airport.

She accepted that Micheál was right in a way, and that she

did tend to be intuitive rather than methodical. In almost every investigation that she had dealt with, however, her intuition had eventually been backed up by solid evidence. She was well aware now that Micheál was doing everything he could to prevent her from being reinstated at Anglesea Street. Perhaps that, more than anything else, was spurring her on to hunt down this Martin Bracken in England. If he really did turn out to be a businessman, or a priest, then she was the Taoiseach's daughter.

Shortly before Kieran arrived, she received another text from Sabrina. She had still not received the payment from Sean Delaney for his Extreme Dreams party. Should he fail to pay today, she would unfortunately have to inform his employers at the Riverview Animal Hospital that he had booked a BDSM party and that she was trying to get in touch with him about it.

Katie read Sabrina's text with a sour sense of justification. Since she was so ready to blackmail one of her partygoers before he had even attended a party, it was highly likely that she had regarded poor Detective Mullan as a prime source of cash.

Now she would have to find a way to prove beyond any doubt that Sabrina had extorted money from him, and that her blackmail had led him to take his own life. She had no intention of paying her just yet, but all the same she opened an online account with her AIB branch in the name of Sean Delaney and transferred €750 of her own money into it, just in case.

16

Kieran arrived a few minutes after five o'clock, looking cheerful. He was carrying a cardboard box with a green satin ribbon tied around it.

'What do you have here?' Katie asked him.

'That's your surprise,' he smiled. 'Could you hold it for a second while I take off my coat?'

Well, I was wrong, and it's not an engagement ring, thought Katie, as she took the box from him. *So much for my incredible intuition.*

They went into the living room and sat down, with the dogs circling around them as if they were hoping that the surprise was something for them. Kieran set the box down on the coffee table and said, 'There, go ahead. Open it up. It's something for our happy future, that's all.'

Katie untied the ribbon and opened up the box. Inside were six champagne flutes with long, elegant stems, all wrapped up in pink tissue paper

'Kieran, they're beautiful,' said Katie, taking one out.

'Antique Waterford crystal,' he told her. 'They're really rare, from 1845 or thereabouts. Well, that's what the auctioneer assured me. I thought they'd be perfect for us to drink a toast on the day we get married.'

'They really are grand. They must have cost you a fortune.

In fact, I can *see* they cost you a fortune, by these labels on them. Two hundred euros each.'

'Yes, I tried to peel the labels off, but they must be stuck with superglue or something like that. I'll have to buy some of that special stuff for removing stickers – Gloo-Off or whatever it's called.'

Kieran held up one of the flutes and said, 'I can see us drinking our health to each other out of these glasses every year for countless years to come. Go *maire tú!*'

They drove into Cobh for dinner at the Titanic Bar and Grill overlooking the harbour. After they had sat down at their table, Kieran nodded towards the waxing gibbous moon that was reflected in the water.

'What do you think of the lighting effect? I arranged for it specially, to make this evening even more romantic.'

Katie smiled at him over the top of her menu. 'Do you know something? I think you're in love.'

'I can't deny it, Mrs Kathleen Connolly-to-be. I find you guilty of stealing my heart, for which I sentence you to a lifetime of companionship, with no possibility of parole.'

After they had ordered, seared sea bass for Katie and a featherblade steak for Kieran, they clinked their glasses together and Katie said, 'Go *lasfaí na réaltaí i do shúile i gcónaí.*' It meant, 'May the stars always shine in your eyes.'

She needed to tell Kieran that she had arranged to fly to England tomorrow, but she waited until the end of the meal because she thought it might dampen the mood. Once their waitress had brought them coffee and chocolate mints, though, she said quietly, 'I'll be away tomorrow, Kieran. I'm going after that baldy fellow that I saw in Ballincollig and

Kinsale. It wouldn't surprise me if he was behind that bombing at Berrings too. Martin Bracken his name is.'

'Sorry, I don't understand. What do you mean, you're going after him? Have you found out where he hangs out?'

'Maybe.' Katie told him that Terry O'Sullivan had been given his address by the UK passport office, and that it was in Erdington, where The Huntsman pub had been bombed in 1972.

'I'll admit that this isn't absolute proof that he was responsible for all those bombings. Of course not. But it increases the likelihood that he might have been.'

Kieran put down his coffee cup and sat back. 'I hope in God's name you'll be careful. You won't be going in any official capacity, will you, so you won't be able to be armed.'

'I need a lead, that's all, Kieran. Whoever's behind these bombings, they're organized and they have a motive. This Martin Bracken can't be doing this entirely on his own.'

Kieran shook his head. 'Honestly, sweetheart. I don't know why you can't leave this to Micheál.'

'Because Micheál won't listen. He doesn't want to listen. He would rather those Dripsey Dozen were all blown to bits than have me proved right. He's investigating, yes. I have to give him that. The trouble is that he's putting this case together as if it's a thousand-piece jigsaw, but he doesn't even have the box with the picture on it. I just don't want to see any more innocent people lose their lives while he's taking so long.'

'Surely they must all be aware of the threat now, mustn't they – what's left of the Dripsey Dozen? Don't tell me they're not keeping their eyes open for anything that looks like it might be a bomb.'

'I'm hoping so, Kieran. But even if they've moved away, it's possible that the bombers might be able to track them down and find out where they've moved to. When they blew up the O'Farrells' house, they made a tragic mistake because they must have believed that the Lyonses were still living there. But it wouldn't surprise me if they've learned a lesson from that. Why do you think that Martin Bracken was following me, with a bomb in the boot of his car?'

'I'm only concerned that these bombers must have realized by now that you're hot on their trail, whoever they are, and that as well as the Dripsey Dozen they'll be coming after *you*.'

'Kieran, I've had all kinds of criminals threatening me ever since I first became a detective. Drug-dealers, people-smugglers, out-and-out psychopathic headers. It wouldn't surprise me if the Kinahan cartel all carry photos of me in their wallets, to remind them of what I look like. I always stay doggy wide, I promise you.'

'Okay, I trust you to be careful. But I still don't want anything horrible happening to Mrs Kathleen Connolly-to-be, not before our wedding day. Well, not after, either! More coffee?'

Katie shook her head. 'If I have any more coffee I'll be awake all night, listening to you and the dogs all snoring the Hallelujah Chorus.'

She bit into another mint, and then she said, 'They're letting Kyna out of Bon Secours tomorrow morning. I've invited her to stay with me for a while, and of course that'll be pure handy tomorrow when I go to England. She'll be able to take care of the dogs while I'm away.'

'You think that's a good idea, having her stay with you? It's because of you she tried to take her own life.'

'That was in a moment of black despair, Kieran. She's had therapy now and she's so much calmer. I think it would do her so much good to see that she and I can get along together simply as friends and colleagues.'

'So how long will she be staying with you?'

'I'm not sure. She wants to rejoin the Garda eventually if she can manage to pass as fit, although she's not so sure that she wants to come back to Anglesea Street.'

Kieran shrugged, but said nothing. Katie could tell that he was not particularly happy about Kyna coming to stay with her, but she thought: *Kyna almost died because of me. Helping her to get back on to her feet is the least I can do.*

Kyna was sitting on the end of her bed with a carpetbag of her belongings next to her. One of her doctors was standing beside her, and they had obviously just shared a joke because both of them were laughing.

'Ah, you must be Detective Superintendent Maguire,' said the doctor, as Katie came in. She held out her hand in greeting. 'I expect you realize that I've heard a fair amount about you, one way and another. But you can rest assured that none of it will go any further. My lips are sealed.'

'Sure, that's a relief,' said Katie. 'Is the patient all ready to be discharged?'

'She is, yes. And I'm thankful that you've offered her a place to stay for a while. I'll be totally honest with you and say that she's still in a fragile state psychologically. It's important that she has calm surroundings and constant reassurance.'

'There you are again,' smiled Kyna. 'Making me sound like a fruitcake.'

The doctor laid her hand on Kyna's shoulder. 'We've discussed the pros and cons of her coming to stay with you, considering her history. But we've agreed that it'll be the best way for her to come to terms with your relationship. If she went off and never saw you again, there would always be an emotional vacuum in her life and that would be no good at all for her underlying mental stability.'

'You see,' said Kyna, standing up. 'She definitely thinks I'm a fruitcake.'

'What's the harm in that?' Katie reassured her. 'I'm pure partial to fruitcake, as a matter of fact. You should have tasted the fruitcake with apricots and whiskey in it, like my mam used to bake.'

Katie shook hands with the doctor again, and the doctor gave Kyna a hug.

'I'm always here if you need me,' the doctor told her. 'There'll never be a night so black that I won't be able to shine a light in it for you.'

Katie and Kyna left the hospital, climbed into Katie's car and made their way back through the city towards Cobh. As they drove, Kyna was softly singing 'Wild Mountain Thyme', her eyes closed as if she were afraid that should she open them, none of this morning would be real and she would be back in her room in the Bon Secours.

'Will ye go, lassie, go…' she sang, and as they passed over the bridge that spanned the Glashaboy River, Katie reached over and squeezed her hand.

'You're going to be grand altogether,' Katie told her. 'One day at a time, darling, one day at a time. And you and me, we're going to stay the best of friends for ever.'

Kyna stopped singing, and nodded. She kept her eyes closed, but her eyelashes sparkled with tears.

The Ryanair flight from Cork to Birmingham was delayed

by three-quarters of an hour, and it was seven o'clock before Katie reached Erdington in her rental car, and it was raining.

She had booked a double room for two nights at the Hardintone Wood, an economy hotel facing the main road, with a grimy lemon-yellow frontage and sagging net curtains at the windows. The reception area smelled of burned sausages, although she was welcomed warmly enough by a fat friendly woman with a prominent mole on her chin and two crochet needles stuck crosswise to keep her hair pinned up.

Upstairs, Katie's room, overlooking the car park, reminded her of the basic accommodation at the Garda Training Centre at McCan Barracks in Tipperary – a bed with a faded patchwork bedspread, a TV and a chilly bathroom with a dripping tap. But it was less than five minutes' walk away from Wood Close, which meant that she could go on foot to take an unobtrusive look at Martin Bracken's house.

Not only that, The Huntsman pub was only another three or four minutes further up the road. Katie was acutely aware that she might be adding two and two together to make five and a half, but it was hard for her to believe it was a coincidence that Martin Bracken lived so close to the pub that the Dripsey Dozen were suspected of having bombed in 1972.

Out of her overnight case she took a shoulder-length brunette wig, which had been made for her by the Cork School of Hairdressing. She had used it only once before, when she had attended a dinner party at the Fota Island Golf Club, where she had been tipped off that two Cork drug-dealers would be meeting a member of the county council. The councillor was suspected of taking bribes and she had wanted to listen in to their conversation if she could, or at least observe their body language. The trouble was that both the councillor and one of the drug-dealers knew what she looked like.

The second part of her disguise was a heavy pair of spectacles with thick black rims. It always interested her that glasses could be almost as effective as a mask. After all, she thought, Clark Kent had worn glasses, and even his friends had failed to recognize that he was Superman.

Although it was past eight o'clock now, and still raining, she decided to take a walk up to Wood Close. She fitted on her wig in the bathroom mirror, pouting at herself because she thought long brunette hair made her look like the Northern Irish actress Laura Donnelly. She also carefully smoothed some foundation cream across the bridge of her nose to cover up her freckles.

It was a dreary, miserable evening outside. She made her way up the road with the rain pattering against her umbrella and for the first time in a long time she felt lonely. She didn't even have her dogs to talk to. Maybe Kieran was right, and she should have left this investigation to Micheál.

She turned into Wood Close. It was bordered on the left by a long privet hedge, which was crackling in the rain as if it was on fire, and then by a row of seven terraced houses. Number 5 had a broken picket fence and a narrow front garden paved with concrete. Behind the curtains of numbers 3 and 7, lights were glowing and televisions were flickering, but in between them number 5 was in total darkness, with blinds drawn down at every window, upstairs and down. It was also the only house with no car parked in the road outside it.

Katie was still standing outside when the front door of number 3 opened up and a grey-haired man came out, smoking a cigarette. He was carrying half a dozen empty beer bottles, which he dropped with a clatter into the wheelie bin beside the porch.

He caught sight of Katie and called out, 'Looking for Martin, are you?'

Katie went across to his front gate. 'I am, yes,' she said, trying to sound clipped and English. 'I have some letters for him. They were sent to the wrong address.'

'Oh, he's not hardly never here these days, Martin. You could try The Huntsman, that's where you'll probably find him. It's the pub just up the road if you don't know it. His mam's the owner and he's been helping her out lately. Stays overnight too, most nights.'

'Thanks. I'll go there and see if I can find him.'

'In case you can't, do you want me to tell him you was looking for him? Give me your contact number or something?'

'No, thanks. But thanks, anyway.'

'You're welcome, love. No worries.' The man took a last drag on his cigarette and then flipped it out into the rain.

Katie walked further up the main road until she reached The Huntsman. She had already seen it on Google, but on an evening like this it looked even more grim than it had on her PC screen. It was a brown-brick Victorian pub, three storeys high, standing on one corner of a five-way roundabout. The sign that hung above its door depicted a man in hunting pink, sitting astride a glossy black warmblood horse. He had his back turned, but he was looking over his shoulder with an expression that Katie thought was strangely malicious, as if he were thinking, *Coming in here for a drink, are you? You'll regret it.*

She put on her glasses and pushed her way in through the heavy front door. Inside, the pub was packed, with loud background music playing so that the customers were all shouting at each other to make themselves heard. It had an old-fashioned mahogany bar, although Katie knew from reading about The Huntsman that this was a replica, just like the stained-glass windows and the chandeliers. As well as killing and injuring so many men and women, the bomb that had been detonated inside this bar in 1972 had devastated its interior and blown out all its windows into the street.

Katie weaved her way across the crowded saloon and two men sitting on stools grudgingly shifted themselves another four or five inches apart so that she could reach the bar. A tall thin woman came up to her and said, 'Yes, pet, what'll you have?'

The man at number 3 had told her that The Huntsman was owned by Martin Bracken's mother, and Katie guessed that this was her, because she looked so much like Martin. Her iron-grey hair was tightly twisted into a coronet, and her face was so pale that she could have been dead. She was wearing a long clinging dress of grey wool, the same colour as her hair, with three buttons at the neck. Her eyes, too, were grey, but a cold glossy grey, like fish skin.

'I'll take a vodka and tonic, please,' Katie told her. 'Just a single.' She never normally drank alcohol on duty, but she thought it would appear odd to have come into a pub and ordered only Coke or sparkling water, and she was anxious not to attract attention to herself in any way at all. Besides, she was not officially on duty.

'I tell you,' said one of the men sitting on stools next to her. 'I had so much booze that night I woke up the next morning feeling like two penn'orth of God help me.'

Once she had paid for her drink, Katie circled slowly around the saloon, looking for somewhere to sit and also looking for Martin Bracken.

Halfway along the bar, she saw a collection of framed black-and-white photographs arranged on the wall. The largest photograph, in the centre, was draped with a black silk cloth, knotted at the corners.

She went along to take a look at them. The largest photograph showed The Huntsman's landlord and his wife, with some of their regular customers standing around them. They were all smiling and lifting up their glasses in salute. The caption underneath read 'Douglas and Hilda Bracken, 5 September, 1972'. Katie immediately recognized the landlord's wife as the same woman who had served her, only plumper and fifty years younger, with curly blonde hair.

The rest of the photographs showed the pub the day after the bombing. Not only had most of the bar been blasted away and all the windows blown out, but part of the ceiling had collapsed so that a leather sofa from upstairs had dropped down at an angle into the bar. Underneath all of these pictures was a brass plaque – '13 November, 1972. Lest We Forget.'

Katie was still looking at these photographs when she heard raucous male laughter from the far end of the bar.

A man's voice said loudly, 'I swear to you, he's so fecking thick, that gobdaw! Thick as bottled shite!' And then he started laughing again.

His accent was unmistakable, not to mention his slang. In a pub crowded with people shouting at each other in that flat Birmingham accent, as if they were keeping their front teeth clenched together, this was a man speaking like a Corkonian.

Katie turned away from the photographs and squeezed past a group of shrieking young women until she could see the men who were laughing. They were sitting around a circular table cluttered with empty and half-empty beer glasses and bottles, and from the way they were still chortling and shaking their heads she could tell that they were well on the way to being langered.

There were four of them. On the left sat Martin Bracken, in a black shirt and a black jacket. He was filling up his glass from a bottle of bitter. The two men sitting on the right and on the opposite side of the table Katie had never seen before. But it was the man who was sitting with his back to her who was talking in a Cork accent. His curly grey hair was thinning on top, and he was wearing a brown coat with a blue check pattern on it.

Although the pub was so noisy, Katie had a feeling that she knew who he was. It was partly his voice, and partly the way he repeatedly lifted his right arm with his fist clenched to emphasize what he was shouting about, like Adolf Hitler.

'I was up to ninety about it, but he wouldn't fecking listen! I said, Jesus, are you deaf or stupid, which is it? Feck off with yourself!'

Katie went up and stood close behind him so that she could listen to more of what he was saying, although she deliberately faced in the opposite direction as if she were waiting for somebody. But when he stopped shouting to listen to one of the other men, she glanced back at him to see if she could recognize him.

It was then that Martin Bracken looked up at her and frowned. She did her best not to change her expression at all, as if she had no idea who he was. She prayed that her spectacles and her brunette hair were enough of a disguise. But Martin Bracken nudged the man in the brown check coat, and he twisted his head around to look at her too, in the same way that the huntsman on the pub sign was looking over his shoulder.

She felt a prickly chill. She did recognize him, and the last thing in the world she wanted was for him to recognize her. But he grinned at her and winked and gave her the thumbs up, and turned back to Martin Bracken, nodding in approval. She could imagine him saying 'nice diddies!' or something else lecherous like that. She raised her glass as if she had caught sight of the person she had been waiting for, and started to push her way back past the shrieking young women.

She left her vodka and tonic on the bar, untouched, and pushed her way out of The Huntsman into the rain. She was trembling so much that she struggled to put up her umbrella.

The man in the brown check coat was Rayland Garvey, who had once been a detective inspector at Anglesea Street. Five years ago, he had been caught taking money from one of Cork's most notorious criminal gangs. He had been accepting thousands of euros not only to turn a blind eye to their protection rackets and robberies, but actively to assist in setting them up. It also turned out that he had been acquiring guns and explosives for a splinter group of the New IRA – again, in return for generous amounts of cash.

A warrant had been issued for Garvey's arrest, but he had several close cronies in the Garda, and somehow he had managed to slip out of the country.

Katie walked quickly back to the Hardintone Wood hotel. As she entered the reception area, the fat woman with the crochet needles in her hair smiled at her and said, 'All right, bab? Brekkie's at seven till half nine. Have a good night's kip!'

As soon as she had returned to her room, Katie sat on the end of her bed and called Terry O'Sullivan.

'Terry? It's Kathleen. I'm in Erdington.'

'Serious?'

'Yes, really. I followed your man here this afternoon. I've seen his house, although his neighbour told me that he doesn't stay there very often. But you won't believe this. I've found out that his mother owns The Huntsman, and that's why he's away most nights, staying with her. She must be in her seventies now, but from what I can see it was she and her husband owned it back in 1972.'

'Jesus. If that isn't a motive for going after the Dripsey Dozen, I don't know what is.'

'Absolutely. And this November happens to be the fiftieth anniversary of the night it was bombed. I don't know if her husband or any other member of her family was killed but I'll be able to check. The pub has pictures on the wall with black curtains around them, like a kind of shrine, so I'm guessing that Mrs Bracken was widowed.'

'So what's your next step?' Terry asked her.

'Wait. I haven't told you the best bit yet. Or the worst, depending on which way you look at it. I saw Martin Bracken in the pub and you'll never guess who was sitting beside him. Two other fellows I didn't know, but Rayland Garvey.'

'Rayland Garvey? *The* Rayland Garvey? You're joking!'

'I wish I was. But it was Rayland Garvey in the flesh, large as life and twice as ugly. He saw me too, and so did Martin Bracken, but I was wearing my long brown wig and my outsize glimmers and I'm sure he didn't reck me.'

'Rayland Garvey, who'd have believed it? We all thought he'd gone off to live in Spain, didn't we, with all the rest of the skangers in exile? What does Frank Magorian call it? "The Costa del Criminal Corkonians".'

'Maybe he does live in Spain. But maybe the Brackens called on him to come to the UK so that he could help them to get their revenge on the Dripsey Dozen. I mean, what was Rayland Garvey most notorious for, apart from giving the O'Flynns and the Keenans a helping hand to run their various rackets? Supplying the New IRA with guns and C-4.'

'But if Martin Bracken is back in the UK, what do you reckon?' asked Terry. 'He could be feeling that he's done enough now to punish the Dripseys, do you know what I mean? Like, he's made his point and he doesn't have to do any more bombing. Or he could be worried because his face has been plastered all over the media, and he's running a high risk of being caught. Then again, he could simply be giving himself a break, like, and he's planning on coming back to Cork and finish the job.'

'There's no way we can say for sure,' said Katie. 'But assuming that he *is* our bomber, what puzzles me is how he found out that it was the Dripsey Dozen behind the bombing of The Huntsman, and not the Provisionals? The Provisionals claimed the credit for it, after all, and it was only that tip-off we were given that pointed the finger at the Dripseys. But of course we never came up with sufficient evidence to take it any further, even though it looked almost one hundred per cent certain that the tip-off was true.'

'Maybe the same fellow who gave us the tip-off gave it to Martin Bracken, too.'

'Maybe he did. Maybe he found out some other way. This investigation has more questions in it than a whole series of *Ireland's Smartest*, I can tell you.'

'When are you coming back?'

'Tomorrow, I expect, or the day after at the latest. I just want to do a little more digging around Erdington. Maybe I can find somebody who has an inkling of what Martin Bracken and Rayland Garvey were up to. It's clear the Brackens are still grieving, and it's hard to believe they haven't said anything at all to anybody about what they were planning to do, especially after a few bottles of lager.'

'Well, good luck, ma'am. And stay safe.'

Next, Katie called Kieran.

'How's it going, sweetheart?' he asked her. 'It's been only a day and a night but I miss you like you've been gone for a week.'

'I'm grand altogether, Kieran, and I've been making some progress.'

She told him what she had found out about Martin Bracken's connection to The Huntsman, and how she had seen him with Rayland Garvey.

'Rayland Garvey? That gowl. Somebody told me years ago that he was dead.'

'It wouldn't surprise me if that was a rumour he was putting around himself so that we wouldn't go looking for him any more. But he's alive all right, and if Martin Bracken isn't our bomber and Rayland Garvey's not the one who's been supplying him with explosives, then you need to buckle me up in a straitjacket and lock me up in Carraig Mór.'

'When are you coming back? I can't say that you don't have me biting my nails.'

'Kieran, believe me, you really don't have to worry. I've been doing this job long enough and if anybody can take care of me, I can. I'll probably see you tomorrow.'

'I love you, Mrs Kathleen Connolly-to-be.'

After she had spoken to Kieran, she called Kyna.

'Everything okay?' she asked her. 'How are my three mad children?'

'Oh, the dogs and me have been having a whale of a time, thanks. The only problem is that they go rushing to the front door every time they hear a car outside. But they've been looking after me better than I've been looking after them. That Foltchain, she's a dote.'

'You're feeling all right yourself?'

'Thanks to you, Katie, for giving me somewhere to stay, and peace. And by the way, they delivered that stuff for taking off labels this afternoon, and I've managed to peel four of them off already. So your glasses will all be ready for us to be drinking a toast at your wedding.'

'That's great, Kyna. Thanks a million.'

'It's more than a pleasure, Katie. I love you, and I always will.'

17

'Aren't you ready yet, bird?' Ronan called out, standing by the open door of their car.

'I'm coming! I'm coming!' Shanessa called back, from the hallway. 'I couldn't find my rubber dollies! Mona left them in the washroom!'

Ronan turned back to Denis and Fergal, who were sitting in the back of their red Mazda hatchback taking it in turns to punch each other in the arm.

'The day that your mam's ready on time, I swear to God it'll be the top story on the Six One News.'

'How long will we have to be staying with Auntie Mona?' asked Fergal. He was seven, and he had recently lost his upper and lower front teeth, so that he spoke with a whistle.

'I'm not sure exactly. Until we hear that it's safe, I suppose.'

'But they wouldn't be blowing up our house, would they? We haven't done nothing.'

'I know, son. But most of the people whose houses have been blown up so far, they belonged to the Dripsey Dozen. I've told you all about the Dripsey Dozen.'

'But Denis and me, we don't belong to them.'

'No, you don't, but your mam does, doesn't she? Our name's Doherty, because that's my family name, but your mam's name before we were married was O'Callaghan. She's related to Daniel O'Callaghan, like I've told you before, and he was one of the five fellows executed for the Dripsey Ambush.'

'But that was *so* long ago, like.'

'Yes, it was, and don't ask me why somebody's taken it into their heads to blow up innocent people who had nothing at all to do with the ambush. But it's better to be safe than blown into dooshie bits and pieces.'

'I don't like it here at Auntie Mona's. I mean I like Auntie Mona, but I hate all her scratchy cats and we don't have a telly in our room so that we can play Minecraft. And I'm supposed to be going swimming on Saturday with Brendan at Churchfield, because it's his birthday.'

'Don't worry, Fergal. I'll take you there so,' said Ronan. 'Ah, look, here's your mam. Five minutes nearer to meeting Saint Peter, as your granpa used to say.'

Shanessa came out of the house carrying three or four shopping bags, still struggling to pull on her sheepskin coat. Ronan opened the passenger door for her, and she climbed in, piling all the bags on her lap.

'We should go to Lidl first,' she said. She tugged down her Aran cable-knit hat to cover up her tangled brown curls. 'Then I want to go to Dunnes and see if they have any of those Kilrush vases left. It's Aoife's anniversary next week and I've been racking my brains what to buy her.'

'Do we *have* to come to Lidl?' Denis complained. 'It's fierce boring.'

'No, you can go and play in the Sail Garden while your mam and I go for the messages, so long as you promise not to fall in the river and drown yourselves.'

He fastened his seat belt, put the key into the ignition, and twisted it to start the engine. It was then that the Mazda blew up. The explosion was so loud that it was heard as far away as Ballymartle, nearly five miles away to the west, and crows flapped up from the trees all around Riverstick in alarm. It shattered the windows in the front of Mona Doherty's house and burst the Mazda apart so its torn sides hung down all around it like the petals of a massive crimson flower.

An orange fireball rolled up out of the wreckage, followed by a pile of thick grey smoke. All that remained of Ronan was one hand still clutching the twisted steering wheel, and his knobbly spine sticking up from the springs of his seat. Shanessa's sheepskin coat and her woven shopping bags had absorbed some of the blast, but she was headless now, and her head was lying in the flowerbed beside the entrance to Cois Bruach, still wearing its Aran hat.

Denis and Fergal in the back seat had been reduced to a bloody jumble of flesh and bones and torn-apart intestines, so that it was impossible to tell which of them was which, especially since both of their faces had been blown off, leaving two skulls resting against each other like two broken jugs, both overflowing with glistening brain matter.

The echo of the explosion died away. The crows settled back into the trees and on to the telephone wires. Footsteps could be heard pattering all around Cois Bruach as the neighbours came running out to see what had happened.

Katie had not slept well. The couple in the room above hers had clearly had a lot to drink, and had argued with each other until well past three o'clock in the morning. Not only did they shout, but they stamped across the room from one side to the other, and repeatedly slammed their bathroom door.

She was so tired that she was tempted to book a seat on the morning flight back to Cork, but she decided that she would be squandering her trip to Erdington if she made no attempt to find out more about Hilda Bracken and the relationship between her and Martin Bracken and Rayland Garvey.

She went down to breakfast in the dingy dining room. The red-and-white check tablecloths were frayed at the edges and the view out of the window was a back yard cluttered with wheelie bins and dismantled beds. She helped herself to a latte from a coffee machine that sounded as if it had asthma, and the fat friendly woman with the mole brought her a plate of solidified scrambled eggs on toast.

She was still eating when her phone played 'The Parting Glass'. It was Sergeant Murphy, and like before, he sounded furtive, as if he was making sure that nobody could overhear him.

'Good morning to you, ma'am. Have you seen it on the news in England?'

'Have I seen what?'

'There's been another bombing, God help us, with four fatalities. A whole family, Ronan and Shanessa Doherty, and their two young children, aged nine and seven. A car bomb this time. They were staying with Ronan Doherty's sister in Riverstick because Shanessa was one of the Dripseys, and they were afraid that their house in Rochestown might be a target.'

'Oh, Jesus. No, I haven't seen the news yet. But I can get RTÉ on my laptop. I'll take a look. What action is himself taking about it?'

'He'll be holding a press conference at midday today. He's admitting now that it looks like a vendetta against anyone related to the Dripseys, but he's still not speculating who's doing it, or what their motive might be.'

Katie pushed her plate away. 'I'll be taking the afternoon flight back to Cork. But I want to go back to The Huntsman pub this lunchtime and see what I can pick up. I'm close to being convinced that it was the bombing there back in 1972 that's the key to these attacks, but I need more evidence. Thank you, Peter, for keeping me up to date. You don't have to, you know that, and I'm well aware of the risk you're taking with DS Ó Broin.' She paused, and then she added, '*Acting* DS Ó Broin.'

The fat woman came into the dining room and stared at Katie's plate.

'You've hardly touched your eggs. Did you not like them?'

'They were grand, thanks. But I'm a little stressed at the moment, and I don't have much appetite.'

'You know the cure for stress, don't you, love?'

Katie was tempted to say, *arresting a serial bomber*, but instead she simply smiled and shook her head.

'Get yourself a tattoo,' the fat woman told her.

'Really?'

The fat woman dragged up her baggy brown sweater to show Katie that she had a man's face tattooed on her left hip, peering over her waistband as if he were hiding inside her slacks.

'That's my ex-hubby,' she explained. 'After he left me I thought it was the end of the world, but then I had him tattooed on my leg so that he'd have to stick with me for ever, rain or shine. Percy his name was. Percy Proctor. What a bastard. But I loved him.'

After she had finished her coffee, Katie went up to her room and logged into the latest news on RTÉ. The bombing at Riverstick was the lead story, and Fionnuala Sweeney was standing beside the police tape that had cordoned off Cois

Bruach, interviewing DS ó Broin. Behind them, Katie could see Garda cars and vans, the khaki truck from the bomb disposal unit, and four or five forensic technicians in their white Tyvek suits. The Dohertys' shattered Mazda was hidden behind a high blue incident screen.

'I'll be making a full statement at our media conference later,' Micheál was saying. 'Meanwhile, I can only express the Garda's sincerest condolences to the family and friends of Ronan and Shanessa Doherty and their two innocent children, taken so young. It's a true tragedy, enough to break anyone's heart.'

'Do you yet have no idea at all who might be responsible for all these bombings?' asked Fionnuala. 'Not even an inkling?'

'We have suspicions about the perpetrators, of course,' Micheál told her. 'But what we're also keen to find out is how they might have acquired the names and addresses of the victims.'

'Can you elaborate on that? Are you trying to say that someone who was involved in the Garda investigation into the Dripsey Dozen might have given them that information, or told them where they could find it?'

Micheál looked directly at the camera, and Katie almost felt that he was looking directly and accusingly at her.

'I'm saying nothing more for the time being,' he said. 'I always rely on solid evidence, and never on theories, unlike some officers I could mention. But as soon as I have indisputable proof that someone passed classified information to the perpetrator, and who it was, I will of course let you know. Let's leave it there for now.'

The report ended. Katie closed her laptop and sat back. She was both puzzled and disturbed by what Micheál had seemed to be suggesting. Would anyone at Anglesea Street really have handed the names and addresses of the Dripsey Dozen to someone who clearly might have been intending to do them harm? If anyone had a legitimate interest in finding out who they were and how to contact them, such as a writer or the producer of a TV documentary, they would have openly contacted Mathew McElvey in the press office.

She booked a seat online on the afternoon Ryanair flight back to Cork. Then she called Kyna, who had just come back from taking the dogs for a walk up to the ferry terminal. Kyna was breathless, but in a cheerful mood, and Katie could hear the dogs scrabbling about in the background. She tried Kieran, too, but his phone was switched off, which meant that he was in court. After leaving him a text message, telling him that she loved him, she fitted on her long brunette wig, shrugged on her coat, and left the hotel. It was not raining as she walked up towards The Huntsman, but it was foggy, and the air felt like a cold wet towel pressed against her face. Before she went inside the pub, she put on her glasses.

The Huntsman had been open for less than half an hour, and yet there were five customers in there already – four men in donkey jackets, who looked as if they should be out filling potholes in the road rather than drinking pints and eating crisps, and a solitary older man in a cloth cap, sitting alone in the far corner with a pint of Guinness and the *Sun* crossword.

Hilda Bracken was behind the bar, polishing glasses, but at the same time her attention was fixed on the television on the wall opposite, which was tuned to Sky News. Katie went up to the bar and asked her for a coffee.

'Right you are, my darling,' said Hilda Bracken, still without taking her eyes off the television. 'Martin!' she called out, to the open door behind her, 'do us a coffee, will you, our kid?' Then, to Katie, 'Sit yourself, down, love, and he'll fetch it to you.'

Katie went over and sat down next to the elderly man in the corner. He looked up from his crossword and said, 'Aye oop, love.'

After a few minutes, Martin Bracken came out from behind the bar, carrying a cup of coffee with a ginger biscuit in the saucer. He looked directly at Katie, but it was obvious that he failed to recognize her in her wig and her glasses.

As he turned to go back into the kitchen, the midday news came on the television, and Hilda Bracken turned the volume up louder. Although she was unable to see the screen from where she was sitting, Katie could clearly hear the anchor saying, 'Terrorists are being blamed for yet another explosion in Cork, in southern Ireland, after a family of four were all fatally injured in a car bomb blast.'

Hilda Bracken clenched both bony fists. '*Yessss!*' she hissed triumphantly, and as Martin Bracken lifted the flap and came back behind the bar, she went up to him and hugged him and kissed him on his cheek.

They both stood behind the bar, transfixed by the television report about the Riverstick bombing, with Hilda still holding Martin tightly around his waist. When the report was finished, Hilda switched off the sound, and they both stood looking at each other and smiling like two people who have just been told that they have won the lottery.

'Did it again!' said Hilda. She turned towards the black-draped photographs on the wall, the shrine to the bombing of 1972. 'Did you hear that, Dougie, we did it again! Five down and only seven left to pay!'

Martin looked around the pub and pressed his finger to his lips. 'Hush, Mum, all right? But Ronnie did bloody wonderful, didn't he? As soon as I get back there, I'll tell him how chuffed you was.'

He said something else, but he had turned his back now, and Katie found it difficult to hear it. All she could pick up was 'Friday, okay?'

The elderly man lowered his crossword and said, 'Paint I'm getting mixed in drums.'

'Excuse me?' said Katie.

'That's the clue, seven across. "Paint I'm getting mixed in drums". Any ideas?'

Katie nodded towards the Brackens behind the bar. 'Does she often get as excited as this?'

'Only when she hears about these bombs going off in Ireland. Gets them going every time. I suppose it's something to do with this pub being bombed, back in the seventies, and her losing her husband. Eye for an eye, if you know what I mean.'

Martin Bracken disappeared back into the kitchen, but Katie could see that his mother was still fired up, pacing up and down behind the bar as she polished the glasses, and repeatedly looking up at the television, clearly impatient for another report about Riverstick.

For Katie, this was the clincher. She had clearly heard Hilda Bracken say '*we* did it again'. She had no way of knowing who 'Ronnie' was, but it had sounded as if he might have been responsible for this particular bombing. Maybe she was putting two and two together and making five again, but she guessed that he was an accomplice who Martin Bracken had left behind in Cork when he came back here.

She finished her coffee, took the cup up to the bar and said, 'How much do I owe you?'

Hilda Bracken was still smiling. 'It's on the house today, love. I'm in too good a mood to charge you for it.'

'Well, that's very kind of you,' said Katie, again trying to sound as English as she could. Before she left the pub, though, she went back to the elderly man in the corner and said, 'Timpani.'

18

Katie was sitting with a cup of coffee in the Caffè Ritazza at Birmingham airport, waiting for her flight back to Cork to be called, when 'Sean Delaney' received another text message from Sabrina.

She was scolding Sean because he had not yet paid the €250 that he owed her, reminding him that this was 'only a reservation fee for his Extreme Dreams session' and that since he had left it so late, he would also be liable to pay for the girls and the men whose services she had already booked, and who she would now have to cancel. This would cost him a further €500.

'Sean, I would hate for you to put me into a position whereby I had to inform your employers that you had defaulted on your debt,' Sabrina warned him. 'Of course I would have to explain to them what the debt was for.'

To Katie, it was beyond any doubt that Sabrina was using her sex sessions as a way of extorting money from her clients, and that her relentless blackmail had led DS Conor Mullan to commit suicide. But now she was beginning to see a way in which she could collect enough documentary and circumstantial evidence to have Sabrina arrested and charged.

As she was queuing up to board her flight, Kieran texted her. He told her that he was 'grievously sorry' but he would not be able to come to Carrig View to welcome her home and spend the night with her. He had a late meeting this evening and an 'insanely' early start the following day. But he should be able to come down tomorrow. 'I might be very late, but I promise you I'll make it up to you, in spades.'

The flight back to Cork was bumpy because of turbulence, and it was raining hard when they landed. Katie arrived back at Carrig View a few minutes before six, tired but glad to be home. Kyna greeted her with a hug, and the three dogs circled around and around her as if they found it hard to believe that she had really returned.

'Did you get what you wanted?' Kyna asked her, as she unpacked her overnight case.

'Not as much as I was hoping for, but enough to start making some progress. Not only with the Dripsey bombings, but poor Conor Mullan too.'

'Would you care for a welcome-home drink in your hand?'

'You read my mind. You always could.'

Kyna hesitated in the bedroom doorway, and when Katie turned around, she could see an expression in her eyes that she could only describe as longing. It was like a child outside a sweetshop window. After Kyna had gone into the living room to mix her a vodka and tonic, she stood still for a moment, with Foltchain looking up at her, and she felt disturbed.

She hoped she had not made a mistake in inviting Kyna to come and stay with her. Yet she was so fond of her, and felt so protective towards her, that it was hard for her to think of telling her to leave.

She went into the kitchen, where Kyna was peeling potatoes to prepare them a supper of colcannon. Sitting down at the table with her laptop and her glass of vodka and tonic, she sent Sabrina a text as if it had come from Sean Delaney.

'I can pay you now,' Sean told her. 'Give me your account details and I'll transfer it to you tomorrow morning.'

It took less than five minutes before Sabrina texted her back, giving the sort code of a branch of Ulster Bank in Malahide, just north of Dublin, and her account number. The account was under the name of ED Holdings.

Katie knew it was possible or even likely that she had not made Conor Mullan pay his blackmail money into the same account. All the same, she had known several fraudsters and money launderers who had not been wily enough to create separate accounts from which it was impossible to trace them or to connect them with other criminal scams that they were running.

She had already transferred €750 of her own money into 'Sean Delaney's' account to cover the €250 fee that Sabrina was demanding. She could only hope that when Sabrina was brought to justice, she would be able to claim it back as 'operational expenses'.

She thought about calling Frank Magorian to find out if there was any news about her reinstatement at Anglesea Street, but she knew that he would have contacted her already if he had received any notification from Dublin about it.

'How's your drink?' asked Kyna. 'You never stop being a detective, do you, even now you're suspended?'

'Oh, stop. You know yourself that it's an addiction,' said Katie. 'Even if there was a cure for it, I'm not sure that I'd want to be cured. But my drink's okay for the moment.'

'You should take some time off. We could go to Dingle together and let the dogs run along Inch beach. I love it there and I know they'd love it.'

'I'd love it, too, but I can't take a break just yet. I'm too near to closing both of these cases – not only the Dripsey bombings but poor Conor Mullan too. I heard Hilda Bracken pretty much condemning herself out of her own mouth, and I'm going to see if I can persuade Sabrina from Extreme Dreams to do the same.'

'How are you going to manage that?'

'Not me, in person. But Sean Delaney.'

'Sean Delaney doesn't exist.'

'Then I'll just have to bring him to life. I've been thinking that one or two of the younger fellows from Anglesea Street might fill the bill, like, do you know what I mean? Hickey or Malloy. Hickey in particular, because you could easily mistake him for the feen in the picture that I sent Sabrina, and he and I worked together like a couple of tennis players. You remember that fearful stabbing in the Voodoo Rooms last year? Hickey was brilliant the way he teased information out of all those young witnesses, even though most of them were pure terrified to say what they'd seen. And when those three Garity gowls were found guilty and sent off to Portlaoise, I made sure that Hickey was given all the credit.'

'You think he'd agree to do it? What if Micheál ó Broin finds out about it and throws a rabie?'

'I can only ask him. And what could Micheál do, really, if he helped me to bring in the woman who had hounded Conor Mullan to death?'

Katie was feeling tired now, but before she shut up her laptop she sent a text to Terry O'Sullivan, telling him how jubilant Hilda Bracken had been when she saw the news on television of the Riverstick bombing. Now she was more convinced than ever that the Brackens were at least partly responsible for the campaign against the Dripsey Dozen, with the connivance of Rayland Garvey. Not only that, she had heard Martin Bracken mention a possible partner in crime called Ronnie, and from what she had overheard, this Ronnie might have planted the explosive device that had killed the Doherty family, father and mother and two young sons.

She also tried to contact Detective Garda Kevyn Hickey, but when he failed to answer his phone, she decided to postpone it until tomorrow. She wanted to speak to him live about the possibility of him acting as 'Sean Delaney', and she was reluctant to leave him a message or send him a text. If he declined to help her, a recorded answerphone message or a text could be produced as evidence that she had interfered in an ongoing Garda investigation while she was suspended.

'Eat,' said Kyna, putting down a plate of colcannon in front of her, and handing her a knife and fork. 'The food of the angels.'

Katie smiled and touched her hand. 'The food of one angel, anyhow.'

The next morning, before they took out the dogs for their morning walk, Katie called Kevyn Hickey again.

'Yes, ma'am. I saw that you called me yesterday evening. My phone was off because I was round the South Docks until half past three, like. I was trying to dig out more evidence against those fecking Hanagans. I didn't think you'd appreciate me calling you back at that time of the morning.'

'How's it going with the Hanagans?'

'So-so. They're fierce tricky, those two, like some comedy double act. You can never work out if they're telling you the truth, like, or if it's all some joke they just made up. I'll nail the pair of them in the end, though, you mark my words.'

'Kevyn, I called you to ask you a favour,' said Katie. 'I want you to understand that if you say no, that you don't want to do it, for whatever reason, I won't hold it against you. Not now, and not when my suspension's lifted and I'm back at Anglesea Street, God willing.'

'I owe you a lot, ma'am. Like, you gave me so much advice and support when I was starting out, but you never asked for nothing in return – never. Ask away. Would it be something to do with dog-fighting, by any chance?'

'Not this time, no. It's to do with Conor Mullan and the reason he committed suicide.'

'DS Mullan? I thought it was depression. We all did, because of his marriage being so rocky.'

'Well, it was in a way, but that wasn't the whole story. His wife, Maeve, found out what it was but she made me swear to God to keep it confidential, for the sake of Conor's reputation. If I tell you what it was, I need you to make the same promise too.'

'I will, ma'am, for sure. I think you know by now that I can keep my lips zippered tight when it's called for.'

Katie explained how Conor Mullan had been tempted by Extreme Dreams and how Sabrina had extorted almost all his savings from him. Then she told him how she had created 'Sean Delaney'.

'What I'm asking you, Kevyn, is whether you would agree to be Sean Delaney and go along to the Abhaile ó Bhaile Hotel for his whipping session. Except that I wouldn't expect you to be whipped – don't worry!'

'So what would I have to do?'

'Try to provoke this Sabrina into threatening you with blackmail, and covertly record it. That would be enough on its own to charge her. But better still, if you could trick her into admitting that she blackmailed DS Mullan. You're a genius when it comes to persuading people to incriminate themselves.

Maybe you could tell her that DS Mullan was a good friend of yours and that he confided in you about going to Extreme Dreams. Maybe you could say how frightened he was that he would lose his job, and that Maeve would find out where all his money had been disappearing to.'

'Sure. I think I could manage something like that. I'll give it a shot any road. You remember that Nola Devine, and how I wangled her into telling us how proud she was about pimping all those girls from Christ King secondary school, and what a rake of money she was making out of it?'

'Oh, I'll never forget that, Kevyn. In fact, I have to laugh when I think about it, the way her face almost dropped down on to the carpet when we told her she was under arrest. Listen, why don't we meet today and I'll give you all the background on Extreme Dreams and show you what Sean Delaney is supposed to look like? Will you be free in an hour's time, maybe? We could get together for a coffee at The Bookshelf.'

'Okay, ma'am. I can be there at eleven-thirty if that suits you.'

'That'll be perfect,' Katie told him. But then she said, 'You do understand what DS ó Broin is going to think about you when he finds out about this, and he'll have to find out about it sooner or later? He's not exactly going to think that you're his bar of gold.'

'Don't worry. He doesn't think that already. Only a couple of days ago he accused me of jumping to conclusions about the Hanagans and their people-smuggling, with only the circumstantial evidence to go on. In fact, he said he could tell that I'd been trained by you. "Pie in the sky policing", that's what he called it.'

'Better than "plodding-along policing", Kevyn. At least

innocent people don't lose their lives while we're trying to find indisputable proof that somebody's out to get them.'

They took the dogs for a walk down to Whitepoint Drive, which had a narrow shoreline that overlooked Cork Harbour and Haulbowline Island. It was a gloomy morning, with shaggy black clouds hanging down low, and the water gleamed as flat and grey as stainless steel.

When they returned to Carrig View, Katie changed out of her waterproof puffer coat and brushed her hair in the mirror in the hallway. Kyna stood watching her.

'Do you know when you're going to be back? I was thinking of making fishcakes for supper.'

'Oh, I won't be back late. Kieran will be coming down this evening. But I'll probably pop into Dunnes Stores once I've finished my meeting with Kevyn, so if there's anything you want.'

'If they still have some of that Jo Malone pomegranate shower gel, yes please.'

The dogs all accompanied her out of the front door as if they expected her to be taking them out for a drive and maybe another walk somewhere. Harvey was the first to trot up to her Audi, but when he reached it he stopped abruptly, and lifted his head. Katie could see that he was sniffing, deeply. His tail was erect and his legs were quivering.

'What's wrong, Harvey?' she asked him. 'It's not Jenny next door cooking that packet and tripe again, is it? What she puts into it I can't even guess, but it always smells like someone's died.'

She approached her car, with her keys in her hand, but Harvey turned around and barked at her.

'Harvey... I have to go to the city to see Kevyn Hickey and so you can't come with me. But I'll be back later, boy, I promise you, and I'll fetch you a treat.'

She took another step towards her car, but Harvey barked at her and kept on barking, and danced from side to side to obstruct her.

When she took one more step, he jumped up at her, again and again, and now she could tell that he was frantic.

'Holy Mary!' called out Kyna, from the porch. 'What's Harvey getting himself into such a heap about?'

Katie hesitated for a moment, and then took a step back. Harvey stopped jumping and barking, but stayed where he was, with his tail still sticking up and his fur all bristling. Katie could tell that he was waiting for her to try and reach her car again, and that he was prepared to jump and bark at her until she gave up.

Without turning around, she said to Kyna, 'He's a sniffer dog, remember. He was always one of the best, that's what they told me at the airport. He could sniff out drugs and money – but explosives, those were his speciality.'

Kyna said, 'You don't think—?'

Katie came back to the front door. 'I don't know. Maybe he's picked up on something that has a similar kind of smell to explosives. You know, maybe there was some toxic chemical spillage lying in the road and I ran over it. But I'll not take the risk. I'm going to call the bomb squad and I'll put Terry O'Sullivan on alert, and Bill Phinner, too, just in case.'

She went back into the house, although she kept on her duffel coat. Harvey stayed where he was, guarding her car, although Barney and Foltchain were both pacing backwards and forwards, obviously wondering why he was not coming in to play with them.

She called Collins Barracks and they put her through to Commandant Brophy in charge of the Explosive Ordnance Disposal team. Kyna watched her as she said, 'Patrick? I'm hoping against hope that somebody hasn't planted an IED under my car. But I really need you to come and check it out.'

'What makes you think that there may be a device there?'

'I have a sniffer dog, and he can smell it.'

'Serious?'

'About as serious as I could ever be, Patrick, I promise you.'

19

Katie and Kyna stayed in the kitchen at the back of the house while they waited for the bomb disposal squad to arrive. If an explosive device had been planted under her car, and it was detonated, it would almost certainly blow in the front door and all the living-room windows, or worse.

Harvey had wanted to stay outside, preventing anyone from coming close to Katie's car, but after Katie had coaxed him and offered him a pig's ear, he relented and trotted back in to join them.

Katie checked her CCTV, but if anybody had sneaked into her driveway in the past ten hours, they had somehow managed to avoid being recorded. It was possible that they had climbed over the fence from next door, keeping themselves hidden behind Katie's car.

She called Kevyn Hickey to tell him that she would be delayed, although she refrained from telling him why. If no explosive device was found under her car, he might think that she was being paranoid, and if there were a device, he might reconsider doing a favour for someone who was a target for bombers. She was confident that Terry O'Sullivan would have kept her bomb alert to himself so far, and would not tell anyone else at Anglesea Street about it – not unless and until the EOD team found that Harvey's warning had been well founded.

'If there is a bomb, then who do you think might have put it there?' asked Kyna.

Harvey looked up at her as if he could understand what she was saying, and gave a gravelly growl.

'I can only guess that the Brackens might have realized that I'm on to them. Maybe their neighbour in Wood Close told Martin Bracken that I'd been looking for him. I tried to sound as English as I could, but Cork's not the easiest accent to pretend that you don't speak like, do you know what I mean?'

'There's nothing wrong with the Cork accent, Katie. It's the rest of the world that speaks funny.'

After only forty-five minutes, Katie's phone played 'The Parting Glass'. It was Commandant Brophy, telling her that the EOD team had arrived at Carrig View and were parked at a safe distance outside. They had already closed off the road and had unloaded a Reamda Reacher robot out of the back of their truck, so that it could come trundling into her driveway and examine her car for explosives.

Katie had no choice but to wait for the robot to inspect her Audi, staying on the phone while Commandant Brophy gave her a running report.

'The Reacher's trying the door handles,' he told her. 'They're locked tight, all of them, so we're sending it now to take a sconce underneath.'

He was silent for over a minute, although Katie could hear him breathing, and then he said, 'Yes. There's a massive lump of white plastic stuck right beneath the driver's seat. It's C-4 by the look of it, about a kilo and a half, I'd say. Enough to send you and your car halfway to Cobh.'

'Jesus,' said Katie. 'I've already alerted DI O'Sullivan and Bill Phinner that my car might have an IED planted on it, just in case. I'll call them again now and tell them it's definite. Can you see how it was going to be set off? Is it on a timer?'

'No. But I can see that there's a remote detonator stuck into it, like a RISE-1. Maybe your bombers were going to wait until you drove off somewhere. It could be that they're watching you, to give themselves the satisfaction of seeing you blown sky-high. On the other hand, maybe they're long gone. Some of these detonators have a range of twenty-five kilometres, so your bombers could be over the hills and far away by now.'

'What are you going to do? You're not going to blow up my car, are you?'

'Here's praying we don't have to. The Reacher's fitted with a pigstick, and the pigstick shoots a fierce powerful jet of water into the IED. That should hopefully disrupt it and make it safe.'

'In that case I'm praying too, Patrick.'

Katie called Kieran to tell him about the bomb under her car. He was in court, but she left him a message and told him not to panic about it, because the EOD team had it well in hand.

She and Kyna waited for another twenty minutes, and then the doorbell rang. When Katie went to answer it, almost tripping over the dogs, Commandant Brophy was standing outside. Not far behind him, one of his team in an armoured blast suit was lifting off his huge protective helmet and wiping his forehead with the back of his hand.

Commandant Brophy was short and thickset, with permanently surprised eyebrows and bulging eyes. He always put Katie in mind of the actor Ernest Borgnine.

'All done and dusted now, Superintendent Maguire. The pigstick blew out the detonator. There's C-4 still stuck under your car, but it's totally stable. We'll leave it there for now so that the technical boys can take a look at it. I shouldn't think it's too likely, but they may be able to find fingerprints or DNA on it.

'I'll say something, though,' he added. 'Judging by the blast pattern, the IED that blew up the Dohertys' car at Riverstick was planted in a pure similar way. So the odds are that you're looking for the same suspect.'

Ten minutes later, three Garda cars arrived, and a few minutes after that, Bill Phinner and the technical bureau van drew up behind the bomb disposal truck. Next, a van from RTÉ appeared, and parked across the road.

Kyna came out and laid her hand on Katie's shoulder. 'What a circus. And there you were, trying to keep everything you've been doing under wraps. But I'm desperately worried for you, Katie. If those people are out to get you, and they know where you live, don't you think we'd better think of moving somewhere else – at least for a while?'

'I'm worried for the both of us,' said Katie. 'You should have seen the houses of those poor Dripsey people after they were bombed. There was nothing left of them. But I'm damned if those shitehawks are going to scare me out of my own house.'

DI O'Sullivan climbed out of his car and came up to her, accompanied by Inspector Barry Walsh.

'I'm relieved that you're safe, ma'am,' he told her. 'It would be hard to imagine a world without DS Kathleen Maguire, I can tell you.'

As soon as he caught sight of the two officers, Harvey came running up to her and stood beside her, softly growling, as if he were guarding her. Katie bent down and tugged at his ears.

'If it hadn't been for Harvey here, I would have been singing with the angels this afternoon,' said Katie. 'If they don't give medals to sniffer dogs, they should. He certainly deserves one. Canine Nose of the Year.'

'Do you have any notion at all who might have planted this IED?' Barry Walsh asked her.

'I do, yes, Barry. I may be wrong, of course. I've upset a whole rake of different criminals during my career, especially the O'Flynns, and I'm sure that they'd love to see me go to meet my Maker. But it's likely the same offenders who've been blowing up the Dripsey Dozen.'

'How about your CCTV?' said Terry O'Sullivan, nodding towards the camera on top of her porch. 'Have you checked it for any sign of your suspect?'

Katie nodded. 'I have, yes. But somehow he managed to stay out of sight. Or she.'

Three more uniformed gardaí had just arrived and Barry Walsh went off to brief them. Terry waited until he was out of earshot, and then he said, 'Of course, DS Ó Broin knows all about this. He told me to tell you that it was like a final warning to you to stop interfering in the Dripsey bombings. He said you were lucky not to have paid the full price. Actually, I missed out a couple of words of what he said, but I expect you can guess what they were.'

'But for the love of God, what progress is *he* making?' Katie asked him. 'That's what infuriates me. From what you've told me and from what I've seen on the news, he doesn't seem to be getting anywhere close to solving this investigation at all. I could almost believe that he *wants* the rest of the Dripsey Dozen to be bombed.'

Terry shrugged, but he had no answer to that. At that moment, Bill Phinner came up to them and said, 'Whoever planted that C-4 knew exactly what they were doing. I'd say you're looking for a soldier, or an ex-soldier, or a miner, or somebody who's worked in the demolition business.'

'How about the New IRA?' asked Terry.

'Very doubtful. Their IEDs were always much more slapdash. That's why so many of them never went off. But this one, believe me. If a signal had been sent to detonate this one, and Superintendent Maguire here had been sitting in her car, we would have been attending her funeral next week, and that's only if we could have found enough bits of her to bury.'

Katie and Kyna had to stay in for the rest of the afternoon. They sat in the kitchen while the driveway outside was bustling with gardaí and forensic technicians. A small crowd of curious bystanders had gathered across the road to see what all the commotion was about.

After two hours, Katie's car was towed away for closer examination at the forensic laboratory in Cork city. Once it had gone, Bill Phinner's team combed the driveway for any trace that the bomber may have left behind when he crawled underneath it to plant his plastic explosive. Using ultraviolet lamps and oblique lighting, they discovered a few stray hairs on the tarmac, as well as some fibres that may have rubbed off a jacket or a coat.

Fionnuala Sweeney from RTÉ texted Katie to ask if she would be willing to come out and be interviewed, but this time Katie said no. Fionnuala would only ask her who she believed had been out to blow her up, and the last thing she wanted to do was provoke the Brackens, if they had been responsible, or further irritate ó Broin.

Although Micheál had made no secret of how badly he wanted to stay as detective superintendent at Anglesea

Street, Katie was increasingly disturbed by his repeated insistence that she should keep out of the investigation into the Dripsey Dozen bombings. So he disliked her personally, and disapproved of her methods of detection, and regarded her as a threat to his career? None of that explained why he would refuse any assistance that she could give him to solve what had now become one of the worst offences in the entire criminal history of Cork.

At about 4 p.m., Bill Phinner came in to say that the examination of the driveway and surrounding area was more or less wrapped up.

'Your neighbour has a video doorbell, and it's recorded an image of a man crossing her front garden. It's brief and it's blurry, so we'll be taking it back to the lab to see if we can enhance it.'

'How long will you be needing to keep my car?'

'Hard to say. A few days at least.'

Terry had entered the hallway and he overheard what Bill Phinner had told her. When he came into the kitchen, he said, 'Don't worry, ma'am. I'll make sure we send you over a replacement tonight from the car pool, and you can keep that for as long as you want to. Unmarked, of course.'

But then he looked around the kitchen and said, 'You're really going to stay here? It might be advisable for you to find somewhere else to go, at least until this case is cleared up.'

'No, I'm going to stay,' said Katie. 'I'm not going to let any scangers drive me out of my own home, ever. I didn't before when I was being threatened with all kinds of retribution by the O'Flynns and the Higginses, and I'm not going to now. You don't have to fret. Kyna and me, you can be sure that we won't try to open any air fryers that we haven't ordered, and we have Harvey here in case there's any whiff of C-4.'

'Well, the best of luck to the both of you, that's all I can say, and may the Lord protect you.'

Kieran rang her as soon as the day's court session was adjourned.

'I'm safe, Kieran. They've taken my car away now but they've just fetched me a Toyota Corolla from the car pool. It has a sensory alarm on it so if anyone even looks at it too closely, it'll go off.'

'Listen, Kathleen, I have some good news for you, in the midst of all this. Judge Collins has handed down his sentences on Muireann Nic Riada and Megan Riordan. He's found them both guilty of manslaughter, but under the circumstances he's given them only five-year suspended sentences. No time in jail. He said their action was extreme but understandable. So that should bode well for you with the Discipline Section, fingers crossed.'

'That's a relief, that really is. Let's hope the officers handling my case agree with him. I'd say that's a cause for celebration. Well, cautious celebration, anyhow. I've no champagne in the house but there's a couple of bottles of prosecco in the fridge. I can't wait to see you this evening. What time do you think you'll be here?'

'Kathleen, I'm mortified, but I've another critical meeting scheduled for this evening, and that means I'll probably have to stay in the city again overnight. This fraud case that I'm hearing at the moment, you wouldn't believe it. It's more complicated than a nest of spiders.'

'Oh, Kieran.'

'I know, sweetheart. I feel like God's punishing me for some reason. I'm missing you so much that it's actually painful.'

'I'm missing you too, Kieran. You'll be able to come down here tomorrow, though, won't you?'

'You can be sure of it, Mrs Connolly-to-be. They could pass a barring order in the district court but that couldn't stop me. But listen, are you sure that it's wise for you to be staying there?'

'Kyna and me, we're keeping sketch, I promise you.'

'I'll try to call you again when the meeting's over, if it's not too late. I have to go now, but never forget how much I love you.'

'I love you too, Kieran.'

She put down her phone and pulled a sad face.

'What's wrong?' Kyna asked her.

'Kieran can't come tonight. He has to go to another stupid meeting. It's all to do with some incredible scam that a building company pulled on the city council's planning department.'

'Oh, no. So it's fishcakes for two.'

Katie gave her a wry smile. 'Do you know, that sounds like a song.'

After their supper, they sat in front of the television for a while, but neither of them could concentrate on what they were watching. It started to rain, hard, and Kyna went to the window, drew back the curtain and stared out into the darkness.

'Supposing they've seen the news, those bombers, and they try again?'

'They won't. They'll know that we're on to them. I'm going to leave the floodlight on all night, and if they even *breathe* on that Toyota, it'll scream like a sow in labour. At least, that's what Terry told me. He wanted to post a twenty-four-hour guard on the house, but there's too many officers off sick with the Covid. A patrol car's going to drive past Carrig View once an hour every hour, which is the best he could manage.'

'I'm still nervous, Katie. Maybe we really should think about moving somewhere else.'

'Kyna darling, like I told Terry, I've been threatened by some of the scariest gangs in Cork, but the minute you show them that they frighten you, that's the moment you start to lose the battle against them.'

Kyna let the curtain fall back. 'When I tried to kill myself, I saw what death looks like. People talk about shining lights, but it wasn't like that at all. It was dark and it was cold, and it came rising up in front of me like a ghost wearing rags. I don't want to see death again. Not until I'm old and I've lived my life out, right to the very end.'

Katie picked up the remote and switched off the television. 'I think we both need a good night's sleep. Why don't you go and take a shower and I'll make us some chamomile tea.'

After Kyna had closed her bedroom door, Katie took a shower too, and put on Kieran's brushed cotton Magee nightshirt because it was warm and it felt like him.

She sat up in bed sipping her tea and listening to *This Is How It Ends* by one of her favourite authors, Kathleen MacMahon. But every now and then she took off her earphones and listened to the rain against the window, although she knew that she was really listening out for the sound of somebody creeping around outside. She felt much more uneasy about their safety than she had been prepared to admit, either to Kieran or Terry or Kyna, and most of all to herself. She had seen blown-apart bodies in the morgue, and she found it impossible not to visualize Kyna and herself as two jumbles of jawbones and ribs and shredded intestines. It was always the staring eyes that horrified her the most: those eyes on stalks that seemed to be asking in bewilderment, *what's happened to me, am I dead?*

Once she'd finished her tea, she went into the bathroom to brush her teeth, and then she climbed back into bed and switched off the lamp. Her bedroom was not completely dark, because of the floodlight that she had left on to deter any intruders, and it was shining through the gap in her curtains. Apart from that, her mind refused to stop racing. Not only could she vividly picture the victims of bomb blasts lying strewn on the examination tables in the morgue, she kept thinking about Hilda Bracken dancing in delight behind the bar of The Huntsman, and singing *We did it again! Five down and only seven left to pay!*

If it had been the Brackens who had arranged for that IED to be planted under her car, she could not stop herself from wondering if they somehow found out that she had gone to Erdington to see if she could gather more evidence against them. She was sure that neither Martin Bracken nor Rayland Garvey had seen through her disguise when she visited The Huntsman, or else they would have confronted her there and then. Or perhaps they *had* recognized her, but had been prepared to wait until they could eliminate her back in Ireland. In Cork, so many convicted criminals bore grudges against her that they would be far from the sole suspects.

An hour went past, and she heard the clock in the living room chime half past midnight. If she switched on her lamp again, and listened to some more chapters of *This Is How It Ends*, maybe she would be able to doze off. Yet even though she was still awake, she felt too tired to try. She would just have to lie here, staring at the raindrop patterns crawling across the ceiling, and hope that she would fall asleep without realizing it.

After a few more minutes, though, she heard her bedroom door open. She raised her head from the pillow in alarm, but immediately Kyna whispered, 'Don't be frightened! It's only me!'

'What's the matter?' Katie asked her.

'I can't get off to sleep for the life of me. I'm too scared that somebody's going to come and blow us up in the middle of the night!'

'I'm sure they won't, darling. But I can't get off to sleep either. It's not every day that you have a bomb planted under your car! Here – get into bed and I'll give you a hug. Maybe I'll even sing you a lullaby. That should send you off.'

Kyna drew back the duvet and climbed into bed beside Katie. She had her hair tied back and she was wearing only a red striped pyjama top. As usual, she smelled of pear and freesia cologne. Katie wrapped her arms around her and gave her an affectionate squeeze, as well as a kiss on the forehead.

'How about I sing you "The Angel's Whisper"? My ma always sang that to me and I was dead to the world in no time. Oh, sorry. I didn't mean it like that. I only meant I fell asleep before she'd even finished singing it.'

'Do you truly think they won't come back to harm us?'

'I don't believe they'll have the nerve, darling. Honest.'

She ran her fingers into Kyna's hair and gave her another kiss on the forehead. She had forgotten how much Kyna attracted her. She was slim and warm and she had the softest skin. Kyna lifted her face and kissed her back, first on the tip of the nose and then on the lips.

'Go on, then, sing me the lullaby before I start getting too excited.'

Katie hesitated, and so Kyna kissed her on the lips again. This time Katie opened her mouth and let the tip of Kyna's tongue slide inside and play with hers. She knew that this was wrong, and they should not be kissing like this, but after today she felt as if she needed loving and she needed comfort and there was something magical about Kyna, as well as earthy and erotic.

Kyna caressed Katie's left breast through her nightshirt, circling her thumb around and around over her nipple until it stiffened.

'Oh blest be that warning, my child,' sang Katie, in a whisper. 'Thy sleep adorning.'

'Don't stop,' said Kyna, running her hand inside Katie's nightshirt so that she could gently massage her bare breast and roll her nipple between finger and thumb.

Katie closed her eyes. She wanted to tell Kyna to stop, but the words refused to climb out of her throat.

'For I know that the angels are whispering with thee,' she sang breathlessly.

They both paused for a moment. They stared into each other's eyes, shining in the half-darkness. They were both panting. Then, without a word, they started to claw desperately at each other, as if they were wrestling, and they kissed each other again and again, deeper and deeper.

Kyna climbed on top of Katie, tugging up her nightshirt so that she could kiss and fondle both of her breasts. She took each nipple between her lips and sucked it against the roof of her mouth. At the same time, Katie lifted Kyna's pyjama top and cupped the cheeks of her bottom in both hands.

Kyna kissed Katie's face all over, forehead and cheeks and lips and chin. 'Oh God I love you Katie and I never stopped loving you.'

With that, she wriggled herself further down the bed. She parted Katie's thighs and kissed her vulva, before starting to lick at her quickly with the tip of her tongue.

Katie gripped Kyna's shoulder with one hand and ran the fingers of the other hand into her hair. She knew that this was wrong, that she should not be allowing this to happen, but she loved Kyna as much as Kyna loved her, and the thrill that was rising between her legs as Kyna continued to lick her was overwhelming.

She closed her eyes tight and felt as if every other sense had shut down – that she was blind and deaf and all she could feel was the ever-tightening grip of her approaching orgasm. But when she was teetering right on the brink, Kyna stopped licking her.

'*Kyna*,' she gasped, and opened her eyes. Kyna was climbing off her, clumsily, almost falling on her side on to the bed and pulling down her pyjama jacket. It was then that Katie saw why. The bedroom door was wide open and Kieran was standing there, staring at them. The shoulders of his mackintosh were sparkling with raindrops.

Katie closed her legs and dragged the duvet across to cover herself up. She heard herself say, 'Kieran,' but her voice sounded as if some other woman was speaking.

Kieran continued to stare at them both without saying a word.

Katie thought, how can I possibly explain this? *It isn't what it looks like?*

But there was no need for her to say anything, because Kieran turned around and left, leaving the bedroom door open and closing the front door behind him very quietly. They heard his Volvo start up and pull away.

Katie and Kyna looked at each other in the dim light of the bedroom, and then they both started to cry, like two children.

Barney and Foltchain came in from the kitchen, followed by Harvey. The three of them stood in the open doorway, as if they were expecting Katie and Kyna to explain why they were so distressed.

20

As soon as she had wiped her eyes and taken several deep breaths, Katie called Kieran. There was no answer, but she knew he was probably driving, so she left a message, pleading with him to call her back.

Kyna was sitting on the end of the bed with a miserable expression on her face. Foltchain was resting her head in her lap and looking up at her every now and then as if she understood her pain.

'It's all my fault, Katie. I've gone and totally banjaxed your relationship with Kieran now. How can you ever expect him to forgive you? I'm such a selfish, selfish bitch.'

Katie sat down beside her. 'Kyna – it's as much my fault as yours, if not more. I'm supposed to be taking care of you and helping you to recover. Inside my head I kept telling myself that I shouldn't be doing this, but I let myself get carried away. I love you, you know that, but if I had really shown you how much I love you, I would never have allowed that to happen.'

'What are you going to do?'

'Well, I've tried calling Kieran. He didn't pick up, but I'll try him again when he's had time to drive back to the city.'

'Oh Jesus, Katie, I've destroyed your whole life.'

Katie had no words for that. She felt as if none of what had happened was real, and that she would wake up soon and it would be morning, and that the rain would have stopped.

Kyna returned to her own bedroom and closed the door. Katie didn't wait any longer but tried calling Kieran again. This time she was told that the person she was calling was busy, and that she could leave a message.

'Kieran, darling. I have to speak to you. I'm in bits here.'

She waited for another half-hour, by which time Kieran should easily have returned to the city centre. He had a suite at the Metropole for the duration of his appointment to the Cork District Court, and so she phoned the hotel reception to see if they could put her through to him.

'I'm sorry, madam. I've not had to let anyone in for over an hour, and there's no answer from his room.'

Mother of God, she thought, where is he?

She was tempted to pour herself a large vodka, but she knew that would be stupid, because she had already decided to drive to the city to arrive at the courthouse before it opened at 10:30 to see if she could find Kieran. Perhaps she would be able to persuade him that what he had witnessed was a kind of therapy – a way in which she had been helping Kyna to overcome the post-traumatic stress of her suicide attempt. She realized that it was an outright lie, and that Kieran would probably think it was absurd, but she could think of no other excuse for being caught in the middle of making love.

She dressed in a black roll-neck sweater and jeans, and then she knocked on Kyna's bedroom door. Kyna opened it, and she looked a mess. Her eyes were red and swollen from crying and her hair was straggly.

'You're dressed,' she said miserably. 'Are you leaving?'

'Not yet, darling. But I didn't feel like going back to bed. I'll be heading off to the city about a quarter past nine. I'm hoping to talk to Kieran before he has to go into court. I have to meet Kevyn, too. He must be wondering what in the name of God is going on with me.'

'Katie, how are you ever going to forgive me?'

Katie opened her arms for Kyna and gave her a hug.

'If anyone's to blame, sweetheart, it's me. If you can just take care of the wild bunch for me while I'm gone.'

'I will of course. Maybe I should call Kieran for you and tell him that you tried to stop me but I practically raped you.'

'It's better if you leave it to me. He's a judge, remember, and he doesn't easily fall for far-fetched excuses.'

Kyna's eyes filled up with tears again. 'But what if he doesn't want to marry you, after seeing us together? What are you going to do then?'

'Let's wait and see. He's a judge, but he's not a hanging judge. Maybe he'll let me off with a caution.'

By the time Katie left for the city it had stopped raining, although the clouds remained low and grey and oppressive. She parked her car behind the Garda station and walked across the street to the district courthouse.

The courts were busy this morning. Today's business included not only the complex fraud case that Kieran was hearing, but the prosecution of five players from the Curraheen hurling team for possession of drugs and sexual harassment after a riotous post-match party.

Katie made her way through the crowd of relatives and lawyers and reporters. She was given smiles and salutes by two of the court ushers, and Dan Keane from the *Examiner* lifted his hand as if to show her that he wanted to talk to her, but she shook her head.

She reached the judges' chambers just as the door opened and Judge Boyle came out, followed by Kieran.

'Ah, Detective Superintendent Maguire!' said Judge Boyle. 'Are you back at the helm yet? We miss you!'

'Soon, I'm hoping, judge,' Katie told him, although her eyes were on Kieran. He had turned his face towards Judge Boyle as if he had failed to see her, or there was nobody else there at all.

'Kieran,' she said. 'Could I have a word with you, please?'

Judge Boyle glanced at Kieran, and it was obvious that he could sense the tension between them. 'I'll be getting on so,' he said, and left the two of them standing in the corridor.

There was an uncomfortable pause, and then Katie said, 'Kieran, you deserve an explanation.'

'What I saw, Katie, that was explanation enough.'

'Kyna desperately needed reassurance. She needed affection. She tried to end her own life, remember. It all went far too far, I admit, and it was my fault for allowing it to happen. But both of us are mortified, and I promise you that it will never happen again.'

Kieran looked at her with a mixture of pain and disdain.

'I really believed that you wanted to be Mrs Connolly, with all your heart.'

'Kieran, I do. You know I do.'

'How can you say that, when you're so ready to share your heart with someone else?'

'That wasn't love. That was therapy.'

Kieran gave a grunt of bitter amusement. 'If that was therapy, the queue for the clinic would stretch all the way to Kerry.'

Katie looked around. One of the ushers was waiting for

Kieran at the end of the corridor, impatiently clutching an order paper.

'Can we meet later, when you've finished court?'

'What for? So that you can invent some other unbelievable reason for cheating on me? I caught you out this once, Katie, but the Lord only knows how many times you and Kyna have been having fun and games together since she came to stay with you.'

'That was the only time, Kieran, I swear on the Bible.'

'People come into my court every day and swear on the Bible that they're going to tell me the truth, but what comes pouring out of their lips? More lies than ants out of an anthill.'

'Kieran—'

'I've nothing more to say to you, and I'd rather not hear from you again. Now, if you don't mind, I have a court to attend.'

'Kieran, please.'

'I'm not blaming you for being who you are, Katie, but you're not the woman I thought you were, and you're not a woman I could confidently marry. If it wasn't Kyna, it could just as easily be someone else, some other attractive girl who took your fancy. I don't want to spend the whole of my married life being suspicious.'

Katie had no words. She watched Kieran as he walked off along the corridor and started to talk to the usher. She felt numb, rather than hurt, and she didn't start to cry. Instead, she wondered if she had been saved from a future life with a man who would little by little have crushed all the spirit out of her.

As she walked back across the entrance hall, Dan Keane caught up with her.

'What way are you, super?'

'Hallo, Dan. Sorry. I've no comment for you today.'

'The word is that you and Judge Connolly have been doing a line. Is that true?'

Katie stopped by the front door. 'Dan – you know what they say. *Níl a fhios ag aon duine an fhírinne ach amháin le Dia.* Nobody knows the truth except God.'

She left the courthouse and crossed back over to the Garda station. It was starting to rain again and she thought, *there, the angels have seen what I've done and they're spitting on me.*

She went upstairs to the first floor and found Kevyn Hickey hunched over his desk, eating a sausage roll and staring intently at his computer screen. Detective Garda Coughlan was sitting on the opposite side of the room and he raised his coffee cup to Katie by way of a greeting.

'Kevyn, how's yourself?' asked Katie.

Kevyn looked up with his mouth full and tried to say, 'Grand altogether,' and swallow at the same time. Katie always thought that he looked too young to be a detective, with short hair faded up at the sides and protruding ears.

'I'm pure sorry about yesterday,' she told him. 'Something came up. Well, quite a few things came up.'

'I heard about the plastic under your car. Nothing more disastrous than that, I hope.'

Katie pulled a face. 'It depends on your definition of "disastrous".'

'Do you have any ideas at all who might have planted it?'

'One or two. But I'm waiting on Bill Phinner to tell me where it might have come from and if he's been able to lift any fingerprints off it, or DNA.'

'I thank God you didn't get into the car and try to drive off.'

'Actually, you should be thanking my sniffer dog, Harvey. But listen, I was wondering if you were still up for this Extreme Dreams operation. I'll understand completely if you've changed your mind. You might not want to be working unofficially and undercover for someone who might be blown up at any moment.'

'No, ma'am, I'm still more than game for it. I love a sting when I'm making out that I'm someone I'm not. Remember that Dooly case last year when I was pretending I was a sax player, even though I couldn't blow a single note to save my life?'

'Don't. It still gives me the shivers. Anyhow, the Extreme Dreams session is booked for tomorrow afternoon at three at the Abhaile ó Bhaile Hotel on Leopold Street. The hotel's run by a fellow named John Quinn. He used to be a priest but he was defrocked.'

'Yes, I've heard about John Quinn. What did his parishioners call him? Father Filthy, wasn't it?'

'That's him. He allows sex parties in his hotel because he says that sex is all about love and the Lord approves of love, no matter how kinky it is. On top of that, I'm sure that Sabrina gives him a generous percentage of what she charges her clients.'

'Now, you mentioned whipping.'

'I did, yes. You're supposed to be Sean Delaney. You're unmarried, and you live with your parents in Carrigaline. You're a vet, and at the moment you're employed at the Riverview Animal Hospital. You say that you're into BDSM because you deserve to be punished for the unclean thoughts you have about women.'

Kevyn grinned. 'I can act that out all right. I *do* have unclean thoughts about women, I admit. But I've never had any women telling me that I ought to be punished for them. Quite the opposite.'

'You don't have to submit to being whipped, don't worry,' Katie told him. 'In fact, the plan is that you'll get yourself into an argument with Sabrina and that you'll encourage her to threaten you with blackmail. You can say something like, oh yes, like you did to my friend Conor Mullan? You'll be wearing a wire, of course, and we need only one admission from her that she extorted money out of him, and we'll have her. We can apply for a search warrant and go through her bank accounts.'

'What if she doesn't admit it?'

'We can still charge her for threatening you, and that'll be enough for a warrant. If we can identify any payments in her accounts that came from Conor's bank, that should be evidence enough to convict her. Even if Conor sent his payments some other way, like PayPal, we should be able to prove that they came from him.'

'Don't worry at all, ma'am. I'm mad for it. I thought Conor was one of the best. Out of all the sergeants, he was the boy. There's nothing would make me happier than to see the hoor who killed him locked up.'

'I'll meet you here tomorrow at two-thirty then,' said Katie. 'I'll take you to Leopold Street and I'll wait outside the hotel while you go in for your whipping.'

Katie was making her way to the lift when she heard DI O'Sullivan calling out to her. She stopped and turned around, and he came hurrying along the corridor to catch up with her.

'Here's a stroke of luck,' he told her. 'I've been looking

through CCTV with Sergeant Murphy, and I was about to text you about it.'

He glanced over his shoulder as if he were making sure that nobody could overhear him.

'Don't tell me,' said Katie. 'You've identified the bomber and it's DS ó Broin.'

Terry smiled and shook his head. 'There's wishful thinking for you. But we believe that we may have a lead on the suspect who planted it. We enhanced the footage that we took from your next-door neighbour's doorbell camera. It was recorded at 3:11 a.m. You can't see the fellow's face, but he's wearing a baseball cap on backwards and the collar of his jacket's turned up.'

'That description fits about seventy per cent of the male Cork population under the age of thirty.'

'It does of course. But we also have footage taken from the junction of the R624 and the N25 East Cork Parkway. The camera's only been recently installed there, after that terrible bus crash. But of course that's the route that anyone would take driving from Carrig View into the city. Lo and behold, the camera's captured a Ford Kuga being driven by a man with his baseball cap on backwards and his jacket collar turned up. It takes exactly ten minutes to drive from your house to the N25, and this footage was timed at 3:24.'

'Did it catch the registration plate?'

'No, because it had been covered over. We're not sure what with, but it looks a lot like brown parcel tape. But that may not matter. This Kuga was a non-standard colour, chrome yellow it's called, according to Garda Glenney, who's a bit of a car buff. Apparently the chrome-yellow Kugas didn't sell too well, so most of the stock was bought up for a knockdown price by EconoCar, the car hire company.'

'So now you're going up to the airport to ask EconoCar if they recognize this man, and did he hire one of their cars?'

'Malloy and Murrish are already on their way.'

'That's grand, Terry, thanks. Keep on keeping me updated, if you can. But keep it low key. I don't want you finding yourself on the wrong side of you-know-who.'

'Never fear,' said Terry. 'When I was in college, I was always so good at keeping my mouth closed they used to call me The Zipper.'

Katie was crossing the reception area when Assistant Commissioner Frank Magorian came in through the front doors and shook out his umbrella.

'Good morning, Kathleen,' he smiled. 'Have you come to reacquaint yourself with your office?'

'Do you think there's a real chance of that?' she asked him.

'As a matter of fact, an excellent chance. I had a call from Pat Devain yesterday afternoon and he told me that the Discipline Section will be holding a final meeting about your suspension today. Now that the judge has let off Muireann Nic Riada and Megan Riordan with suspended sentences, it looks almost a hundred per cent certain that you'll be reinstated.'

'They weren't put off by my shooting that Rathkeale feen without giving him a warning?'

'Apparently not. Pat said that Micheál should have been thankful you saved his life.'

'I doubt if Micheál has ever been thankful for anything, not since the day he was born.'

'Oh, come on. Whatever you think about him, you can't criticize his track record. Some of the best detectives are the grumpiest.'

Katie was tempted to reply to that, but she didn't want to sound bitter. In any case, she was too gratified by the news that today she might have her suspension lifted and be able to return here to Anglesea Street.

Frank Magorian laid his hand on her shoulder as if he were a priest giving her a blessing.

'I'll call you as soon as I hear from Pat for definite. It should be late this afternoon sometime.'

'What about Micheál? Are you going to warn him that he needs to start packing his bags and booking a taxi back to Limerick?'

'I'll be giving him the heads-up, of course.'

Katie thought: *I wish I could be there when you do. I'd love to see the expression on Micheál ó Broin's miserable face.*

21

'Oh, I wouldn't mind if we stayed here for ever and never went back home,' said Grainne, crossing over to the window and looking down at the River Lee six floors below. 'I feel like the Queen of Cork up here.'

'And I'd be the King of the Empty Bank Account,' said Declan, bouncing up and down on the black leather couch like an impatient child waiting for his dinner. 'If Redmond and Darragh hadn't offered to find us somewhere to stay and pay for it, I don't know what we would have done. Slept in Dunnes' doorway, most likely.'

He stopped bouncing and looked around the apartment with its parquet flooring and glass-topped coffee table and its abstract print on the wall.

'Even so, love, I wasn't expecting a penthouse at Lancaster Gate. Do you have any idea what the rent is? One thousand nine hundred and fifty, every month. Every single month! I mean, Holy Saint Joseph and all the carpenters, that's nearly twice my pension.'

Grainne came away from the window and sat down on the couch next to him. Her white hair was fastened in a complicated bun and she was wearing a black ankle-length dress with wide sleeves. Declan called it her 'funeral outfit'.

'I'm still scared sideways, though,' she told him. 'Look what happened to poor Ronan and Shanessa and their two wains, and they'd moved down to Riverstick in case someone tried to blow up their house in Rochestown. How in God's name did the bombers know where they'd gone to?'

'I haven't a bull's notion,' said Declan. 'Maybe they followed them down there, the bombers, do you know what I mean? But I can't see how anyone can find out that we've moved here. Only the guards know, apart from Redmond and Fergal. And I can't see how anyone could plant a bomb up here in the penthouse. Nobody can get in here without buzzing the buzzer from downstairs, can they? And we've not had any suspicious packages delivered. Air fryers the guards told us to watch out for, didn't they, and microwaves. If anyone tries to deliver anything like that, we'll tell them what they can do with it.'

'I don't know,' said Grainne. 'I can't stop seeing their faces in front of me, all those dear beloved friends we've lost. Derry and Fidelma and Brendan and Tommy and Bridget and Nessa and Bryan and now Ronan and Shanessa. I mean, we're family, aren't we, the Dripsey Dozen, and what have we ever done to deserve to be murdered, like, do you know? We've only been keeping the flame burning so that nobody ever forgets the Dripsey Ambush. It gives me such a terrible sickness in my stomach.'

'Well, I know you've been off your scran since all this bombing started. But you really should eat something, love. You need to keep your strength up. You don't want the bombers to kill you of starvation, even if they can't blow you up.'

Grainne gave Declan a slap on the arm. 'You have a twisted mind, do you know that?'

Declan stood up. 'Talking of food, I had no breakfast, did I?

How about I heat up a couple of those beef and Beamish pies? I could eat a nun's arse through a convent gate.'

'Not for me, thanks, and you know my cousin Rose is a Poor Clare so I wish you wouldn't say that,' Grainne admonished him. 'I might have some of that lentil soup later. This has all been too stressful, and I think I left my reading glasses in the bedroom at home.'

Declan went into the kitchen, with its shiny cream appliances and its black granite worktops. They had visited the English Market before they came here, and stocked up with everything they needed for the next few days, tea and bread and apples and milk. Declan rummaged in the shopping bag until he found the pies, and then he switched on the oven.

The explosion was devastating. It ripped the flesh off Declan's skeleton into bloody tatters and demolished half of the kitchen wall. Grainne had been rising off the couch to come into the kitchen and help Declan to empty the shopping bag. She was blasted through the glass door that gave out on to the balcony and into the air, high up over the river, her arms spread wide like a great black crow.

Passers-by who were walking along Lancaster Quay looked up in shock when they heard the bang. They saw Grainne tumbling out of the sky in a cloud of glittering glass fragments and dropping into the water with a sound like a sharp slap. Dense black smoke was billowing out of the penthouse apartment, with licks of orange flame.

A man who had been rowing along the river in a kayak turned around and paddled frantically to the spot where Grainne had fallen. As he reached it she rose up to the surface, face down, her black dress floating around her. He managed to reach over the side of his kayak and roll her over, but she was staring blindly at nothing at all, and it was obvious that she was dead.

All he could do was shout out to the people who were beginning to gather by the railings, 'She's gone!'

He started to paddle to the bushes that lined the riverbank, dragging her along with him. Two young men climbed over the railings to beat their way through the shrubbery and lift her out of the water.

Meanwhile, the sound of fire-engine sirens could already be heard from the direction of Anglesea Street, and ambulance sirens from the station on Kinsale Road.

Katie was pulling on her boots to take the dogs for a walk when her phone played 'The Parting Glass'.

It was Sergeant Murphy. 'I don't have much detail yet, ma'am, but there's been another bombing. Yes, and it's two more Dripseys, so far as I know. Declan and Grainne O'Brien.'

'Holy Mother. When did this happen?'

'Less than half an hour ago. But the thing is, they weren't bombed at home. They live in Carrigaline, but just to be safe they'd moved themselves into a top-floor apartment at Lancaster Gate. You know, down along the Western Road.'

'So they weren't even in their own house? That's the same as the Dohertys. They'd gone to stay with Ronan Doherty's sister in Riverstick, hadn't they, in case they were bombed?'

'From all the reports that I've seen coming in, the blast was humongous. Their apartment at Lancaster Gate was totally wrecked. Liam Coughlan said that Declan O'Brien was in more bits than a jigsaw, and would you believe that Mrs O'Brien was blown clear out of the window and into the river.'

'Jesus. I'm sure it'll all be on the news tonight. But the

Dripsey Dozen's new locations – or what's left of the Dripsey Dozen – they're supposed to be completely confidential, aren't they?'

'I reckon there's a leak somewhere,' said Sergeant Murphy. 'But listen, I have to go. I'll let you know if anything new comes up.'

'Thanks a million, Peter. You'll have your reward in Heaven, or in El Fenix bar, anyhow.'

She was tempted to take off her boots and go back into the living room to switch on the television news, but she knew there was nothing she could do until she was given a full forensic report on how the O'Briens had been bombed. Even then she would be limited in what action she could take, unless Frank Magorian called her and told her that she had finally had her suspension lifted. Besides, Barney and Foltchain and Harvey were gathered together by the front door, their tongues hanging out, panting to be taken for their walk.

Katie knocked on Kyna's bedroom door. 'Kyna? Are you coming out for a scove?'

'No, thanks, Katie. I think I'll just stay here feeling sorry for myself.'

Katie opened the door. Kyna was sitting on the end of her unmade bed, her hair tangled and her eyes red from crying.

'Come on, girl. The fresh air will do you the world of good.'

'I'm surprised you even want to talk to me.'

'Kyna, what's for you won't go by you. We all have to float on.'

'You're only trying to stop me feeling guilty, aren't you? But I can guess how much you're hurting inside.'

Katie paused for a moment, and then she said, 'All right. It wasn't raining when I was driving back from the city, but I admit that my eyes needed windscreen wipers.'

Kyna stood up, came up to Katie and put her arms around her. She kissed her lightly on the cheek and said, 'Sure, I'll come for a scove with you. All the fresh air in the world won't stop me from blaming myself but if it makes you feel better. Have you heard any more about that bombing? I thought you might have gone to see it for yourself.'

'No. There isn't much I could do there, sweetheart, even if I did go. Terry O'Sullivan and Bill Phinner will feed me all the gory details, as and when they get them. Also, I think the media have got wind of the bad feeling between me and Micheál ó Broin and I don't want to put his back up too much. It won't do either of us any good. Besides, if I get the call this afternoon that they've lifted my suspension, I can go back to Anglesea Street and take charge of this bombing investigation from the top.'

'It gives me the shivers, though. If it hadn't been for Harvey, *you* could have been blown up too. Did you know them at all, those two who were killed?'

'I met Grainne O'Brien once, at ChildVision, where they were holding a fundraising sale for blind children. The reason I remember her is because she gave such a moving speech that everybody was in floods. It's tragic.'

'That's why I don't agree with you when you say "what's for you won't go by you". You escaped but she was killed, and what had she done? Nothing at all, except to honour the memory of five men who didn't deserve to be killed either.'

'Well, there's a bit more to it than that,' said Katie. 'There's some people in this world who are bitter, through and through. They can never forgive, not ever, and they can never forget.'

'I hope to God that your Kieran's not like that.'

'We'll have to wait and see, won't we?'

Katie gave Kyna a hug and then called out to Barney and

Foltchain and Harvey, 'It's all right, you three scruffs! We're coming!'

They left the house and walked all the way down to Richie's Steps, overlooking the harbour. A stiff southerly wind was blowing, which ruffled the surface of the water and blew the seagulls around like scraps of paper.

'Do you think you'll hear from Kieran?' asked Kyna. 'He does love you, you know. He was mad for you to marry him. I'm sure that once he's over the shock, he's bound to come round.'

'I don't know, Kyna. But sometimes it feels like there's two of me. One of me feels like my heart's been torn apart, but the other me feels like I might have had a lucky escape.'

Kyna turned her face towards the wind. 'I'm the last person to tell you which one of you is right. I've never been able to understand what men want out of women, apart from their loolahs. I don't think that men understand themselves what they want, or what women could give them. Otherwise they wouldn't leave them for hours on end, would they, and go off to play golf. My friend Maolisa used to say that it was like they were sneaking off to pleasure themselves with a bent stick.'

In spite of herself, in spite of her pain, Katie shook her head and couldn't stop smiling.

At five minutes past five, the call came at last from Frank Magorian.

Katie was watching a live news broadcast from Lancaster Gate, which was still cordoned off and surrounded by fire engines and bomb disposal vans and Garda patrol cars. Even from a distance it was possible to see the blackened hole where the penthouse apartment had been, with all its windows blown out and its concrete balcony hanging down over the windows of the apartment below.

Her phone played 'The Parting Glass' and Katie picked it up, although she was still watching the television. She could see Micheál ó Broin standing in the background, waiting to make a statement. She wanted to hear him explain how a couple who had been moved away from their own house in case they were bombed had been blown up on the same day in the so-called safe haven that had been found for them.

'Kathleen? It's Frank. I expect you have your eye on the news. This latest bombing, God in Heaven. Are they not going to stop until every one of the Dripsey Dozen have been killed?'

'I'm praying that this is the last, sir. I'm finding it fierce hard to understand why we haven't yet been able to arrest even one suspect. You keep telling me what a fine detective Micheál is, but if you ask me he couldn't find a piglet if it was hiding down his own trousers.'

'Now then, Kathleen. Let's not be derogatory about our fellow officers. But you'll be happy to hear that you'll soon be in charge of finding and arresting the suspects yourself. Pat Devain called me not five minutes ago to tell me that Chief Superintendent Griffin has evaluated the report from the Discipline Section and has finally agreed to lift your suspension.'

'Thank the Lord. Those are the words I've been waiting to hear for too long.'

'The officers looking into your case carefully considered all the circumstances surrounding the shooting of Thomas O'Flynn and Barry Riordan. Both Muireann Nic Riada and Megan Riordan pleaded guilty, and the only way in which you could have prevented the two men from being shot would have been to shoot the two women instead. In the light of that, their decision was that you found yourself in an almost impossible situation and took the most reasonable course of action.'

'Did they have anything to say about my shooting the fellow who tried to kill Micheál?'

'It's mandatory to give an armed suspect a warning before opening fire. But that presupposes that you're given enough time. This was a sudden and unexpected attack and your response was both prompt and appropriate.'

'I hardly know what to say, sir. What happens next? When can I return to Anglesea Street?'

'Micheál's out at Lancaster Gate at the moment, but as soon as he comes back I'll be advising him that your suspension has been lifted. You can start first thing tomorrow morning if you like. You and Micheál will need two or three days working in parallel, as it were, so that he can get you up to speed on all the investigations that he's been handling. Then you'll be back in your office once again and I presume that he'll be returning to Limerick.'

'As it happens, I'm watching Micheál right this minute on the news. I only wish I could phone him and tell him right now. I'd love to be able to see his expression.'

'Now then, Kathleen. An Garda Síochána was created to hand out justice, not vengeance.'

'Yes, sir. But there are times when it's a pleasure to see somebody thrun on the bed that they've made for themselves.'

'I'll see you tomorrow,' said Frank Magorian, and she could tell by his tone of voice that he was smiling.

Because she had been talking on the phone, Katie had missed the beginning of Micheál's statement, but she was able to hear him saying, '—we've been doing everything in our power to keep the Dripsey relatives safe from harm, believe me. Yet the last two bombings took place even after we had made sure that the victims had moved to new locations, and these locations were supposed to be confidential. Because of that, we have a strong suspicion that someone has been surreptitiously passing the details of these locations to the bombers.'

'Do you have any notion at all who this "someone" might be?' asked Dinny O'Rourke from the *Echo*.

'We have some possible leads, yes,' said Micheál. 'Right now, I can't tell you any more than that.'

'Could it be one of the Dripsey Dozen themselves, DS ó Broin? One who might be holding a grudge for some reason against the others?'

'Like I say, Dinny, that's all I can tell you for now. I'm waiting on developments myself.'

Katie watched with grim satisfaction as Micheál returned to his car and drove off. Within less than twenty minutes he would be told by Frank Magorian that his time as acting detective superintendent at Anglesea Street was over. She knew that when he returned to Limerick he would be exposed to greater danger from the Rathkeale gang and other criminals, but she found it hard to feel much sympathy for him after he had treated her with such contempt. If he had been less dismissive of her intuition and not so reliant on his own dogged procedure, it was possible that the lives of at least some of the Dripsey Dozen could have been saved.

Kyna came into the living room. 'Would you take a cup of coffee?'

'No, no thanks. Maybe a treble vodka and tonic.'

'You have a queer look on you, if you don't mind my saying so. Who was that on the phone?'

'Frank Magorian. To be honest with you, I don't know whether to laugh or cry. My suspension's been lifted and I'll be going back to Anglesea Street tomorrow.'

'Oh, Katie, that's brilliant!' said Kyna. She sat down on the couch beside her and gave her a hug and a kiss. 'You never deserved to be suspended, you know that. But why would you cry?'

'Because of Kieran. It gives me one more reason to stay here in Cork when he goes back to Dublin. I feel like fate's making up my own mind for me. Fate with a capital "F".'

'But surely you could arrange for a transfer to Phoenix Park in Dublin, couldn't you?'

'What's the point, if he doesn't want to marry me any more? He doesn't even want to speak to me, for God's sake, let alone walk down the aisle with me and put a ring on my finger.'

'He'll get over it, I'm certain he will. He'd best get over it, anyhow, or else I'm going to spend the rest of my life feeling mortified for wrecking yours.'

Katie's eyes were suddenly brimming with tears. 'I was even hoping that we might have a child together. A little boy, like Seamus. Of course he could never replace Seamus, but he could play with Seamus's toys and sleep in his crib and I'm sure that Seamus would look down from Heaven and be happy for him.'

'You should try calling Kieran again.'

'I have, three times. He didn't pick up.'

'Then text him, or send him an email. Tell him that there's only one love in your life, and that's him.'

Katie took hold of Kyna's hands and clung on to them tightly, as if she were trying to save herself from falling backwards off the top of a ten-storey building. *If only that were true*, she thought, but she didn't say it out loud.

22

Detective Garda Kevyn Hickey called Katie later that evening. He had heard that her suspension had been lifted and that tomorrow she would be back at the station.

'Congratulations, first of all, ma'am. But what about our operation at Extreme Dreams? Will that mean we have to postpone it? You'll be up the walls, surely.'

'No, Kevyn. I still want us to go ahead with it. I promised Conor Mullan's wife that I'd find out who was responsible for blackmailing him, and make sure that they were arrested, and I intend to do just that. Apart from anything else, we owe it to him, or to his memory at least. His funeral's on Sunday. I don't want to be standing over his grave thinking that we haven't done everything we possibly could to punish the woman who led him to take his own life.'

'Fair play to you, ma'am. I'll see you tomorrow then. Or "Sean Delaney" will, anyhow.'

Katie and Kyna ate a light supper of cheese omelettes and salad, their plates on their laps, watching *First Dates Ireland*. One of the contestants was a thirty-one-year-old garda from Mayo and even Kyna had to admit that he was attractive.

'Pity about his accent, though.'

'Ah, shtop,' Katie teased her. 'Hish accent wouldn't worry you for a shecond if you were kishing him.'

Kyna smiled. 'At least you're feeling a dooshie bit more cheerful.'

But after Kyna had showered and retired to her bedroom, Katie went into her own bedroom and picked up her phone. She sat on the end of the bed, holding the phone in her hand for more than half a minute before she eventually decided to prod out Kieran's number.

To her surprise, it rang only five times before he picked up.

'Katie,' he said. His tone was totally flat.

'Kieran, we need to talk. You must have seen the texts I've been sending you. We can't let it end like this. I love you.'

'I know,' said Kieran, clearing his throat. 'And you know that I love you, too. But it's never going to work. You have natural urges inside you that you can't control, and that's always going to mean that I can't trust you to be faithful.'

'Kieran, I swear to you that I *can* control them. And there's something else. Frank Magorian told me today that my suspension has been lifted. I'll be able to go back to Anglesea Street tomorrow.'

'I'm very pleased for you. You deserve it.'

'But listen to me. I'm completely prepared to give it all up and not go back at all, so that I can come to Dublin with you. I can be your wife, Kieran. I can make a fresh start altogether.'

There was a long silence. Katie was afraid for a moment that Kieran had simply hung up.

'Kieran?'

'I'm sorry, Katie. You could give up your job, but it couldn't last. It was tragic that I caught you the way I did, but at least it saved me from entering into a marriage with a woman who could never be altogether mine. It's happened to me before, for a different reason, but I don't want to go through all that pain a second time.'

'Kieran, from the moment I say "I do", I promise you that I'll be yours and yours alone.'

'I wish I could believe you, Katie, but I can't. Imagine how *you* would have felt if you had come home and surprised me in bed with another man, *in flagrante*.'

Katie was crying now. 'I'd forgive you, if I found you like that. We're all complicated human beings, and we all make mistakes. I love you, can't you understand that?'

'I do, Katie. And the feeling is mutual. But I should have realized from the day I took you to visit Kyna at the hospital that there was no hope for us being happily married. I shouldn't have allowed myself to get carried away. I've only ended up hurting us both.'

Katie was about to answer him, but she opened and closed her mouth and said nothing. Over the years she had interviewed murderers and frauds and thieves and drug-dealers, and she could tell when a man was never going to change his mind, no matter how much the evidence was stacked against him.

'I'm sorry,' Kieran told her. 'I'm truly, truly sorry.'

'Are you?' Katie retorted. 'I don't think you've ever been sorry for anything. I don't think you could have been, because it sounds like you've never really been in love. Love isn't ownership, Kieran. You talked about me being altogether yours, and right from the very moment you proposed you started calling me Mrs Connolly.'

'Well, if that's the way you feel, it looks like you never will be, doesn't it?'

Without giving her the opportunity to reply, Kieran hung up. Katie stared at her phone for a moment, tempted to ring him back, but she knew in her heart that it was all over.

She heard tapping at her door.

'Is everything all right?' Kyna asked her.

'You can come in if you like,' said Katie.

Kyna opened the door and came in, holding a glass of water. 'I was passing on my way to the kitchen and I heard you on the phone. Was that Kieran you were talking to?'

Katie nodded, and tossed her phone on to the bed. 'Let's just say that it's a good thing I haven't been along to Diamond Bridal yet to order my wedding dress.'

The next morning, Katie went up first to Frank Magorian's office. Over the years she had confronted some of the most venomous criminals in Cork, and yet for some reason she felt nervous about facing Micheál ó Broin.

Frank Magorian was standing by the window, drinking a cup of coffee.

'Ah,' he said, when Katie knocked and came in. 'You're all ready to take up the reins again?'

'I can't wait. How did Micheál take it when you told him that I'd been reinstated?'

'It seemed like he was expecting it. All he said was "oh", and then he asked when you'd be coming in, that's all.'

'Serious? I thought he might be more upset.'

'Well, let's go down and see if he's really philosophical about it. By the way, take a sconce at all those hooded crows sitting on top of that roof over there. That's supposed to be some kind of bad omen, isn't it?'

Katie looked out of the window. She had seen these hooded crows gathering like this before. This morning there must have been at least a dozen of them perched along the roof ridge. She was not superstitious, but almost every time they had settled on the rooftop opposite the Garda station, something disastrous had happened, such as one of her detectives losing his life.

She said nothing, but she hoped that if they were a bad omen, these hooded crows, that they were a bad omen for Micheál and not for her.

They went downstairs together to Micheál's office. Katie's PA, Moirin, saw them through her open door and gave Katie a happy little wave. Katie waved back.

Micheál was sitting at his desk with a smouldering cigarette in the ashtray beside him, talking on his phone. When Katie and Frank Magorian came in, he said, 'Okay, Pat, that's grand altogether. Listen – I have to go for now. I'll call you after,' and at the same time he crushed out the cigarette. Then he stood up, pushing back his chair and greeting Katie and Frank Magorian with a strange self-satisfied smile. There was a glitter in his eyes that made him look even more witch-like than usual.

'Good morning to you, Micheál,' said Frank Magorian. 'Terry O'Sullivan should be joining us shortly, so that the two of you can bring Kathleen up to date on all your current cases. Including these terrible bombings.'

'Yes, these *terrible* bombings,' said Micheál, still smiling that eerie smile, and there was an intonation in his voice that made Katie think that he had repeated those words for a very specific reason. If she had been asked to describe it, she would have called it 'triumphant'.

'How about that Lancaster Gate bombing?' asked Frank Magorian. 'Have we made any progress with that yet?'

'Maybe you should ask Kathleen,' said Micheál.

'I'm sorry,' said Katie. 'What exactly do you mean by that?'

'I might as well tell you straight out what I've discovered,'

Micheál replied, keeping his eyes on Frank Magorian and not once looking at Katie. 'I'm afraid that when the Discipline Section are informed about it, they may sadly decide to postpone Kathleen's return to this office. In fact, they may decide to take even more drastic steps and cancel her reinstatement altogether, although whatever they choose to do of course is entirely up to them.'

'What in the name of God are you talking about?' Katie demanded. 'What have you discovered?'

'Yes, what exactly?' asked Frank Magorian.

'You should know, Kathleen,' Micheál continued, still without looking at her. 'Yesterday evening, after Assistant Commissioner Magorian told me that your suspension had been lifted, I asked Moirin to give me access to all your previous emails. I wanted only to make sure that I hadn't missed any critical details in those investigations that I inherited from you, and which are still ongoing – like, for instance, the Deeley-Gavigan protection racket or all that immigrant smuggling through Harty's Quay.

'I blame myself entirely. I should have looked through your emails earlier, although I hadn't thought that it was necessary before. If I had, God help me, I would have found out what I found out yesterday evening, and we could have been saved a whole rake of death and destruction.'

'Go on,' said Frank Magorian coldly. 'Don't keep us in suspense.'

'I checked your deleted emails as well as those that you'd saved. And would you believe it, I came across a message that you'd sent to Rayland Garvey.'

'Rayland Garvey? Are you mental? Why would I ever send an email to Rayland Garvey?'

'You're not talking about DI Garvey?' asked Frank

Magorian. 'He was sacked years ago. If he hadn't managed to sneak out of the country, he was going to be charged with corruption and extortion and gun-running and who knows what else. Jesus – he was more of a pooka than a police officer.'

'I never sent any message to Rayland Garvey,' said Katie. 'Why would I?'

'Do you want me to show it to you?'

'You're off your head. I knew Rayland, of course I did. But once he was gone, I never heard from him again, and why would I? And why would I send him an email?'

'For money? From what you said in that email, it was obvious that he was going to pay you, and pay you well.'

'I'm not going to listen to this,' Katie snapped at him. 'This is pure invention, and malicious invention at that.'

'Not half as malicious as what you were up to,' said Micheál. He sat down again, and tapped with two fingers at the keyboard of his desktop computer. While he did so, Katie looked across at Frank Magorian and shook her head in complete bewilderment. Frank Magorian looked back at her and shrugged.

Katie wondered if it was sheer coincidence that she had come across Rayland Garvey in the The Huntsman pub in Erdington, or if there was some inexplicable connection. After all, she had neither seen him nor heard anything about him for well over five years.

Micheál turned his computer around so that Katie could see the screen. Frank Magorian came up closer, too, so that he could read the email on it.

Hi Rayland. Herewith all the names and addresses from our file on the DD. Looking forward to your generosity! X K.

A PDF was attached, and when Micheál opened it, Katie saw a list of all the members of the Dripsey Dozen. It started with Brendan McCarthy of Merrion Court, Montenotte, and ran down through Derry O'Brien of Ballincollie Road and Thomas O'Mahony of Berrings and all the other descendants of the five men who had been executed for their part in the Dripsey Ambush – those who had already been bombed and those who were still alive.

'This is a fake,' said Katie. 'This is a complete and utter fake.'

Micheál turned his computer back around. 'I found it in the recoverable items folder and it looks genuine enough to me. Look – you can scroll down and there's several other deleted emails of yours. So it must be genuine.'

He sat back, lacing his fingers together.

'Are you seriously trying to suggest that I would sell a list of potential victims to one of the most corrupt and devious men that I have ever come across?' Katie asked him. She was trying to stay calm, but she felt as if a wet ice cube were sliding all the way down her spine, and her throat was tight. 'So what about the last two bombings, the Dohertys and the O'Briens? Those were carried out at different addresses, weren't they? How could Rayland Garvey have found out where those victims had moved to?'

'Who knows?' said Micheál. 'Maybe *you* told him.'

'Oh yes? And how did I know where they'd gone?'

'Don't ask me. Maybe we have a grass somewhere in the station, and they tipped you off. There's no telling what people will do for a little remuneration.'

'This is insanity, sir,' said Katie. 'How can I be expected to work with a man who's making fairy-tale accusations against me like this? If anyone's a pooka, he is.'

'I'm sorry, Kathleen,' said Frank Magorian. 'This has put me in a fierce awkward situation. I can't really allow you to return to the station until this email has been looked into. I can't imagine myself that you really sent it, but I'll have to notify Internal Affairs.'

Katie turned to Micheál. 'Are you satisfied? Are you listening to me? I said, are you satisfied?'

Micheál looked past her at Frank Magorian and gave a troubled little shake of his head, as if to say, *women, they shouldn't promote them, it only causes ructions for everybody.*

'Right, that's it,' Katie snapped at them. 'I'm leaving, and I'm not coming back until you've sorted this out. I don't know how this email was added to my station account, but someone must have hacked into it. It's a fake and a forgery.'

She stalked out of the office that had once been hers, leaving the door open behind her. She was so angry that she couldn't even wave goodbye to Moirin.

Before she left the station, she found Detective Garda Hickey in the canteen. He was having a late breakfast or an early lunch, rashers and eggs and sausages and Clonakilty black pudding.

'Don't get up, Kevyn,' she said, as he started to stand.

'Well, welcome back, ma'am,' he told her. 'Maybe life is going to get back to normal now. We can go back to hauling in scumbags whenever we're suspicious of them, and stop worrying that we might be infringing their rights.'

He prodded at one of his sausages. 'Would you believe we have a fellow in custody who bit his wife's breast but DS ó Broin said that our evidence of his toothmarks won't be admissible because we didn't have his teeth examined by a qualified dentist.'

'I'm sorry to say that life won't be getting back to what you call "normal", not just yet,' said Katie. 'There's been a hitch in my reinstatement.'

'You're joking, aren't you? What's wrong?'

'I can't tell you what the problem is exactly. An accusation has been made against me but it's such a joke that Brendan O'Carroll would probably want to steal it for *Mrs Brown*. I'm confident that I'll be able to return to duty very soon, but it won't be today.'

Kevyn looked at Katie intently. 'You're raging, aren't you, ma'am?'

'You're a good judge of mood, Kevyn. I'm trying not to be up to high doh about it, but this accusation is so nonsensical that I simply can't help it. Look, anyway, don't let me keep you from your breakfast or your dinner, whichever it is. I'll be outside the front of the station at two-thirty, like I promised.'

'Do you think I'm dressed for the part? I think this corduroy jacket makes me look like a bit of a masochist.'

'It's perfect,' Katie reassured him. 'You're looking like a genuine masochist while I'm only feeling like one. I'll see you later so.'

23

At ten minutes to three, Katie parked opposite the Abhaile ó Bhaile Hotel. A soft rain was falling so that she kept her windscreen wipers working with a monotonous squeak.

'Are you nervous?' she asked Kevyn.

'Oh, not at all. I can't wait to tell a whole bunch of sadists that I don't really fancy being whipped after all.'

'You have your pen?'

Kevyn took the black pen out of the pocket of his corduroy jacket and held it up. Although it looked like a pen and could actually be used to write notes, it was a voice-activated microphone with twenty hours of recording time. Katie had used one several times before, most successfully when she had arrested a South Mall lawyer for perjury in a complicated fraud trial.

'If you can wangle an admission out of Sabrina that she blackmailed DS Mullan, you'll be a hero, and I'll make sure that you get commended for it. But even if you can only record her blackmailing you, that'll be more than enough to have her hauled in.'

Kevyn crossed himself and said, 'All right then, ma'am. Here goes nothing!'

He climbed out of the car, hurried across Leopold Street and entered the musty hotel lobby, with its suffocating smell of stale cigarettes and cheap perfume. John Quinn was standing behind the reception desk, his pen poised, frowning down at the *Examiner* crossword as if every clue were a personal insult. Eventually, he looked up and said, 'Help you?'

'I've an appointment, like,' said Kevyn.

'Ah. An appointment.'

'Yes. With Sabrina.'

'In that case you'll be taking the lift up to the second floor, turning right and then left and it's the door at the end of the corridor. *Bain sult!*'

Kevyn stepped into the old-fashioned lift with its collapsible gates. He inspected himself in the mottled mirror at the back of the lift as it whined unsteadily upwards, and he couldn't help thinking that he made a very believable masochist. Apart from his corduroy jacket, he had brushed his hair forward into a fringe and loosened his tie and adopted a round-shouldered posture so that he looked like a man who spends his whole life feeling humiliated, and actually enjoying it, because he knows that he will never achieve any kind of success or attract any pretty young women.

He walked along the second-floor corridor with its threadbare carpet, turned left and then knocked at the door at the end. The door was opened instantly, and there stood a bosomy redheaded woman in a turquoise satin blouse and black tights. Her arms were thrown wide to greet him, as if he were a dear friend she hadn't seen for decades. Apart from her sticky crimson lipstick and all the gold chains around her neck, Kevyn couldn't help thinking how much she resembled Katie.

'Sean! Welcome, welcome, welcome to Extreme Dreams! Come in, my darling, and meet your new masters and mistresses!'

Kevyn stepped cautiously in through the door and found

himself in the living room of a shabby hotel suite. Its walls were painted sea-green, although the ceiling was yellow from years of nicotine. It was furnished with two sagging sofas, both upholstered in dark-green velvet, and two overstuffed armchairs. Its window overlooked Leopold Street, so Kevyn knew that if he looked out he would be able to see Katie's car.

'Ladies! Gentlemen!' called out Sabrina, in a throaty whoop. 'Come out and meet your new slave, Sean!'

The bedroom door had been slightly ajar, but now it was opened wide. First of all, out came a short well-built woman with cropped blonde hair. She was wearing a tight black corset with her breasts almost spilling over the top like the foam from a glass of Murphy's, as well as black fishnet stockings and suspenders and stiletto-heeled shoes.

She was followed by a tall lanky girl whose head was completely covered in a black latex fetish mask with a zipper across her mouth. Her small uptilted breasts were bare, with pale pink nipples, but she was wearing black high-waisted control knickers and thigh-length black latex boots. She was carrying a braided leather whip.

Behind her came a muscular man with a shaved head and a beard and a hairy chest. Kevyn thought he looked Greek or Turkish. He was wearing only a pair of shiny black latex underpants, and boots with no laces in them, and in one hand he was carrying a wooden paddle, which he was repeatedly smacking into the palm of his other hand.

Another man brought up the rear. He was bulky rather than muscular, and although the top of his head was shaved in a circle, he had greasy shoulder-length curls and a face like a pug dog. He reminded Kevyn of the porn star Ron Jeremy. He was wearing a grubby white flannel bathrobe with a studded leather belt around his waist, and Kevyn guessed that he was naked underneath it. Most disturbingly, he was holding a cat-o'-nine-tails, which he was swishing around in the air as if he could hardly wait to start their whipping session.

'You can undress in the bedroom if you're shy,' smiled Sabrina. 'Or Mary and Neave will give you a helping hand if you're not. And we have handcuffs ready for you, and a dog-collar. And a king-size dildo. And, don't worry, a jar of Vaseline, too.'

The two women and the two men all crowded up close to Kevyn, so close that he could smell their perfume and their body odour. The short blonde woman tugged at the lapel of his corduroy jacket as if to straighten it for him before he went off to school, and in a grating voice the man in the grubby bathrobe said, 'What shall we call you, boy? Ma's Mope? Or Pooley Pants?'

Kevyn ignored him and looked across at Sabrina, who had sat down now on one of the sofas with her legs crossed and was lighting a cigarette.

'As it happens, I've changed my mind,' he said, very quietly, but firmly.

Sabrina almost choked, and coughed up smoke rings. 'What? What the feck are you talking about?'

'I've changed my mind. I don't want to be whipped. Not by this crowd of goms, anyhow.'

'Hey, who the feck are you calling goms, you fecking gom?' blustered the man in the grubby bathrobe.

Sabrina stood up. 'You're serious? You really don't want to be whipped?'

'How many times do I have to tell you?'

'Ah, but whether you get whipped or not, Sean, you still have to pay. I'll be needing seven hundred and eighty euros altogether. That's a hundred and ten each for your masters and your mistresses here, and ninety for the hotel suite, and two hundred and fifty cancellation fee.'

'I've already paid you two hundred and fifty.'

'That was the reservation fee.'

'Well, sorry, but that's all you're going to get out of me. I'm not going to pay you seven hundred and eighty euros for a service I never had, like, same as I wouldn't pay a restaurant for a meal I never ate. Besides, I don't have seven hundred and eighty euros. Not to spend on you and this collection of weirdos, anyhow.'

The man in the grubby bathrobe growled, 'Watch it, you gobshite—!' and the girl in the latex mask prodded Kevyn sharply in the hip with her whip handle. He took two steps back.

Sabrina was puffing quickly at her cigarette in a way that told Kevyn she was actually quite stressed. 'If you don't pay, I'm sure the Riverview Animal Hospital will be fierce interested to find out that you're in debt for such a large sum of money, and especially what it is that you owe it for.'

'Isn't that what they call blackmail?' said Kevyn. He was trying to sound as if Sabrina had really worried him, although in reality he was delighted that she had come out with her threat so soon, and that he had recorded it.

'Not paying your debts,' said Sabrina, 'that's what they call defaulting.'

'Well, for sure. But you wouldn't take me to court for not paying you, would you? Whereas I could report you to the guards for blackmailing me. Same as you blackmailed my friend Conor.'

'Conor? Conor who? I know dozens of Conors. I have no idea who or what the hell you're talking about.'

'Conor Mullan. He was a guard. A detective. And one of your clients.'

Sabrina stared at Kevyn as if she were trying to stop his heart.

'Come on, love, you must remember Conor Mullan,' Kevyn coaxed her.

But Sabrina didn't answer him. Instead, she turned to the man in the grubby bathrobe. 'Finn,' she said, 'give him what he's refusing to pay for. It's on the house.'

Katie looked at her watch. Kevyn had entered the Abhaile ó Bhaile Hotel over forty minutes ago, and she was beginning to wonder if she should go across and check up on him. If he had not yet managed to inveigle Sabrina into admitting that she had blackmailed DS Mullan, then what was he doing?

She had opened her car door, ready to climb out, when her phone rang. It was DI O'Sullivan, and he was sounding even more serious than usual.

'Frank Magorian's told me what happened when he took you back to your office. He can't believe it and neither can I, and neither can anyone else here at the station.'

'Terry, it's an obvious fake. Why in the world would I send all the details of the Dripsey Dozen to a shitehawk like Rayland Garvey? And of course I never did.'

'So how did that message turn up among your emails, that's what I'd like to know. I've seen it myself and it has all the appearance of being genuine.'

'I'll tell you what I believe. If Micheál didn't tamper with my emails himself, then he knew somebody or found somebody who could. It was my duty account, of course, so Moirin was probably happy to give him my password. She wouldn't have imagined for a moment that he was going to have it hacked into, and that he was trying to make it look like these bombings were all down to me.'

'I asked Micheál what possible motive you could have had,' Terry told her. 'I mean, you're not stupid. You would have guessed that Garvey intended to do them some kind of harm, even if you didn't realize that he was actually aiding and abetting someone who was out to have them all killed.'

'What did he say?'

'He suggested you did it because you were frustrated that your investigation into the Dripsey Dozen two years ago had come to nothing.'

'What? I was part of that investigation, sure, but I didn't head it up.'

'Maybe not. But Micheál said you were raging because you hadn't been able to find enough concrete evidence to prove that the Dripsey Dozen had been responsible for bombing The Huntsman pub. Either the current Dripseys, or their parents.'

'I was disappointed, for sure. But The Huntsman bombing was fifty years ago. It wasn't just a cold case, it was frozen solid, and the evidence simply wasn't there any more.'

'But Micheál said you never believe that hard evidence is necessary so long as you're sure that you're right. "That Maguire woman, she's her own judge and jury", those were his exact words, and you could have felt that the Dripseys deserved to be punished, even if it couldn't be proved beyond a reasonable doubt. Either that, or Rayland Garvey offered you a generous amount of money to send him their addresses. Or both.'

'Terry,' said Katie, 'you and I both know that Micheál would sell his mother if it saved him from having to go back to Henry Street. And I think I'm well paid enough not to be tempted by a bribe, even with three hungry dogs to take care of.'

'I'm pure sorry about this situation, anyhow,' said Terry. 'I know Frank Magorian is doing everything he can to get it straightened out. But the real reason I called you was because of that IED that was planted under your car.'

'Really? How's that going? Did Malloy and Murrish find out anything from that car hire company?'

'Yes, they did. That particular yellow Kuga was rented out to a fellow with a UK passport. His name was – hold on, I have it written down here. His name was Ronald Smith, and he gave his home address as Greenhill Road, Handsworth, near Birmingham. He told EconoCar that he was staying at the REZz hotel on MacCurtain Street, but when Murrish checked they told her that they had nobody of that name staying there.'

'The REZz? That's the hotel with the teeny-tiny rooms, isn't it? A bed and a shower and a toilet and that's about it. Maybe he checked in under a false name.'

'No. They said they had nobody staying there who answered his description. And they have no parking facility there, so they wouldn't have seen his car.'

'Does he still have the car?'

'Yes. He rented it for a whole month.'

'In that case, Sergeant Murphy can watch out for it from the communications room, can't he?'

'I've briefed him about it, and he's doing that already, but no luck so far.'

'What does DS ó Broin have to say about this, if anything?' asked Katie.

'He said not to waste too much time on it. He doesn't think the fellow in the baseball cap who was caught on CCTV on the N25 bears too much of a likeness to the fellow who was caught by your neighbour's doorbell camera.'

'He's joking, of course. Don't tell me that in Cobh at three o'clock in the morning two totally different men were both wearing baseball caps backwards.'

'Well, anyhow, ma'am, if and when we do find the fellow, we should be able to identify him. Bill Phinner tells me that they found numerous patent prints in the C-4 that was stuck underneath your car, and they managed to take high-res photographs of nearly all of them. They found traces of DNA too.'

'That's grand. Did he give you any idea when he might be fetching my car back?'

'I didn't ask him that, but I will.'

'Thanks for bringing me up to date, Terry. I appreciate it.'

'It's not a bother at all, ma'am. I can't tell you how much we were all looking forward to having you back in charge today, and I think you know it. Let's hope we can get this Rayland Garvey email business cleared up as soon as possible.'

'You and me both, Terry. Right now I could use some fierce complicated cases to concentrate on.'

'Is everything okay with you?' Terry asked her cautiously. 'It's none of my business, like, but I've heard some gossip, and if there's anything I can do to help.'

'Not unless you have a time machine, Terry, and you can take me back two days.'

By the time Katie had finished talking to DI O'Sullivan, almost an hour had passed since Kevyn had entered the Abhaile ó Bhaile Hotel. He had still not reappeared, and neither had he sent her any phone calls or text messages.

She was growing increasingly anxious. It could be that Kevyn was successfully stringing Sabrina along, and convincing her that he had simply changed his mind about being whipped. Maybe he was still arguing with her about paying her. If that were the case, she was reluctant to go into the hotel and interrupt him because that would reveal that his whipping session had been a sting from the start. On the other hand, she was concerned that he might be in some kind of trouble.

She decided to give him five more minutes, but then she saw two women coming out of the hotel, putting up an umbrella, and walking quickly away together in the direction of MacCurtain Street. Almost immediately afterwards, two men appeared, gave each other a high five, and went off in opposite directions.

Katie was now beginning to feel that something had gone badly wrong. She climbed out of her car into the drizzle and crossed over the road. She had taken the first step up to the hotel's front door when an ambulance turned the corner into Leopold Street with its blue lights flashing. It sped up to the hotel and slithered to a stop, and two paramedics jumped out, one of them carrying an EMS bag.

'Excuse us, love,' said one as they hurried up the steps, pushed open the doors and entered the hotel lobby.

Katie could see that John Quinn was standing inside, and that he had obviously been waiting for them. They conferred for a few moments, and then John Quinn led the paramedics to the lift. They closed the gates behind them and all three of them disappeared upwards.

Katie went inside. She stood alone in the musty lobby, and she could hear the lift whining and the gates clanking somewhere upstairs as they were opened again. She took out her phone and rang Sergeant Murphy at Anglesea Street.

'Peter? It's Superintendent Maguire. Have you received an emergency call from the Abhaile ó Bhaile Hotel on Leopold Street?'

'No, ma'am. Nothing like that at all.'

'Well, consider this to be one. I'm not sure exactly what's going on yet but there's an ambulance crew here already. I think something may have happened to Detective Garda Hickey.'

'Do you have any idea what?'

'No, although I hope to soon. Can you ask Inspector Walsh to send out a couple of officers urgent-like. And also inform DI O'Sullivan that we might have some kind of incident here.'

'You have it, ma'am, don't worry.'

Katie heard the lift whining down to the lobby again. When the gates clattered open, John Quinn appeared. He looked pale and badly shaken, and when he saw Katie waiting for him he gave an involuntary jerk with his left leg, as if he had stepped on a slug.

'Jesus, my nemesis,' he said. 'What are you doing here?'

'What's the story upstairs? Why is there an ambulance crew here?'

'There's been an accident.'

'What sort of an accident? Anything to do with Extreme Dreams?'

'I'm not saying,' John Quinn told her, lifting the flap of the reception counter.

'You don't have to say, but you do have to show me,' said Katie. 'Before you go sneaking off into your back room, I want you to take me up there.'

'And if I won't?'

'If you won't, I'll arrest you for obstructing a Garda officer in the course of her duty. Do you want a €500 fine or six months in prison, or both?'

'All right. But don't expect me to take another look. It's grim, what's happened up there. I was close to gawking and it wouldn't surprise me if you feel the same.'

He led Katie to the lift and they went up together to the second floor, with him sniffing constantly all the way. Then he walked beside her along the corridor, but as soon as they reached the corner he stopped.

'That's it, that's as far as I'm going, like, and if you want to fine me or lock me up because I won't take you any further then that's up to you.'

From where she was standing at the corner, Katie could see that the door to the suite at the end of the corridor was wide open. She could also see the back and the boots of one of the paramedics, so he must be kneeling down. She turned to John Quinn but she stayed tight-lipped, although her heart was thumping and she was breathing hard. She felt like ripping into him because he had encouraged Sabrina to hold her Extreme Dreams orgies here in his hotel, even though he was a former priest. But she would have to save her anger for later. Right now, she needed to see what had happened to Kevyn, and why he had failed to reappear or contact her.

She walked quickly along the corridor and into the suite. Both paramedics were on their knees, and one of them looked up and said, 'Hey, no, you can't come in here. This is an emergency.'

'I'm a senior Garda officer,' she told him. She tugged her ID card out of her coat pocket and held it up. 'Detective Superintendent Maguire. I'm looking for Detective Garda Kevyn Hickey.'

One of the paramedics stood up, and it was then that Katie

could see Kevyn lying face down on the floor. He was almost completely naked, with his trousers pulled right below his knees. His back and his buttocks were a ploughed-up mess of grisly flesh, and the carpet all around him was soaked in his blood.

Blood was splashed all over the sea-green walls, like poppies, and there was even a spattering of blood on the ceiling.

'Mother of God,' Katie whispered. 'Is he still alive? What's happened to him?'

'He's unconscious and he's lost a lot of blood,' the paramedic who was still kneeling told her. 'We're trying to stabilize him and then we'll take him straight to the ED.'

'It's almost certain he's been whipped,' said the other paramedic, a woman. 'See, look at these deep parallel lacerations all across his shoulders and his middle back? Only a whip could do that.'

She stepped back, so that Katie could see him more clearly. 'See here, he's been cut right through to his spine. You can actually see his vertebrae. I worked in South Africa once, and I treated patients who had been whipped with sjamboks, but I swear to God I never saw whippings as traumatic as this. Not ever.'

'Apart from blood loss, there's a serious risk of acute renal failure,' his companion put in. 'He'll most likely need haemodialysis, if he survives.'

Katie could see that Kevyn was trembling, and that his eyes were half open, even though he was unconscious.

She heard squeaking in the corridor, and a third paramedic appeared, pushing a trolley.

'Right,' said one of the paramedics, 'let's get him to the Uni, pronto.'

Between them, the paramedics lifted Kevyn on to the trolley, still face down, and covered his bloody back with a sterile cellophane wrap.

After they had wheeled him away, Katie remained in the suite, not only shocked but flooded with guilt. If only she hadn't persuaded Kevyn to pretend to be 'Sean Delaney', he would still be safe and well and back in his office at Anglesea Street. She prayed to the Blessed Virgin that he wouldn't die, and that his appalling wounds would heal, although there was no question that he would be scarred for life. She had realized that Sabrina was ruthless after the relentless demands she had made on Conor Mullan, but she could never have imagined that she would unleash such a vicious punishment on Kevyn.

She looked around. Kevyn's jacket, sweater and shirt had been tossed on to the floor behind the sofa. She picked up his jacket, and was relieved to find that his pen was still stuck in his breast pocket. Whatever had happened here, it would all have been recorded.

Extreme Dreams? she thought. I'll give you nightmares, Sabrina, and whoever whipped Kevyn like this. I'll give you nightmares you'll never forget.

24

Katie went back down to the lobby. As she stepped out of the lift, two uniformed gardaí were coming in through the front doors. John Quinn was still standing behind his reception desk, gnawing at one of his thumbnails, and he glanced across at her nervously, but said nothing.

'Superintendent Maguire,' said one of the gardaí, in surprise. 'I thought—?'

'What you thought doesn't matter right now,' Katie told him. 'Detective Hickey's been attacked and critically injured. Did you see the ambulance outside?'

'Sure, yes, we saw it shooting off, just as we arrived.'

'Put in a call to DI O'Sullivan. I believe he's already aware that we have an incident here. Tell him to send backup, urgent-like, and that we'll be needing forensics too.'

'How about DS ó Broin? He'll be wanting to be informed, won't he?'

'Never mind about DS ó Broin. I'll do that myself. Meanwhile, if can you cordon off the hotel entrance to make sure that nobody else enters.'

She went over to the reception desk. John Quinn stopped biting his thumbnail and stared at her through his rimless glasses, although they were reflecting the light from the open doors, so that he looked blind.

'I don't think I ever knew what it was like to be truly angry until now,' said Katie. 'What has happened here today is more than a tragedy. You disgust me, John. What you've regularly allowed to take place in this hotel disgusts me. Because of you, I've lost two of the best officers I've ever had the privilege to work with. One dead, by suicide, and the other so badly injured that he'll probably never be able to work again, even if he's lucky enough not to die.'

'How was I to know that he was a guard?' John Quinn retorted. 'Your man came in like every other gom and told me he had an appointment with Sabrina. It's not my place to make moral judgements. Only the Lord can do that.'

'It's not your place to run what amounts to a brothel, either. I'm going to make it my business to see that this hotel is closed down and that you receive the punishment you so richly deserve. Where's Sabrina now?'

'How should I know? She did a legger out through the back door. You'd have thought all the bats in hell were chasing after her.'

'I saw two women and two men leaving out the front. I'm assuming all four of them were hired by Sabrina. Do you know who they were?'

'I haven't a notion.'

'But they weren't guests here?'

'I've seen one of the women before. But no.'

'Do you have any guests staying here at the moment?'

John Quinn opened up the register on the counter in front of him. 'I have five altogether. Three for tonight only, two staying for the Jobs Expo on Saturday, and one till next Wednesday. I think he's a musician. He didn't say so, but he was toting one of them huge great double-bass cases that hardly fit into the lift, so that was kind of a giveaway.'

'Are any of your guests here now?'

'No, they all went out after breakfast. I don't expect to see them back until this evening.'

'What about cleaning staff? Are any of them still here?'

'No. The last one, Hinaya, she always leaves about two. She has to pick up her weans from low babies.'

'All right, John. You need to stay here, but don't you go back up to that room again. There's more officers on the way, as well as forensic technicians.'

John Quinn took off his glasses. 'I want you to know that I had nothing whatsoever to do with your man being beaten like that. Nothing like this has ever happened here before.'

'And nothing like this is ever going to happen here again,' Katie told him. 'You can bet your life on that.'

Ten minutes later four more uniformed gardaí arrived, followed only a few minutes later by Detective Sergeant Begley, as well as Detectives Malloy, Coughlan and Murrish.

'Kevyn Hickey's been assaulted, and he's in a serious state altogether,' Katie told them. 'He's been taken off to the ED at the University Hospital and by the looks of him it's touch and go, because he's lost so much blood.'

'Jesus,' said DS Begley. 'Where did this happen? Do you know who attacked him?'

'Second floor, end room on the right. And yes, I do know who's responsible, or at least who's mainly responsible. But look, here's DI O'Sullivan. I need to have a word with him first. Why don't you go up and have a sconce for yourselves?'

Terry O'Sullivan came across the lobby looking grim. He glanced across at John Quinn, but John Quinn turned away and disappeared into his office behind the counter, although he left the door ajar.

'What's the story, ma'am?' Terry asked Katie. 'Do I have to ask what you're doing here?'

'Come in here where it's quiet,' said Katie, and she led him through to the hotel's shabby dining room, with its dusty brown velveteen curtains and its view of the rainy street outside. On the wall hung a painting by Jessica Baron of an isolated thatched cottage in Kerry with the caption *Abhaile ó Bhaile*.

Katie pulled out a bentwood dining chair and sat down, and Terry sat down opposite her.

'I thought I was acting in the best interests of Conor Mullan and his dear wife, Maeve,' said Katie. 'She begged me to protect his reputation, for the sake of herself and their son but mostly for Conor's own honour. But for once I underestimated who I was dealing with. And I mean badly.'

As concisely as she could, she told Terry all about Extreme Dreams and how Sabrina had blackmailed Conor almost into bankruptcy, and that was why he had drowned himself. She explained how she had then come up with the idea of 'Sean Delaney' and how she believed that Detective Garda Hickey could trick Sabrina into confessing what she had done.

'But Holy Mother of God, why did I say that this Sean Delaney wanted to be whipped? It could have been any other perversion and it wouldn't have near killed him. But it was the first thing that came into my head.'

Terry picked up the cheap glass salt cellar on the table as if it were a chess piece and he was debating with himself how to play it.

'You'll be telling all this to Assistant Commissioner Magorian?'

'I'll have to. I'm not at all sure where I'll be standing in all this, legally. I don't know if it's going to affect my returning to duty. Like, it's already been delayed by Micheál ó Broin's false accusation that it was me who passed the addresses of the Dripsey Dozen to Rayland Garvey. I mean, what madness is that?'

'I'm not certain what your position is either, to be honest with you,' said Terry. 'There may be a case for misconduct, but technically you're no longer suspended, and I can't see that you've broken the law in any way. What Detective Garda Hickey volunteered to do, that wasn't strictly against the law, either. It was chancy all right, and it probably would have been more sensible to open a formal investigation against this Sabrina woman, but who knows? If we had done that, could we have found a way of proving that she was blackmailing DS Mullan?'

Katie held up the pen that she had taken from Kevyn's jacket. 'See this? With any luck, we'll have all the proof we need on here. And this Sabrina shouldn't be too difficult to track down.'

'You know what she looks like?'

'There's CCTV in the lobby, so she should be recorded on there, if it's working. But if not, she shouldn't be too difficult to find. I have her bank account details, and not only that, although I hate to say it, she's the bulb off me.'

Katie stayed at the Abhaile ó Bhaile Hotel while DI O'Sullivan and the other detectives questioned John Quinn and Bill Phinner's forensic technicians examined the room where Kevyn Hickey had been whipped.

She called Kyna to tell her what had happened and that she would probably be home quite late.

According to John Quinn, the CCTV camera in the lobby was 'awaiting repair', but there was another camera in the lift that was working, and the technicians were able to download footage from the past twelve hours.

It was dark and still raining by the time Katie and DI O'Sullivan drove to Anglesea Street. There, Katie went up to Frank Magorian's office. He had put on his raincoat and was about to leave for the day.

'I'm sorry, sir. But I expect you've heard that Kevyn Hickey's been assaulted and seriously injured. You need to know the full story.'

Frank Magorian put down his briefcase and took off his raincoat. Katie sat down in front of his desk and told him everything about her scheme with Detective Garda Hickey to inveigle Sabrina into incriminating herself.

When she had finished, Frank Magorian looked across at her and shook his head. 'To be honest with you, Kathleen, I don't know what in the world to think. I can understand you wanting to protect DS Mullan's reputation, but look at the consequences. You could almost say that two birds have been killed with the same stone. Although pray God that Kevyn Hickey pulls through.'

'I'll be giving a full statement to DI O'Sullivan, sir. And of course we'll be putting out descriptions of Sabrina and the four others who were involved, the men and the women. John Quinn gave us an address for Sabrina in Mayfield, although I doubt we'll find her there, even if it's genuine.'

'Sure, look, let's leave it there for now,' said Frank Magorian. 'I want you to know that I'll have to be sending off a report to the Data Protection Commissioner on Monday about that email you were supposed to have sent to Rayland Garvey. But I also want you to know that I find it pure hard to believe that you really sent him such a message. I've asked Sergeant Murphy if there's anyone down in communications who can check if it's authentic, and he tells me that they'll be able to do it within the next couple of days.'

'I've been trying myself to think who might have done it, and how it was done.'

'And do you have any ideas?'

'I do, yes, sir. But for now, I think it's best if I keep them to myself.'

She drove home through the rain, feeling exhausted. All the way back along the N25, another car was close up behind her, almost dazzling her with its headlights, and she was relieved when she turned off towards Fota Island and it kept on going along the parkway and disappeared into the darkness.

When she opened the front door at Carrig View, the dogs were all tail-wagging in the hallway, and from the kitchen came the smell of carrot and coriander soup. Kyna came out, wearing an apron and with her hair braided up.

'It's been on the news,' she told Katie, giving her a kiss and helping her to unbutton her coat. 'They didn't mention you, though.'

'Thank God for small mercies. I'm flahed out.'

She sat down in the living room. The news was still on, but they were reporting on a man who had been sent to prison for stealing two fifty-litre kegs of beer from outside the Welcome Inn pub in Cork city centre. He had pleaded that he had 'something of a problem' with alcohol.

Kyna brought Katie a vodka and tonic and sat down on the couch next to her.

'Have you heard any news about Kevyn? He's such a sweet feen, I'm praying that he recovers.'

'No. Nothing more, although Terry's promised to call me as soon as he knows anything. But Jesus, you should have seen the state of him. His back had been whipped all the way down to the bone.'

'That's heartbreaking, that really is. I hope we find the beasts who did it to him and lock them up for the rest of their lives.'

'Some hope. They'll probably plead insanity and get packed off to a comfortable room at the Carraig Mór.'

Kyna watched Katie sipping her drink for a while.

'What about this email that Micheál ó Broin claims that he's found? How can he seriously expect anybody to believe that you would have given the Dripsey Dozen's home addresses to a piece of shite like Rayland Garvey?'

'Maybe he couldn't think how else he could delay my return to Anglesea Street. In fact, he's delayed it already. If I can't disprove that I wrote to Rayland Garvey, it might even mean that I won't be allowed back at all, ever. Apart from being charged with misconduct in office, I might even be accused of aiding and abetting the worst series of homicides ever, in the whole history of Cork.'

'You know it's not true, though, and that you never sent such an email.'

'Of course I didn't. But I've seen it for myself, and it looks real enough. At least it seems to be the only evidence that Micheál has against me, God rot him.'

'I came up with an idea as soon as you called me about it,' said Kyna. 'About last April it was, I caught this young fellow for hacking into the accounts of shops in Cork and having them send him all manner of stuff like computers and TVs and even jewellery, all for free. Sergeant Murphy said he was one of the cleverest black-hat hackers he'd ever come across, and I have to confess that we caught him only by the sheerest accident. He came into Gentleman's Quarters to pick up a leather jacket that he'd ordered on a false account, and I was in there at the time.'

'I think I remember the case. What happened to him?'

'He was given two years suspended. But I was wondering if we might ask him to hack into your account and delete that email as if it never existed – erase any trace of it.'

'Surely I can simply delete it myself. Is that not good enough?'

'No, it won't be. If you delete an email it goes into a deleted items folder, doesn't it, and you can recover it up until thirty days afterwards. After that it's supposed to be automatically lost for ever, although there are still ways of finding it again. You can permanently delete it before the thirty days are up, but if you do that it's still held in a recoverable items folder, which is where Micheál ó Broin says he found yours. You have to purge it from there too. But even then you can find it, if you have the know-how. So what you need is to erase it beyond any recovery.'

'And you think this young fellow can do it?'

'If anyone can, I'm sure he can. You still have the password, after all, and now your suspension has been lifted you should be able to get access to your account again. Or *he* could, even if you can't.'

Katie stared at Kyna with disbelief that she could even consider hacking a Garda computer, but also with a measure of admiration. She had always been an unorthodox detective, and highly successful too.

'I can't see how that's doing wrong,' said Kyna. 'If you never sent it, then it never was, and it's not against the law to remove something that was never there in the first place.'

'That's making me almost as sneaky as Micheál,' said Katie. 'Talk about the dog calling the cat's behind hairy.'

'I still remember the young fellow's name, Dillan Plunkett. And it shouldn't be difficult to get in touch with him. His dad and mum run Plunkett's Chip Bar in Blackpool, and he lives with them over the shop.'

'Well, we have a little time,' said Katie. 'One of Bill Phinner's computer experts will be checking the email, apparently, but he won't be able to do that for a day or so, and Frank Magorian won't be reporting it to Internal Affairs until they're back in the office on Tuesday. And you're right. If it isn't there to be checked and it isn't there to be reported, there's nothing to stop me from being reinstated.'

She paused, and then she said, 'Only my own conscience.'

'So you don't want me to call Dillan Plunkett?'

'No, call him. See what he says. Although I feel like I'm entering the shady world of Garda corruption.'

Kyna picked up her phone, found the number of Plunkett's Chip Bar and called it. After more than half a minute, a woman answered, sounding flustered.

'Would Dillan be there, by any chance?' Kyna asked her.

'Dillan? He's out this evening and he won't be back till late. He's gone to Popscene so far as I know, and Popscene don't close till three or four, do they? Who wants him?'

'Kyna my name is. We met each other in the spring, like. You don't have his mobile number, do you? I did have it, but I lost it.'

'Hold on a couple of seconds.'

Kyna finger-waved to Katie and said, 'Pen,' and after

waiting for a moment she wrote a number down on the back of her hand.

'Thanks a million,' she said, and put down her phone. Then she looked steadily at Katie as if she were a doctor about to give her some bad news about her health.

'You're sure you want to go ahead with this? The way I see it, Katie, you don't have any choice. What if Sergeant Murphy's computer whizz examines that email and can't find any indication at all that it's a fake? Your career's going to end up in shreds. Worse than that, you could even end up being prosecuted. Even if you can prove that you had no idea at all what Rayland Garvey wanted those addresses for, you're going to have this hanging over your head for the rest of your life.'

'Let's talk to this Dillan Plunkett then. If he can erase that email without anyone finding out what he's been up to, then there's no harm done.'

'I was hoping you'd say that. I've ruined your life already, Katie. If there's anything I can do to make up for it, even in a small way.'

Katie put down her glass and reached over to give Kyna a hug. 'How many times do I have to tell you that what happened wasn't your fault? And I haven't given up on Kieran, not completely, not yet. I'm hoping he's beginning to miss me.'

Kyna tried calling Dillan Plunkett's mobile number but he didn't pick up. Either the retro music at Popscene was too loud and he was unable to hear his phone ringing, or he was too busy dancing.

'I'll try him again later. If not, I'll call him in the morning first thing. Can I fetch you some soup?'

'No, no thank you. Not yet, anyhow. I don't think I've ever had less of an appetite in my life.'

*

Kyna called Dillan Plunkett the next morning while she and Katie were drinking coffee and eating bowls of granola and blueberries in the kitchen.

He answered almost immediately, although he gave her a very weary sounding, 'Yeah? Who is this?'

'Dillan? I don't know if you remember me, but I was one of the detectives who caught you hacking Gentleman's Quarters and Castle Jewellers last year. Kyna Ní Nuallán.'

'Serious? What do you want now? I've done no hacking at all since then. I've found myself a job at PC Genius and I've been clean as a whistle, like, I swear it.'

'You're not in any trouble, Dillan. You probably won't believe this but we're looking for someone to help us with some hacking. Do you think we can come and talk to you about it? We'll make it worth your while.'

Kyna looked across at Katie for approval and Katie nodded, even though she felt that she was becoming entangled in a situation that was ethically dubious, to say the least. Despite that, she was convinced that Micheál had faked that email to keep her from returning to Anglesea Street, and her years of experience had taught her that the most effective way to deal with frauds was to play them at their own game and out-fraud them. It was just that she had never had to out-fraud a fellow Garda officer before now.

After they had finished their breakfast and taken the three dogs next door for Jenny to look after, Katie and Kyna drove into the city. They parked on Parnell Place, outside the wide frontage of PC Genius computer store. Dillan Plunkett was waiting for them in the back of the shop, a pale and skinny young man in his early twenties with a vertical shock of black hair, a large nose and deep-set near-together eyes.

Kyna introduced Katie to him. Then she nodded towards the shop's manager and said, 'Would your boss mind if we went to the pub next door for a few minutes, so that we can have a bit of a chat in private?'

Dillan went over to ask his manager, who said, 'Okay, we're quiet at the moment. But only something soft if you're having a drink.'

Coincidentally, the pub next door to PC Genius was the Welcome Inn, which had featured on the news last night because of the beer kegs that had been stolen from it. The three of them sat in a narrow booth by a stained-glass window and ordered two coffees and, for Dillan, a Lucozade Energy.

Katie said, 'I'm only going to tell you half the story, Dillan, because the rest of it is confidential. But I'm the detective superintendent at Anglesea Street and someone has criminally hacked into my working account. They've planted an email message in it that is intended to compromise my position there.'

Dillan stopped sucking at his Lucozade and blinked at her. 'What does that mean, like?'

'It means that there's another officer in the Garda who's allergic to her and he's trying to make her look bad so that she loses her job,' said Kyna. 'All we need you to do is hack into her account and purge that email so that nobody will know it was ever there. And make sure that the same person is blocked from doing it again.'

'I still have the password,' Katie told him. 'You won't have to be phishing for that, or however it is that you hack people's passwords.'

'I won't land myself in any kind of shite for doing this?' Dillan asked her. 'Remember I had to swear to the judge that I'd stop hacking for good and all, otherwise she'd have had me banged up.'

'You won't be hacking to steal goods this time, Dillan,' Kyna reassured him. 'You'll be hacking to save Detective Superintendent Maguire from a fierce unjust attack on her reputation.'

Dillan frowned and sucked at his drink and had a lengthy think. At last, he said, 'You said on the phone that you'd make it worth my while, like.'

'Fifty euros?' Katie offered him.

'Could you stretch to a hundred?'

'Okay. A hundred. When could you do it?'

'The shop's quiet this morning. I could have a go at it as soon as I go back. I'm supposed to be downloading some new software so it'll look as if I'm doing that.'

'You're sure you can actually manage it?'

'It won't be a bother at all. Give me your password and tell me which email you want me to delete, and I promise you that nobody will never be able to find it again. And I mean that. Never. I'll wipe it off the face of the earth, like, do you know what I mean?'

25

Katie and Kyna were still finishing their coffee in the Welcome Inn when Sergeant Murphy called from the communications centre. At 8:20, one of his morning shift had noticed a chrome-yellow Kuga turning out of John Redmond Street in Shandon. He had tracked it crossing the River Lee by the Christy Ring Bridge, then back again over Patrick's Bridge, and eastwards along the Lower Glanmire Road to Kent railway station.

The Kuga had parked outside the station for a little over ten minutes, without the driver getting out. Then, after a train had arrived, a man had come hurrying out of the booking hall, crossed the car park and climbed into the passenger seat. The Kuga had then immediately driven off and doubled back over the river, the way it had come.

'There's no CCTV up John Redmond Street, ma'am. But that's a rental car, right? So the odds are that whoever rented it is only a visitor. If he's only a visitor, then he's probably staying at a hotel, and the only hotel up John Redmond Street is the Maldron.'

'Did you manage to get a look at the driver, or the man he picked up at the station?'

'Not the driver, no. There was too much reflection on the window. But the fellow who came out of the station was tall and bald and carrying like an overnight case.'

Katie put her hand over her phone and said to Kyna, 'Jesus. I think that Martin Bracken's come back.'

To Sergeant Murphy, she said, 'Peter, thanks a million for that. If you can keep an eye on John Redmond Street for me, in case that Kuga comes out again. You've told DI O'Sullivan what you've seen?'

'I have of course.'

'And DS ó Broin?'

'DS ó Broin isn't here. Moirin said he went off to Dublin this morning for some kind of a meeting with the Deputy Commissioner. He may not be back today at all.'

Katie put down her phone. She wondered why Micheál would have gone to see Deputy Commissioner Anne McMahon at Phoenix Park. She had an unpleasant feeling that he may be trying to undermine Frank Magorian for supporting her during her suspension. Maybe he was also complaining that Frank Magorian had failed to act promptly and decisively enough about the incriminating email that she was supposed to have sent to Rayland Garvey. Since Frank Magorian was an Assistant Commissioner, Anne McMahon was the only person apart from the Commissioner himself who had the authority to reprimand him or even to sack him.

Katie realized that she might be too suspicious. Maybe Micheál had gone to see her only for some mundane administrative reason. But by suddenly producing this fake email, like some cheap conjuror, he had made it clear how desperate he was not to be sent back to Limerick.

He had pretended not to be disturbed by the Rathkeale gang attempting to shoot him, but Katie was sure that underneath his insouciance he was terrified. It was possible that he bore her no ill will at all, not personally, but he could think of no other way of staying at Anglesea Street except to make sure that her career was demolished, and that she was unable to return there.

She called DI O'Sullivan. She asked him first if he had any news of Kevyn, but all he could tell her was that he was receiving intensive treatment at the University Hospital, which had the only level 1 trauma centre in the whole of Ireland. The latest he had been told was that Kevyn was 'critical', but at least he was still alive.

'I've said a prayer to Saint Raphael,' Katie told him. 'I can only hope against hope that he's heard me.'

'We all do, ma'am, believe me.'

'Apart from that, Terry, Sergeant Murphy has given me the heads-up about that chrome-yellow Kuga. I expect he's told you that the driver might be staying at the Maldron.'

'That's right.'

'Has he also told you that he's been joined by a fellow who could well be our suspect Martin Bracken? This fellow came in by train, so he wouldn't have had to go through security at the airport.'

'Murphy's brought me up to date, yes. And I'll be sending Malloy and Murrish to check out the Maldron. If it turns out that Bracken is staying there, I've told them to take no further action for now. So long as you agree with it, my plan of action is to stake out the hotel until the suspects leave, and then tail them. If they head for an address where any of the Dripseys have relocated, we'll have reason to pull them over. All we need to do is catch them in possession of explosives, and they'll be toast.'

'Exactly what I would have suggested, Terry. Good man yourself.'

Terry hesitated for a moment, and then he said, 'If you don't mind me asking, ma'am, what's all this about an email? I tried to find out more about it from DS ó Broin yesterday, because it's all over the station, but he would only say that it's serious, and that he wasn't sure when you'd be coming back, if at all.'

'What email?' asked Katie, looking across the table at Kyna and giving her a thumbs up.

'You don't know?'

'No, Terry. I have no idea at all what you're talking about.'

'Are you serious? It's going around that you sent an email to Rayland Garvey, giving him all the Dripseys' addresses.'

'What! You're slagging, aren't you? Can you really believe that I'd do something like that?'

'Well, no. Of course not. But the word seems to be that DS ó Broin has proof of it.'

'Pff, it sounds to me like he's having a bit of a joke, that's all. Maybe he's trying to brighten up your day.'

'If I thought you were gone for good, ma'am, that wouldn't brighten up my day at all. Between you and me and the gatepost, DS ó Broin runs investigations like he's building a house out of Lego. It's one small brick at a time, and you're not allowed to guess what the finished house is going to look like until the last brick's in place.'

Katie gave an ironic shake of her head. So many of her fellow officers had made it clear when she was first appointed detective superintendent how much they resented having a woman in charge. Now it seemed as if they would do anything to have her back.

'Terry, don't you worry. You haven't seen the last of me, I promise you. But you'll keep me informed about Kevyn, won't you? They still don't allow visitors at CUH so I can't go to see how he's getting on.'

'Of course, ma'am. We're all thinking of him. He's one of ours.'

★

Katie and Kyna left the Welcome Inn and went back to the PC Genius shop. They found Dillan Plunkett sitting in a niche at the back, behind a stack of computers, staring at a laptop screen with both hands poised above the keyboard.

'What's the story, Dillan?' said Kyna. She looked at his laptop screen and it was filled with slowly spinning planets.

'Oh, sure, I've sorted it for you, no worries at all. I was about to head next door and tell you, like, but my boss told me to download all this software first.'

'You've totally erased it, that message?' Katie asked him. 'You're quite sure of that?'

Dillan glanced across the shop to make sure that his manager was busy with a customer, and then he switched the computer screen to the recoverable items folder of Katie's work account. Katie could see for herself the genuine messages that she had deleted before and after the fake message to Rayland Garvey had been inserted, but that had now disappeared.

She was unable to stop herself from feeling a grim sense of satisfaction. Micheál would return from his meeting with the Deputy Commissioner to find that the evidence of her corruption that he had so magically conjured up had magically vanished.

'Dillan, I'll need you to forget that you ever did this,' she told him. 'It never happened, do you have that? It was all a dream.'

Dillan held out his hand like a waiter expecting a tip. Katie opened her purse and counted out eighty euros and Kyna was able to make up the other twenty.

'Next time I need a black-hat hacker, I'll know where to come,' Katie told him.

'You're welcome, like,' said Dillan, standing up and stuffing the money into the back pocket of his jeans. 'That was a piece of piss, to be honest with you. It was for me, anyhow.'

She and Kyna left the shop. The pavement was starting to be spotted with rain, so she opened up her folding umbrella. 'Are you going to go back to the station?' Kyna asked her. Anglesea Street was only a few minutes' walk away on the south side of Parnell Bridge, and the Garda station was almost in sight.

'Not today. I don't know how many people Micháel might have shown that email to. Frank Magorian saw it. Terry O'Sullivan knew about it, even if he hadn't actually seen it. If I go waltzing back in there right now, all cheerful, like I *know* that it's been erased, they're going to suspect that I might have been up to something fishy, even if they can't work out what it is. No – I'm going to wait until Bill Phinner's computer expert has a look for it and can't find it. And the same like I did today, I'm going to make out that I never knew it even existed. Well, that's true, of course. I didn't.'

They drove back to Carrig View. Katie was feeling much more confident now that she would be able to return to Anglesea Street, maybe tomorrow or the day after. She was relieved that she had managed to outwit Micheál, but her sense of malicious satisfaction had faded. Her thoughts were now dominated by her worry about Kevyn, and a terrible guilt too, because of the way in which her plan to trap Sabrina had led to him being so brutally thrashed.

If he were to die, she didn't know how she would ever be able to forgive herself.

When they arrived back at Katie's house, she was shocked

to see that Kieran's silver Volvo was parked in the driveway outside.

'Wow,' said Kyna. 'Maybe he's come to make up with you.'

Kieran was sitting behind the steering wheel, scrolling through his phone. When Katie's car drew up beside him, and she climbed out, he dropped his phone into the breast pocket of his coat and climbed out too.

'Kieran,' she said.

Kyna kept well back, and said, 'Listen, I'll take myself off next door to Jenny's and fetch the dogs so.'

'Yes, please, Kyna.'

Kieran came around his car, holding up a door key.

'Here, Kathleen, I came to return your key. It brought me nothing but trouble, after all. Or maybe it brought me the truth.'

Reluctantly, Katie took the key, looking up into his eyes for any clue as to how he was really feeling. She thought she could see pain, and regret, but could she also see forgiveness?

'Why don't you come inside?' she asked him.

'I'll need to. I left my waterproof jacket here, didn't I, and my walking boots. And I think I also left that book about the *Titanic*.'

'You did, yes.'

Katie opened the front door and Kieran followed her into the hallway. He lifted his olive Jack Murphy jacket off the peg, and picked up his hiking boots.

'Your book's in the living room,' said Katie. 'I'll fetch it for you.'

She came back holding the book close to her chest, as if she were reluctant to give it to him.

'When do you go to Dublin?' she asked him. 'Have they told you a firm date yet?'

'January the second, so far as I know. I hear that your suspension's been lifted. Have you started back yet?'

'There's been a slight hitch, but it should be soon. Early next week maybe.'

They stood looking at each other in silence for a few moments. Then Katie said, 'You really can't forgive me?'

'You don't need forgiving for doing something that comes naturally to you.'

'Don't you believe that I love you?'

'I do, yes. But I also believe that you love Kyna just as much, and I can't share you with anyone else.'

'You wouldn't have to. I promise you.'

'See look, Kathleen, you can say that. But even if I hadn't caught you and Kyna together, you still would have made love to her. I wouldn't have known about it, but my not knowing about it wouldn't have changed the way you feel towards her, or any other woman who might take your fancy.'

'So this really is the finish of us?'

Kieran nodded, solemnly, as if he were handing out a sentence in the District Court.

'Here,' said Katie, holding out his book for him. 'Perhaps you'll learn a lesson from it. Like how to stay alive, even when you're sinking.'

She had a lump in her throat, but she was determined not to cry. When she had first seen his car in her driveway, she had thought for a moment that he might have come to be reconciled, but she knew for an absolute certainty now that their relationship was over.

She heard panting and scrabbling outside the front door, and she saw that Kyna had brought the dogs back. They came snuffling up to Kieran, but he backed away, giving Katie one last rueful raise of his eyebrows, as if to say *sin é an saol* – such is life.

'Is that it?' said Kyna, as he returned to his car, climbed in, and started up the engine.

'Yes, that's it,' Katie told her. 'He's not changed his mind.'

'Oh God, Katie, what have I done to you?'

'I did it just as much to myself.'

'But I've destroyed your whole future. Your marriage, your house together, your social life, your holidays. The children you could have had. And when will you ever meet a man like Kieran again?'

'I need a drink,' said Katie.

26

Early the following morning, while Katie was still standing in the kitchen in her white fluffy dressing gown with a mug of coffee, looking out at the rain, Assistant Commissioner Frank Magorian rang her.

'Will you be able to come in today, Kathleen? It would seem that everything's settled.'

'Meaning what? That I'm officially reinstated?'

'You are, yes. It's all pure baffling, but it turns out that Bill Phinner's computer expert was unable to find any trace of that email you sent to Rayland Garvey. Well – that email that DS ó Broin alleged that you'd sent to Rayland Garvey.'

'I never sent any email to Rayland Garvey.'

'So what Micheál ó Broin showed us was some kind of optical illusion? Kind of a mirage, like?'

'I can only repeat, sir, that I never sent any email to Rayland Garvey.'

'Fair play to you, Kathleen. But if you can come in, anyhow, we can get the wheels turning at full speed again. This has all been a fierce unwelcome distraction.'

'Does Micheál himself know about this?'

'I've called him and texted him, but I've had no response. I gather he spent last night in Dublin. If he doesn't know yet, he'll find out soon enough when he shows up at the station.'

Kyna came into the kitchen, accompanied by Foltchain. Her hair was tangled and she looked pale and exhausted. Foltchain kept glancing up at her as if she were worried about her.

'Oh, Kyna,' said Katie. 'You look like you haven't slept a wink.'

'I haven't. I couldn't. And when I did drop off, I kept having nightmares, and they woke me up again.'

'I hope it wasn't nightmares about me and Kieran.'

'What else? I kept dreaming that you were coming into my room and you were sobbing your heart out.'

Katie went up to her and gave her a hug. 'You have to stop feeling so bad about yourself, you really do,' she told her, stroking her hair. 'I've lost Kieran but maybe I'll find myself another judge one day soon – one who isn't so possessive and so strait-laced.'

'Oh, come on. Where are you going to find another judge like him? All the rest of them are about a thousand years old and smell of Voltarol.'

Katie couldn't stop herself from smiling. 'Here – let me fetch you a mug of coffee in your hand. I've heard from Frank Magorian. It's worked, our deleting that email. Bill Phinner's IT expert had no luck at all in trying to find it, and he's one of the best. Frank wants me to go back to Anglesea Street this morning and pick up where I left off before I was suspended.'

'That's wonderful, Katie. At least you have your job back.'

'Kyna, I'm not going to pretend that I'm not devastated about Kieran, but what option do I have? He doesn't want me and I'll have to get over it, that's all.'

'I suppose.'

'I'd best go and take a shower and get myself ready. I think I'll wear my black suit today. I want to look like I mean business, you know? And a bit scary. Would you look after the wolf pack for me while I'm away? And listen – you take care of yourself too, sweetheart.'

'I'll have a quiet day,' said Kyna. 'Maybe I'll finish taking the labels off those champagne glasses for you. At least Kieran has left you with something to remember him by, apart from a broken heart.'

When she entered her office, Frank Magorian was already there waiting for her, as well as DI O'Sullivan, DS Begley and detectives Coughlan and Murrish. Her personal assistant, Moirin, came in too, and they all gave her a little smatter of applause.

'I think I speak for everyone in the station when I say welcome back, Detective Superintendent Maguire,' said Frank Magorian. 'Sure we've had our disagreements in the past. There's no question that there were times when you conducted your investigations in a way we all thought was wildly unorthodox – I might even say supernatural. But your way almost always turned out to be highly effective, and we've learned to appreciate that. You have a rare nose for the rotten smell of crime, if you don't mind my saying so.'

'Thank you, sir,' said Katie. 'All I can say is that regardless of my rare nose, I can't wait to get my teeth into our ongoing cases – especially, of course, the Dripsey Dozen bombings.'

She paused, and then she said, 'I also want to express my deep concern for Detective Garda Kevyn Hickey, and to pray that he makes a full recovery.'

'Amen to that,' said Frank Magorian. 'Now you'll forgive me. I have a meeting with the Lord Mayor.'

Once he had left, Katie went around the desk. Micheál ó Broin's notepad was lying there, open at a page of meticulously numbered comments about the stealing of diesel from O'Connell Transport at Tivoli docks, how many litres and when. Next to his notepad, his ashtray was still crammed with half-smoked cigarette butts, and there was a framed photograph of an elderly woman, frowning fiercely into the camera. Katie guessed that it was Micheál's mother.

'As soon as DS ó Broin gets back, we can start bringing you bang up to date on all the investigations we're working on at the moment,' said Terry. 'I can tell you now, though, that we've been keeping a twenty-four-hour watch on the Maldron Hotel in Shandon. Murrish and Malloy will be heading off there in a minute to take over the next shift.'

'We have a list of all the remaining Dripsey Dozen who have moved to safe houses,' said Bedelia Murrish. 'We thought they were safe houses, anyway. If there's any sign that our suspects are heading towards any of those locations, we'll be stopping them.'

'No sign of them yet?'

'Not so far,' said Bedelia. 'They checked in as – hold on—' She took out her phone and quickly scrolled through it. 'Yes, they checked in as Ronald Brown and John Banks. They said they would be staying at the Maldron for at least ten days.'

'Ten days would give them long enough to blow up the last remaining Dripseys, wouldn't it?' said Terry. 'That's if they are who we suspect they might be.'

'Have you googled those names?' asked Katie. 'Sometimes offenders pick a pseudonym that they're familiar with. You remember that attempted bank robbery in South Mall last October? The leader of the gang had opened an account there in the name of John Roberts after John Roberts Square in Waterford, where he came from. His real name was Something MacCauley.'

'I've not googled them yet but I will,' said Bedelia.

'Also – if they come out of the hotel and they give you any reason at all to think that they're on their way to do something suspicious, like you say, then please let me know at once. And I mean, instantly. If one of them happens to be the suspect who I believe it could be, I'll be able to make a positive ID.'

She turned to Terry. 'What's the story with Sabrina from Extreme Dreams?' she asked him. 'Any sign of her yet?'

'We're still looking for her. We found her address all right. Her full name's Sabrina Berrigan and she lives on Ard na Laoi in St Luke's. When we went there, though, her house was all locked up. Her neighbour said that she'd seen her leaving with a suitcase, like the Devil himself was breathing down her neck. We have the registration number of her car so I'm confident that we'll be catching up with her sooner rather than later.'

'And we have CCTV of her from the Abhaile ó Bhaile Hotel – from the lift, anyway?'

'That was no help. In all the footage in which she appears, she always has her back turned or she's wearing a hat with a brim so that you can't see her face. It's my guess that she's been perfectly aware all along that these sex sessions of hers were on the wrong side of legal.'

Katie dropped Micheál's ashtray and all his cigarette butts into the wastepaper basket. 'I'll tell you what you can do. You can ask Bill Phinner to send up his forensic photographer to take a picture of me. Then you can put that out as a picture of Sabrina. We could be twins, that woman and me.'

'Oh, and what if some overenthusiastic guard arrests *you*, by mistake?' grinned Terry.

'Unlikely. But I think I can prove that I'm not an orgy organizer. I'm sure the Very Reverend Casey from St Colman's Cathedral will vouch for me.'

She sat down behind the desk that was now hers again. 'Once we've caught her, we should be able to identify the two women and the two men I saw leaving the hotel, if they're the ones who whipped poor Kevyn, which I strongly suspect they were.'

Detectives Murrish and Coughlan both gave Katie a respectful nod and left the office.

While she was opening the drawers of her desk to see what Micheál might have left in them, DS Begley came up to her.

'I thought you might like to know that I was given a tip-off today about one of your favourite bunch of chancers, the Cooney gang. They've been lying low for a while, like, but I was told they've started up a racket stealing expensive watches. I don't know if you saw it on the news but Derek Finnerty the golfer was threatened with a machete last Friday on Paul Street and had his Rolex taken off him. He bought it five years ago for €21,000 but today it must be worth at least three times that. And that's the third watch theft this month.'

'Right,' said Katie. 'I'll have a word with Jim Cooney. If it's the Cooneys behind it, I'll start by warning him off. He's usually reasonable if he knows that we've rumbled him.'

She was still talking to DS Begley when the door opened and Micheál walked in. He was wearing his long black raincoat and clutching his grey woollen beanie tightly in his left hand as if he were trying to crush a squirrel to death. His expression was one of barely suppressed fury.

'Well, Kathleen,' he said, and his voice was shaking. 'I see you've wasted no time in evicting me from my chair.'

'I'm not throwing you out, Micheál. We have a rake of cases to be going over together before you leave, and I'll be needing your help to bring me up to date. But, yes, I have been reinstated here now, and it's official.'

'We have to thank you for taking over while Kathleen was suspended,' Terry put in. 'You've done some valuable work here, Micheál, and it won't be forgotten.'

He paused, and then he said, 'I hear that you met with the Deputy Commissioner yesterday. Anything I should know about?'

'Routine,' said Micheál, his teeth clenched, without taking his eyes off Katie. The last time any man had stared at her like that was when she had arrested the gangster Gerard Connolly, and he had been sentenced to five years in prison for causing serious harm to a shopkeeper with a brick.

Terry glanced from Micheál to Katie and back to Micheál. He could obviously sense the hostility between them. 'In that case, I should leave you and Kathleen to catch up,' he told him. 'Come up to my office after so that we can discuss your return to Henry Street, and when that might be.'

Micheál said nothing as Terry and DS Begley left the office and closed the door quietly behind them.

'Well?' said Katie. 'Aren't you going to take off your coat? It's dripping on the carpet.'

'I'm here to pick up my personal possessions, that's all.'

'But, come on, Micheál, we have at least five major investigations to go over. What about the Dripsey Dozen bombings? What's the latest with them? Have we collected any more evidence from Lancaster Gate – eyewitness or forensic?'

'I don't often make mistakes,' said Micheál. 'This time I can't forgive myself.'

'What do you mean?'

'I mean I should have taken a screenshot of your email to Rayland Garvey and printed it out, or saved it on a USB.'

'I never sent an email to Rayland Garvey, and you know that as well as I do.'

'Oh no? I saw it, clear as day, and so did you, and so did Frank Magorian.'

'All I can say to you, Micheál, is prove it.'

'I don't know how you managed it, but I won't forget this. Do you have any idea what it was like to go all the way to Phoenix Park to have a special meeting with the Deputy Commissioner so that I could show her the evidence of your passing all those addresses to Rayland Garvey? Except that there *was* no fecking evidence. I switched on my laptop and it was gone.'

Katie found it hard to understand why Micheál was telling her this, but he must be feeling so angry and so humiliated that he had to tell somebody.

'It was fecking *gone*!' he snapped. 'It was gone like it never fecking existed!'

'Do you know why?' said Katie, standing up. 'That's because it never *did* exist.'

Micheál's chest was rising and falling so that his raincoat rustled, and he was screwing his beanie even tighter. He was trying to answer her, but he had no words. It was obvious that he was just as angry with himself as he was with her, maybe even more so.

'Are you going to take off your coat now and start updating me on all our current cases?' Katie asked him. 'Or are you just going to collect all your personal bits and pieces and go storming out through the door?'

'I wouldn't update you on my latest shite. Not if you were the last woman on earth. Have your minions do that for you.'

'All right, then. If that's the way you feel. You tried to banjax my career, and if you've wound up wrecking your own career instead, then all I can say is that you deserve it. I'll ask Moirin if she can find a box you can put your things in.'

★

Katie left Micheál to pack up his belongings. She went down first to see Bill Phinner in his laboratory to ask if his forensic technicians had found any more evidence from any of the Dripsey Dozen bombings, and in particular the last one at Lancaster Gate.

According to their analysis of the blast damage, the bomb that had killed Declan and Grainne O'Brien had been packed with almost twice as much C-4 as the bomb that had blown up the Doherty family in their car, possibly as much as five kilos. It had completely devastated their apartment and caused significant structural damage to the apartments directly below it, and on either side.

'The only difference from all the other bombings was that it was set off by the oven door being opened,' Bill Phinner told her. 'All the others were set off remotely, at a moment of the bomber's choosing.'

Katie was looking through the photographs of the wrecked apartment. 'It's a penthouse, isn't it? My guess is that the bomber wouldn't be able to see from the street if the O'Briens were at home or not, or where in their apartment they were, and so he wouldn't have been able to pick the exact moment to make the maximum impact. That's probably why he used more explosive, too, in case one of them was in another room, and was shielded from the blast by the intervening wall. I mean, look at the state of this place. There's nothing left at all, like. Even the bed's been reduced to splinters.'

'Considering that C-4 is generally used to demolish houses and blow up tanks, that's not surprising.'

'Do you have any notion where it might have come from?'

'Not to begin with we didn't, no – not until we recovered

that sample from underneath your car. Once we had that, we were able to make a chemical analysis with time-of-flight secondary ion mass spectrometry, and XPS. I won't bore you with the details, but we found that the atomic concentration was consistent with C-4 manufactured in the Czech Republic.'

'I thought all plastic explosives had to contain some kind of security marker – you know, so that we could tell where they were made.'

'They're supposed to, yes. The UN drew up an international convention about that – in 1991, I think it was. But this C-4 had no such marker, so we needed to analyse it to find out where it came from. We ran its composition through our records, too, and lo and behold, it's a match to several bricks of C-4 that we took off the New IRA when we raided that builders' merchants in Farranree five years ago. They were made in the Czech Republic, too.'

Katie put down the photographs. 'You're joking. That C-4 was smuggled into Cork by DI Garvey. That was one of the illegal activities he was arrested for. Along with all the others, of course. Did you tell DS ó Broin about this?'

'Yes, as soon as we'd confirmed the test results.'

'What was his reaction?'

'He asked if we were sure. When we said we were, one hundred per cent, he said that we shouldn't be jumping to conclusions. It might match the C-4 from the New IRA, that's what he said, but that doesn't mean that it was supplied by DI Garvey.'

'So what did you say?'

'I said I was aware of that, but the binders and plasticizers in this C-4 were identical in every respect to the ones we confiscated from Farranree, so the odds were that somewhere along the line, the same person was involved.'

Katie interrupted him. 'And then *he* said, "But Superintendent Maguire isn't one of the Dripsey Dozen, is she? So what grounds do you have for assuming that the same batch of explosive that was planted under her car was used to bomb *them*? Or even that the same suspects were behind the attempt to blow her up?" Or words to that effect.'

Bill Phinner blinked at her. 'How do you know he said that?'

'Because I know what he's like. Everything has to be utterly logical. Unless he's sure that his case is watertight and leakproof, he won't make an arrest and he won't bring it up in front of a judge.'

'To be fair, I've seen a few cases that would have benefited from that kind of an attitude from the prosecution. You remember that shooting on Winthrop Street?'

'Oh, do I! We proved that the suspect was carrying a gun, and that it had been fired all right, but the defence showed that the bullets they took out of the victim were a different calibre.'

'But why do I have the feeling that you're sure about this one?'

Katie was about to tell Bill Phinner that she had seen Rayland Garvey talking to Martin Bracken in The Huntsman, and that was what led her to believe that it was one of the Dripsey Dozen bombers who had planted C-4 under her car.

'Listen,' she said, 'Two days ago I visited Birmingham, or Erdington to be more accurate, and—'

And at that moment her phone rang. When she answered it, Detective Garda Murrish spoke to her, breathlessly.

'The two of them came out the hotel about five minutes ago, ma'am. We weren't sure where they were going at first because they were heading east on the Lower Glanmire Road.

But now they've turned north at the Dunkettle Roundabout, and that means they're on their way up to Glanmire.'

'There's members of the Dripsey Dozen in Glanmire?'

'Cormac and Niamh Fennelly. Cormac's descended from the Lyons family on his mother's side, according to my list.'

'And what address are they staying at?'

'Eleven, Gleann Caoin.'

'I'll be right with you.'

27

She drove along the Lower Glanmire Road at more than a hundred kph, swerving in and out of the slow-moving traffic, so that a chorus of angry motorists blew their horns at her. It took her only twelve minutes altogether to speed up the Glashaboy river valley and reach Glanmire Village.

Detectives Murrish and Coughlan were parked in a sloping side road a short way south of the residential cul-de-sac that was Gleann Caoin. Although they were hidden behind trees and bushes, they could still see the chrome-yellow Kuga, which had turned into the entrance to Gleann Caoin but then stopped.

Katie drew up behind Murrish and Coughlan and climbed out of her car. The two detectives climbed out too.

'They're still sitting there, having a smoke,' said Liam Coughlan. 'Maybe they're waiting for the Fennellys to leave the house.'

'I don't think there's much doubt why they're here, though,' said Katie. 'What other possible reason could they have for coming here to Glanmire, if it wasn't to blow up another one of the Dripsey Dozen? I'd sorely like to know who gave them this address, though.'

'Me too,' said Bedelia Murrish. 'Only six of us were given a list of the safe houses that the Dripseys had moved to, and we were all warned that it was not to be shared with anyone else.'

Katie shook her head. 'After that bombing at Lancaster Gate, didn't DS ó Broin think of arranging a twenty-four-hour watch on each of these addresses, or moving the Dripseys yet again?'

'He said that it wasn't necessary. In his opinion, one of the bombers probably recognized one or both of the O'Briens when they were moving into Lancaster Gate, and that's how he found out where they were. He said there was no conclusive evidence that the new addresses had been leaked.'

'Him and his conclusive evidence,' said Katie, watching the cigarette smoke rising from the Kuga's half-open windows. 'Innocent people have died because of him and his conclusive evidence.'

'What's the plan, then?' asked Liam Coughlan.

'Like I say, there's not much doubt why they've come here,' said Katie. 'And that fellow sitting in the passenger seat, I can see that he's bald, although I can't see his face. My main suspect, Martin Bracken, he's bald. If I can make a positive ID, and it's him, then we'll have grounds to search that car, and take them in for questioning too.'

She reached into her coat and unfastened the stud that held her Sig-Sauer subcompact automatic in its holster.

'I'll walk up to them until I'm close enough to have a clear view of his face. You follow behind me, in your car. Even if it isn't Martin Bracken, we can still ask the two of them what they're doing here, and what they're waiting for.'

Detectives Murrish and Coughlan climbed back into their car, while Katie crossed the road and started walking up towards Gleann Caoin. As she approached the chrome-yellow Kuga, the passenger window was put right down, and the bald man twisted around in his seat to drop his cigarette butt into the gutter.

It was Martin Bracken. And as he put up his window again, he raised his eyes and caught sight of Katie walking towards him, not twenty metres away.

She heard him bellow '*Go!*' and the driver started the Kuga's engine. Before they could pull away from the kerb, she ran up to the Kuga and banged with her fist on Martin Bracken's window.

'*Stop!*' she shouted. At the same time, Liam Coughlan had seen what was happening. He sped up to Gleann Caoin and swerved around in front of the Kuga so that it was blocked in.

'Martin Bracken! Get out of the car!' Katie ordered him.

Martin Bracken sat motionless for a few seconds, as if he hadn't heard her.

'I said, get out of the car!'

Another few seconds passed, and then he suddenly swung his door wide open, hitting Katie hard on the hip. He rolled sideways out of his seat like a parachutist rolling out of a plane and then he scrambled to his feet and pushed her in the chest, so that she staggered backwards. Then he started to run up the cul-de-sac, towards the houses.

Liam Coughlan started to run after him, and Katie reached into her coat, tugged out her automatic and fired a shot into the air. Two seagulls were scared off and flapped away.

'Stop!' Katie screamed.

As soon as she did that, though, there was a loud bang from inside the Kuga, and a bullet hit the fence right behind her. She ducked down behind the open passenger door, and there was another bang. The door shook as it was struck by another bullet.

'Super!' cried out Bedelia. 'Keep your head down!'

She stayed where she was, crouching on the pavement. Then she heard a sharp crack and glass splintering and an odd thumping sound.

There was a pause. From her crouching position, she looked up Gleann Caoin and saw that Liam had caught up with Martin Bracken and was making him stand with his hands up, while he quickly frisked him.

'You're grand now, super, you can come out now,' Bedelia called to her, although her voice sounded shaky.

When Katie stood up, she saw that the Kuga's driver was slumped forward with his forehead pressed against the steering wheel. He was wearing a baseball cap on backwards, which was soaked in blood, and there was blood sprayed over the windscreen in front of him. The window next to him was smashed and sparkling shards of glass were scattered across the shoulders of his grey North Face anorak.

In his lap he was holding a Glock automatic pistol, although his fingers were slowly opening like the legs of a dying crab. Bedelia was standing outside with her own pistol raised in both hands.

'You saved my life there, Bedelia,' said Katie. 'God bless you.'

'I didn't warn him. I don't think he would have heard me, even if I had. But he's the first person I've ever shot.'

'You did the right thing, believe me.'

'Oh, Jesus. I can't believe I actually aimed at his head and pulled the trigger.'

Katie turned to see if Liam was bringing Martin Bracken back down. Liam still had his gun pointing at him, but Martin Bracken no longer had his hands up.

Got him, thought Katie. *On my first day back as detective superintendent, I've got him.* It's no consolation to all those members of the Dripsey Dozen that he's killed, but it's justice, if nothing else.

Martin Bracken was still too far away for her to read the

expression on his face, but she hoped that he felt utterly crushed. As he came nearer, though, she saw him dip his right hand into the pocket of his black leather jacket. She had an instant flashback to that time when she tried to stop him at Ballincollig, after he had crashed his Honda. He had reached into his pocket then, and she had mistakenly thought that he was going to pull out a gun. But this time she guessed what he was actually about to do.

'Bedelia!' she shouted at her. 'Run! As fast as you can! *Run!*'

She started to run herself, back along the main road towards Glanmire Village, and Bedelia sprinted after her, and even caught up with her. When they were about two hundred metres away, Katie stopped, panting, and turned around.

The explosion was so loud that Katie felt as if it had burst her eardrums, and both she and Bedelia were hit by the shock of it as if they had been standing in the sea and were struck by a massive wave. The chrome-yellow Kuga was blown apart, and the unmarked Garda car beside it was sent tumbling across the road, wheels over roof, ending up in the hedge.

An orange fireball rolled up into the sky, followed by a biblical pillar of dark-grey smoke, and fragments of metal and rubber and glass began to rain down in a tinkling shower.

'Liam,' said Katie, although her own voice sounded far away.

'What?' said Bedelia, screwing her finger into her ear.

Katie began to hurry back to the corner of Gleann Caoin. The shattered remains of the Kuga were blazing ferociously, and the driver's headless body was sitting behind the twisted steering wheel, his clothes already charred black. Bits and pieces of debris were still dropping down all around them, and the broken lid of the Kuga's glove box fell at Katie's feet.

She looked up the cul-de-sac and Liam was coming down

towards her, his hands spread wide as if he were appealing to be forgiven. There was no sign of Martin Bracken.

'What happened?' Katie asked him, as he came up to her. 'Where's Bracken?'

'Gone! He's legged it!' Liam shouted, because he had been deafened too. 'This godalmighty bang and then he knocked the gun out of my hand and went running off! By the time I'd picked it up, he was gone.'

He shook his head, trying to clear his hearing. 'I'm sorry, but that fecking explosion. It almost knocked me off my feet.'

'Which way was he headed?' asked Katie, taking out her phone. 'I'll call for an APB.'

'He went running down the slope there, between the trees, down towards the road.'

Residents were emerging from their houses along Gleann Caoin, all of them looking shocked and bewildered.

Katie raised her hand and called out, 'We're Garda! There's nothing for you to worry about! Please go back inside! It was fierce frightening, I know that, but it's all over now!'

She could see that Cormac and Niamh Fennelly were standing in the porch of number 11. They were a short, fiftyish couple, both wearing cardigans. They reminded Katie of the little figures that came out of a chiming clock.

She called for an all-points bulletin to be sent out for Martin Bracken, and for backup, and forensics, and the fire brigade. Once she had done that, she would go up and talk to the Fennellys. She would have to explain to them what had happened, and that the explosives had almost certainly been intended to kill them.

At least she would be able to reassure them that, from now on, armed gardaí would be keeping a watch on their house, twenty-four hours of the day.

Without a car, Martin Bracken would not be able to get far, not at first. But he had been friendly with Rayland Garvey, and Katie guessed that Rayland Garvey might still have contacts in Cork who would be willing to drive out and pick him up, and give him sanctuary.

She was not going to underestimate how ruthless Martin Bracken was, and how critical it was that he was caught. He had been too far away from the Kuga to see if the driver had been shot dead or simply wounded, and yet he had still detonated the explosive to help him escape.

'Oh, Mother of God,' said Bedelia. 'Will you look over there, at that hedge?'

Katie turned around and saw that the driver's head was embedded in the centre of the hawthorn hedge beside the road. He was thirtyish, with a thin moustache on his upper lip, the sort that Cork people called a 'thirsty eyebrow'. His eyes were open and he appeared to be smiling, as if he were playing peek-a-boo, but that was probably the result of his face muscles reacting to the bullet in his brain.

'I'll be having nightmares about this for ever,' said Bedelia. She pressed her hand to her mouth, and then she crossed over to the gutter, bent over it and retched.

Nightmares? thought Katie. *You and me both. And it isn't over yet.*

It was dark by the time Katie returned to Anglesea Street, and raining. When she went up to her office, she found that Micheál had emptied all the drawers in her desk, but he had left them all hanging open. He had also taken the bulb out of the desk lamp, as if to suggest that the only light had been his, and that Katie would only bring back guesswork and uncertainty.

Garda patrols had been criss-crossing the area all around Glanmire, but Martin Bracken had not yet been sighted. She called DI O'Sullivan and asked him to fetch her the confidential list of safe houses to which the six surviving members of the Dripsey Dozen had been moved. When he had printed that out and brought it around to her office, she went along the corridor to see Superintendent Pearse.

'How's it going, Michael? As you can see, I'm back in harness.'

'Well, it's grand to have you here again, ma'am. But I know that look. You're going to ask me for something that's next to impossible.'

She handed him the list of addresses. 'These are the safe houses where the six surviving members of the Dripsey Dozen have been moved to. The Boyles are back from Tenerife this evening so we've included their address. The thing of it is, I'm not at all sure how safe they really are, or if someone's leaked them to the bombers. So, as a precaution, we'll be needing to post round-the-clock watches on every one of them.'

Michael Pearse sucked in his breath. 'I'm not sure if I have the officers to spare, to be honest with you,' he told her. 'And it'll be stretching my overtime budget way beyond the limit.'

'You'll be saving at least a dozen innocent lives,' Katie told him. 'On top of that, you'll be salvaging our reputation. Have you seen the comments on the news about the way we've been handling these bombings? People are saying that we've failed to prevent the worst series of murders in Cork since 1922, and it's true. We were even criticized in the Dáil on Wednesday by Mary Lou McDonald.'

'I saw that,' said Michael Pearse. 'She said that if she could catch the coronavirus so easy, why was it so hard for us to catch the bombers? So far as she could tell, they'd left evidence littered around like Covid viruses.'

'That's going to change now, Michael,' said Katie. 'I'll be giving a full briefing tomorrow morning on everything that I've found out about these bombings. I'm also going to be contacting the police in the UK to liaise with them, because there's no question now that they're some kind of revenge attacks originating from England. I don't want even one more member of the Dripsey Dozen to die, not a single one.'

'Very well then, sure, I'll go along with that. You'll have your surveillance, starting tonight. I'll manage to somehow. And by the way, welcome back. I have to tell you in confidence that it's not been the easiest of times, working with DS ó Broin. Bit of a stickler for detail, you might say, to be charitable.'

After arranging round-the-clock surveillance with Superintendent Pearse, Katie was kept busy for the rest of the evening, until late. First of all, Mathew McElvey called her from the press office for a media statement about the explosion at Gleann Caoin. Then Bill Phinner's deputy, Roger Deeley, sent her a message about the preliminary forensic findings from the blown-up Kuga. The explosive had been C-4, and probably as much as two and a half kilos.

Before she had gone for the day, Moirin had made sure she left Katie up-to-date information on all the ongoing investigations, as well as the latest messages from Phoenix Park and Cork City Council.

It was 10:45 before Katie decided that enough was enough, and it was time to go home. As she buttoned up her coat, though, she realized that her day had given her excitement and fulfilment, even if it had exposed her to danger too. She looked around her office and knew that this was the place where she was meant to be, doing what she had always been destined to do. In a way, it made the pain she was feeling about Kieran slightly more bearable.

Before she left, she phoned Kyna to tell her that she was on her way, but there was no answer. She guessed that Kyna was probably asleep by now, after a hard day taking the dogs out.

When she arrived home, she was surprised to see that the house was in darkness. She would have thought that Kyna would at least leave the porch light on for her, and the light in the hallway too, even if she had gone to bed.

She opened the front door, and was surprised again that Barney, Foltchain and Harvey didn't come scrambling out from their beds in the utility room to greet her.

She switched on the light. The house was silent. She didn't call the dogs because she knew that if they hadn't appeared, they were probably still at Jenny's next door. But why would Kyna have left them there?

She went along the hallway to Kyna's bedroom and very quietly opened the door. It was dark in there, but there was enough light from the hallway for her to see that Kyna's bed was still neatly made, and empty.

'Kyna?' she called out. She was beginning to grow anxious now. What if the people who had planted that explosive under her car had come back, with the intention of finishing her off? She knew that it couldn't have been the driver of the chrome-yellow Kuga. His head had ended up in that hawthorn hedge in Glanmire. But there could well be others who were helping Martin Bracken to exact his revenge on the Dripsey Dozen.

The living-room door was closed, which was unusual. When she opened it, she saw that it was in semi-darkness, although the television was still on, with the sound muted. By almost supernatural coincidence, her own face was being displayed on the screen, with the caption *Have You Seen This Woman? Contact An Garda Síochána on 112 or 1800 666 111.*

She switched on the overhead light. At once, she saw that Kyna was lying on her side on the couch, her eyes closed, still wearing her fluffy pink sweater and her jeans. On the coffee table next to her stood the champagne flutes that Kieran had given to Katie as an engagement present. One of them was lying on its side, and its stem was broken.

Katie bent over Kyna and gently shook her shoulder.

'Kyna? Kyna, wake up!'

Kyna's eyes remained closed and she dribbled out of the corner of her mouth. Katie shook her again, harder this time, but she still failed to respond.

'Kyna, wake up! What's happened?'

Katie knelt down beside the couch, and it was then that she noticed the bottle of Goo-Gone lying on the carpet, where Kyna must have dropped it. It had no lid on it, and when she picked it up she saw that it was empty. She had read the label when she bought it, and she knew that if it was swallowed, and entered the lungs, the effects could be fatal.

'Kyna!' she shouted at her, shaking her again. 'Kyna, wake up!'

A bloody bubble formed on Kyna's lips. She was still breathing, but in shallow gasps, with a catch in them.

Katie knew that it was crucial not to make her sick, as it might damage her airways even more. She took out her phone and called 112 for an ambulance. Then all she could do was stay beside her, holding her hand and talking to her soothingly, although she doubted that she could hear her.

28

A Medicall ambulance arrived from Glounthaune within ten minutes. The two paramedics strapped an oxygen mask on to Kyna and then immediately lifted her on to a stretcher and carried her out.

Katie followed them. She handed them the empty Goo-Gone bottle so that the doctors in the emergency room could see what Kyna had swallowed, and then she climbed into her car. Once the ambulance had pulled away, with its blue lights flashing, she swerved backwards out of her driveway and then stayed close behind it as it sped towards the city.

It took them only fifteen minutes to reach the University Hospital. Kyna was wheeled into the emergency department, while Katie went into the waiting room. There was only one other person in there, an elderly man with hair like a dandelion puff. He looked infinitely sad and he never once looked across at her.

An hour went by. Katie went out to the reception desk to ask if there was any news about Kevyn Hickey. The receptionist called the night duty nurse in intensive care, and after a short wait, she rang back to report that Kevyn was still critical but stable. A plastic surgeon was coming to see him in the morning to assess if he required skin grafts.

Another hour went by. A woman doctor came into the

waiting room and sat down next to the elderly man, speaking to him very quietly. The elderly man nodded and nodded but said nothing. Then they both got up and left. Katie could only guess what tragedy she had just witnessed.

At last, at nearly 2:30 a.m., another doctor came in. He was Indian, with sorrowful eyes and baggy green scrubs.

'Ms Maguire? My name is Doctor Kapoor. It was you who came in with Ms Ní Nuallán?'

'It was, yes. How is she?'

'We did everything we could, Ms Maguire. But she had ingested a mixture of toluene, acetone and methanol. If this mixture is swallowed, it can cause severe distress to the stomach lining, but the real danger is if it enters the airways.'

Katie stared at him. She felt as if an outside door had suddenly banged open, and an icy draught had blown through the waiting room.

'Excuse me. When you say you did everything you could—?'

'I'm afraid so, Ms Maguire. She passed about ten minutes ago.'

Katie was aware of the tears trickling down her cheeks, but otherwise she was numb. She could almost believe that she was not actually here in the hospital at all, and that she was simply having a bad dream after such a gruelling day at the station.

She heard the doctor saying, 'It was drastic respiratory failure, I'm sorry to say.'

'Can I see her?'

'Yes, of course. If you come with me, I will take you to the ED.'

Katie followed him out of the waiting room and along the corridor. She could hear hospital noises like distorted voices and a phone ringing and the sound of trolley wheels squeaking, but she could still believe that she was dreaming.

Doctor Kapoor led her into the emergency department. Kyna was lying on the operating table, covered up to the neck by a green sheet. Her face was as white as a marble statue. Katie went up to her and now she knew that this wasn't a dream.

Oh dear God, she thought. If only she had understood the true depth of Kyna's guilt and how much mental pain she was in. Kyna had first attempted suicide when she had lost Katie's love to Kieran. Then, after Kieran had caught them together, she had insisted repeatedly that it was entirely her fault that Katie's future with him had been destroyed, no matter how much Katie told her that the blame was hers too. But she had still believed that she had ruined the life of the woman she loved more than anyone, and it must have been more than she could bear.

'May I kiss her?' she asked Doctor Kapoor.

'It is safer if you don't, Ms Maguire. She vomited the toxic liquid and it could still be on her lips.'

Katie stayed beside the operating table for another five minutes. Under her breath, she whispered a farewell prayer. 'Receive your beloved servant Kyna into the arms of your mercy, o merciful Saviour, into the blessed rest of everlasting peace, and into the glorious company of the saints in light.'

It was the same prayer that she had said over the tiny white coffin of her little Seamus. And as she prayed, she couldn't stop herself from thinking how much she had hoped that she might have another child with Kieran. On that night of lovemaking with Kyna, though, that hope had died too.

★

When Katie returned to Carrig View, it was gradually beginning to grow light. She went first into the living room to collect up the five unbroken champagne flutes that Kyna had left on the coffee table and put them back into their box. She would return them to the auctioneers where Kieran had bought them, and ask if they would pay her whatever they were worth. She would then donate that money to the Irish Society for the Prevention of Cruelty to Children.

After she had drawn open the curtains, she saw that there was a white envelope lying next to the flutes. She opened it up, and found a letter inside. All it said was, *Sorry. K.*

She sat down on the couch and now she started sobbing, so loudly that it hurt her chest. She felt as if she were a female version of the Dullahan, the driver of the mythical death coach, who would have only to speak someone's name and they would die.

After a long while, she eventually stopped crying, and wiped her eyes with a tissue. She reminded herself that she was a detective superintendent, and that most lives were tragic in their different ways, and it was her calling to deal with such tragedies, even her own.

She went into Kyna's bedroom and opened her wardrobe, to see what clothes she would have to dispose of. Her dresses and her folded sweaters smelled of that floral perfume she always wore. In her chest of drawers she found her jewellery, and her diary, and an album of family photographs. When she opened up the album, the first picture she saw was of Kyna, aged about three or four, standing on the seashore in Kerry, laughing and holding up a string of seaweed.

She closed her eyes tightly for a moment and said to herself: *You're not going to start crying again, Kathleen Maguire.*

At 7:30 she went next door to Jenny's to collect Barney,

Foltchain and Harvey. The three dogs came bustling out to greet her, their tails flapping and their tongues hanging out.

'Thank you so much for taking care of them all night,' said Katie.

'Oh you're grand. I love them. And so does my Reilly. He keeps asking if we could have a dog of our own, but we don't really need to, not with your three toppers.'

'What time did Kyna fetch them around to you?'

'About half-past eight I think. Just after the *Hidden Camera* show.'

'Did she say why she needed you to look after them?'

'Something about a family emergency, that was all. She didn't say what it was, but I thought she had quite an anxious head on her.'

'I'm afraid I have some sad news for you. Kyna passed away last night.'

Jenny stared at her and said, 'No! You can't be serious!'

'I'm afraid I am. They rushed her into the emergency department at CUH but she couldn't be saved.'

Jenny crossed herself twice. 'Holy Mary, I can't believe it! Reilly told me that he'd seen an ambulance outside but when I went to look there was no sign of one. What happened to her?'

'She'd been depressed for a long time. I knew that she was, but I never realized how much. I'm sorry to say that she took her own life.'

'That's pure tragic. Really. I had a friend at school who hanged herself and we could never understand why. She always seemed so happy, like your Kyna, but I suppose it must have all been an act, so that we never knew how desperate she was.'

'I'm back at Anglesea Street now, Jenny, full time. Yes, I've been granted absolution. So I hope you don't mind if the dogs stay with you today. I'll feed them now and take them for a scove up to Flowerhill, and then I'll fetch them back.'

'Of course. But I'm knocked sideways by Kyna. The poor, poor woman. I just hope she finds some peace in Heaven.'

When she arrived at Anglesea Street, Katie immediately contacted West Midlands Police in Birmingham. She was transferred from one officer to another, but she was finally put through to Detective Inspector Robert Charles. He told her that he had investigated several cases of suspected terrorism, including the bombing of the Elswood mosque three years before, in which three Muslims had been killed.

Out of interest, he had been following the reports about the Dripsey Dozen bombings on the UK news. But he was surprised and disturbed when Katie said that they might have been instigated by Hilda Bracken from The Huntsman pub in Erdington.

'I can see that she might have a motive, seeing as how her husband was killed, but it was a hell of a long time ago, wasn't it? And it's one hell of a way of getting your own back.'

'As soon as I have more information for you, I'll let you know,' Katie promised him. 'Meanwhile, I'll email you copies of all the files we have on the bombings so far, including all the forensic reports.'

'I happen to know The Huntsman. A pal of mine had his fortieth birthday party there. I'll drop by there later and have a quiet nosy around.'

When she had finished talking to DI Charles, Katie started to sort through all the investigations that her team of detectives were currently working on. She was keen to take full control again as soon as possible, and it was one way to keep her mind off Kyna.

In some investigations, she saw that Micheál ó Broin's step-by-step way of gathering evidence had made reasonable progress. This was especially noticeable with organized crimes such as fraud and money laundering and illegal drug manufacture, including the production of fake vapes.

When it came to the more spontaneous offences, though, such as gang shootings and political riots and vandalism by activists and domestic abuse, it was very different. No matter how irrational it was, he insisted on finding a logical and explicable motive for every single act of law-breaking before he would consider making an arrest. More often than not, he was unable to find one.

Katie could remember him saying, 'If you want to be sure of a conviction that suits the offence, you have to be able to prove two things in court beyond a shadow of a doubt. Not only what offence was committed, but why the offender committed it.'

After seeing him shot at by one of the Rathkeale gang, Katie wondered if the real reason for his extreme caution was because he had arrested several of their gang members in times gone by, only to see them released for lack of evidence. He could have been frightened that once they were free, they would come after him, looking for revenge. Two Garda inspectors and a sergeant had been killed in Limerick in recent years, and although their killers had never been caught, it was suspected that they had been victims of criminals who had been charged but then let off because nobody had dared to speak out against them.

She was looking through a case of people-trafficking when DI O'Sullivan knocked at her door.

'I heard the sad news about Kyna Ní Nuallán,' he told her. 'You have my condolences. She was such a bright light.'

'Thank you,' said Katie. 'Did you know that she was seriously thinking about reapplying for duty? She could have had a brilliant future in the Garda.'

She refrained from adding, *but I took her future away from her, because of my own selfish lust. Not only her future career, but her whole life.*

Terry could obviously sense that she was thinking about something upsetting, because he waited respectfully for a few moments. Then he said, 'You'll be pleased to know anyhow that I've received a message this minute from Superintendent Doyle at Rosslare Harbour Garda station. A customs officer recognized you trying to board a Stena Line ferry for Fishguard, and you've been arrested. Well, your twin sister, that is.'

'Sabrina Berrigan? Now that is good news.'

'They're fetching her here, so she should be with us early this afternoon.'

'That's grand. With any luck she'll give us the names of those gowls who whipped poor Kevyn Hickey near to death.'

After Terry had left her office, Katie stood up and went to the window. The hooded crows were clustered again on the rooftop opposite. She wondered if they were an omen for her, or whether they meant that justice was coming for Sabrina Berrigan, or for Martin Bracken and Rayland Garvey.

She was still standing there when her phone played 'The Parting Glass'. She thought that she should change it, since it was a song about a final farewell to the ones we love, either to leave them for ever or to die. It was a song about accepting blame, too. *All the harm that e'er I did, alas, it was to none but me.*

'Kathleen? It's Michael Pearse. I've had an urgent call from

Garda O'Keefe up in Ballyhooly. He's watching the bungalow in Árd Abhainn where the Brennans have been moved to.'

'Not bad news, I hope?'

'Well, it depends. He's just seen a car driving up and down Árd Abhainn and slowing down to a crawl when it went by the Brennans'. It had to pass him twice because Árd Abhainn's a dead end, like. He checked the number plate and it was registered in the name of a Margaret Dowd, from Blackstone Bridge, but he thought he recognized the driver of the car as Jimmy Gerrity. I don't know if you remember Jimmy Gerrity yourself, but he was one of the detectives who was sacked along with DI Garvey for taking thousands in sweeteners from the O'Flynns.'

'I do remember him, sure. Flaming red beard like someone had set fire to his chin.'

'That's your man. And the passenger next to him was a baldy. So that could well have been your Martin Bracken fellow. I may be wrong, but it sounds to me like they were checking out the Brennans' place to see how best they could plant some kind of device there.'

'It does sound like that, Michael, I agree with you. Listen, look, I'll go up there myself and see if I can't arrange some kind of reception for them, if they come back looking to blow the place up.'

'O'Keefe's staying wide, anyhow, and he'll alert us immediately if he sees any sign of them again.'

Katie went to find DI O'Sullivan. She told him that she intended to go up to Ballyhooly because of her suspicion that Martin Bracken might be intending to kill Niall and Dolores Brennan. Dolores was distantly related to the Dripsey martyr Thomas O'Brien.

She also told him that Martin Bracken's appearance at

Ballyhooly had reaffirmed another suspicion of which she had been almost sure. After the Fennellys, the Brennans were second on the list of members of the Dripsey Dozen that Terry had given her. This suggested that it must have been an officer at Anglesea Street who had passed their addresses to Martin Bracken. Maybe Micheál ó Broin would have said that she was jumping to wild conclusions again, but was it a coincidence that Martin Bracken was going after them in the same order?

'I agree with you,' said Terry. 'I mean, who else had that list of addresses, but half a dozen of us here at the station?'

Katie said, 'Okay. I might not be here when Sabrina Berrigan arrives. But you have all the details, don't you? Charge her under the Sexual Offences Act with selling sexual services. Process her, and see if she wants a lawyer.'

'Anything else?'

'If I'm not back, ask her how we can find the two men and the two girls who I saw leaving the Abhaile ó Bhaile Hotel shortly before we found Detective Hickey. I'll bet money that they were the ones responsible for whipping poor Hickey. Tell her it'll make things a whole lot easier on her if she does.'

'I suppose you have no idea how long you might be up at Ballyhooly?'

'Terry, I'm going to stay as long as it takes. Martin Bracken has murdered more innocent people than anyone else in the history of Cork, forty-two so far. Forty-two! Catching him and everyone who might have helped him is my number one priority. Nothing else comes close. I find it so hard to believe that Micheál ó Broin treated all those bombings as if they were no more serious than – I don't know, fly-tipping, or stealing the wheels off people's cars. I mean, Jesus, it's almost genocide.'

'Well, you're right,' said Terry. 'I must say that DS ó Broin's attitude had me scratching my head too. By the way, if you're wondering where your man is, I was told that he'd called in sick with the Covid, so we won't be seeing him again for a week at least.'

'Really? There is a God, after all.'

Once DI O'Sullivan had left, Katie went to find Detectives Coughlan and Murrish. She told them that she needed them to help her to stake out the Brennans' bungalow, and for each of them to pack an overnight bag in case they had to stay for longer than a day. She would arrange for the Brennans to be accommodated at a hotel in Mallow for as long as their stake-out lasted, and for their own safety.

She agreed to rendezvous with Coughlan and Murrish up at Ballyhooly, since she wanted to go home to Carrig View first, not only to pack a bag for herself but to pick up Harvey. It was unlikely that explosives had already been planted in the bungalow, as they had been at Lancaster Gate, otherwise Martin Bracken would not have needed to be checking it out. But even if they had, Harvey would almost certainly be able to sniff them out.

Bedelia said, 'I'm so sorry about Kyna. Has her family been told?'

'She told me that her parents and her brothers turned their backs on her years ago, but I'll be writing to them anyway.'

'That's sad. A life is a life, no matter what. It's nobody's business who you love, only your own, and the person you're in love with.'

'Yes,' said Katie, although those last words hurt her like a knife in the heart.

29

Ballyhooly was out in the countryside forty kilometres due north of Cork city. By the time Katie reached it, Detectives Coughlan and Murrish had already arrived. They were parked next to Garda O'Keefe in the driveway of another bungalow three doors down from the Brennans, on the opposite side of the road.

'The Brennans left about twenty minutes ago,' Liam Coughlan told her. 'They weren't at all upset that we've put them up at the Springfort Hall. They said they needed a holiday after all the stress they've been going through, like.'

'You've seen no more sign of Jimmy Gerrity and that baldy fellow?' Katie asked Garda O'Keefe.

'No, I've not. In fact, the only person I've seen since this morning was an old biddy pushing leaflets through the doors from the Nativity of Our Lady, and I didn't reckon that she was too much of a threat to life and limb.'

'Right, we'll go over now and make ourselves at home,' said Katie. 'When will you be relieved?'

'At four. Then if I'm still needed I'll be back here tomorrow morning at eight.'

'Let's pray you're not.'

Katie let Harvey jump out of the back of her car, and then she and Bedelia and Liam went across to the Brennans' bungalow. Once they had let themselves in, Liam opened the garage and drove Katie's car inside. When he and Bedelia had arrived, he had swapped cars with the Brennans so they could leave their own car outside and not arouse Martin Bracken's suspicion that they were no longer there.

They all went into the bungalow's living room. It was wallpapered with pale grey dahlias and furnished with fat mushroom-coloured sofas from EZ Living. Over the fireplace hung a dismal painting of sheep under a grey sky.

'Jesus! Whoever decorated this room must have been suicidal,' Liam remarked, and then abruptly realized what he had said. 'I'm fierce sorry, ma'am. There's me opening my mouth and sticking my left boot in it, as per usual.'

Katie waved her hand to show him that he was forgiven. Then she sat down and took her laptop out of her shoulder bag, as well as a packet of Irish Rover dog treats for Harvey. While she was here, she was going to carry on catching up with all of the investigations that were still outstanding. There had been a recent spate of shoplifting in the city centre that appeared to be highly organized, and it was costing jewellers and fashion stores thousands of euros every day.

Bedelia and Liam had brought their own laptops and they continued to work on their current assignments. The living room fell silent except for the tapping of keyboards and Harvey snoring.

The afternoon went by. Shortly after 4 p.m., they could see that another unmarked car had arrived across the road to relieve Garda O'Keefe. It was dark already, and a soft drizzle was falling.

'I fetched some ham and cheese and bread from home,' said Katie. 'How about some sangers?'

'That would be more than welcome, ma'am,' said Liam.

'I've not eaten since breakfast and then I had only a slice of cold pizza left over from last night.'

Katie went into the kitchen, and Bedelia came to help her. She took plates and cups out of the cupboards and filled the kettle so that they could have tea.

'Do you really think they'll come back and try to blow the place up?' asked Bedelia. 'Maybe they've gone scouting around to all the other addresses, too, to see which would be the easiest to get access to, do you know what I mean?'

'You may be right,' Katie told her, 'but I have a sixth sense about this. I might be totally mistaken, but I don't believe it's a coincidence that Bracken's come looking for the Dripsey Dozen in the same order as they appear on our list of addresses.'

'You think that he could have got hold of the same list somehow?'

'Like I say, it could be a coincidence. But in any case, all these addresses are supposed to be confidential, so how do they know where they are? DS Ó Broin suggested that Bracken or one of his pals may simply have recognized the Fennellys going into Lancaster Gate, but how did he find out that the Brennans were moved way up here to Ballyhooly?'

The kettle started to whistle, but at exactly the same moment they heard a sharp double knock at the front door. It gave her the same eerie feeling she had experienced when she had walked into her living room at Carrig View and seen her own face on the TV screen.

Harvey came trotting out into the hallway, and looked up at Katie as if he were asking her what she wanted him to do. Liam came out, too.

'Amazon!' called a muffled voice from the other side of the front door.

Katie said, 'I'll go. But be ready for anything.'

She reached out and opened the front door wide. A large cardboard box had been left up against the doorstep, but she saw at once that it had no address label on it, and no distinctive Amazon arrow. A tall man in black was walking quickly away from the bungalow with his shoulders hunched. It looked as if he was heading for a grey van that was parked a little way down the street.

Harvey took a few tentative steps towards the cardboard box, sniffing at it. He barked, and barked again, and then jumped up at Katie as if he were trying to push her back into the hallway.

Katie resisted his frantic jumping up and stayed where she was. She unfastened the stud on her holster and tugged out her revolver.

'Martin!' she screamed out. 'Martin Bracken!'

The man was just about to step off the kerb, but he stopped, and turned around. He was wearing a black leather cap that shaded his face, and the only light came from the streetlamp on the other side of the road behind him. All the same she could see at once that she was right, and it *was* Martin Bracken.

'Put up your hands!' she shouted at him. 'Put up your hands and keep them up!'

Liam came up close behind her, and he had drawn out his pistol too. Harvey continued to bark, and bark, and jump up and down, trying to force them both away from the cardboard box.

'Now, walk towards us!' Katie shouted. 'Slowly, and keep your hands up!'

'That's him?' said Liam. 'That's Bracken?'

'Yes. And Harvey can smell explosives in that box.'

'Hey, maybe I should kick it out the way.'

'Don't even touch it,' she warned him. Then, to Martin Bracken, 'Did you not hear me? I said, walk towards us!'

She was thinking that the nearer he came to the box, the less likely he was to detonate it remotely, in the same way that he had done at Ballincollig and Glanmire. But he stayed where he was, on the pavement, about twenty-five metres away, although he kept both hands raised.

Bedelia had sent an alert to the garda who had relieved O'Keefe. He climbed out of his car, slamming the door behind him, and came across the road towards them. He was a big burly man, also armed, and he was holding up his automatic pistol in both hands. Martin Bracken turned his head and saw him approaching, and then he turned back to look at Katie standing in the open doorway, with the box in front of her, and Harvey jumping up and down.

Katie had been in so many situations before in which offenders had been cornered, and she could guess what he must be thinking: *It's now or never. Either I surrender or I take the risk.*

His right hand dropped towards the pocket of his leather jacket. She shouted at him, *'Don't!'* but she knew that a second's hesitation could be fatal for all of them, and she shot him at the same time. He jolted backwards as if he had been punched and dropped into the road. Almost as soon as he had fallen, though, he lifted up his head and tried again to reach for his pocket. Katie fired two more shots in quick succession. One of them hit him in the shoulder and the second one hit him high in the forehead, so that his cap was blown off. He lolled back and lay still.

As soon as he had heard the shots, the driver of the grey van started up his engine and began to reverse down Árd Abhainn. The garda took three bounding steps sideways and intercepted him, knocking on his window and pointing his pistol at him. The driver stopped and switched off the engine.

'Now we need to get out of here, fast,' said Katie. 'God alone knows how much explosive is in that box. If Harvey's planking it then so am I.'

The three of them stepped carefully around the box. When they reached the pavement, Katie looked down at Martin Bracken to make sure he was dead and there was no more chance of him setting the explosives off by remote control. His cap was lying in the gutter, with some of his brains inside it, because her last shot had taken off the top of his skull. With a sick feeling in her stomach, Katie couldn't help thinking that it looked like a half-finished bowl of lumpy porridge.

They crossed the road, with Harvey scampering after them. The garda had made the van driver stand with his hands pressed flat against the side of his van, and was about to cuff him.

'Fetch him over to your car,' Katie told him. 'Quick, now. If that box goes off, this van could flatten the both of you.'

The van driver turned around, and she saw that Garda O'Keefe had identified him correctly. He looked much older than she remembered him. His face was more wrinkled, like the skin of an overripe nectarine, and his hair was white and wiry, but it was Jimmy Gerrity all right, one-time detective sergeant from Anglesea Street, and partner in bribery and racketeering with Rayland Garvey.

'Well, well, Detective Not-so-Superintendent Maguire,' he said, in the clogged-up voice of a heavy smoker. 'I should have known. Rayland always said that it was the worst mistake the Garda ever made, promoting women. They'd be a curse for ever after, that's what he said.'

★

Within an hour, Árd Abhainn was cordoned off and brightly illuminated with LED lamps. The eight-man bomb disposal team had arrived from Collins Barracks in their khaki truck, as well as an ambulance from the Mercy, the forensic technicians' van and five Garda patrol cars. The families living directly opposite and on either side of the Brennans' bungalow had all been evacuated.

Katie waited with Bedelia in one of the patrol cars. Liam and the garda who had caught Jimmy Gerrity had taken him together down to Anglesea Street to be formally charged.

It was almost midnight and it had stopped raining when Commandant Brophy from the EOD came over. Katie climbed out of the patrol car to meet him.

'You were fierce lucky that you stopped that fellow before he could set that off,' Commandant Brophy told her. 'We found a wireless detonator in his jacket pocket, and I'd guess that there's at least twenty kilos of C-4 in that box, easy. Even if you'd left it outside where it was, and not taken it indoors, there wouldn't have been much of that bungalow left. The blast from only one kilo of C-4 can kill you at a distance of thirty metres.'

'Thank the Lord,' said Katie. 'And let's pray that this is the last attempt to blow up the Dripsey Dozen.'

'Do you know for sure now who was behind it?'

'A Brit called Martin Bracken. That was your man with the detonator in his pocket. He was the son of a woman called Hilda Bracken, who runs a pub near Birmingham.'

'What was his motive?'

'Revenge, more than likely. The pub was bombed in the early seventies and Hilda Bracken's husband was killed, as well as a fair few other people. We had a tip-off a few years ago that it wasn't the IRA who bombed it, but the Dripsey

Dozen. They were supposed to have done it as payback for the five men who were executed after the Dripsey Ambush. The trouble was, we could never prove it.'

'So you think these Brackens decided to punish the Dripsey Dozen themselves?'

'That's what it looks like, even though the pub was bombed fifty years ago, and not many of today's Dripsey Dozen are the same people who might have actually done it – only their sons and daughters and cousins.'

'That's pure mental. Talk about bearing an everlasting grudge.'

'There's someone else we have to find, as a matter of priority,' said Katie. 'That's a fellow called Rayland Garvey. He used to be a detective inspector at Anglesea Street until he was found taking backhanders from some of the local gangs. I saw him in England, but he may be back here now.'

'That name rings a bell. Wasn't he caught smuggling Semtex for the New IRA?'

'Semtex and C-4, that's right, and we're fairly sure that it's Rayland Garvey who's been supplying the Brackens with their explosives.'

Commandant Brophy turned around and saw that his men had taken off their blast-proof helmets and were closing the doors at the back of their truck.

'Good luck with snaring him, then. Meanwhile, it looks like we're all finished here. We'll examine the device to weigh up exactly how much C-4 is in it and how it's been constructed, and forensics will be analysing where the C-4 originated from. I'll send you a full assessment of it as soon as I can.'

He took a step back and gave her a light-hearted salute. 'Now I'll say what I always say after we've made safe some explosive or other. "Thank you once again, dear Lord, that we haven't all been blown into a thousand bits."'

It was nearly four in the morning before Katie returned home. She took a quick shower and put on a pair of pink striped pjyamas, but before she went to bed to snatch an hour or two of sleep she sent an email to DI Robert Charles in Birmingham, bringing him up to date on the night's events.

> With the grace of God, it looks like we have at last been able to put an end to this series of bombings of the Dripsey Dozen. However, we still need to locate and detain Rayland Garvey for the suspected supply of contraband explosives, and we also need to interview Hilda Bracken on suspicion of conspiracy to commit multiple homicides. I will apply to the Department of Justice for an extradition warrant first thing in the morning, on the grounds of dual criminality.
>
> Hilda Bracken will also have to be informed that her son Martin was fatally wounded by a Garda officer while attempting to detonate an explosive device that could have caused several fatalities and serious injuries.

Once she had closed her laptop, she sat on the side of her bed for a few moments, thinking: *How could I have shot and killed a man today and yet feel so cold and detached about it? It's almost as if someone else killed him, not me. But then it was justice, and that's what my life is all about.*

Harvey was already settled in his bed in the utility room and Katie went to look in on him. As she watched him sleep, she found it impossible not to be moved by the fact that this little dog had twice saved her, and the lives of others too. She wondered if dogs dreamed, and if they did, what he was dreaming about.

She arrived at the station at 10:30 the next morning, still feeling tired but grimly satisfied that she had been able to put an end to the bombings. There would have to be a formal inquiry into her shooting of Martin Bracken, which meant that she would have to surrender her revolver for forensic examination. While the remaining members of the bombing conspiracy were still at large, though, she was permitted to continue to carry a weapon for her personal protection.

Before she had even taken a sip of her first cup of coffee, she contacted the Department of Justice in Dublin to start the procedure of applying for an extradition warrant from the UK for Hilda Bracken. Next, she arranged with Mathew McElvey to hold a media conference at noon about the attempted bombing at Ballyhooly. Then, after catching up with her messages, she went downstairs to the holding cells with DI O'Sullivan to confront Jimmy Gerrity. He was sitting on his bunk looking sulky, with the remains of his breakfast on a plastic plate next to him. He had left all the baked beans.

'He's asked for a lawyer,' said Terry. 'Apart from that we've not heard a squeak out of him, have we, Jimmy?'

'His lawyer's on the way?'

'Shelagh Murphy from McCloskey and Murphy. She'll be here at eleven.'

'If you don't care for baked beans, Jimmy, we can always find you something more to your liking,' Katie told him. 'We're pure amenable here, you'll find. If you were to give us some helpful information, I'm sure we can make your life easier for you. You're charged with being an accomplice to attempted murder, and that's an offence that judges don't regard at all kindly, I can tell you that for nothing.'

Jimmy Gerrity said nothing, but folded his arms and looked away, as if he had heard enough.

'Have it your way,' said Katie. 'We'll see you later so.'

She left the holding cells with Terry and they went back upstairs together to interview Sabrina Berrigan. This morning, Sabrina resembled Katie far less than she had before. She was wearing a hairy grey jumper and no make-up, and she had bags under her eyes. Katie imagined that this was what she might look like when she was approaching sixty.

Her lawyer was there too, Patrick McAleese, and Katie knew him well. He always reminded her of a ferret, if a ferret were ever to be caught wearing rimless spectacles.

Katie and Terry sat down opposite Sabrina and Patrick McAleese, but Sabrina kept staring down at the table.

'You'll be relieved to know that Detective Garda Hickey will survive the injuries that you and your friends inflicted on him,' Katie told her. 'He's still in intensive care, and he'll need numerous skin grafts, and it's unlikely that he'll ever be able to resume his career as a detective.'

Still without raising her eyes, Sabrina said, 'I never touched him.'

'Shh,' said Patrick McAleese, touching her sleeve. 'You're not obliged to make any comment at all.'

'You may not have touched him, but your friends did,' said Katie. 'They almost killed him. And even if you didn't physically touch him yourself, you arranged the whole event and you stood by watching them while they whipped him. It was you who encouraged them to start whipping him and at any time you could have told them to stop. That means that you're equally liable for their assault on him and you should know that you're facing at least twelve years in jail for assaulting a police officer and a possible life sentence for causing grievous bodily harm.'

'But I never once touched him myself. I'm not to blame.'

'Shh!' repeated Patrick McAleese. 'Don't you be saying another word!'

'Well, we can let a jury decide who's to blame,' said Katie. 'And don't forget you'll be facing additional charges under the Sexual Offences Act 1993 for selling sexual services. You could face another year in jail for that.'

Sabrina looked up now. Her eyes were glistening with tears. 'I only wanted to give people the kind of sex they dreamed of but couldn't find anywhere else. I thought I was doing something good, not something criminal. And I needed the money.'

'For Christ's sake, Mrs Berrigan, that's enough,' said Patrick McAleese. Then he turned to Katie and DI O'Sullivan. 'You can't deny that this was a trap, set up by the police with the deliberate intention of provoking my client into incriminating herself. It was never her intention that Detective Hickey should be harmed, but, after all, she was led to believe that he had specifically asked her to be whipped. In fact, you had paid a substantial deposit on his behalf for him to be whipped. If it all went a little too far, then that could hardly be considered to be my client's fault. She may have been in charge, but she wasn't holding the whip hand herself, so to speak.'

'"A little too far"?' said Katie. 'Detective Hickey was thrashed so severely that his spine was exposed. It's a miracle that Sabrina isn't sitting here today charged with murder.'

Terry looked across at Katie and she gave him a discreet nod.

'Sabrina,' he said, 'I asked you yesterday if you would be willing to tell us the names of the two men and the two women who actually carried out the whipping. You refused, because you said it would be disloyal. But I hope you've had a chance to reconsider, like. If you do, there's a fair chance that the assault charges against you could be substantially reduced, or even dropped altogether.'

There was a lengthy silence between them. Katie drummed her fingers lightly on the table and Sabrina dragged out a tissue and blew her nose. Patrick McAleese looked across at Sabrina with both of his eyebrows raised as if to say, *Go on then, you know it makes sense, how many years do you want to spend in the Dóchas Centre?*

Eventually, Sabrina said, 'Have you a piece of paper and something to write with?'

Patrick McAleese passed her his open notebook and his pen, and they all watched as she wrote down four names, and a number.

'You'll find their contact details on my phone,' she said, passing the notebook back. 'I've given you the passcode here.'

When she had done that, she closed her eyes and clasped both her hands together as if in prayer. 'God forgive me. And they didn't even give me thirty pieces of silver.'

Katie was buttoning up her coat to go to the Abhaile ó Bhaile Hotel when her phone played her new tune, 'The Rose of Allendale'.

It was DI Robert Charles. He had received her email about Martin Bracken and he had gone to The Huntsman pub to inform Hilda Bracken about his death, and then to arrest her on a charge of conspiracy to commit multiple homicides.

'She wasn't there,' he told Katie. 'There was a relief manager in charge behind the bar and he told me that she'd taken at least ten days off. She left him her phone number in case of any problems, but he had no idea where she'd gone.'

'Well, two guesses,' said Katie. 'Either she's taken herself off to some country that doesn't have an extradition agreement with the UK, or else she's heard what's happened to her son already and she's come here to Cork to collect his body and take him back to England for a funeral. I'll check with border control.'

'Meanwhile, we're on the lookout for that Rayland Garvey,' said DI Charles. 'But if Hilda Bracken's gone, I think the odds are that he's flown off somewhere too.'

'You're probably right. I just want this case all tied up. I was feeling pure relieved last night but this morning I still feel uneasy, like we haven't heard the last of this yet.'

'Let's hope that you're mistaken, superintendent. But I'll keep in touch.'

Katie had made it to the door when Superintendent Michael Pearse knocked and entered.

'Oh, Kathleen, I'm glad I caught you. I've been told what happened at Ballyhooly last night, so congratulations. Well, commiserations, too. None of us ever want to take a life, whoever it is. I mean, heaven forbid.'

'Thanks, Michael, I was coming down to give you a full briefing later, before the media conference.'

'Sure look, now that you've wrapped it all up, I'm presuming that there's no further threat to the Dripsey Dozen – or what's left of the Dripsey Dozen.'

'I'm hoping there's not, of course.'

'What I mean is, they'll be able to leave their safe houses now and return to their own homes, yes? And my officers won't have to keep round-the-clock surveillance on them any longer? We've been stretched desperate thin, I can tell you, and we have the hurling semi-finals at The Park this weekend. We've heard rumours of trouble between the supporters, so I'll be needing every guard I can call on.'

'We could let the Dripseys return to their own homes, yes,' Katie agreed. 'I'll be discussing it with Chief Superintendent O'Leary when I get back. It's almost certain now that someone from this station leaked the addresses of all their safe houses to the bombers, so there's no point in them staying where they are.'

'You've more or less closed this case, haven't you, so what danger are they in?'

'I don't know, Michael. They're probably in no danger at all. We've taken out Martin Bracken, but I'd still feel happier if we kept a constant watch on them, do you know, at least for the time being. We've yet to arrest everyone involved and I have a feeling in my stomach about it, that's all, like when you've swallowed an oyster and you're not sure it's going to stay down.'

'Fair play to you. I'll wait until you come back from wherever you're going and give me the full briefing. But so long as the Dripseys stay cautious when they return home, and don't accept any strange packages they never ordered, I don't see that it'll be necessary to keep watching them twenty-four hours of the day.'

'I'm not saying you're wrong,' Katie told him. 'Maybe Micheál ó Broin was right about me all along, and I rely too much on my gut feelings.'

Michael gave her a wry smile. 'So let's keep our fingers crossed, shall we, and hope that the oyster stays where it is.'

30

Katie pushed open the doors of the Abhaile ó Bhaile Hotel with a feeling of reluctance but also inevitability.

For the past few years, the Garda had mostly turned a blind eye to the shelter that John Quinn had given to the drug addicts and prostitutes who needed somewhere safe to stay. Even so, Katie had always feared that the day would come when his Christian charity led to a minor tragedy of one kind or another. Perhaps one of his guests would be seriously hurt, or die, either from a drunken attack or an overdose of drugs or accidentally setting fire to their room. She had never guessed that the first casualty would be one of her own detectives.

As usual, the lobby smelled of mustiness and cigarettes and cheap perfume, and the radio was playing 'Why Worry?' There was nobody behind the counter, so Katie went up and pinged the bell. After a few moments John Quinn appeared, and as soon as he saw her he closed his eyes and let his head drop in resignation.

'You know why I'm here, John?'

'I've been expecting you. I was surprised you didn't come by earlier.'

'I had other business to attend to. More serious offences than yours. But you know I'll have to arrest you for allowing this hotel to be used for the selling of sexual services by more than one individual, which legally amounts to running a brothel.'

'If it's illegal to give people the love and comfort and succour that they desperately lack, then yes, I'm guilty.'

'Detective Garda Hickey wasn't given much in the way of love and comfort and succour, was he?' Katie retorted. 'If you believe in miracles, then it's a miracle that he's still alive. I'm still considering if I can charge you for having some liability for the injuries that he suffered.'

She looked around the shabby lobby. 'Do you have any guests staying here at the moment?'

'Three paying guests. And one addict who's in recovery from adulterated crack.'

'I'm afraid that all of them will have to leave as soon as possible and you'll have to close this place down. I'll give you some time to do that, but I'll expect you over at Anglesea Street later today for all the formalities. Make sure you show up. Meanwhile, I'm charging you under the Sexual Offences Act. You are not obliged to say anything unless you wish to do so, but whatever you say will be taken down in writing and may be given in evidence.'

'Dear Lord please forgive me for whatever sins I have committed with the best of intentions.'

'Is that all you have to say?'

John Quinn nodded, and crossed himself.

The conference room was already packed when Katie arrived with DI O'Sullivan, as well as Detectives Murrish and Coughlan. The TV lights had not yet been switched on so that she could clearly see her old nemesis Dan Keane from the *Examiner*, as well Ruari Mackey from the *Irish Sun*, Johnny

Bryan from Cork FM and Douglas Kelly, who was a stringer for the *Irish Times*. Sitting right at the front, as usual, was Fionnuala Sweeney from RTÉ Six One News.

Once everyone had settled down, Katie picked up her microphone.

'I want to say first of all how delighted I am to be back here at Anglesea Street after my brief suspension. I have to thank Micheál ó Broin from Limerick for covering for me while I was away. Unfortunately, he can't be with us today because he has gone down with the Covid. However, I appreciate the contribution he made towards resolving our investigation into the bombing campaign against the Dripsey Dozen, and I wish him a speedy recovery.

'I can announce today that after all the tragic loss of life that was inflicted by the bombers, we have at last managed to bring their vendetta to an end, and as far as we can tell it *was* a vendetta. A premeditated series of murders in revenge for a bombing that occurred in England way back in 1972.

'The principal offender was a British national called Martin Bracken, fifty-four years old. He was the man shot dead last night in Ballyhooly. He was taken down to prevent him from detonating an explosive device that contained over twenty kilos of C-4.'

'I gather that you and other officers were lying in wait for him,' called out Ruari Mackey. 'An ambush, like. Is that right?'

'Give me a moment and I'll explain exactly how our operation was planned and what transpired,' Katie told him. 'You're welcome to ask questions after I've done that. This has been an extremely complex case and I can't tell you how relieved we are that we have managed to close it.'

It was then that Chief Superintendent O'Leary entered the conference room with a serious look on his face. He went up to Katie, bent over her and said something quietly in her ear. Katie listened, shocked. She said something back to him, and then she stood up.

'I'm afraid to say that I'll have to bring this conference to a premature close,' she announced. 'Chief Superintendent O'Leary has just brought me unconfirmed news that there's been an explosion up by the Lough. It's in Hartland's Avenue, and it's at an address that's being temporarily occupied by Cathal and Orla O'Mahony, who are members of the Dripsey Dozen.'

'Were the O'Mahonys at home at the time?' called out Dan Keane.

'I don't know, Dan. I'll be going up there now directly to see what damage has been done.'

Douglas Kelly held up his hand. 'Does this mean that you've not been able to put an end to this bombing campaign after all?'

'We'll have to see, Douglas,' Katie told him. 'As soon as I know what's what, Mathew here will be in touch with you all. Right now, as you can imagine, I have to leave you.'

When she arrived at Hartland's Avenue, she found that it had already been cordoned off, and a small crowd had gathered. The bomb squad and the fire brigade had arrived, as well as three ambulances, and when a uniformed garda unhooked the police line tape to let her pass, the forensic van followed her through and parked up close behind her.

Even before she opened the door of her car, she could smell the distinctive walnutty aroma of a C-4 explosion, and when she saw what had happened to the semi-detached house in which the O'Mahonys had been staying she could barely believe it. The left side of the house, where they had been living, had been completely flattened, leaving only heaps of rubble. The explosion must have been devastating, far more powerful than was needed to bring that side of the house down, because the road was strewn with bricks and debris, and all the windows of the houses opposite were shattered. Most of the party wall had been blasted into the living room and kitchen and bedrooms of the house next door, and Katie could see a child's cot hanging precariously from the edge of an upstairs floor.

A blue Honda Civic was resting on its side in the driveway next to the house, its windscreen smashed, its doors dented and its paintwork thickly coated in dust.

At least twenty gardaí and fire officers were clambering over the broken bricks, trying to find any trace of Cathal and Orla. Commandant Brophy was standing in the front garden with three members of his bomb disposal team. As Katie carefully stepped over the rubble towards him, he held up a hand-held explosives detector.

'No trace of any secondary devices,' he told her. 'But this was one hell of a blast, and no mistake.'

'Have you been able to work out where the device was planted?'

'At the back of the house, that's what we reckon. All these properties were built with coal sheds at the back, from the days before they had central heating. We haven't completed a full survey yet, but we've found some metal fragments and it looks almost certain that the ED was placed in there. We don't know yet if it was detonated by a timer or whether it was set off remotely.'

The garden fence was lying flat on the grass, and Detective Sergeant Behan was standing next to it, talking to Superintendent Pearse and Inspector Montague. As Katie went over to join them, a van stopped on the other side of the road. Garda Harrington from the dog unit climbed out, and opened the back doors so that Cody the German shepherd could jump down. Cody was specially trained to find missing persons.

Katie reached down to give Cody a tickle under his chin as he trotted past her, and then she turned to Tom Behan.

'Were the O'Mahonys at home?' she asked him.

'So far as we know,' Tom Behan told her. 'That's their car there, what's left of it. We haven't yet found them, but I shouldn't think there's much left of them, either.'

'What about the neighbours? Any injuries?'

'The wife next door was in her kitchen and she sustained some cuts from flying glass. The two little weans were lucky. They were down at the end of the garden having a teddy bears' tea party inside their wooden playhouse. The blast knocked the playhouse over but they weren't injured at all. They're fierce traumatized, though, all three of them, shaking like jellies, and they're all suffering from temporary deafness.'

'Where's the officer who was keeping watch? Didn't he see anything suspicious?'

Superintendent Pearse gave an embarrassed cough. 'Erm, I'm afraid to tell you that there *was* no officer on watch.'

'What? I thought you agreed to keep up the surveillance until we were certain that it was safe.'

'Garda Brogan called in sick this morning and since you'd taken out that Bracken feen, I thought there'd be no real need for me to post anyone else in his place. You know how short-staffed I've been. Obviously, that was a bit of an error.'

'A bit of an error?' said Katie. 'Holy Mother of God.'

She looked at the gardaí and the fire officers still picking through the bricks, and Cody sniffing in a zigzag pattern from one side of the demolished house to the other. 'Let's pray that the O'Mahonys were out for a walk somewhere.'

'They would have needed to walk a good couple of kilometres away not to hear the bang of this one,' said Inspector Montague.

'Any witnesses at all? We need to start a door-to-door as soon as we can, and checking any CCTV or doorbell cameras.'

'I came up here with Cooper and Joyce,' said Tom Behan. 'They've already been talking to some of the neighbours.'

'Good. Coughlan and Malloy and Murrish should be here any minute. They were all out on Pana and Oliver Plunkett Street this morning trying to collar those shoplifters.'

It started to rain, very softly. Katie could only stand with her hands in her coat pockets, staring at the ruins of the O'Mahonys' house and feeling utterly mortified. She should have realized how determined the bombers were to wreak their revenge on the Dripsey Dozen. Anyone who would go to the lengths of blowing up innocent people, regardless of the collateral risk to life and property, was not simply vengeful, they were obsessive. She was sure now that at least one of the offenders responsible for these bombings was a psychopath, and she could guess which one it was. Of course, Micheál ó Broin would have wanted a birth certificate, a written confession and a complete psychiatric report before he would have called anyone a psychopath. But Katie wished only that she had trusted her intuition earlier.

After ten minutes, Detective Garda Joyce came up to her, accompanied by a middle-aged woman in a hooded raincoat.

'Superintendent Maguire? This here is Shelagh Laferty. She clocked two people outside the O'Mahonys' house this morning while they were out. Shelagh, this is Detective

Superintendent Maguire. Maybe you could tell to her what you told to me.'

Before she said anything, the woman looked over at the rubble and pressed her hand over her mouth in distress.

'They've not been found yet?'

'No,' said Katie. 'We're hoping they weren't at home.'

'Oh, but I'm sure they must have been. They went out together for the messages about nine, but after they came back I was in my front room the whole time and I never caught sight of them going out again.'

'So who were these two people you saw?'

'It must have been about half-past nine. They drove up and stopped outside and both got out of their car, but only one of them went up to the front door and knocked. A woman it was, in a brown coat. Of course, neither Orla nor Cathal came to answer it because they were out.'

'If you saw this woman again, do you think you'd be able to identify her?'

'Sure I couldn't be certain of that. But I'd say she wasn't in the first flush of youth, like, judging by the kind of coat she was wearing and her old-fashioned kind of a hat.'

'So she knocked and nobody answered. What happened then?'

'She turned around and it was like she was calling out to the person standing by the car that there was nobody in.'

'The person by the car. What did they look like?'

'It's hard to say if it was a man or a woman. They were tall, like, but they had on a black coat that reached almost down to the ground, like a woman's coat. Anyhow, the woman by the door called out to them and they opened up the back of their car and took out a box. They carried this box round the side of the house, while the woman stayed by the front door like she was keeping sketch, like, do you know what I mean?'

'Then what?'

'Then they both got back into their car and drove away.'

'What did the box look like? How big was it?'

'It was cardboard, so far as I could see,' said Shelagh Laferty, and she held her hands about sixty centimetres apart to give Katie some idea of its size.

'How about the car? Would you know what make it was?'

'I wouldn't have any idea. But it was grey, like, and it had a Cork number plate.'

'You wouldn't remember the number, by any chance?' asked Detective Garda Joyce, although he was only trying to lighten the mood.

'I only wish I had the photomagraphic memory. I mean, Jesus Christ, look at what they've done to that house. And the poor Whelans next door. They'll have to move and that's for sure, but thank God they're safe. If that had happened at night, they would have been killed in their beds, the children, too.'

Katie was about to ask her if she could describe the tall figure in the black coat in more detail, but she was interrupted by a shout from one of the gardaí searching through the rubble. When the bomb had exploded at the back of the house, the kitchen wall had fallen flat on to the floor, almost intact. Cody was snuffling at the edge of it, and Garda Harrington was unable to pull him away.

'There'll be somebody underneath here!' called Garda Harrington, and Cody barked twice, as if in agreement.

'Hold on there!' Two fire officers clambered over the bricks to their fire engine, and came back carrying two Holmatro ram jacks. They wedged the jacks under the narrow gap between the fallen wall and the floor, and then they gradually raised the wall, at an angle. As soon as they had lifted it up high enough, Cody dived underneath it.

With a loud crack, the wall started to break in the centre, and bricks dropped down on either side. The fire officers immediately stopped jacking it up any further, but Katie was able to see that Cody was crouching down protectively next to a man and a woman, who were lying side by side, face down on the floor. Neither of them appeared to have been mutilated, and they were still fully dressed. They had obviously been shielded from the lacerating effects of the blast by the wall collapsing on top of them. The man had his arm around the woman's shoulders, but only as if he were being affectionate, and just about to tell her that he loved her cooking.

The two fire officers bent down and dragged the man and the woman out from under the wall and on to the bricks. While they were doing this, four paramedics had brought over two stretchers. The man and the woman were lifted on to them and turned to face the sky. The man's eyes were open, while the woman's were closed. Their lips were blue, as if they had been drinking ink, and their faces were dead white. They may not have been dismembered by the force of the explosion, but it would still have been more than enough to kill them instantly.

Katie crossed herself and whispered a blessing. '*Ar dheis Dé go raibh a anam.*'

Over on the other side of the rubble she could see Superintendent Pearse turning away, so that he would not have to face the two bodies. She could guess how guilty he was feeling because he had failed to make sure that a round-the-clock watch was kept up on the O'Mahonys' house. She felt guilty enough herself for assuming that by taking down

Martin Bracken she had put an end to the bombing, even if she had not yet managed to apprehend everyone involved in it.

Detective Behan came up to her.

'Cathal and Orla,' he said, looking down sadly at the two bodies, side by side on their stretchers. 'What in the name of God did they ever do to deserve an end like this?'

'Sometimes I think we shouldn't teach history in schools, only forgiveness,' said Katie. 'The past is the past, like. It's gone. We weren't even there. We shouldn't allow ourselves to feel bitter about it for ever after.'

'What's the plan, then?'

'We carry on knocking on doors to see if we can find any more witnesses. We check every CCTV camera all around the Lough. And I'm going to have a word with Lorcan O'Neill, God help me. We need to find out where this C-4 is coming from. Maybe Rayland Garvey's been smuggling it in new from the Czech Republic, like he did before. But maybe he's been calling in a favour and the New IRA have been letting him have some, out of the stocks that he gave them before. If that's the case, Lorcan might possibly be able to tell me where he is.'

'Good luck with that, ma'am. If I was going to have a word with Lorcan O'Neill, I'd make sure I was wearing my bulletproof sweater.'

Late in the afternoon, Katie returned to the station to give a statement to the media in time for the Six One News and tomorrow's papers.

She did no more than tell the small crowd of reporters that Cathal and Orla O'Mahony had been victims of an explosion in the house by the Lough in which they had been staying temporarily, and that they were members of the so-called Dripsey Dozen.

'Was no security watch being kept on the house?' asked Dan Keane.

'I've no comment about that, at this time,' said Katie.

'But it was supposed to be a safe house, was it not? If that was a safe house, Jesus, I'd hate to be living in a dangerous one.'

'Again, I've nothing to say, Dan. I'm still waiting for the EOD and our forensic team to give me a full report on the cause of the explosion.'

'You were telling us earlier that you'd put a stop to the bombing campaign against the Dripsey Dozen. It's looking as if you've done no such thing. What steps are you taking now to find who's responsible, before they've all been killed? There's not too many of them left, like.'

'What happened to the O'Mahonys was a tragedy, and we're offering our heartfelt condolences to their families and their loved ones. Believe me, we're doing everything we possibly can to make sure that they're the last of the Dripsey relatives to die.'

'Should we have a bet on that?'

After the reporters had left, she drove to Shandon Street and went into the Old Dependable pub. Because it was early in the evening it was mostly empty, but she knew that she was likely to find Lorcan O'Neill sitting in his usual alcove at the very back.

The Old Dependable was long and narrow and divided into booths, with engraved mirrors on the walls. It was over twenty years since smoking had been banned in Irish pubs, but it was still redolent of stale tobacco. Katie guessed that came from the breath and the clothing of its customers.

Sure enough, Lorcan was sitting with two friends and they were playing cards together. He was in his early forties, Lorcan, with a black temple fade haircut and a deeply-furrowed forehead. As soon as he caught sight of Katie, he flipped over the ace of diamonds and said, 'Uh-oh, boys. *Póilíní*. Keep your language respectable, like.'

'What's the story, Lorcan?' said Katie. 'Is it okay if you and me have a quiet word together?'

'Sure. Could you two boys give us a moment alone? It'll only be business, like. Nothing romantic.'

Lorcan's two friends stood up and went across to the alcove on the opposite side of the pub. Katie sat down and said, 'Sorry to interrupt your card game. But I guess you've heard that there's been another bombing and two more of the Dripsey Dozen are dead.'

Lorcan looked at Katie suspiciously. 'I have of course. Why have you come to talk to me about it?'

'All the bombs so far have been made from C-4. I've been wondering where it came from.'

'Not from us, I can assure you of that.'

'Really?'

'Oh come on, them days are long gone. We could do far more damage by hacking than bombing. And we could do it from the comfort of our own homes. That's only if we wanted to, like. I'm not saying we're actually doing it.'

'So you can swear to me on your mother's life that none of the C-4 that caused the Dripsey Dozen bombings came from you?'

'Cross my heart and hope to fart.'

'Fair play. I believe you,' said Katie. 'But have you seen Rayland Garvey at all?'

Lorcan stared at her for a few seconds without saying anything, as if he were trying to work out why she had asked him that, and what he should tell her in reply.

'Rayland Garvey,' he repeated.

'That's right. I mean, he was the one who was caught supplying you with C-4, wasn't he? And you were dead lucky the judge was sympathetic and believed your cock-and-bull story about wanting it for your demolition business.'

'If I told you I'd seen him, what would be in it for me? Not saying that I have, of course. But if I had.'

'I might consider dropping our investigation into those two AK-47s that were found at your brother's house. We've confiscated them, after all.'

'Them? We've no notion at all where they came from. We reckon they were planted there by the Provos to drop us into the shite. Or even by you peelers.'

'That's your story. But I'm prepared to close the case if you can give me some genuinely helpful information. And I might even treat you to a pint of gat.'

Lorcan looked across at his friends, perhaps to make sure that they were both engrossed in their card playing. It was doubtful that either of them could lip-read, but perhaps he was afraid they would see something in his expression that gave him away.

'Rayland's back here, in Cork,' he said. 'He came in here to see me at the weekend. He's growing himself a bushy old beard, like, so I didn't recognize him at first. I thought Santa had showed up a month early.'

'What did he want? Or was it just a social call?'

'He asked me if I could spare him some plastic, like you said. He said he'd pay me well for it. But I had to tell him no, I had none left at all.'

'Was that true? Or did you tell him no because you didn't want to be implicated in whatever he was going to do with it?'

'It was true. I'll tell you what I did with it if you swear that you'll take no action.'

'Go on, then.'

'I sent the last of it up North to our boys in Armagh. They wanted it for knocking out a polling booth before the last election. The army found it, though, and disarmed it, so nobody was hurt and no damage was done.'

'Where do you think Rayland might have found C-4 if he couldn't get any from you?'

'You probably know that better than me. But let's say there's no love lost between me and Arthur McCrohan at McCrohan's Demolition and Arthur's been known to be generous with the plastic, like, if anybody wants some for political purposes or to settle a score. Provided you cross his palm with enough yoyos, that is. But I'm not saying for sure that's where Rayland went next, so don't quote me for the love of Jesus Christ.'

'All right, Lorcan. My lips are sealed. Let me ask you one more thing, though. Do you have any idea where Rayland might be staying while he's back here in Cork?'

Lorcan shook his head. 'Not for sure. But are you really going to forget about those AK-47s?'

'If your information turns out to be helpful, then yes.'

'Then you might try that woman he had an affair with before he got kicked out of the guards. Shayla something. She used to live up in Croppy Boy on the Lower Kilmore Road. I don't know the exact address but right opposite the Centra.'

'Thanks, Lorcan. And I hope you trust me to keep my word.'
'You're a fecking detective superintendent. Why wouldn't I?'

31

When Katie returned to Anglesea Street, she found DS Begley waiting for her.

'You're looking fierce pleased with yourself, Sean,' she said, sitting down at her desk. 'Did you manage to track down those Extreme Dreams suspects?'

'Three out of the four of them, ma'am. The two men and one of the women. We arrested them on suspicion of assault causing serious harm and they're downstairs right now. The other woman's in Kenmare today as far as we know, but I reckon we'll have her when she comes back to Cork tomorrow.'

'Have any of them said anything?'

'Not a word except to ask for legal representation and the toilet. Their lawyers should be here later. But you're going to be shook when I tell you who they are. Or rather, *what* they are.'

'Go on, surprise me.'

'Well, the woman won't surprise you. She's working as a part-time barmaid at the Black Cat in Blackpool. But you'll never believe where we picked up the two fellas. The contact address they'd given to Sabrina turned out to be St Joseph's old folks' hospice at Clogheen Cross. They don't live there, though. They'd only been helping out there now and again.

In fact, they're both Benedictine monks from the Holy Mount monastery in Carrignavar, and that's where we found them, right in the middle of None.'

'You're serious? They're *monks*?'

'I know. I could hardly get my head round it myself. But I suppose that a monk's the same as any other man, like, do you know? Now and again he'll feel a bit of a stirring underneath his habit.'

'I'm not shook, Sean. I'm totally stunned. What time are you expecting their lawyers?'

'Not till seven or eight at least. The monks wanted that Ryan Nolan from Nolan and Sharpe. You remember him. He got that priest off, the one who molested all those convent school girls.'

'Oh well, that'll give me just enough time to go out looking for Rayland Garvey.'

'Rayland Garvey? Don't tell me that piece of something unpleasant's back here in Cork.'

'I'm afraid so. I've been given a tip-off that he's not only back here, but he's been trying to lay his hands on plastic explosives. It's more than likely he supplied the C-4 that blew up the O'Mahonys' house. In fact, I'm ninety-nine per cent sure of it. I saw him with my own eyes in the UK having a drink with Martin Bracken. And guess who tipped me off? Lorcan O'Neill, of all people.'

'Lorcan O'Neill? Holy Jesus. Lorcan O'Neill? Has he seen the light?'

'Well, we did a bit of a deal, to be honest with you. But he also told me where I might find Garvey. It's possible that he's staying up in Croppy Boy with one of his old girlfriends. I'll be going there in a couple of minutes with Bedelia, and I'm praying that we find him. I can't tell you, Sean, putting an end to this bombing, it's a million times more critical than anything else.'

'That Rayland Garvey, he's a curse,' said Sean Begley. 'He always was. There's always some police officers who think that the law applies to everyone else but not to them, like, and he was a classic example. Mind you, there's one or two I could put a name to now. Present company excepted, of course.'

Katie drove with Detective Garda Murrish up to the Lower Kilmore Road. She took Bedelia with her rather than a male detective to avoid Rayland Garvey's former woman friend feeling threatened in any way. She clearly remembered Rayland from his time at Anglesea Street, a misogynist and a sarcastic bully, and she would not be at all surprised if he had treated this Shayla in the same way.

They stopped at the Centra convenience store and went inside to ask the gingery woman behind the counter if she knew where Shayla lived.

'So who wants to know?'

'We're old school friends of hers. Haven't seen her for donkey's years.'

'Oh, she'll be made up to see you, then. She lives right over there, see, that house with the yellow door and the grey bin outside.'

As Katie and Bedelia crossed the road, a fine sparkling rain was falling. Lower Kilmore Road was high up to the west of the city with daytime views in the distance as far as Ballincollig and the hills around Blarney. It was bleak, though, with rows of shabby terraced houses painted pink and green and half-finished building sites and a concrete water tower like a Martian from *The War of the Worlds*.

They climbed the steps to the yellow door and Bedelia rang the bell. They could hear the muffled sound of a television somewhere inside, and after a few moments a light was switched on in the hallway.

'Who is it?' asked a woman's voice.

'Shayla?' said Katie. 'I hope you don't mind us disturbing you, but we need to have a chat.'

'Who are you?'

'Friends of Rayland's. We heard he was back in Cork and we'd like to see him if we could.'

The chain was taken off the door and it was opened up. A short woman in a maroon sweater dress was standing in the hallway with a brindled cat dangling under her arm, as if she had just scooped it up from the floor. She looked like Sophia Loren's younger but plainer sister.

Katie said, 'My name's Katie and this is Bedelia and we used to know Rayland well. Is he here at home with you now?'

'He's back in Cork, yes,' said Shayla. 'But he's out just now on some business or other. Shall I tell him you called to the door to see him? Maybe you could leave me your mobile number.'

'Is he staying with you now that he's back here?' Katie asked her. 'Weren't you and he doing a line together once, before he left for wherever it was that he left for?'

Shayla frowned at her, and put down the cat. 'I thought you said you knew him well, like. Where was that from?'

'We worked together for two or three years.'

'But he was an officer in the guards.'

'And so was I, Shayla, and I still am. Detective Superintendent Maguire. And I'm looking for him. Did he tell you where he was off to tonight?'

'No. I don't stick my nose into his private business. I never did.'

'Did he give you any idea when you could expect him back?'

Shayla was about to answer when a white Opel Insignia drew up outside the house, with its windscreen wipers squeaking from side to side, and stopped. The driver's door opened and a grey-bearded man climbed out. Katie failed to recognize him at first, like Lorcan O'Neill, but then she recognized his coat. It was brown, with a blue check pattern on it. The same coat that he had been wearing at The Huntsman when she had seen him drinking with Martin Bracken.

'Rayland!' she called out, and started back down the steps, but in the same instant that she had recognized his coat, Rayland Garvey had recognized her. He ducked back down into his car, slammed the door, and started the engine up again.

'Bedelia!' said Katie, and as the Opel squealed away from the kerb, the two of them ran up to their own car, opened the doors and threw themselves in. Katie twisted the key in the ignition and stamped on the accelerator so that they slithered at an angle on the wet road surface, but then they straightened up and went speeding after Rayland Garvey's red tail lights. They were only seconds behind him.

'There's guilty for you!' panted Bedelia, as Rayland took a sharp left down Courtdown Drive towards Hollyhill.

'God, he needs to slow down,' said Katie. 'He'll be after killing someone at this speed, if not himself. Call for backup, will you?'

Rayland took a left and a right down Hollyhill Lane, past the Mercy University Hospital. It was one-way and he was driving against the traffic, but fortunately the road was empty except for a Tesco delivery van. At the bottom of the hill, he turned into Blarney Street. This would take him directly into the city centre, although it was lined on both sides by single-storey terraced houses and rows of parked cars, and it was so narrow that two cars coming in opposite directions were unable to pass each other. A Land Rover approached Rayland's Opel with its headlights flashing, but instead of slowing down he drove up on to the pavement, and then off again. Katie had to follow him, with her car's suspension banging and both she and Bedelia jolting in their seats.

'He's taking a right down Shandon Street towards the North Gate Bridge,' Bedelia told the communications centre. Then, to Katie, 'Why in heaven's name doesn't he cop on that he's never going to get away?'

'He's probably panicking,' said Katie, as she steered right and left to avoid a parked pizza van. 'There's still a warrant out for him for all the racketeering he was tied up in before he was found out and fired.'

Rayland drove over the bridge and through the red stop light on the opposite side. He accelerated eastwards alongside the river, but Katie accelerated too. As they reached Coal Quay, she was so close behind him that she could have collided with his Opel's rear bumper if she had wanted to. If the pavements had not been crowded with evening shoppers, she would have done.

Nose-to-tail, they crossed back over the river at Patrick's Bridge, running through another red traffic light and arousing a chorus of angry horn-blowing from other drivers. As they turned eastwards again, along MacCurtain Street, Katie saw blue flashing lights in her rear-view mirror. They had been joined by two Garda patrol cars, and she expected that there would be more on the way.

Rayland sped out of the city and kept on heading eastwards on the Lower Glanmire Road. He was driving at over 140 kph, weaving in and out of the traffic, but Katie was not going to let him go. She had three patrol cars close behind her now, so that the rain on her windscreen was glittering sapphire blue, but she was not going to move aside to let them overtake her. To her, this pursuit was personal.

They were almost three kilometres away from the city when Katie saw that there was no traffic coming in the opposite direction, at least as far as the railway bridge up ahead of them.

'Hold tight,' she told Bedelia, and she pressed her foot right down to the floor, even as Rayland was slowing down slightly to negotiate the tight S-bend over the bridge. Her Toyota rammed into the back of his Opel with a loud buckling sound, and he swerved out of control, first to the left and then to the right.

Katie slammed on the brakes so that her car slid sideways to a stop beside the highway, facing the wrong way, but Rayland's Opel went careering on. It knocked down a row of metal posts outside the gates of the Port of Cork 2000 Garden and then it smashed through the wrought-iron gates themselves, leaving them wildly tangled like a spider's web.

Even the gates were not enough to bring his Opel to a halt. It went skidding across the grass verge beyond the entrance, and then it crashed through the bushes that bordered the river and vanished into the darkness.

'Jesus, he's gone in,' said Bedelia. Both she and Katie scrambled out of their car and hurried to the river's edge. At the same time, the three patrol cars arrived, their lights flashing.

The Opel was already sinking fast. Katie could see only its roof and its red tail lights glimmering under the water. She and Bedelia were joined by five uniformed gardaí and two of them were carrying LED lamps. They shone them on the Opel and one of them said, 'No wonder he's going down so quick. Look – his window's open and the water's pouring in.'

'Yeah, the water's pouring in but he's not getting out,' said the garda next to him. 'Maybe he's out for the count, like.'

Without saying a word, Bedelia unzipped her puffer jacket and wriggled out of it. Then she kicked off her leather boots.

'Bedelia,' said Katie. 'For the love of God be careful. That water's freezing.'

'I went swimming in the Lough on Saint Stephen's Day, didn't I?' said Bedelia.

She hopped her way through the prickly knee-high bushes and then without any hesitation she jumped into the water.

'Christ almighty,' said one of the gardaí, shining his lamp on Bedelia as she dived down next to the Opel. By now it was completely submerged, but even though that one open window meant that it had sunk right down to the riverbed, it had made it possible for her to open up the door.

She reached inside to unlock it, and when she had opened it, Katie could see Rayland slumped over a deflated airbag. Bedelia caught hold of Rayland's sleeve and started to drag him out of the driver's seat, two or three centimetres at a time. It seemed to Katie that it took her for ever, and she found it hard to believe that she could hold her breath for that long. But Bedelia lifted her leg and pressed her foot against the side of the car to give her extra leverage, and at last she managed to wrestle Rayland completely out of the door. He started to rise slowly, and Bedelia clung on to his collar as she beat her way up to the surface.

Two of the gardaí stripped off their coats and pulled off their shoes and jumped into the water to help her to keep Rayland afloat. A third garda had run to fetch the lifebelt that was hanging on a post halfway along the garden. He threw it down to Bedelia and the two gardaí and they clung on to it together so that they could keep Rayland's head out of the water.

At last, gasping and snorting with cold, Bedelia and the two gardaí heaved Rayland up on to the riverbank, and the other gardaí assisted them to drag him through the bushes. His brown coat squelched as they laid him down on the grass. One of the gardaí tilted Rayland's head back and gave him five rescue breaths, and then started chest compressions.

Bedelia was shivering wildly. Katie helped her to put on her puffer jacket and zip it up, and then she took her back to the car and switched on the engine to warm her up.

'You deserve a medal for what you just did,' she told her. 'That's if you hadn't saved one of the most evil men who ever was.'

Bedelia looked across to Rayland lying on the ground, with the garda still pumping his chest. They could hear an ambulance siren heading their way along the Lower Glanmire Road.

'Is he breathing?' she asked. 'I mean, he's not dead, is he?'

Almost as if he had heard her, Rayland spluttered and coughed.

'At least we'll be able to haul him up in front of a judge and jury,' said Katie. 'It looks like even the Devil doesn't want him. Not yet, anyway.'

Rayland was breathing harshly but normally now, although he was still concussed, with his eyes rolled up into his head so that only the whites showed, like two hardboiled eggs. The paramedics fitted an oxygen mask on to him, wrenched off his sodden overcoat and then carried him over to the ambulance.

It was still raining, but only softly, like thistledown. After the ambulance had left, the gardaí cordoned off the entrance to the garden and tied the twisted gates together with nylon cord. Katie sat in her car and called Superintendent Pearse. She asked him to send at least two officers to the emergency department at CUH to keep a watch on Rayland Garvey in case he tried to escape once he had recovered from his concussion or in case one of the remaining bombers tried to smuggle him out.

Next she rang Tim Deeley, the manager of the crane hire company in Carrigtwohill, to see if he could arrange for Rayland's Opel to be lifted out of the river. She knew Tim well, from all the other cars and vans that had ended up at the bottom of the Lee, some by accident and some deliberately, fourteen altogether since she had been serving at Anglesea Street.

'Unless there's somebody still sitting in it, like, it's going to be safer and more practical to leave it until tomorrow,' Tim Deeley told her. 'But don't you worry, detective superintendent. As soon as we've had our breakfast in the morning, we'll be right there with the thirty-tonne Liebherr, I promise you.'

Katie and Bedelia drove back to the station. Katie sent Bedelia off for a warm shower and a change of clothes, and then she went up to her office to catch up with any messages. Detective Coughlan had sent her a report about two shoplifters he had arrested in Dunnes stores with their bags full of stolen perfumes. She was still reading it when DS Begley knocked at her half-open door.

'I heard about Rayland Garvey, ma'am. If ever it paid off to follow your intuition, it did this time, for sure. I mean, of all the people on God's earth I never would have thought of asking Lorcan O'Neill where he was. Lorcan O'Neill, holy Mary.'

'If you want the dirt, Sean, sometimes you have to go down the sewer. When Rayland's out of the ED, I'm hoping that we can persuade him to give us the names of everyone else involved in this bombing.'

'You could threaten to have those two monks give him a whipping.'

'That's too much of a good idea to be funny,' said Katie. 'By the way, has their solicitor showed up yet?'

'That's why I've come up to see you. He's just arrived with one of his assistants and he's talking to them now, if you want to go down and start to give them a grilling.'

'What about the woman?'

'She's still waiting for her brief. But she can't stop keening. If you ask me, you'll get a confession out of her easy.'

'Right,' said Katie, 'let's go and have a word with the heavenly twins.'

32

The two monks were sitting in the interview room with their solicitor, Ryan Nolan, and his young woman assistant. Both monks were still wearing their long black hooded habits, and both smelled faintly of incense and stale body odour.

Ryan Nolan was silver-haired and smooth, with a precise Dublin accent. He was formally dressed with a bow tie and a waistcoat with a watch chain, which he always wore when he appeared in court. His assistant had upswept spectacles and protruding front teeth and spoke with a lisp.

'Fathers, this is Detective Superintendent Maguire,' said Ryan Nolan, standing up. 'Superintendent Maguire, this is Father Rowan and Father Finn.'

'Of course, I was given your full names by Sabrina Berrigan,' said Katie. She sat down and opened her notebook. 'Rowan Gribbin and Finn Hanlon. I'm not sure she was even aware that you were monks. But if you prefer to be addressed as Father This and Father That, then that's all right by me.'

Sean Begley sat down next to her, switched on the audio-visual recorder, and announced the time and the date and the names of those present.

Although they were both wearing habits, Katie found it hard to think of the monks as men of the cloth. Father Rowan reminded her of one of the waiters in the halal restaurant in the middle of the city and Father Finn, with his broken nose, had the appearance of an all-in wrestler who was past his prime.

'You've both been charged with assault causing serious harm,' she told them. 'There's no question that it was you two. You were positively identified by Sabrina Berrigan, who organizes sex sessions known as Extreme Dreams. She paid you to give a masochistic whipping to one of her clients.'

'Excuse me, let's get this straight, shall we?' Ryan Nolan interrupted her. 'My clients had no way of knowing that your man was a Garda officer acting undercover.'

'He clearly stated that he had changed his mind. We have it on record.'

'If he did, my clients didn't hear it. Both of them sincerely believed that they were doing nothing more than giving him a sexual experience that he not only wanted but craved.'

'I hope you're joking,' said Katie. 'These two holy fathers gave Detective Garda Hickey far more than a sexual experience. They lacerated him so badly with their whips that they almost killed him. He's had to undergo numerous skin grafts and he's still in a critical condition.'

'I'm aware of that, detective superintendent, but let's be fair. It was you who deliberately exposed him to the danger of being whipped. You set up this whole incident to encourage Sabrina Berrigan and anybody who she employed to break the law, so that you could arrest them. It was a sting, if you want to call it that. If you hadn't arranged it, Detective Garda Hickey would never have been injured and my clients would not be here today, facing this spurious charge of assault.'

'The entire hotel room was sprayed with blood and Detective Hickey's back was lashed so hard that his vertebrae were exposed,' Katie retorted. 'I hardly call that "spurious".

And these are supposed to be men of God. Don't they have anything to say for themselves for what they did?'

'He blasphemed!' Father Finn shouted out, banging his fist on the table. 'He took the name of the Lord in vain! That was why we punished him! We followed the example of Jesus Christ, who whipped the moneylenders for besmirching his Father's sacred place!'

He banged the table again. '"And when he had made a scourge of small cords, he drove them all out of the temple!"'

Ryan Nolan pressed his hand against his forehead, as if he were suffering from a migraine.

'Father Finn,' he said. 'I thought I specifically instructed you to keep your religious rants to yourself.'

'No, come on,' said Katie. 'I'd like to hear it. What did Hickey say that upset you so much that you almost killed him?'

Ryan Nolan waved his hand from side to side to indicate that Father Finn should say nothing more, but Father Finn was shaking his greasy curls in rage.

'I whipped him once. Just the once. But he shouted at me, "In the blank name of God, you blank, don't you do dare to do that again!" So I saw red, and so did Father Rowan, and we gave him the thrashing he deserved.'

He took a breath and added, 'I'll admit that both of us had some drink taken.'

'Father Finn,' said Ryan Nolan despairingly.

But Katie said, 'Let him speak, Mr Nolan, if he wants to. Otherwise I'll have to ask you to leave.'

'I've nothing more to say anyhow,' said Father Finn. 'We've both already been to confession and admitted what we did, even though I believe we were pure justified. It's blasphemy that's turned the world into the living hell that it is today, and those who blaspheme need to be punished every time they insult the Lord Our God.'

'You're preaching morality,' Katie replied. 'But you and Father Rowan here were both dressed up in bondage gear and taking part in a kinky sex session. Aren't Benedictine monks supposed to follow the rules of prayer, humility, obedience and work – not to mention chastity?'

'Our sexual desires were given to us by God. Father Rowan and I believe that we have a duty to help people if they are unable to fulfil those desires, no matter what they are, and for whatever reason – loneliness, disability, or the inability to find a partner who wants to share what excites them. Everyone should be able to experience the bliss that God gave us the capacity to enjoy.'

Katie closed her notebook and stood up, nodding to Sean to switch off the audio-visual recorder.

'Is that all?' asked Ryan Nolan. 'Don't you have any more questions?'

'For now, no,' Katie told him. 'What I'm going to do next is arrange for Father Finn and Father Rowan to be seen as soon as possible by one of our consultant psychiatrists.'

'*What?*' Father Finn demanded. 'Just because we believe in the joy that God's gifts can bring to us, you think that we're insane?'

'I'm not saying that, Father Finn. But I do think that you and your friend here have allowed your beliefs to go to your head. God knows what your abbot will say when he finds out about all your unholy shenanigans – that's if he hasn't found out already.'

Before she went home, Katie went down to the custody suite

to see the girl who had been arrested along with Father Rowan and Father Finn. Her name was Neave Blaney, and she was twenty-three years old. Her solicitor had been unable to come out so late and now she was asleep, her dyed black hair spread out on the grey blanket beneath her, sucking her thumb.

Next, Katie looked in on Sabrina Berrigan. She was due to be interviewed about the blackmail demands she had made on Detective Mullan, but her legal representative for this investigation had also been delayed until the morning. She was awake and sitting up, staring at the wall of her cell.

'How's yourself, Sabrina?' she asked her, but Sabrina simply snorted and turned away.

'She's fierce crabbit, that one,' said the duty sergeant. 'I asked her if she'd care for a mug of tea and she almost bit my head off. You'd think I'd offered her a mug of arsenic.'

It was nearly midnight by the time Katie drove back to Carrig View. She could see that Jenny's bungalow next door was in darkness and her living-room curtains were drawn, so she decided not to collect the dogs until the morning.

She undressed and took a long hot shower to try and wash the day away. When she closed her eyes she could see Cathal and Orla O'Mahony lying dead on their stretchers, with their chalk-white faces, both of them coated in dust.

Even when she went into the bedroom to sit in front of her dressing-table and smooth on her night-cream, she could almost imagine that Father Rowan and Father Finn were standing behind her and making faces at her in her mirror, like two characters out of some grotesque Punch-and-Judy show.

She had been so impatient during her suspension to return to Anglesea Street, but she had to admit that these past two days had shaken her. After all the years she had served in the

Garda, she still found it hard to believe that anyone could deliberately set out to commit such atrocities.

How could they have felt so vengeful that they were determined to kill more than forty innocent people and devastate the lives of so many others? And how could anyone really believe that God would be so offended by having His name taken in vain that He would approve of somebody being whipped on His behalf to the point of death?

She went into the kitchen and brewed herself a mug of mango and strawberry tea. She took it back into the bedroom and lay down on her bed to scroll through her phone.

She woke up at a quarter past five. Her bedside lamp was still on. Her phone had dropped on to the floor. Her mug of tea was untouched, stone cold, with the teabag still floating in it.

She could hear rain pattering against her bedroom window, and she thought: *Here we go, another day in purgatory.*

She dressed and hurried next door in the rain to collect Barney and Foltchain and Harvey.

Jenny said, 'If you ever grow tired of them, Kathleen, we'll take them off your hands. It's like they're our children now!'

'I'll need you to look after them today, Jenny, if you don't mind, once I've fed them and taken them out for a scove.'

'I saw you on the telly talking about that bombing,' Jenny told her. 'I honestly don't know how you manage that job of yours without having nightmares.'

Katie was busy patting all three dogs as they snuffled around her. She looked up to Jenny and said, 'Believe me, I do have nightmares. Almost every night.'

She led the dogs back to her kitchen and opened up three

packets of venison and strawberry leaves for them. Then she made a toasted cheese sandwich and a cup of lemon tea for herself. She was about to sit down to eat when her phone played 'The Rose of Allendale'. It was DI O'Sullivan, to tell her that Rayland Garvey had been discharged half an hour ago from the emergency department at CUH. He had immediately been arrested on suspicion of conspiring to cause an explosion that would endanger life, and escorted to Anglesea Street.

Not only that, but both solicitors representing Sabrina Berrigan and Neave Blaney had arrived, and were preparing their clients to be interviewed.

'Give me forty minutes and I'll be with you,' Katie told him. She could see that Barney and Foltchain and Harvey were licking the last of their breakfast out of their bowls and she could eat her sandwich in the car on the way to the city. She shrugged on her raincoat again and took the dogs back next door.

'I'm sorry, Jenny, but I won't have time to take them out. And it's lashing, too. But I'll fetch you back some of that Limerick ham you like from the English Market.'

'Come on, you three!' said Jenny to the dogs. 'Walkies! But you'll be needing your bathinas!'

Katie was sorry to leave them. She loved walking the dogs, even in the rain. It gave her time to think about everything – about the messages she needed, and what she was going to cook this week, and what she was going to report to Assistant Commissioner Frank Magorian about the O'Mahony bombing and the arrest of Rayland Garvey, and whether any more bombers were still on the loose.

And of course it gave her time to think about Kieran, and how she could have been Mrs Kathleen Connolly-to-be, and how she should already have been planning what to wear for her wedding. And about the dull numbing pain she felt for Kyna, and knew that she would always feel.

When she arrived at Anglesea Street, Terry came in to see her right away.

'We're making a fair bit of progress,' he told her. 'Sabrina Berrigan's lawyer has told us that she's prepared to plead guilty to the charges against her for blackmail and sexual offences, provided we drop any charges of threatening behaviour that might have led to Kevyn Hickey being injured.'

'Is she serious?' asked Katie. 'Her blackmail led to poor Conor Mullan taking his own life. Surely that comes under threatening behaviour? Even if it doesn't, the judge has to take that into account.'

'Sure, I agree with you, but we'll have to wait and see,' said Terry. 'As for Neave Blaney, she swears that she whipped Kevyn Hickey only twice, and only lightly – "playful-like" is how she described it. According to her, it was the two men who inflicted the most serious lacerations. But Sabrina Berrigan is prepared to testify that all three of them whipped him with equal ferocity. She insists that she called on them to stop when his back started to get bloody. However, Neave Blaney denies this and claims that the bloodier it got, the more Sabrina Berrigan appeared to be enjoying herself.'

'There's no recording of her telling them to stop,' said Katie. 'What about the holy fathers? Have they gone for their psych tests yet?'

'Dr Narwaz will be coming here at two.'

'Good, I'm glad it's him. I'd rather they were tested by a Muslim than a Catholic. I wouldn't want a psychiatrist who was even slightly tempted to believe that God wants us all to dress up in rubber and handcuff ourselves to the bedpost.'

'Do you want to go down now and see Rayland Garvey?' Terry asked her.

'Has he said anything so far?'

'Nothing, except that he doesn't want legal representation because he's done nothing wrong.'

'Nothing wrong? It depends if you think there's anything wrong in supplying C-4 explosive to somebody you know to be determined to blow up at least a dozen innocent people. Not to mention their wives and husbands and children and anybody else who happens to be unlucky enough to be standing close by.'

'Murrish is a brave girl all right, but I don't know why she didn't let him drown. It would have saved us a rake of bother and at least we wouldn't have had to pay to keep him in Portlaoise for the rest of his miserable life.'

Rayland Garvey was sitting reading the *Examiner* when Katie entered his cell. He took off his reading glasses when she came in, folded the paper and set it down on the bunk beside him, patting it as if he were telling it to behave itself and stay where it was.

'Kathleen Maguire,' he said, grinning and showing the gap in his tawny-coloured teeth. 'This is an expected pleasure. You've come quite a way up in the world, haven't you, since I was last here in Anglesea Street?'

'Better up than down, Rayland,' Katie replied. 'DI O'Sullivan tells me you've waived your right to a solicitor.'

'Why should I need a solicitor when I'm pure as the driven snow?'

'How can you say that when you've been supplying explosives to Martin Bracken and whoever else has been involved in bombing the Dripsey Dozen?'

'Come on, who told you that?'

'I have it on good authority that you came back here to Cork looking for C-4. Now why would you do that unless Martin Bracken had asked you to find some for him?'

Rayland pulled a face. 'I've no idea at all what you're talking about, Kathleen. And who's this Martin Bracken you keep talking about? I know nobody called Martin Bracken.'

'You're not telling me the truth, Rayland. I know you know Martin Bracken. I saw you with my own eyes having a gat with him in The Huntsman in Erdington.'

Rayland stared at Katie as if she had made a pint of Murphy's appear out of thin air. But then he shook his head and said, 'No, that couldn't have been me. Maybe some fella who happened to look like me, that's all. Besides, I've never been to – where did you say it was?'

'The Huntsman pub, in Erdington, near Birmingham. You were sitting at the table at the end of the bar with Martin Bracken and two other fellows and you were drinking out of a bottle.'

'I never saw you there.'

'How do you know you didn't see me there if you weren't there not to see me?'

'I meant I wasn't there so that's why.'

'Jesus Christ,' said Terry. 'I've heard some mad excuses in my time, but this one takes the biscuit.'

Katie said, 'Listen to me, Rayland. You've not only been arrested on suspicion of illegally supplying explosives for the purpose of causing death or serious injury. You must be aware that there are still outstanding warrants for your arrest for bribery, fraud, extortion and the illegal supply of firearms without a licence. They're all indictable offences, so you know yourself that there's no time limit for taking you to court.'

'Maybe so. But you'll have one hell of a job proving them, I can tell you that for nothing.'

'Oh, I believe I can. I've been looking through the file that was compiled shortly after you were dismissed from the force and conveniently managed to vanish into thin air, or Spain, or wherever it was.'

Rayland folded his arms, like a schoolteacher who has heard enough stories about dogs eating homework. 'I always had a feeling that you were going to be a thorn in my flesh, Kathleen, from the moment I first saw you at work. "Here's a woman who will never take no for an answer," I told myself. "The trouble is, she will never take yes for an answer either."'

'I'm going to give you a chance to have some of your charges dropped,' said Katie. 'You must realize that if you're convicted for every offence that you've been charged with, you'll be locked up for the rest of your life, even if some of the sentences run concurrently.'

'What do I have to do? Take you to bed?'

'No, with grateful thanks to Saint Agnes. All you have to do is tell us who you've been supplying C-4 to. How many are left, now that Martin Bracken has gone, what their names are, and where we can find them. We also urgently need to know if they're planning any more explosions, and where.'

'And if I don't give you all this information, it's more than likely that I'll end up in jail for life?'

Katie nodded.

'But if I do, I'll be signing my own death warrant, you know that, don't you? So what's better? Being stuck behind bars for forty years or being stuck in a box for all eternity?'

'If you didn't supply C-4 to anyone, like you claim you didn't, why would you be worried about anyone coming to kill you?'

'For the same reason you think you saw me in that pub. Sometimes people get the idea that you've done something when you haven't, or even if you have done it, they don't understand why, which is almost the same thing as not having done it at all.'

'Have a think about the deal we're offering and we'll come back later,' Katie told him. 'So far we haven't informed the media that you've been arrested – only that we fished a father of two out of the Lee when he lost control of his car.'

She and Terry left Rayland's cell and walked back through to the reception area.

'Do you know something?' said Katie, before she went back up to her office. 'I'm beginning to think that Dr Narwaz should be coming to see Rayland too.'

33

Jenny and Reilly took the three dogs down to Whitepoint Drive so that they could enjoy a run along the strand. The rain had cleared, and a watery sun was making an appearance behind the clouds. Reilly's cold was almost better now, except for an occasional nose-blow.

As they came to the railings that ran along the shoreline, they turned around and saw that they were being followed only a short distance away by a man and a woman. Both of them were tall, and the woman was wearing a long mustard-coloured overcoat while the man's black raincoat came almost down to his ankles.

What was disturbing was that they were both wearing black Covid masks over their faces. Apart from that, they were not talking to each other, or admiring the view, but looking ahead at Jenny and Reilly, and walking directly towards them.

They came right up to them, and Jenny said cautiously, 'Top of the morning you two. What way are you?'

'We're taking the dogs,' the man told her.

'Excuse me?'

'We're taking the dogs. So give them a whistle, will you, and clip their leads on for us. No messing. We don't have all day.'

'Are you off your heads? There's no way in the world you're taking these dogs.'

'Oh, please, bab,' the woman put in. 'You're not going to have a benny, are you?' Behind her mask she had a strange flat accent, as if she were talking with her teeth together. 'Just call them and fix on their leads and we can get away from here without any fuss.'

'They're not even my dogs,' Jenny protested. 'They belong to a Garda officer and she'd be down on you like a ton of bricks, I can tell you.'

'We know full well who they belong to,' said the woman. 'Now, are you going to put their leads on or do I have to take the leads off you and do it myself?'

Reilly said, 'I'll tell you what you can do. You can feck the feck off.' He took out his phone and held it up. 'I'll count to three and then I'm calling the guards.'

Almost wearily, the man reached into his raincoat and took out an automatic pistol. He pointed it at Reilly and said, 'You touch one button of that phone, boy, and that'll be your call to the cemetery.'

Barney and Foltchain and Harvey, meanwhile, had seen that strangers had arrived and they came running back along the strand and up on to the pavement. They clustered around Jenny, tails wagging, panting and staring up at the man and the woman with their usual curiosity. They had not yet sensed that Jenny and Reilly were being threatened.

'I can't let you take them,' said Jenny, in a shaky voice. 'I simply can't.'

The man pointed his pistol at her face. 'If you don't, then I'll kill the two of you and take them anyway. That's your choice. I would have thought that was a no-brainer. Well, you'll be the no-brainer if you keep on saying that I can't have them.'

Reilly reached out and took hold of Jenny's hand. 'Mam,' he said gently, 'they're dogs. I know they're not ours and we're supposed to be taking care of them and we love them, but they're dogs, and you're my mam.'

'He's talking good sense, your lad,' said the woman.

The three dogs were becoming unsettled now, especially Barney, and he gave three or four aggressive barks. Jenny put her finger to her lips and shushed him, and then she took the dogs' leads out of her coat pocket and clipped them on to their collars.

She had tears in her eyes as she handed the leads over to the woman.

'I swear to God if you harm one single hair on their precious coats, I'll make sure that both of you suffer for it for the rest of your lives.'

'If their owner's sensible, then no harm will come to them at all,' the man replied. He began to back away, but he still kept pointing his pistol at Jenny and Reilly, waving it from one to the other, and Jenny was convinced that if either of them tried to run forward and snatch the dogs' leads out of the woman's hands, he really would shoot them.

All three dogs were bewildered by what was happening, and kept turning around and around and looking for Jenny to come and rescue them. But the woman was yanking repeatedly at their leads and Jenny waved her hands to them and said, 'Shoo, go on, shoo! Off you go, Barney! Off you go, Foltchain! Go on, off you go, Harvey! Shoo!'

Still holding on to his pistol, the man took out his phone and thumbed out a number. Within a matter of less than fifteen seconds, a white van came speeding around the curve of Whitepoint Drive. It slewed to a stop, and a young man in a green anorak and a high fade haircut jumped out and swung the rear doors open. The woman dragged Barney and Foltchain and Harvey round to the back of it, and the two men heaved them inside. Both Barney and Foltchain were barking furiously in protest, and Harvey was yipping in fright, and Jenny could hear their claws scrabbling on the van's metal floor. There was nothing she could do. The van's doors were slammed shut, the men and the woman climbed into it, and it reversed along the drive. It U-turned at the end, and then it drove away up Whitepoint Moorings, and was gone.

Jenny took out her own phone, although her hand was trembling. 'Jesus, Kathleen's going to be in bits,' she told Reilly. 'You heard what that gowl said to me. "If the owner's sensible." You can be sure that he'll be wanting her to do something or other to get her dogs back, though God alone knows what.'

Katie was on her way to the interview room to talk to Sabrina Berrigan and her solicitor when her phone played 'The Rose of Allendale'. She recognized Jenny's number and stopped in the corridor to answer it.

'Jenny? Is something wrong? Please don't tell me that Barney's gone running off after that bitch from Knockeven House again.'

'It's worse than that, Kathleen.'

Between sobs, Jenny told her what had happened. Katie listened with a chilly feeling coming over her, especially when Jenny described the man and the woman who had taken the dogs. Although she said nothing, they sounded exactly like the man and the woman who had planted the bomb behind the O'Mahonys' house on Hartland's Avenue.

'The fellow said that no harm would come to the dogs if you were sensible. He didn't explain what he meant by that, but maybe he's going to get in touch with you and ask you for something. That's what it sounded like to me, anyhow.'

'That's what it sounds like to me too, Jenny. Oh God, I'm so sorry that you were put through such a frightening ordeal like that. At least you and Reilly weren't hurt.'

'They must have followed us until we ended up somewhere quiet, where nobody would see what they were doing.'

'Yes, but what I'm asking myself is, how did they know they weren't your dogs, but mine?'

'Most people around Carrig View know that they're yours.'

'Well, of course. But there's not many armed gangsters living round Carrig View, are there?'

'I'm so sorry I didn't get the van's number plate. I was too shocked, to be honest.'

'It can't be helped, Jenny. Don't go blaming yourself. There's scores of white vans around Cork, but you've described the driver so I can tell our patrols to keep an eye open for it all the same, and of course to look out for the dogs. I'll come and talk to you and Reilly later so. Meanwhile, I think it's best for me to wait here and see if these gowls try to get in touch with me. What they want should give me a good idea of who they are.'

'I'll be saying a prayer for Barney and Foltchain and little Harvey, Kathleen. May Jesus fetch them safely home.'

Katie reported the dognapping to Superintendent Pearse and then gave the details to Sergeant Murphy so that he could put out a bulletin about it, with descriptions of the three dogs. There was little else she could do, even though she was feeling both angry and worried sick that Barney and Foltchain and Harvey might be hurt, or that she might never see them again.

Her interview with Sabrina Berrigan was short and

unpleasant. She had never liked her solicitor, Colin McEndry, who had a habit of constantly wiping his hands together as if they were greasy, but who had a matchless knowledge of the law. He argued that Sabrina's demands for money from Detective Sergeant Mullan could not be construed as blackmail since she had provided all the sexual services that he had demanded from her. Therefore, she could not be held liable for his suicide.

'He may well have felt guilty for what he did, but by no stretch of the imagination does that mean that Mrs Berrigan has anything to feel guilty about. She was doing no more than he asked, and was obviously prepared to pay for. If he was unable to afford it, that was hardly her fault.'

After half an hour of discussion, it was agreed that she could be released on conditional bail to appear in front of the District Court in the second week of January.

Katie spent the early part of the afternoon catching up on current investigations, although she kept stopping to think about her dogs and wondering when the dognappers might try to contact her. At two o'clock, Dr Narwaz arrived to interview Father Rowan and Father Finn, and she had a short talk with him in her office.

Dr Narwaz was neat and small and bearded, in a grey three-piece suit, and the way he spoke was soft and monotonous.

'I must admit that these are the first monks I have ever been called to examine,' he told her. 'I have had to deal with three or four parish priests and church wardens who went off the rails. Paedophilia is the usual problem. But it is my understanding that if a monk misbehaves, his abbot will punish him in private, inside his abbey, and the outside world will never get to hear about it. I am guessing that they do not wish to give their orders a bad name.'

Katie said, 'They're Benedictines, and Benedictines are usually modest and humble and obedient. But for some reason these two have got it into their heads that God created sex for us to enjoy it, no matter who with, and no matter how kinky our tastes might happen to be.'

'I do not know of any religions that approve of that,' said Dr Narwaz. 'Even the most tolerant of Hindus expect *kama* to be confined to marriage, between a man and a woman, and only then when they reach the state of *grihastha*. But I have occasionally found that men who have been forced by their circumstances to be chaste for most of their lives will unexpectedly commit the most extreme acts of sexual abuse. They seem to believe that they are entitled to it, after all their years of chastity.'

'Well, I shall be interested to hear what you make of Father Rowan and Father Finn,' said Katie. 'Just watch out for Father Finn. He may be a man of God, but if you upset him he'll eat the head off you.'

Dr Narwaz went off to assess the two monks and Katie went back to her desk. She could see that there was only one hooded crow on the rooftop opposite, looking bedraggled and lonely. She had picked up the file on organized shoplifting when her phone rang.

It was Moirin. 'There's a call for you, ma'am. The switchboard put it through to me because they wouldn't give a name. They're saying that it's urgent and that you'll want to answer it because it's about what happened at Whitepoint Drive.'

'Whitepoint Drive? Put them through.'

'You're sure about that?'

'Yes, Moirin. Put them through.'

There was a click, and then she heard a croaky man's voice say, 'Hallo? Is that Detective Superintendent Maguire?'

'It is, yes. Who is this?'

'You don't need to know my name, super. All you need to know is that I am the present custodian of your three dogs.'

'Are they safe? You haven't hurt them at all, have you?'

'Oh, they're safe all right. I wouldn't say they're happy, but they've come to no harm.'

'You realize you've committed a serious offence and you're not going to get away with this.'

'It's not so much of an offence as a trade-off. You've taken something that belongs to us so we've taken something that belongs to you. All we have to do now is arrange for a swap, and both of us will be happy.'

'So what is it you want? As if I couldn't guess.'

'If you're guessing what I guess you're guessing, then you're right. We want you to release Rayland Garvey, and drop any and all charges against him. We know there'll be a few complications, like – superior officers to give their approval, and so forth – so we'll give you twenty-four hours from now.'

'And if I refuse?'

'You won't, because if you do, your three dogs will end up with bricks tied to their collars and going for a swim in the Lee.'

'Do you have any idea how serious the charges are that Rayland Garvey is facing? He's suspected of supplying the explosives that have killed forty innocent people. Not to mention historic charges of extortion and corruption and fraud.'

'None of it proven, super. None of it proven.'

'Who is this?' Katie demanded.

'Who I am is not important. All I'm asking you to do is release Rayland Garvey, and then you can collect your dogs safe and well from a prearranged location.'

'If you harm my dogs I'll find you, I swear to God, and I'll make sure that you're given the maximum punishment possible. I'll find you anyway, because if you're involved with Rayland Garvey then you must be party to these bombings in one way or another, and we're closing in on you, you can count on that.'

'I don't think you are. In fact, I know you're not. And you can threaten me as much as you like, because that's not going to alter the offer you have on the table right now. It's Rayland Garvey or your three beloved dogs. The choice is yours.'

Katie bit her lip. She was raging, and at the same time she was terrified for Barney and Foltchain and Harvey, but she was determined not to show this croaky man any weakness.

'How can I get in touch with you?' she asked him.

'You can't. This is a burner phone, so you won't be able to trace it. I'll give you another call in the morning to see if you've decided to let Rayland Garvey go. Like I say, you have until tomorrow. After that, if you haven't released him, then it's swim time.'

'You—' Katie began, but then she heard a click and knew that he had hung up on her.

She went along the corridor to see Chief Superintendent O'Leary. He was telling Inspector Kelly about a woman who had drunk too much prosecco last weekend at the Fota Island Golf Club and ended up dancing on the table, and then falling off. They were both laughing, but as soon as Katie came in, they immediately stopped, and made an effort to look serious.

'Kathleen,' said Brian O'Leary. 'Any news of your dogs yet?'

'In a way, yes,' said Katie, and she told him about the call that she had received, demanding the release of Rayland Garvey in exchange for the dogs' survival.

'Oh Jesus. I can't even guess how you must be feeling right now. You didn't happen to recognize this fellow's voice at all?'

'No. He sounded kind of robotic, do you know? But I noticed that he called me "super", which would be unusual for somebody who wasn't acquainted with the Garda or a Garda officer themselves.'

'So he's going to call back tomorrow morning to find out if we're going to let Rayland Garvey go?'

'That's what he said.'

'You understand that we can't do that. Garvey's charged with conspiracy to commit multiple homicides. You can imagine the uproar if we let him go to save the lives of three dogs.'

Katie nodded, and swallowed. She was doing her best not to cry.

'I can understand how much you love them,' said Brian O'Leary. 'We're out looking for them and maybe with luck one of our patrols will spot them. Otherwise, we can only hope that this evil character doesn't really intend to do what he's threatening to do. He must realize that what he's demanding is totally unrealistic.'

'You said the way he called you "super" made you wonder if he might be connected with the Garda,' said Inspector Kelly. 'Is there anybody you can think of who might fit that description?'

'Only one. And he even fits my neighbour's description of him, wearing a long black raincoat. But there must be hundreds of men who wear long black raincoats and I can't seriously see him being involved with someone like Rayland Garvey, or the Dripsey bombers.'

'I think I know who you mean,' said Brian O'Leary. 'He wasn't too happy when you were reinstated, was he? But he has an exemplary record, even if he's not exactly Prince Charming. And at the moment he's down with the Covid, so I can't see him making threatening phone calls.'

Katie said, 'All I can do is pray for my dogs and hope that somebody sees them, or that somehow they manage to escape.'

'By the way,' said Brian O'Leary, as she turned to leave, 'all the remaining Dripsey Dozen families are being moved again today, to new addresses, and they're all going to be given round-the-clock surveillance. One couple have upped sticks altogether and gone to stay with relatives in Scotland, at least until they're sure that the bombers have all been caught.'

'That's some relief, I suppose.'

When she returned to her office, Katie sat down and thought about the call that she had received from the muffled man calling her 'super', and about the description that Jenny had given her of the man in the long black raincoat. It sounded so much like Micheál ó Broin, and yet how and why would a senior Garda detective be a party to the Dripsey Dozen bombings? It made no sense at all, and as much as she disliked him, she found it almost impossible to believe that he could have been involved in the wanton murder of over forty people.

At the same time, she found it hard not to recall his reluctance to give the Dripsey Dozen an early warning of the danger they could be in, and his reluctance to assume that they were the victims of some kind of vendetta. Not only that, he had been one of the few officers at Anglesea Street who knew the addresses of the safe houses to which they had been moved for their protection.

But really? There was no question that he possessed a snide and unpleasant demeanour, and that he had deeply resented having to surrender his position in Cork as Katie's stand-in. But as Brian O'Leary had pointed out, he had an impressive record for closing some highly complex cases of fraud and robbery and drug-running, and he had brought some of Limerick's most notorious gangsters to justice.

Katie continued to think long and hard, and then she decided to call him. She was not entirely sure what she was going to say to him, but if he had been involved in the bombings in any way, she thought she might catch him off guard. She was willing to try anything that might give her a clue as to what had happened to Barney, Foltchain and Harvey.

She found his number and was about to dial it when Moirin came in.

'You'll have to forgive me, Kathleen, but I listened in to that call about your dogs. You must be scared sideways. Do you have any notion at all who that was?'

'No, I don't. But I may be about to find out.'

'I'm praying for the poor creatures. Can I fetch you a lemon tea? It's supposed to be good for the nerves, like.'

'No, thank you, Moirin. What I really need now is a double vodka.'

She dialled Micheál's number. It rang for so long that she was about to give up when he answered.

'Yes?' he said, clearing his throat.

'Micheál, it's Kathleen. Kathleen Maguire.'

'Oh, yes?'

'Micheál, I'm only calling to see if you've recovered from the Covid.'

'Are you now? And why would you be interested to know?'

'Come on, we've had our ups and downs, but there's no point in either of us bearing a grudge. We may need to work together in the future. You never know.'

'I doubt it.'

'Why do you doubt it? Aren't you going back to Henry Street?'

'Are you serious? I'd be knocked off by the Rathkeale Mob as soon as I showed my face out the door.'

'So what are you going to do?'

'What do you care? And why would I want to work with you anyhow, you and your divine inspiration? Not having much luck with the Dripsey bombers, are you?'

'I don't know. We haven't announced it yet, but we've arrested Rayland Garvey – Detective Inspector Garvey as was. We're pretty sure that he was the one who was supplying the bombers with their explosives.'

'Oh, yes? And how long do you think you'll be able to hold on to him?'

'What do you mean by that?'

'I mean what evidence do you have that he was supplying explosives, apart from one of your wild female guesses?'

'Don't you worry. I'll have my sniffer dog Harvey have a snuffle round where Garvey's been staying. If there's any trace of C-4 there, he'll find it.'

Micheál was silent for several long seconds, as if he was undecided how to answer that, if at all. Katie waited to hear what he would say, but the longer he was silent, the stronger her feeling was that he knew. *I'm sure he knows. Even if it wasn't actually him who took my dogs and called me to demand that we release Rayland Garvey – he knows.*

'So what are you going to do?' she asked him at last. 'Retire? Get yourself a job? I hear that Carrigaline Court Hotel are looking for a night porter.'

'Do you know something?' said Micheál abruptly. 'You always were a sarcastic wagon.' With that, he hung up.

34

'Those cops,' said Tim Lyons. 'They're about as useful as a pair of shoes to a snake.'

He was rummaging through a large suitcase in the bedroom, trying to find the trousers that matched the pyjama jacket he had just taken out.

'If you'd only packed a bit neater, instead of throwing everything into the case in a rage,' Nola admonished him.

'If only we hadn't had to move here at all. One minute the cops are telling us they've ended the bombing and we're all safe and the next minute Cathal and Orla get blown to high heaven.'

'Well, I know, Tim. It's tragic. And I'm going to miss Orla so much. She was a dote.'

'God knows when we'll be able to move back to Barley Grove. Let's pray that the pipes don't freeze in the middle of winter and we end up flooded like we did that time in Coachford.'

He rummaged some more, and then he said, 'No, they're not in here. They must be in that other case downstairs. There's no way I'm going to bed tonight with no pyjama bottoms on.'

Nola gave him a playful pat on the back. 'You haven't asked *me* if I'd like it.'

'Behave yourself, woman.'

Tim went downstairs to the living room. Compared to their house at Barley Grove, this end-of-terrace property on the Old Youghal Road in Mayfield was cramped and small, with low ceilings, and only a shower instead of a bath, but it had been the best that the Garda could find for them at short notice.

As he picked up the suitcase that he had left on the sofa, there was a knock at the front door. He put down the suitcase again and went to answer it, but before he opened the door he called out, 'Who's that?'

Detective Inspector O'Sullivan had warned him to be ultra-cautious, even though he and Nola had been moved nearly fifteen kilometres away from Ballincollig, to the north-east of Cork city.

'Amazon,' came the reply. 'I've a delivery for your neighbours but they're not in, so can I leave it with you?'

Tim opened the door. Standing on the step outside was a young man in a green anorak, holding a large cardboard box. Behind him, a white van was parked at the kerb with its engine running.

'They said to leave it next door if they were out.'

'No, I'm sorry, I don't think I can take it in,' Tim told him. 'I've only moved here today so I don't know them at all. What is it, anyhow?'

'It's only a microwave oven.'

At that moment, the uniformed garda who had been watching their house from the corner of New Road appeared. He was short and broad-shouldered and approached with a businesslike swagger.

'Who are you and what's that you have in that box, then?' he demanded.

'Amazon. I'm only asking this fellow if he could take this in for his neighbours, because they're out.'

The garda glanced next door. 'Their lights are on and I can hear their TV. They don't look very out to me. And that's not an Amazon van. I want you to lay that box down real careful-like and then take at least five steps back.'

The young man appeared to be undecided for a moment, but then he turned towards the van. Tim could see the driver, and he was leaning forward and making a flapping motion with his hands.

'I said, lay the box down,' the garda repeated. 'I'm not telling you a third time.'

'Okay, whatever,' the young man told him. But then he lifted the box up over his head and threw it through the open door. It hit Tim a glancing blow on the shoulder, but then it dropped on to the floor behind him, tumbled along the hallway and ended up in the kitchen.

The young man ran towards the van, opened the passenger door and scrambled inside. The van immediately pulled away from the kerb, with the passenger door still swinging open. As it swerved into New Road, the box exploded with a bang so loud that it was heard in Glanmire, three kilometres away.

Tim's head, arms and legs were torn off. His dismembered trunk hurtled across the road and struck the living-room window of the house on the opposite side of the street, cracking the glass and splashing blood all over it. The garda was knocked backwards and killed instantly when his head hit the edge of a kerbstone and broke his skull. Upstairs, Nola was blasted through the plaster ceiling into the attic before the whole house collapsed in a heap of bricks and tiles and doors and broken windows and shattered lumps of concrete.

The lights instantly went out in the house next door and the TV was silenced, but all the way along Old Youghal Road lights were switched on and doors were opened as people came out to see what had happened. Within only a few minutes, the evening air was filled with the sound of sirens – police cars and ambulances and fire engines all competing in a haunted chorus.

Katie stood on the corner in her red duffel coat, staring at the smoking ruins of the house and feeling a wretchedness that she had not experienced in years. If only she had been able to track down all of the Dripsey Dozen bombers, Tim and Nola Lyons would never have died such a sudden and horrendous death, and neither would the garda who had been posted to keep a watch on them. She had known him well. His name was Tadhg Daley, and he was the father of two children and only thirty-three years old.

DI O'Sullivan came across the road, treading carefully through the scattered bricks and lumps of concrete.

'Nobody saw nothing, nobody heard nothing, and there's no CCTV,' he told her. 'Not even a doorbell camera. Garda Daley was wearing a body cam but it's totally banjaxed.'

'He must have been alerted to something,' said Katie. 'Otherwise why did he leave his car and come over to the front of the house?'

'We'll check the CCTV from all the surrounding streets. We may be lucky and pick up some vehicle that must have left here about the same time that the bomb went off.'

Katie could see two paramedics lifting a stretcher out of the ruined house. Its black vinyl sheet was covering what was left of Nola Lyons.

'Holy Mary. To think I congratulated myself because I saved their lives when they were living in Ballincollig. The real question is – how did the bombers know that we'd moved them here? There was me half suspecting that it might have been Micheál ó Broin who slipped them the addresses of all the safe houses, either deliberately or accidentally, but he'd quit Anglesea Street before we moved the Lyonses to this new address, so how could he have known it?'

'You think there's someone else at the station who's been ratting?' Terry asked her. 'I can't understand what their motive could be. This bombing campaign's done nothing but ruin our reputation – not only in Cork but all over – even abroad. Mathew McElvey told me yesterday that they'd run a special programme about it last week on the Sky News. And, Jesus, this bombing isn't going to make things any better.'

'Do you know what I'm thinking of doing?' said Katie. 'Moving the few surviving Dripseys yet again, but giving out false addresses, and putting them under even more intensive surveillance.'

She could see Fionnuala Sweeney and Dan Keane on the opposite side of the Garda cordon, and she knew that she would have to go over and give them some kind of statement, although she had no idea what she could say. *Another bombing's taken us by surprise and we still don't know for sure who's planting these bombs or how they're doing it. Does that satisfy you?*

Terry said, 'What about your dogs? Any more news?'

'I'm trying to put them out of my mind, Terry. As the chief says, we can't release Rayland Garvey for the sake of three dogs. Imagine what would happen in the future. Every time we arrested some gowl, his friends would be round to my house stealing my dogs and demanding that we let him out.'

Katie was unable to sleep that night. It was almost midnight when she arrived home from the crime scene in Mayfield, but even though she was exhausted she was too disturbed by the bombing and by the loss of Barney, Foltchain and Harvey.

She put in a late call to Michael Pearse to see if they could arrange for the few remaining members of the Dripsey Dozen to be moved yet again tomorrow morning, and for the watch on them to be intensified. Then she brewed a mug of mango and strawberry tea, even though she was tempted to pour herself a large glass of vodka.

She sat in the living room with the flute and harp music of Tim Janis playing quietly in the background to relax her. She sipped her tea and looked through all the photograph albums of herself and her dogs, and the copy of *Our Dogs Ireland* magazine in which she had appeared with Barney and Foltchain last year as 'the dog-friendly detective'.

It was then that she saw an advertisement in the magazine for a miniature GPS dog tracker, the PitPat. She remembered Garda Harrington from the dog unit telling her about them, and how he had fitted one on Cody's collar so that he would always know where he was, even when Cody was searching through a collapsed school building or an unlit block of flats or a factory after a fire.

The tracker was only sixty millimetres long and weighed less than thirty grams. Katie got up and went to the hallway and measured the heels of her rubber boots. Then she went back into the living room and called Michael Pearse again.

'Michael, I'm so sorry to disturb you so late.'

'No, you're grand altogether. I'm in bed and the old doll's fasters but I've been reading.'

'Who do you have on duty tonight?'

'Tom Hackett.'

'Listen, can you have him call Garda Harrington from the

dog unit. It doesn't matter if he has to wake him up. I know that Garda Harrington has some of these tiny GPS trackers that he uses to make sure he knows where his dogs are. They're called PitPats.'

'Okay. I have that. PitPats. And then what?'

'One way or another, get hold of one of these trackers, and wake up whoever it is we use for any small repair jobs. It's that fellow with a stammer from Ardpatrick, as far as I remember. He mended the lock of my desk once. Rayland Garvey will have had his shoes removed while he's held in custody. Ask our repair man to cut a hole in the heel of one of his shoes and insert this tracker.'

'Serious? Then what?'

'Then we can let Garvey go and with any luck I'll be having my dogs back. As soon as they've been safely returned to me, though, we can track him down and arrest him again. But it's not so much about my dogs, Michael, as much as I love them. It's about the rest of the Dripsey Dozen. If we can follow where Garvey goes, we'll have a reasonable chance of finding the rest of the bombers, and that'll finally put an end to all these killings.'

'Well, that's a plan all right, Kathleen. But supposing Garvey changes into a different pair of shoes?'

'He's come sneaking back into the country undercover, hasn't he? I doubt if he's fetched too many pairs of shoes with him. In any case, even if he does change them, we should be able to locate where he's staying.'

'Fair play to you, Kathleen. I'll get this set in motion right away. I expect we'll be cursed to the ends of the Earth and back for disturbing all these fellows' sleep, but like you say, if this can stop these bombings, it'll be worth a million times more than a few hours in bed.'

Katie sent text messages about the dog tracker to Chief Superintendent O'Leary and DI O'Sullivan. After that, there was nothing more she could do except wait to hear that Inspector Hackett had managed to contact Garda Harrington and get hold of a PitPat, and that it had been successfully inserted into the heel of one of Rayland Garvey's shoes. She was still unable to sleep, though, and she spent the early hours of the morning sitting with her feet tucked up on the couch watching repeats of the quiz show *Ireland's Smartest* and the fire brigade drama *999 Faoi Oiliúint*.

It was not until 8:15 that her phone played 'The Rose of Allendale'.

'Kathleen? Michael here. You'll be happy to hear that it's all done and dustificated. There was a rake of grumbling all right but we got hold of a PitPat, and your man from Ardpatrick was able to fit it into one of Garvey's shoes. A pure neat job he made of it, so Tom Hackett said. He glued the bottom of the heel back in place so you'd never guess that anything had been hidden inside it.'

'Thank you so much, Michael,' said Katie. 'And thanks to Tom and everyone else. I know there's no guarantee that this is going to work. If we let Garvey go and he manages to disappear without a trace, then I know who'll have to shoulder all the blame for it, and that's me.'

'Yes, but if we catch the rest of the bombers, you'll take all the credit for it, so keep your fingers and toes crossed. By the way, have you heard yet about your shooting that Bracken feen?'

'Not officially. But Assistant Commissioner Magorian gave me a hint that I was totally justified in taking him down. After all, for God's sake, he was only a second away from blowing up the whole house, and us with it.'

'You've heard what they're calling you, have you, down in the canteen? Quick Draw Maguire.'

The call came at 10:05, when Katie was making herself a cheese roll to take to work. The caller had the same robotic-sounding voice as yesterday.

'Good morning, super. Have you come to a decision yet? Will you be releasing Rayland Garvey or will your dogs be going for a swim?'

'Are they safe, my dogs? You haven't hurt them, have you?'

'Oh, they're safe enough. They're pining for you, no doubt about that, but they ate a hearty breakfast.'

'You realize how difficult this is, what you've been asking for?'

'Did I say it was easy? Of course it's not easy. But so many people love their dogs so much more than their fellow humans, and I reckoned that you were one of them. You know, given your history.'

'What do you know about my history?'

'More than you'd think. But then you're reasonably famous around Cork, aren't you? I'd say a fair proportion of the population know the name of Detective Superintendent Kathleen Maguire. You're quite a star. Except among the criminal community, of course. They're not too fond of you.'

'You realize that the final decision on releasing Rayland Garvey is not mine to make.'

'You're pure persuasive, though, aren't you? I'm sure you've been able to convince your superiors that the lives of your three lovely dogs are worth much more than keeping some disreputable ex-police inspector in custody.'

'Rayland Garvey helped to take the lives of innocent human beings.'

'Well, as I said before, super, you have no way of proving that, and even if he had, it would have been an eye for an eye.'

'What do you mean by that? You're saying that all of those people were murdered out of revenge?'

'I meant nothing. A figure of speech, that's all. What I need to know now is if you're going to release Rayland Garvey before your twenty-four hours are up. I'm not a great animal lover, I have to admit, but I wouldn't like to frighten your dogs more than necessary by drowning them in the dark.'

Katie took a sharp breath, and then she said, 'We're going to release him.'

'What? You're not slagging?'

'Slagging? No. This is a fierce serious situation, whoever you are, and it doesn't call for any kind of jokes. We'll release Rayland Garvey as soon as I get to the station this morning and make sure that all the paperwork's in order. I've received permission from the chief superintendent to let him go. There'll be no publicity – none whatsoever. We haven't yet informed the media that we've arrested him and we're not going to inform them that we're letting him out. The only thing I'm going to say to you is that we're not dropping any of the charges against him – either the new charges or the charges that were made against him before he disappeared five years ago. So he'll have to make himself scarce.'

'Oh. That's not too generous of you.'

'I think that releasing a suspected conspirator to mass murder is more than generous enough. We want to make absolutely sure that we don't see his face again, that's all. Now, are you going to return my dogs to me?'

'We will. As soon as Rayland gets in touch with me to say that he's out, I'll call you and tell you where you can collect them from.'

'You won't be leaving them anywhere where they might get hurt, or stray away?'

'You keep your word, super, we'll keep ours. There's only one thing I have to warn you about. If we catch any indication at all that you're following Rayland after you've released him, and I mean like only the slightest hint of it, then your dogs will be taking that swim after all. Otherwise it's been grand doing business with you.'

He hung up. Katie picked up her knife again to spread butter on her roll and her hand was shaking.

She entered Rayland Garvey's cell just as he was lacing up his brown leather brogues.

'I have the paperwork here, Rayland. I'll need your signature to confirm that you've been released and that you're not holding us liable for wrongful arrest. Mostly because it wasn't wrongful.'

'If it wasn't wrongful, then I'd be interested to know why you're letting me out,' said Rayland. He stood up and fastened the buttons on his brown check coat, although he still refused to make eye contact with her.

Katie handed him the clipboard and a ballpoint pen. 'Yes, sign it down there at the bottom. Where it says "Agreed by". Apparently, the powers that be are concerned that the new evidence against you is insufficient for a conviction. On top of that, the offences that you were alleged to have committed when you were serving as inspector here are almost out of time and in any case they would probably cause more embarrassment than they were worth. That's the impression I was given, anyway.'

Rayland scribbled his signature and handed the clipboard back, still without facing her. He made her feel that if he allowed her to look into his eyes, she would be able to see that he was guilty of everything with which he was charged, and maybe more.

'Right,' she said. 'You know where the front door is.'

Rayland stepped outside the cell into the corridor, but then he stopped.

'I suppose before I go you want me to offer you my heartfelt gratitude for saving my life,' he said. It sounded almost like a challenge.

'That won't be necessary,' Katie told him. 'We've fished far more repulsive things out of the Lee than you, and not expected any thanks for it.'

'I wouldn't have crashed into the fecking river if you hadn't been chasing after me.'

'Rayland, you've been released. Now go. But I warn you. We never want to see you again, like ever.'

Rayland still hesitated, and Katie had the feeling that he was regretful that he had to leave, because he had achieved considerable success here at Anglesea Street. That was before he had become involved in fraud and extortion and sold his soul to the O'Flynns and the Keenans and other Cork gangs.

But then, without saying anything else, he walked out of the custody suite on his squeaky-soled brogues and across the reception area. He pushed open the front doors and without looking back he went down the steps into a grey November day that looked like a black-and-white crime film.

35

Katie went upstairs immediately to the communications room. Sergeant Murphy had picked up the GPS signal from the tracker in Rayland's shoe even before Rayland had put it on and laced it up.

Now he and Katie sat down in front of the monitor screen and watched the triangular blip cross over Anglesea Street and make its way north to Union Quay. It stopped at Charlie's Bar, overlooking the river, and Katie guessed that Rayland was going to wait there for somebody to come and collect him.

The blip stayed there for over a quarter of an hour, and while Katie was still sitting there waiting for it to move, Moirin called her.

'Dr Narwaz has come in to see you, ma'am. He says he's completed his examination of the two monks and he needs to talk to you about it.'

'Okay, Moirin, that's grand. Tell him I'll be with him directly.'

She looked at the blip on the monitor and it was still not moving.

'Keep an eye on him for me, Peter, will you? I shouldn't be long, but if he starts to shoot off let me know at once.'

She walked back to her office and found Dr Narwaz

standing by the window looking out at the hooded crows that were clustered on the roof opposite.

'Fascinating, those crows,' he said, as Katie came in. 'Do you know that crows bury their dead and hold funerals for them? In the Quran, Allah expresses his regret that he did not bury his dead brother in the same way that the crows would have done. And in Islam they are a symbol of bad luck and bad fortune. Do you ever ask yourself why they gather outside your window like that?'

'Dr Narwaz, believe me, I don't need crows to tell me that I'm having bad luck. How did things go with the heavenly twins?'

'Very interesting. Father Rowan experienced some trauma in his childhood because his father was an alcoholic and a violent bully. The effect that had on him was to make him withdrawn and mistrustful of other people. However, it also encouraged him to dedicate his life to helping others who had been made to feel worthless because of constantly being browbeaten and abused.

'Father Finn has what you might call a superiority complex. He considers that he was brought into this world to teach the rest of us how to behave. He believes in God, but he thinks of himself as personally chosen by God to carry out His wishes. In Father Finn's view, God gave us our ability to feel sexual excitement, and therefore we should enjoy his gift to the full, or else we are being ungrateful to the One who put so much thought into creating us. He thinks that anyone who tries to deny us this enjoyment is doing so only in order to impose their own will on us, in the same way that some religions repress women or condemn homosexuals.'

'I think Father Finn's behaviour was pretty much

self-explanatory,' said Katie. 'What I really need to know is, are they barmy, those two, or are they sane enough to stand trial?'

'I assume you are Catholic, and that you strongly disagree with their interpretation of God's intentions.'

'My religious beliefs don't enter into this, doctor. If I arrested people every time they transgressed against Catholic doctrine, the prisons in Ireland would be too crowded for anyone to breathe. You'd have only to blaspheme against the Holy Spirit and you'd find yourself locked up for the rest of your life.'

Dr Narwaz smiled. 'The answer to your question is that both Father Rowan and Father Finn passed every psychological test that established their sanity beyond any question. Their view of God's wishes may be unusual, but you have to admit that it has a certain logic to it, and it is certainly not insane. I will of course be writing you a full report on the pair of them, giving you my official opinion that they are mentally sound and able to stand trial.'

'That's what I was hoping.'

'Times have changed, superintendent. These two men are not being condemned for their sexual proclivities, or for taking the Lord's name in vain. Their only sin under the law was to whip your colleague close to the point of death.'

Moirin brewed Katie a cup of lemon tea and she carried it back up to the communications centre on the top floor. Rayland Garvey was still at Charlie's Bar, unless he had taken off his brogue with the PitPat in it and left it there. Sergeant Murphy had gone back to watching the main shopping streets, but he had given Garda Lilian Lennon the job of keeping an eye on Rayland's blip.

'There's been slight movement, like,' said Lilian quietly, as Katie sat down next to her. 'But I reckon that's nothing more than him going to the bar for a drink and back.'

They waited for another ten minutes, but then the blip suddenly left the bar and went out on to Union Quay. Rayland was clearly picked up by someone in a car, because the blip then travelled westwards along the quay at speed, crossing the south branch of the Lee over Parliament Bridge and then heading north on Grand Parade.

When it passed the Roundy pub and turned into Cornmarket Street, it stopped in what Katie guessed was one of the disabled parking spaces.

'You know what I think he's doing?' she said, putting down her cup of tea. 'The street's fierce narrow there, and only one-way, and he's double-checking that he's not being followed.'

After about a minute, the blip started going again. It crossed the north branch of the Lee at North Gate Bridge and then turned west on Blarney Street, following the same route in reverse that Rayland had taken when Katie and Bedelia had been chasing him in his Opel.

'I have a fair idea where he's going. Lower Kilmore Road, where his old girlfriend Shayla lives.'

She was right. The blip turned northwards again towards Croppy Boy and within a few minutes it had stopped at Shayla's house opposite the Centra store.

Sergeant Murphy had left his console to stand behind them.

'Don't you think he'd guess that we'd be keeping a watch on that address? I mean, if we hadn't fitted that tracker on him, we would've been, wouldn't we?'

'Of course,' said Katie. 'But whoever picked him up must have told him by now what the deal was to release him, so he'll be feeling safe enough until I get my dogs back. You'll see.

In any case, I doubt if he'll be staying with the lovely Shayla for too long.'

Again, she was right. Only ten minutes after it had stopped at Shayla's house, the blip was off again, this time travelling east, towards Fair Hill.

'With any luck, he'll be heading now to wherever it is that the other suspects have been hiding themselves.'

Sergeant Murphy shook his head in admiration. 'If this works, we ought to find a way to hide one of these PitPats inside the shoes of every criminal in Cork. We'd only lose track of them when they went to bed.'

The blip continued east until it reached Spring Lane, an uphill boreen that led towards Ballyvolane. It stopped opposite Spring Lane Park and right next to a railway bridge. From its next movement, it appeared that Rayland was entering a house there.

'Right,' said Katie. 'I'll ask Superintendent Pearse to have that area surrounded, but with every officer out of sight until I give the word to go in. It could be that Rayland's making just another temporary stop, but I have the strongest feeling that this is the location where we're going to find the others. Spring Lane's out of the way, like, and it has houses only on the one side so it's not overlooked. That's where I'd choose to stay if I didn't want any nosy neighbours to see me coming and going.'

Katie contacted Superintendent Pearse and brought him up to date with Rayland's location. She asked him to deploy officers not only at both ends of Spring Lane, but also on Dublin Street and the North Ring Road. She was taking the precaution that if and when they raided the house, Rayland and any other suspects might try to make a getaway on foot through Spring Park or the grounds of the Glen Boxing Club.

She could tell by the tone of his voice that Michael Pearse was impatient to send in his officers immediately, without delay, regardless of what the consequences might be for Katie's dogs. They were only dogs, after all, and the suspects were serial killers. But he would be aware that if he gave the order to go in now, he would risk losing her trust and her close co-operation, perhaps for ever.

Besides, it was possible that the dogs were being held at a different location altogether by another member of the bombing gang, and that this suspect had not yet released the dogs and returned to Spring Lane. These bombers were a greater threat to innocent lives than any terrorist they had ever had to deal with, and it was essential that they caught every one of them.

Katie took a look at the house on Google. It stood right next to the railway bridge, the only two-storey building at the end of a long terrace of single-storey dwellings. Its façade was pale grey and flaking, as if its owners had neglected to paint it in decades, and all its windows were covered with drooping white curtains. Katie thought that it looked like a house out of a ghost story.

The blip stayed where it was and so she waited in the communications centre for nearly an hour. It was hushed in there, as the duty officers sat watching their screens. There was no small talk, only an occasional softly spoken comment about what their CCTV cameras had picked up. A reporter for the *Examiner* had once described the atmosphere in the communications centre as being 'like a funeral home'.

Shortly after noon, Chief Superintendent O'Leary came

in. Katie was showing him the image of the house when her phone rang.

'Am I speaking to Detective Superintendent Maguire?' came the robotic voice.

'You are so,' she said, lifting her hand up to show Brian O'Leary that this call was critical.

'You've stuck to your side of our agreement, super, and I thank you for that. So we've stuck to ours.'

'My dogs are all safe and well?'

'Safe and well, never fear. In fact, they're more than safe and well. They're positively pampered.'

'When are you going to return them? And where?'

'You'll find them in the loving care of the Pawfect Pooch dog grooming parlour in Riverview Gardens, by the Glen River Park. Don't you go giving the owner a hard time because she has no idea about our arrangement. She thinks we owned them, and that we simply dropped them off for a wash and a fluff-up and a nail-clipping. She's probably done it all by now, so be prepared to pay her for it.'

'You'd better pray to God that you're telling me the truth.'

'Go and find out for yourself, super. It's been a pleasure doing business with you.'

As soon as the caller had hung up, Katie turned to Brian O'Leary. 'He's told me where my dogs are, and he swears that they're safe. I'll go now and collect them, and the second I'm sure that he's kept his word, we can enter that house and see if we can't put an end to this bombing for good and all.'

'Jesus, I hope so, Kathleen. I've never known our reputation so low. Did you see Patrick Kielty on the *Late Late Show* last night? He said the Cork Garda hadn't been able to catch a single soul for setting off all those illegal firecrackers around the city over Hallowe'en, so what earthly hope did we have of arresting somebody who was causing real explosions?'

'Really? No, I didn't see that. And I used to think he was funny.'

'Good luck,' said Sergeant Murphy. 'Even if Rayland does move on somewhere else, you'll be able to follow him on your laptop.'

Katie took Murrish and Coughlan and together they drove up to Riverview Gardens. The grooming parlour was in a neat bungalow with a red roof, overlooking the park. Katie went up to the front door and rang the bell. She could hear barking somewhere inside, and she could feel her heart beating hard. What if her robotic-sounding caller had been lying to her, and that her dogs were not really here after all? What if they had been drowned almost as soon as they were stolen?

The door opened and a young blondish woman in a purple jumper greeted her with a smile.

'Can I help you at all?' she asked, looking left and right to see if Katie had brought a dog with her.

Katie held up her ID. 'Detective Superintendent Maguire. I've been told you've had three dogs fetched here for washing and grooming. A red setter, a red-and-white setter, and a brown-and-white springer spaniel.'

The young woman nodded. 'Yes, they're here. I've just finished fluffing them up. Is there something wrong? They're not stolen or anything, are they?'

'Let's say they were borrowed without their owner's permission. Their owner being me.'

'Are you serious? Well, do come on in, anyhow. They're all

ready for you. Lovely creatures, all three of them, and I can tell they've been well looked after.'

She led Katie through to a large back room, where a teenage assistant was on her knees, blow-drying a fluffy white Samoyed. Around the corner of the room, Barney and Foltchain and Harvey were lying together on the carpet. Harvey was gnawing on a squeaky plastic bone while Barney and Foltchain were staring out of the window into the garden with what Katie could only interpret as an air of resignation.

'So there you are, the three of you!' said Katie. They all turned their heads and instantly jumped up, rushing towards her with their tails furiously wagging. She was almost knocked over as they clustered around her, huffing and snuffling with delight. She tugged at their ears and stroked them and patted them, but they were still so excited that they circled around and around her until she had to say, 'Sit! Sit! For the love of God, *sit*!'

They sat, but kept twitching and quivering, with their tongues hanging out. Katie thought that they really must have believed they were never going to see her again.

She turned to the young woman, still tugging at Barney's ears. 'It's too long a story for me to explain it all to you, but the people who fetched my dogs here had stolen them.'

'It was only the one woman. I have to say that I did wonder about her, and whether the dogs were hers, because there didn't seem to be any affection between them, do you know what I mean? Usually a dog will look confused or upset when their owner leaves them here, but these three seemed to be glad to see the back of her.'

'Can you describe her?'

'Tall, she was, with grey hair tied up in a knot, and with

such a pale face that you'd swear she'd never seen the sun since the day she was born. And she had on a long brown coat. Her accent was some kind of English, although I wouldn't like to guess where from. She spoke with her lips tight together like she was afraid that her false teeth would fall out.'

'Thanks a million,' said Katie, thinking *Hilda Bracken, no question about it*. 'Did she leave you any kind of contact details?'

'Only a phone number,' the young woman told her. She went over to her desk and came back with a slip of paper. The number written on it was Irish, so Katie could only presume that it was either the mobile phone of one of Hilda Bracken's associates, or else it was false.

'I need to ask you a favour,' she told the young woman. 'We have some urgent police business to sort out now that we've found my dogs, so I wonder if you could look after the two setters for maybe an hour or two more. The spaniel I need to take with me.'

'That's no bother at all. I'd be delighted. I can give them something to eat if that's all right with you.'

Katie crouched down next to Barney and beckoned Foltchain to come closer.

'Listen, you two,' she said softly, tickling them both under the chin. 'I'll be leaving you for just a while with this lovely young lady, the same as I leave you with Jenny next door, but I promise you that I'll be back for you. Do you have me?'

Whether they understood her completely or not, both setters backed away when Katie stood up again, and looked up at her with expressions of obedience. She gave a quick breathy whistle to Harvey, as she always did, and he came trotting up to her, his tail wagging, ready to go.

'I'll make sure that you receive some payment for this,' she told the young woman. 'Once this business is all over, I'll tell you how important it is, what you're doing to help us, and it's much more than you can guess, believe me.'

The young woman looked down at Barney and Foltchain and smiled and shook her head. 'I don't need paying for doing something I love.'

36

After they had left the Pawfect Pooch parlour, Katie alerted Superintendent O'Leary that her dogs had been found safe and that it was time for them to break into the house on Spring Lane.

Spring Lane was one-way, so they should have taken a circuitous route by way of Hawthorn Estate and the Dublin road, but Detective Coughlan switched on the blue flashing lights in his radiator grille and they sped there against the oncoming traffic, although that amounted only to a tractor towing bales of hay and a minibus from the Ballyvolane Retirement Home.

'You really think we'll find the rest of them here?' asked Bedelia Murrish, leaning over from the back seat. 'I mean the whole gang, like?'

'I'm praying that Hilda Bracken came back here to join them,' said Katie. 'Like I said, I'm one hundred and ten per cent sure that it *was* Hilda Bracken who left my dogs at that grooming parlour. An elderly woman with a dead-white face. I very much doubt that it was Fionnula Flanagan.'

When they reached the railway bridge, they found that it had already been blocked by two Garda patrol cars, and that two more patrol cars were blocking Spring Lane on the opposite side. At least twenty uniformed gardaí in ballistic vests were gathered on the boreen itself and on the grassy slope of Spring Park, although they were positioned so that nobody in the grey-painted house would be able to look out of the front windows and see them.

Katie climbed out of her car and Harvey jumped out after her. She walked under the railway bridge, where Superintendent Pearse was standing with DI O'Sullivan and Inspector Hackett.

'I'm glad to hear your dogs are all safe and sound,' said Michael Pearse.

'They are, thank God, and I've fetched Harvey along with me to sniff out any explosives. But have you seen a woman come here to the house in the past half-hour? An elderly woman in a brown coat?'

Terry shook his head. 'There's been nobody. There's no question that Rayland Garvey's in there still because we're continuing to pick him up on the GPS, and whoever came to pick him up is still in there, too, because nobody's come out and the van hasn't moved.'

'But no sign at all of this woman? From the description I was given at the dog grooming parlour I'm convinced it was Hilda Bracken, and I'm sure that she's been behind all these bombings, one way or another. She has the motive, after all. Her pub was bombed and her husband killed, and there's a rake of evidence that it was the Dripsey Dozen who did it, or at least some members of the Dripsey Dozen.'

'So what do you want to do?' asked Michael Pearse. 'We could withdraw, like, and wait for her to show up, but then there's always the risk that the others may find a way of sneaking out.'

Katie knew what Michael Pearse had deliberately omitted to add. There was no way of telling how long they might have to wait for Hilda Bracken to appear, or even if she would. If they had to keep up their surveillance on the suspects' house for an unlimited time, the cost in overtime would be punishing, and they might even have to replace the team who were here already.

She thought to herself: at least we're reasonably sure now that she's wholly or partly responsible for this bombing vendetta. All we have to do is find her, and we may be able to do a deal with Rayland Garvey or one of the other bombers to tell us where she is. Maybe she's heading back to Erdington already, in which case Detective Inspector Robert Charles could probably arrest her at The Huntsman.

'Fair play, Michael,' she said. 'Let's go in now. But let's be doggy wide. There could be explosives in there and we don't know how mental these characters are. I'll let Harvey here have a good sniff around before we start any serious searching. And remember that they're armed, or at least one of them is. My neighbour was threatened with a firearm when my dogs were taken off her.'

Superintendent Pearse switched on his RT and called all his officers forward to the front of the house. He warned them that the suspects could be armed, and to be wary of explosives. They would break down the front door with a battering ram, while at the same time they would kick in the side gate and six of them would hurry round to the back of the house to make sure that none of the suspects escaped through the garden.

A helmeted garda came forward carrying a red steel enforcer. He positioned himself on the step and when Superintendent Pearse gave the order, he swung the enforcer and hit the door lock with a force of nearly three tonnes. With a splintering crack, the door burst open, and five gardaí immediately went charging into the hallway, their weapons raised, with the sergeant in front of them screaming, '*Armed Garda! Armed Garda!*'

Katie waited with Harvey by the broken door. She heard no shots, and no shouting. After only two or three minutes, the sergeant came out, lifting off his helmet.

'They're ready and waiting for you, ma'am,' he told her.

'They didn't resist?'

'No resistance whatsoever. But you'll understand why, like, when you see who they are. They know full well what we'd do to them if they tried to act the maggot.'

Another garda came up behind him and he was holding up an automatic pistol between finger and thumb, as if he were holding a dead mullet by its tail.

'Is that the only firearm they had on them?' asked Katie.

'Yes, ma'am. Well, unless you count this, whatever it is.'

He lifted his other hand, in which he had a red plastic toy that looked like a pistol, except that it had a wide trumpet-like barrel. Katie took it from him, clicked its yellow switch and spoke into it.

'It's a voice changer,' she told him in an amplified growl. She had known what it was immediately, because Jenny's younger son had been given one for his last birthday, and when she was sitting out in her garden he had annoyed her with it for hours. A child could use it to speak in a deep lion-like roar or a shrill falsetto or a silly giggle. Or in a flat, mechanical monotone, like a robot.

'Is that all?' she said, switching the voice changer off. 'No remote detonators?'

'Not on them, and they've all been thoroughly frisked. We've taken their phones and their wallets and their keys, too. There might well be detonators and explosives in the house somewhere, but we won't start looking until your dog has had a good snuffle around the place.'

Katie entered the hallway, with DI O'Sullivan and Detectives Coughlan and Murrish close behind her. She unclipped Harvey's leash from his collar and said, 'Off you go, boy! *Search!*'

Harvey started furiously sniffing along the hallway, past a toilet and a dilapidated staircase, until he reached the open door of the living room at the far end. Katie could only guess what he could smell, but to her the house reeked of mould and decay, and judging by the peeling green wallpaper and the worn-out carpets, it had not been occupied for years.

She followed Harvey into the living room. It was illuminated only by two table lamps, one with a dusty fringed shade and the other with no shade at all. The furniture consisted of a sagging maroon couch and two kitchen chairs, one with a broken back.

Standing in the middle of the room, each with a garda beside them, were Rayland Garvey and the young man with the high fade haircut who had driven the van for the dognapping. Next to them, in a baggy black turtleneck sweater, his eyes fixed on the opposite side of the room as if none of this arrest had anything to do with him, was Micheál ó Broin.

Katie approached Micheál first. She stood staring at him for almost half a minute without saying a word. Should she be feeling utter disbelief that a senior Garda detective could be involved in the worst series of killings that Cork had ever suffered? Or should she be gloating that her suspicions about him had all proved to be true – especially since he himself would have sneered at them as 'baseless speculation'?

She held up the voice changer, although he still kept looking away.

'Micheál,' she said at last. 'It was you, wasn't it, who made me all those threatening phone calls? For the love of Jesus, how did you come to be involved in this bombing? Don't you remember a single word of the oath you took when you joined the Garda?'

'I've nothing to say to you, Kathleen,' Micheál replied.

'Then all I can say to you is that I am arresting you for murder. You are not obliged to say anything unless you wish to do so, but whatever you say will be taken down in writing and may be given in evidence.'

'I know that caution better than the Lord's Prayer, thank you.'

She stared at Micheál a few moments longer, and then she turned to the young man. He was pale, although his cheeks were red-spotted with acne. His high fade hairstyle was lopsided, as if he had been sleeping on it. Unlike Micheál, he was glaring at Katie and grinding his teeth, either in frustration or in anger.

Katie thought that she might have seen him before, but then she realized that he closely resembled Martin Bracken, only younger and spottier.

'So what's your name?' she asked him.

'Why don't you go and fuck yourself?' the young man retorted.

'All I can say is that you look like a Bracken to me.'

'Well, good for you, you Irish slag. And what are you going to do, arrest me for murder as well?'

'It depends if you've had any part in all these bombings.'

'Oh, I see! You're going to arrest *me* for murder, when it was you who murdered my dad?'

'So you are a Bracken?'

'Yes, and proud of it. Neil Bracken, if you must know. And

I've come here to get my own back on all you fucking Irish. You blew up my grandpa and then you shot my dad in cold blood.'

'I hope you realize that you've freely admitted your own guilt,' said Katie.

'You think I feel guilty? You slag.'

'I don't care how you feel. I'm thinking of all the innocent people you helped to kill, and their families who are going to be grieving for them for evermore. Neil Bracken, I am arresting you for murder. You are not obliged to say anything unless you wish to do so, but whatever you say will be taken down in writing and may be given in evidence.'

'Fuck off.'

'Was it your grandma who encouraged you to help with this bombing? If it was, you know, you can tell that to the judge. It could well mean that you're given a much lighter sentence.'

'I said fuck off.'

'You say that now, but you won't be saying that when the judge gives you forty years to life in Portlaoise Prison. Why don't you tell me where we can find your grandma, so that we can bring her in too? I mean, why should you take all the blame, like, when she was the one who persuaded you to do it? If you can tell me where she is, I promise you that I'll put in a good word for you when you're taken to court.'

'Neil,' said Rayland. 'Don't! I used to be a cop and I know what a cop's promise amounts to. One and a half of feck-all.

Rayland looked at Katie and gave her a bitter smirk. 'Haven't we kept our side of the bargain, and let your mutts go? But have you? Micheál always said he could never trust you. He said he'd never ask you to pour him a cup of tea in case you dropped something nasty in it.'

Michael Pearse came back into the living room. 'Your

sniffer dog's going barmy in the kitchen, Kathleen. He's found more than twenty blocks of C-4 in the press, all wrapped up in Mylar plastic, and a box of detonators too.'

'And you're accusing *me* of something nasty?' Katie told Rayland. 'Would you call Commandant Brophy, please, Michael, and ask him to send his EOD team across here as quick as he likes. While you're doing that, I'll call Bill Phinner for the forensics. Then let's take these three down to Anglesea Street and let them contact their lawyers. If ever anyone needed legal representation, they do, for all the good it'll do them.'

By 9:30 that evening, the other fifteen monks in the dormitory at Holy Mount monastery were asleep. Some of the older ones were snoring. One of the younger ones was urgently whispering, as if he were having a conversation with someone in a nightmare.

Father Finn raised his head from his pillow. A lamp was kept burning in the dormitory all night, so he could see Father Rowan on the opposite side of the room. Father Rowan was already sitting up, his hands pressed together in prayer.

Both of them had been allowed out on bail, on the condition that they remained in the monastery until the date of their court hearing. Their abbot had also demanded that they go to confession twice each day, and that they mortify their palates by eating only the most repulsive food, including fish heads and tails, chicken necks and gizzards, and the peel that had been cut from the vegetables served to their brother monks.

Father Finn eased himself out of his bed. From his bedside table, he picked up the knife that he habitually carried, but which he took off at night in case he cut himself while he slept. He crossed the dormitory and stood by Father Rowan's bed, waiting patiently until Father Rowan had finished his prayer, crossed himself and opened his eyes.

It was time. Father Rowan picked up his knife, too, and swung his legs out of bed. Father Finn laid a reassuring hand on his shoulder for a moment. Then, as quietly as they could, the two of them padded on their bare feet out of the room and along the chilly corridor.

They reached the bathroom, which was cold and silent except for the persistent dripping of a tap. The only light came from a small high window, but a waxing gibbous moon was shining brightly through it, as if God had arranged for them to have some holy illumination for what they intended to do next.

Father Finn and Father Rowan stood facing each other. Together, they loosened the cords around their waists and then dragged their black hooded habits up over their heads, although they held on to their knives. Once they had dropped their habits on to the floor beside them, they were both standing in the bathroom naked. They wore underwear only for visits outside the abbey, and even then they had to wash it after their return and give it back to the abbot. They owned nothing, not even their own clothing.

Father Finn was paunchy, with a hairy crucifix on his chest, and plump man breasts. Father Rowan was thinner, with a prominent ribcage and legs like a chicken.

'We have experienced the ultimate pleasures that the Lord has granted us,' Father Finn intoned. 'But, in grievous error, we have sinned against a fellow human being. For that, we will now do the ultimate penance.'

Both monks raised their knives, looking directly into each other's eyes. At the same moment, a cloud passed over the moon.

*

After the three suspects had been brought down from Spring Lane to Anglesea Street, the station was unusually hushed. There was utter disbelief that Micheál ó Broin could have been involved in the bombing vendetta against the Dripsey Dozen, and that Rayland Garvey could have returned from his self-imposed exile to take part in it too. Several officers passed by the interview room just to look inside and confirm that it was really them.

Katie sat in the interview room while Sergeant O'Driscoll and Garda Walsh processed the three of them, taking down all their personal details and removing their belts and their shoes and Micheál ó Broin's blue Masonic tie.

'Do any of you have anything you wish to say to me?' she asked them. 'If so, you can speak to me in confidence, individually, although I have to advise you that what you tell me may still be used in evidence.'

'Oh, do one, will you?' Neil Bracken spat at her, while Rayland Garvey and Micheál ó Broin gave her no indication that they had even heard her.

'Are there any specific solicitors that you want to call? How about Phelim O'Neill?'

Katie was taunting them. Phelim O'Neill was the best criminal defence solicitor in Ireland, specializing in serious crime and renowned for giving expert advice during Garda station interviews.

Again, Rayland Garvey and Micheál ó Broin both failed to respond to her, while Neil Bracken gave her the finger.

Katie stood up. 'In that case, I'll leave you in the capable hands of our custody sergeant, and wish you as many nightmares when you go to sleep tonight as you gave to the Dripsey Dozen.'

★

She collected Barney and Foltchain from the dog grooming parlour and paid for their washing and fluffing. The three dogs sat up in the back of her car, panting, all the way home to Carrig View. Usually, they would fall asleep, but it seemed to Katie as if they wanted to stay awake in case their rescue from their dognapping had been nothing but a dream.

She fed them and then she took a shower and put on her poppy-print pyjamas. She was exhausted, and she was suffering from a headache, but she knew that she would not be able to fall asleep until she had calmed herself down. Although she had harboured such suspicions about him, she was still shocked that Micheál ó Broin had assisted the bombers. Rayland Garvey had shocked her too. She knew that he was guilty of corruption and fraud, but he must have the coldest indifference to human life to have knowingly supplied the explosives that had murdered so many people, none of whom had ever done him the slightest harm.

For herself, she still felt desperately guilty about shooting Martin Bracken, even though he had given her no alternative. It was her calling and her career to protect lives, not to take them.

She was listening to harp music and making notes about what she was going to announce to the media in the morning about the arrests when her phone rang. She was almost tempted not to answer it but it kept on ringing, so she reached across and picked it up. It was DI O'Sullivan and he sounded as tired as she was.

'Ma'am? Sorry to disturb you. We've had an emergency call from the Holy Mount monastery in Carrignavar.'

'That's where our two sadistic monks live, isn't it?'

'Not any more they don't.'

'What do you mean? Don't tell me they've jumped their bail.'

'No. They've both been found dead.'

'Oh, Jesus. Don't tell me they've committed suicide. They're Benedictines, aren't they? I thought they weren't allowed to take their own lives, or else they'd end up in hell.'

'It's worse than that, ma'am, if anything's worse than killing yourself. They were found in the monastery bathroom, and they'd bled to death, the both of them. The abbot said that they were naked, and lying side by side on the floor.

'They'd castrated each other.'

37

Katie had never known a media conference so crowded. Not only could she recognize the usual faces, like Dan Keane and Fionnuala Sweeney and Rionach Barr, she could see reporters from the *Irish Times* and the *Irish Sun* and the *Irish Mirror* and *Sunday World*, as well as the *Breaking News* website. There were also some reporters she had never seen before, stringers from the British and the European press.

As soon as she walked into the conference room with Chief Superintendent O'Leary and sat down behind the desk, the TV lights were switched on so that she had to shield her eyes, and there was a clamour of questions from every side.

She raised her hand for quiet, and then she said, 'Good morning, everyone. I have statements to make about two events. One concerns the arrest of three men suspected of involvement in the bombing of members of the Dripsey Dozen. The other is about the discovery last night of two men suspected of causing severe injury to a Garda detective.'

'They were monks, weren't they, those two?' shouted a reporter from the back of the room. 'From what I've heard, they cut off each other's shillelaghs!'

'And one of the three bombing suspects was your replacement here when you were suspended, am I right?' called out another reporter. 'Detective Superintendent Mícheál

Ó Broin, from Limerick? They used to call him Fear Grinn, didn't they, the gangs in Rathkeale?'

'I'll be answering your questions after I've made my statements,' Katie told them. She had heard only once of Micheál being called 'Fear Grinn' but he was always so humourless that she could understand why. In Gaelic, it meant 'comedian' or 'clown'.

Katie gave the media as much detail as she reasonably could, but until she managed to catch Hilda Bracken her investigation into the Dripsey bombings was still ongoing. She was also careful not to say anything that might prejudice the court proceedings against the three suspects in detention.

More than anything else, she tried to emphasize that while Rayland Garvey and Micheál Ó Broin had both held senior ranks in the Garda Síochána, their involvement in the bombings had come as a complete shock to their fellow officers.

After Katie had been answering questions for over half an hour, Fionnuala Sweeney stood up.

'What you haven't yet come close to telling us, ma'am, is why two Irish men should have actively assisted in what appears to have been a revenge killing of Irish people by somebody British. Let alone two members or one-time members of the Garda. Like, *why?*'

'The answer to that, Fionnuala, is that we don't really know,' said Katie. 'Not yet, anyway. But you know what they say. *Tarlíonn gach rud le haghaigh cúis*. Everything happens for a reason, and sooner or later we'll find out what that reason was.'

Shortly after midday, Ryan Nolan and another solicitor arrived to advise Micheál and Rayland and Neil Bracken during their interviews. Ryan Nolan as neat and precise as ever, while the other solicitor was fat and bumbling with grey curly hair and kept dropping his papers on the floor.

Each interview lasted over an hour, with Katie repeatedly asking Micheál and Rayland the same question that Fionnuala Sweeney had put to her.

'Neil Bracken's motive I can just about understand,' she told them. 'It looks as if the Brackens were out to take a long-belated revenge on the Dripsey Dozen for bombing their pub. But you two are Irish. Why in the name of Jesus did you supply them with explosives so that they could kill so many innocent men, women and children, and cause such disastrous damage?'

Each of the three suspects remained silent. Their solicitors had cautioned them that the charges against them were so serious that it was in their own interest to say nothing at all. Katie could tell that Neil Bracken was bursting to come out with a string of expletives, but he bit his lip and jiggled his feet and looked up at the ceiling and kept quiet.

It was nearly six o'clock by the time Katie could call it a day and drive home. Of course, it was dark, but at least it had stopped raining. She felt mentally exhausted, but much calmer now that she had managed to bring an end to the bombings. She was sure that there would be intensive government and Garda Ombudsman inquiries into the way that the investigation had been carried out, especially since the detective superintendent in charge of it was suspected of actively assisting the perpetrators.

She had come across several cases before in which gardaí or customs officers had turned a blind eye to drug runners or diesel thieves or people-smugglers, in return for a kickback. But she had never come across a case in which senior detectives had conspired to carry out a murder, let alone a series of murders.

As soon as she had parked outside her house, she went next door to Jenny's to collect Barney and Foltchain and Harvey. They were even more excited to see her than they had been at the Pawfect Pooch parlour, as if they had been worrying all day that she might never come back for them.

'Come on, you three mischiefs,' she said, as they milled all around her. 'Let's take a scove up to the ferry port while I still have my coat on and I still have the energy.'

The dogs waited for her in the porch while she went inside to switch on the lamps and draw the curtains. Then she came out and closed the door behind her and they all started walking up the road. The evening was chilly enough for their breath to look as if they were all smoking, but there was no wind.

While she was walking, Katie thought about Hilda Bracken, and how obsessed she must have become with the death of her husband after The Huntsman was bombed. She also thought about all the descendants of those five men who had been executed for their part in the Dripsey Ambush in 1921, and the simmering need for vengeance that they must have held for over fifty years.

She thought about Kyna, too, and she felt a lump in her throat and cold tears clinging to her eyelashes; and she thought about Kieran, and wondered if she would ever be able to forget him.

They had crossed over Carrigmahon Place and almost reached the ferry port when Katie became aware that a car was driving very slowly up the road about fifty metres behind her. She turned around and saw a green Nissan with dipped headlights, creeping along at the same pace that she and the dogs were walking.

She stopped and frowned at it, trying to see who was sitting behind the steering wheel, but there was too much reflection from the streetlights. When she stopped, though, the Nissan stopped too, so it was immediately obvious that it had been following her.

She whistled to her dogs and called out, 'Hold on a second there, gang!', and all three of them stopped and waited for her, looking at each other as if they were thinking *what's she up to now, for goodness' sake?*

Katie started to walk back towards the Nissan, but as she did so it revved its engine and sped another hundred metres towards the ferry port. It went no further than that, though. Its brake lights flared red and it halted again. Almost at once its door opened, and its driver climbed out.

The driver reached back inside and took out a large brown canvas bag, which he slung around his shoulders. Then he slammed his door shut, crossed the road and started to walk along the pavement towards Katie and her dogs. He was coming towards her with a firm, determined walk, as if nothing was going to stop him from meeting up with her.

When he came under the first streetlight, though, Katie saw that he was not a man at all, despite being tall. It was Hilda Bracken, in her familiar brown coat, except that she was no longer wearing her chocolate-cake hat but a shiny grey spotted headscarf, knotted at the back like a gypsy or a pirate. She came marching up to Katie and stood only two metres in front of her, breathing hard, her eyes glittering with hostility.

'Got you, you murdering Irish hammie!' she announced. Her voice was thick and blurry, as if she had been drinking. 'Thought you'd catch me, did you? Thought you'd stop me from getting my own back, did you? You killed my Martin, you hammie. He was my beloved son and you shot him dead.

And now you've locked up my Neil. Well, now you're going to pay for that. You're going to pay for everything.'

'Hilda,' said Katie, trying to sound reasonable. 'Hilda, calm down. We can talk this over, I promise you.'

But Hilda Bracken said '*Pah!*' and pulled open the canvas bag that was hung around her neck. As she started to fumble around inside it, though, Harvey lifted his head and sniffed, and sniffed again. Then he looked up at Katie and barked sharply.

Jesus, thought Katie, *he can smell something. Supposing it's explosives?*

Harvey barked again, and again, and even Barney and Foltchain must have realized that there was something wrong, because they both nervously jumped back. Katie shouted '*Run!*' and started to sprint back along the pavement towards Carrig View. All three dogs turned around and ran along beside her.

'Come back here, you hammie!' Hilda Bracken shrieked at her. 'Come back here and get what you deserve!'

She started to run after Katie and the dogs, although she could only run with an exaggerated limp, because her heavy bag was swinging from side to side. As she ran, she kept on shrieking.

Katie and the dogs ran back over Carrigmahon Place. Katie caught her heel in the drain cover and stumbled, but she managed to wrench it out and keep running. After eighty or ninety more metres, she quickly turned her head and she could see that Hilda Bracken was still coming after them, but she was slowing down. All the same, she was carrying a bag full of explosives, and she was a critical danger to anyone who might come within range. If her explosives detonated when a car or a bus was passing close by, the result could be tragic.

Katie took her phone out of her coat pocket and jabbed 112 while she was still running.

'This is Superintendent Maguire!' she gasped, when the operator answered. 'I'm at Carrig View, in Cobh, and I'm being pursued by a woman with a bag full of C-4 or some other kind of explosive! I need backup now, and the EOD, fast!'

Katie turned her head again, to see if Hilda Bracken had managed to come any nearer. She had limped as far as Carrigmahon Place, but she had stopped shrieking now, probably because she was tiring, and out of breath.

It was then that she tripped on the kerb, and fell forward, holding out both hands to save herself. That was the last Katie saw of her. As she hit the ground, there was a devastating explosion, a bang so loud that Katie was deafened. The shock wave knocked her off her feet and into the road. The three dogs, too, were sent tumbling along the pavement, yelping and whining and scrabbling to find their feet.

A cloud of grey smoke rolled up into the evening air. Bruised and disorientated, Katie lifted herself out of the gutter, her ears still singing from the blast. She called out to Barney and Foltchain and Harvey, and they gathered around her. All three of them were trembling and their tails were down between their legs, but they seemed to be unhurt.

All the way along Carrig View she could see that porch lights were being switched on and front doors opened, and residents coming out to see what had happened. She walked slowly back towards Carrigmahon Place, talking to the emergency operator on her phone, and telling her what had happened.

'I heard it so,' said the operator. 'Even on the phone, I heard it.'

Katie approached the kerbside where Hilda Bracken had fallen. Five or six kerbstones had been shattered, and the surrounding area was glistening with blood. Lumps of flesh were scattered all around, as well as a long pale convoluted string that must have been Hilda Bracken's intestines. Her ribcage was lying on the opposite side of the road, like an abandoned basket.

Katie crossed herself.

Dear Lord, she thought, *please let this be the end of revenge. Why must the people You created always be so set on punishing each other, even after so many years? Why can't we put the harm that's been done to us behind us, and forget it? What happened to forgiveness?*

She had no sleep that night. Gardaí came from Cobh and cordoned off the road, and then DI O'Sullivan and Detective Coughlan and Inspector Hackett and more uniformed gardaí arrived from Anglesea Street. They were followed by the bomb disposal squad and the forensic team and the media, and then an ambulance came from the Mercy to pick up Hilda Bracken's pieces. Carrig View was lit up all night like some kind of grisly festival.

As tired and distracted as she was, Katie had been thinking again about why Micheál ó Broin and Rayland Garvey would have agreed to assist Hilda Bracken in her vendetta against the Dripsey Dozen. It seemed to make no sense. It went against all their loyalty as Irishmen and the solemn oath they had taken when they joined An Garda Síochána to uphold the law and respect human rights, so help them God.

Hilda Bracken must somehow have persuaded them to help her, but how? It was too late to ask her.

*

By nine the next morning, all the emergency vehicles had left Carrig View and the blood had been hosed off the road. The only signs that there had been a major explosion were the broken kerbstones and a deep gap in the hedge on the corner of Carrigmahon Place.

Before he left, Bill Phinner had told Katie that Hilda Bracken's bag must have contained at least four blocks of C-4 and a remote detonator, although he was not entirely sure yet how the detonator had been activated. Only one block would have been more than enough to kill both Hilda Bracken and her, and the dogs too, if they had been standing anywhere within twenty metres of the blast.

'You say she fell over. It could be that she set it off on purpose, hoping you were close enough. You were lucky that you were out in the open air and no debris flew your way.'

'I can't imagine what must have been driving her to do what she did.'

'Oh well,' said Bill Phinner. 'Maybe she just wanted to go out with a bang.' Then, 'Sorry, you can get fierce cynical in this job, can't you?'

Once she had drunk two cups of coffee and taken the dogs next door, Katie left for Anglesea Street. She had made herself a ham and cheese sandwich, but she was unable to stop picturing Hilda Bracken's bloody remains lying in the road, and she had no appetite for it, so she left it in the fridge.

First, she went in to see Chief Superintendent O'Leary to give him a full briefing on what had happened last night. Hilda Bracken's explosive death had already been reported in the morning news on both TV and radio, but Katie would have to hold a media conference later. Until the three suspects had been taken to court, though, she would still have to be guarded about what information she gave out.

Once she had caught up with all her emails and text messages and left another cup of coffee to grow cold, she went down to the custody suite to talk to Micheál ó Broin.

He was writing with a stubby pencil in a notebook when Katie was let into his cell, and he carried on writing without looking up at her. She thought he looked less like a witch today and more like a sad skinny vagrant.

'What's the story, Micheál?' she asked him, sitting down on the other end of his bed.

'Same as before,' he replied, emphatically underlining his last sentence and closing his notebook so that Katie was unable to see what he was writing. 'I've nothing to say to you without my solicitor being present, and even then I've nothing to say to you.'

'I came to tell you that Hilda Bracken's dead.'

38

Micheál turned around slowly to stare at her. She was trying to read his expression, but it was an extraordinary combination of shock and disappointment and what she could only assume was anger. She could see no grief there, not even a slight quiver of his lips.

'You're joking, aren't you?' he asked her. 'You'd better be joking.'

Katie shook her head. 'Sorry, Micheál, it's true. She took her own life last night. I'm not at liberty to tell you how or where, not yet. But I can definitely confirm that she's passed.'

Micheál sat silent for a long time, but Katie stayed sitting where she was. She had a feeling that he needed to tell her something important, and that he was silent only because he was trying to find the right words.

'That screws it up for good and all,' he said at last. He sounded almost as if he were going to start crying. 'I mean, that really screws it up. That's my whole life down the jacks.'

He was silent again for over a minute, but then he turned back to Katie again.

'I'll have to talk to you now. You can record this if you want to, because this is what I'll be saying to the judge.'

'Don't you want your solicitor here?'

'There's no point. He'd only tell me to shut my bake, but this is my only chance to have my sentence reduced.'

'You're sure about that?' said Katie, and when he nodded she took out her phone and set it to record.

'I met Rayland about eight years ago at a Garda function in Phoenix Park. We compared notes, like, because we were both trying to tackle organized gangs – Rayland here in Cork and me in Limerick, mostly the Rathkeale Mob. The problem that we were both experiencing was that nobody dared to give us any evidence against them, and so they were getting away with murder. Like, literally.'

'I thought you'd been scoring good results against the gangs in Limerick. Like, we don't call it "Stab City" any more, do we? I've heard nothing but compliments about all the cases that you were closing while you were there. Rayland had an excellent record too, until it was found out that the gangs were paying him off, and that he was supplying guns and plastic explosives for the New IRA. God alone knows what else he was up to.'

'But that was the way we decided to control the gangs, don't you see?' said Micheál. 'We knew that we would never be able to break them up, because we couldn't persuade anyone to testify against them in court. So we decided to play them at their own game. We offered them immunity from prosecution if they kept their activities down to a reasonable level, like the drug-running and the protection rackets and the prostitution. Like, all those things would be going on anyhow. You know and I know that no matter how many of those shitehawks you arrest, there's always another one who's going to take over. Drug addicts never stop needing their drugs and shop owners always need protection and lonely men are always looking to get their hole from some brass or other.'

'But how did that lead to you two helping Hilda Bracken?'

Micheál shrugged. 'The trouble was, we got too good at it, Rayland and me. We started demanding payment from the gangs for giving them immunity. Then we started demanding a percentage from their drug sales and their brothels. Then we found we could make even more if we cut the gangs out of it altogether and took a percentage from the drug manufacturers and the brasses themselves. On top of that, Rayland found out that the New IRA would pay him silly money for guns and C-4.'

'We were fetching in a fortune every week until Rayland was caught out by Internal Affairs and I was seen by the Rathkeale Mob doing a deal with their main crack supplier. Why do you think they came after me, that day outside the station?'

'I had my suspicions, I have to admit,' Katie told him.

'Any road, three different gangs started to come after us, wanting their money back. Two gangs from Cork and one from Rathkeale. Between the three of them, they reckoned we owed them more than a quarter of a million euros.'

'Don't tell me you'd spent it all.'

'Most of it. A lot of it went on gambling. Rayland bought a six-bedroomed house in Youghal but of course he couldn't sell it because he was wanted and he was out of the country. As for me, I'd bought my Mercedes and taken a holiday in Thailand and I had only a few thousand left. But then we were offered a way out.'

'Which was?'

'Rayland had already heard from Lorcan O'Neill that Hilda Bracken was looking to take her revenge on the IRA for blowing up the place fifty years ago and killing her husband. Believe it or not, she'd been saving up the pub's profits for all that time, for that purpose alone.'

'But as far as we know, it wasn't the IRA who blew it up,' said Katie.

'Exactly. But Lorcan got to hear from some old IRA pals that she and her son, Martin, were trying to find the addresses of all the IRA members who had been involved in the bombing, so that she could have them all blown up in retaliation. So Lorcan sent his brother Finbarr over to England to tell her that it was the Dripsey Dozen who had done it, because it was.

'Finbarr put Hilda Bracken in touch with Rayland because he could supply her with all the explosives she wanted, and Rayland got in touch with me. When he told me how much she was offering, I really had no choice. She was going to pay each of us almost half a million euros.'

'So that's why you were investigating the bombings at such a snail's pace?'

'Sure look, there was no need for me to hurry along, was there? I knew already who was behind it.'

'Did you have no conscience at all about what you were doing?'

Micheál shrugged again. 'It was their lives or mine. It's as simple as that. You saw already that the Rathkeale Mob are out to kill me, and it's not only them. There's two other gangs that are after me and Rayland if we don't pay up.'

'But now Hilda Bracken's dead, you won't be paid, will you?'

'Why do you think I'm telling you all this now? If I'd had the money, I could have skipped the country. Then again, I could say nothing at all and plead not guilty, which was what that Ryan Nolan wants me to do. But let's be realistic. I know that there's far too much evidence against me, and I can't trust Rayland not to rat. If a judge understands the kind of pressure I was under, and still am – if he can see that I'm under constant threat of being killed – then at least there's a chance he'll take that into consideration when he's passing sentence. I would rather be locked up in isolation in Portlaoise for thirty years than lying in a coffin in Mount Saint Lawrence graveyard.'

'Fair play to you,' said Katie. 'You're aware that I'm going to log everything that you've told me this morning as evidence against you.'

'Yes, Kathleen. And I've learned one bitter lesson.'

'What's that, Micheál?'

'It sticks in my throat to say this. In fact, it almost makes me gawk. But you can help me with first-hand evidence that somebody tried to take my life, because you were there, and you saved me. So I'll tell you now that I'll never underestimate a woman, never again. Especially Detective Superintendent Kathleen Maguire.'

Katie returned home late that evening. She took the dogs for a short walk, although not in the direction of the Passage West ferry port. The broken kerbstones and the damaged hedge would be too vivid a reminder that Hilda Bracken really had blown herself up only a hundred metres away from her.

When she came back, she poured herself a vodka and tonic and sat down in the living room to open her mail. There were two bills, an offer from Specsavers to have her eyes tested, and a white envelope with black edging. She opened up the envelope and found that it contained a card, also with black edging.

Kathleen Maguire is invited to the funeral service for Kyna Ní Nuallán at Saint Fin Barr's Cemetery, Glasheen Road, Cork, at 3 p.m. on 17 November.

Barney, Foltchain and Harvey must have heard her sobbing, because they all came trotting in from the kitchen, and Barney rested his head in her lap, the way he always did when he felt that she needed comforting.

Katie left the chapel at St Fin Barr's Cemetery after the short service that had been held for Kyna and stepped out into the sunshine.

This was the first funeral she had ever attended when it wasn't raining, but she thought that Kyna deserved a bright and sunny day like this.

Only seven people had turned up for the service, including Katie. Three of them were old school friends of hers, two were cousins, and one was an attractive young woman in a black coat who sat at the back of the chapel and remained silent.

They all stood around the grave as Kyna's coffin was lowered into it. Katie had brought a small bunch of white roses, Kyna's favourite, and dropped them on to the coffin lid.

'Eternal rest grant unto her, O Lord, and let perpetual light shine upon her,' the priest intoned. 'May she rest in peace, amen, and may almighty God bless us with his peace and strength, the Father, and the Son, and the Holy Spirit.'

Katie stood by the grave while the other mourners walked away. She heard a hooded crow cawing, and she looked up and saw it perched on top of the rocket-like spire of the chapel. *You're always watching me, aren't you*, she thought. *You'll probably be up there watching when they bury me next to Kyna.*

She walked back between the trees that lined the cemetery path. It was here some of the most famous Irishmen lay buried, including Jack Lynch the Taoiseach and Terence McSwiney, the Lord Mayor of Cork who had died on hunger strike in Brixton Prison. On one side of the cemetery was a Republican plot where members of the IRA were interred.

She reached the gates, and turned around for a moment to whisper a last goodbye to Kyna.

She was still standing there when a familiar voice called out, 'Katie?'

Walking towards her in a brown derby hat and a camelhair overcoat, like a character in a sentimental Hollywood movie, was Kieran.

He came up to her and took off his hat. 'They sent me an invitation to the funeral, too, but I didn't want to intrude.'

'So… then why did you come here?' Katie asked him.

'I came here because I needed to see you. The past – well, it's buried in there, isn't it? I came here to tell you that I can't live without you.'

About the Author

GRAHAM MASTERTON is best known as a writer of horror and thrillers, but his career as an author spans many genres, including historical epics and sex advice books. His first horror novel, *The Manitou*, became a bestseller and was made into a film starring Tony Curtis. In 2019, Graham was given a Lifetime Achievement Award by the Horror Writers Association. He is also the author of the Katie Maguire series of crime thrillers, which have sold more than 1.5 million copies worldwide.

Visit www.grahammasterton.co.uk

DISCOVER THE OTHER THRILLING BOOKS IN THE MILLION-COPY BESTSELLING KATIE MAGUIRE SERIES

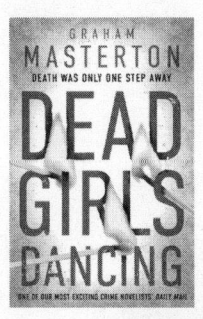